Satan's MORTGAGE

Satan's MORTGAGE

by Robin S. Payes and Richard I. Payes

iUniverse, Inc.
New York Bloomington

Satan's Mortgage

This is a work of fiction. All of the characters, names, incidents, organizations, and dialogue in this novel are either the products of the author's imagination or are used fictitiously.

iUniverse books may be ordered through booksellers or by contacting:

iUniverse
1663 Liberty Drive
Bloomington, IN 47403
www.iuniverse.com
1-800-Authors (1-800-288-4677)

ISBN: 978-1-4401-2443-3 (sc)
ISBN: 978-1-4401-2445-7 (dj)
ISBN: 978-1-4401-2444-0 (ebook)

Library of Congress Control Number: 2009922451

Printed in the United States of America

iUniverse rev. date: 3/19/2009

I.
Ballad of the Landlord

Landlord, landlord,
My roof has sprung a leak.
Don't you 'member I told you about it
Way last week?

Landlord, landlord,
These steps is broken down.
When you come up yourself
It's a wonder you don't fall down.

Ten bucks you say I owe you?
Ten bucks you say is due?
Well, that's ten bucks more'n I'll pay you
Till you fix this house up new.

What? You gonna get eviction orders?
You gonna cut off my heat?
You gonna take my furniture and
Throw it in the street?

Um-huh! You talking high and mighty.
Talk on—till you get through.
You ain't gonna be able to say a word
If I land my fist on you.

Police! Police!
Come and get this man!
He's trying to ruin the government
And overturn the land!

Copper's whistle!
Patrol bell!
Arrest.

Precinct station.
Iron cell.
Headlines in press:
* * *
MAN THREATENS LANDLORD
* * *
TENANT HELD NO BAIL
* * *
JUDGE GIVES NEGRO 90 DAYS IN COUNTY JAIL

—Langston Hughes

Satan's Mortgage

Mortgage: from old French; mort, death and gage, pledge; a pledge unto death

Prologue

He was about a block away from the building, the one Al Pollock owned in the South Bronx. Peller could see the giant mural on the wall, a depiction of a black Jesus bowed under the weight of the cross on his back. The names of three young people who had been pointlessly gunned down on the spot were painted in bright colors on the brick wall of the apartment house: Rest in Peace Luis 1974–1993, Angel 1973–1993, Paulo 1974–1993. The proliferation of such wall coverings in this part of New York City was a poignant reminder of life and death in the barrio.

Louis Peller's company, the American National Mortgage Association, had lent Pollock the money to buy this place, and Pollock couldn't keep up with the payments, so Louis Peller had to sit on his borrower a little, twist his arm to get Pollock to pay on the loan. Standard operating procedure according to the Amie Mae manual, *Cash is King: Get the Borrower to Pay.*

It was noon when Tommy, Peller's driver, dropped him off at the corner. Peller told Tommy to meet him back at the same corner at two thirty sharp. No dillydallying in this neighborhood, especially not after three in the afternoon when the hoodlums got out of school and the dope dealers and their couriers took up residence on every other street corner.

Despite the squalor of the street, Peller was savoring the sunshine on this brilliant blue spring day. The sidewalks, for once, were deserted. This part of the Bronx was generally teeming with life whenever he came to check out a building, boiling over with tension. Peller liked to get in quick and get out. But today, Peller was in no hurry to descend to the cellar to inspect the boiler or to feel his way across the tar paper roof, checking for cracks and leaks.

Suddenly, he heard an explosion, the shattering of glass, and the crash of brick on concrete. It sounded like a bomb detonating in his path. As he looked up, he witnessed the top two floors of the six-story apartment house crumble right before his eyes. As he watched, dumbfounded, he saw the upper third of the mural fold in on itself, leaving only the names and the lower third of the cross to mark the memory of the young victims of poverty. No rest in peace.

Peller immediately ran, thrusting himself to safety. He crouched behind a dumpster, the closest cover he could find. He smelled fire. The air was blistering. Through his nostrils, he breathed in acrid smoke. He could almost feel the air singe his eyebrows. Chunks of brick and mortar rained down around him. He crouched down farther still, searching for somewhere safer to hide, some cover to protect his head. All the while, he was thinking, *I should have taken the cellular phone for safety as Steve and Vicki insisted. Where was my head when I left the office for this godforsaken slum?*

He could hear people wailing, whimpering, and weeping nearby. Looking up at the luminous sky again, now choking with flame, he had to shield his eyes against the debris. When he dropped his gaze, he observed people crawling from the building on hands and knees like animals, choking in the smoke-filled air, screaming as panic flowed into the street. He could make out the smoky silhouettes of mothers with babies clutched in their arms, their shadows cast against the sidewalk, partially obscured by the billowing smoke and yellow flames that were breaking out in what remained of the top two floors.

God, it was hot. Peller was frightened, trembling. He had

to get away. He decided to make a mad dash, even though he was partially sheltered now from the fallout of the apartment building. The conflagration was all too close for comfort. His heart was racing. It was difficult to breathe. He must make it out of there, quickly.

No. He felt guilty for his selfish impulse to flee when people's lives were at stake. He was quick and strong. They looked so helpless. Could he … dare he run back to help?

Maybe he could dart between the falling rubble to save that one mother, frozen there, screaming. He could carry her and her baby to safety. Yes, he must help. He hesitated, his stomach tied up in knots, trying to think. What to do …

"Quit wasting time, Peller," he lectured himself angrily. "Do something, the right thing." He closed his eyes and took a deep breath.

He ran.

Peller felt his heart racing. He forced open his eyes in fear. He was sweating, trembling.

It was dark. He felt an eerie quiet around him. He was alone. He took a deep breath and shuddered. What was happening?

That dream. Again.

Chapter 1
Love this Job

Peller was flying, still half asleep, not thinking about heading into La Guardia on the eight o'clock shuttle. He roused himself reluctantly for the descent. Peering out through the small, scratched porthole, he managed to get an airborne glimpse of the Big Apple in all its glory before fully waking up to the truth of New York City in July, 1993: a tired-out shell of a city, sheltering a buzzing mass of humanity in the shadow of falling prosperity. New York today was more like a third world capital than the hub of the world's greatest nation. Peller pictured Rome's slow burn as Nero fiddled; the ancient urbe could not have fallen hotter or into greater decay than this megalopolis.

Louis Peller was tired. He had been up since the marbled gray-pink dawn of five ante meridian; make that ante-aurora. To make the eight o'clock out of Washington National Airport from his home in suburban Maryland, he reluctantly emerged from the shadowy intimacy of the bed where his wife, Lana, slumbered on serenely, her inviting warmth encouraging him to snuggle just a little longer against her languorous, sensuous body. He dressed hurriedly and fumbled through the dark house, children stirring briefly as he tendered silent kisses and Manny-dog leaping against him in a sad-eyed farewell for the day, until he pulled out of the driveway of their comfortable four-bedroom home only to reemerge a brief plane ride later in a hard, unforgiving world.

It was Peller's job to settle defaulted mortgage loans, to play the good guy to humanity's tired, poor, and humble masses, teeming in crumbling postdepression high-rise apartment buildings now passing for habitable housing owned by slumlords who could no longer make payment on their mortgage loans. At least, that's how he liked to view the job. Every week, he flew up to New York to hammer away at yet another borrower who had defaulted on his loan from Amie Mae, the quasi-governmental, billion-dollar lending institution. The American National Mortgage Association Company—whose acronym, Amie Mae, like that of its competitors Fannie Mae and Freddie Mac, conjured up freckle-faced playground pals—employed him to negotiate, mediate, and arbitrate with borrowers not paying on apartment buildings and cooperatives in this godforsaken city.

At nine forty-five in the morning, in the front of the cabin, Peller barely registered the flight attendants preparing for landing. Flying, to Peller, was a grind, like commuting on the Washington Beltway, a monumental waste of time. Now he could see the heat rising in waves from the runway as the USAir jet touched down. He imagined the smell of burning rubber as the wheels gripped the pavement to drag the unwieldy silver bird to a stop. He thought ahead to his to-do list for the day. Tommy, his driver/bodyguard, was to meet him at the airport to escort him into the New York office of Amie Mae. There he was to meet with a borrower, a Hasidic Jew who hadn't paid the bank for ten months and claimed he had no capital and no way to raise any to pay on his "measly, little thirty-two-unit apartment building that no one else would want" in the Bronx.

"Of course. I understand your position, Mr. Pollock," Peller had harrumphed.

The company had hired him, Peller knew, in part because he was Jewish; none of the gentiles in the office could speak the language of New York's peculiar Jewish apartment owners who had purchased so many of these buildings in the seventies and eighties. "Tell me, Mr. Peller," Alvin Pollock would say. "Will you come to synagogue with me this morning to make our minion? After, I take you to Ratner's on Orchard Street. Maybe a blintz, a little lox, some onion rolls … we talk business."

Oh, yes, Peller understood that language well, had grown up with it, in fact. Certainly he could relate far better than any Texas boy with a wild hair or the pale Hoosier whose worldly exposure omitted Jews, Italians, blacks, or any other ethnic Americans who made up New York's fastest-growing populations. Talk about white bread. Peller got a kick out of the fact that he was one of a few token Jews at Amie Mae headquarters in the suburbs outside Washington DC. He didn't mind the role as long as they also understood that he was professional, strong-minded, and able to negotiate with the toughest of them. That his bosses back at the home office couldn't appreciate those ethnic traits (he had a strong streak of independence) was a constant source of friction between them. They expected a good bureaucrat in the office, and a renegade when negotiating deals with borrowers.

Fortunately for Peller, he wasn't right out of Central Casting. His brown, wavy hair, dark complexion, and strong nose could as easily be Greek or Italian as Jewish. He could move adroitly between the ethnic and corporate worlds, thanks to an upbringing that stressed a healthy respect for the Almighty and pragmatism above all else. He was schooled in the customs of the Jewish community and the rules of the secular one. Accustomed to straddling the line, Peller felt comfortable dancing between both worlds.

For his finesse, Peller had been given Amie Mae's worst loans in New York's toughest neighborhoods. There were many of these high-risk loans in the mortgage lender's portfolio. Amie Mae had gotten caught in the fast-paced, high-risk lending environment of the 1980s. Property values had plummeted later in the same decade, leaving most real estate in New York City seriously overleveraged. Appraisers, banks, and Amie Mae miscalculated the market; they overestimated the value of properties, failed to predict the impact of the recession on real estate, and simply lent too much money to unscrupulous slumlords. Landlords in Brooklyn, Harlem, and the Bronx were losing money by the barrelful now. Monthly rents in these low-income buildings never came close to covering expenses. The heavy debt service left landlords strapped; they stopped repairing properties and started milking the buildings for whatever cash and profit they could eke out of them. Profit—the major impetus for guys buying these properties (they typically *were* men) to take on such crime-ridden, headache-inducing, decrepit buildings—was virtually impossible, so these landlords abandoned any pretense of making them livable or safe.

And the prognostications were gloomy; the burgeoning number of mortgage defaults by borrowers was driving properties into foreclosure and real estate investors into bankruptcy. During the boom times, only three years before Peller joined up with Amie Mae, many New York landlords had paid out two and three times what a building was worth now. Since the 1987 stock market crash, rent had declined by as much as 30 percent. The New York City real estate market was decimated, left in a state of economic depression to a degree unmatched by any other major city in the United States. The high rate of defaulting loans on rental apartment buildings was shaking the foundations of the city's real estate and banking industries.

Amie Mae needed people to work out its huge backlog of loan defaults on rental apartments and cooperatives in New York City.

As a result, workouts were the only decent real estate jobs available these days, and Peller felt fortunate to be bringing home a paycheck. He'd been out of work for almost a year before the job with Amie Mae came up, and even though he thought his bosses to be small-minded technocrats at a company that was, at best, unenlightened, some income was better than living off the wife's salary.

Enter Louis Peller, real estate workout maven and negotiator par excellence.

"Hiya, Louie," called Tommy Romano as Peller appeared through the tunnel from the shuttle. The big, burly New Yorker walked up and slapped his client on the back. It was Tommy's job to drive Peller and his colleagues around town and, incidentally, to protect them from harm in parts of New York where Caucasian Americans were an endangered species.

As the two set out for the clunky white Chevrolet Impala in the parking lot, they caught up on news. Tommy proudly informed Peller about a recent win on the horses at Saratoga, and Peller filled his driver's ear with office gossip. Walking to the parking lot, the duo made an unlikely sight: Louis, short and slight at five and a half feet on a good day, and Tommy Romano, a puffy dough boy of a man, six feet tall and round from neck to ankle. Still, the two had a simpatico relationship, and the bigger man felt a protective affection for his little customer. Peller thought of Tommy as a real diamond in the rough.

"What fun do we have in store for us today?" asked the big man.

"An easy day, Tommy. We're going into Manhattan, to the office, I'm meeting with a borrower, then, if we have time later on, there's a building I want to check out in Harlem before I take off again into the wild blue yonder. I need to be on the four o'clock shuttle."

"My time is you'eh time, Louie." Tommy thought of Peller as a pampered younger brother, and he protected him like a father. And where Peller was going, he needed all the protection he could get.

"But listen, Louie," Tommy warned. "If you want to go to Harlem, fa'gedaboutit! We'd betteh be out of theyah by tree o'clock, tops. You know I don't like hangin' out in that parta town after school lets out. Too many punks with nothin' but time on their hands and guns in their pockets."

"Fine, fine. We'll be out by three." Peller set his briefcase on the back seat and climbed in next to his driver, noticing, as always, the woven straw crucifix stapled to the felt ceiling of the car and the rosary beads dangling from the dashboard. Peller was used to Tommy's superstitions, found them rather comforting, in fact. For, truth be known, Peller did not feel completely at ease going into the ghetto to visit his buildings. He thought of these buildings as his, though God only knew he would never invest in such properties; that took a real New York gambler with lots of *chutzpah* to assume that kind of risk. And, although Peller liked taking some risks, the risk of losing money—big-time, down a sinkhole—wasn't one of them.

"Wanna stop for some good java and a coupla bialys on the way, Chief, per usual?" Tommy inquired.

"You know me well, Tom. Would hit the spot."

As they began the familiar drive from the airport to the city, Peller felt the weight of this other world enshroud him. He was going to dance with the devil. Each pothole jolted him from his mental rehearsal of the exacting tap he must execute with seasoned slumlords who monthly stared destitution and despair in the eye to demand from poverty's inmates a rent check. Peller needed to be just as hardhearted with these masters of manipulation, even when they were down on their luck.

A few miles later, driving across Manhattan, Tommy pulled over to a bagel place on the corner of 42nd Street and Park Avenue, near Grand Central Station. "Right back, Lou."

Peller reached back for his briefcase and took out a legal pad with pages and pages of notes on it. A year earlier, he had begun to jot down his impressions of these weekly jaunts to New York, thinking someday there might be something in it worth recording for posterity. The cast of characters and their stories were positively unimaginable to anyone who didn't dip into Manhattan's indigenous culture. This world was fertile with literary possibilities. He reread some of his notes about the property inspections he had made on his last visit.

> Bronx prop'ty, Grand Concourse: replace boiler. Brass risers pipes leaking. Walls—H_2O seeps into apts. Flr. in apt. 3B bows fr. water rot. Elevator not operating … helped old woman down 4 flts. to lobby. Rats in basement; exterminate.

That was all for the official report.

> Sm. kids (3 or 4 yrs.) playing in stair. No parents. MT crack vials, used colored condoms, MT 22 cal. shells on stairs. Mural painted on the ext. wall: In Memoriam, to D'Monroe, 1975–1993: "We love you, D'Mon." Painting of yg. black man, wearing leather jkt., chains and baggy jeans. D'Mon left his marker. Prob'ly drugs.

Witnessing such misery was disheartening. Peller tried not to dwell on it too much. The faces of the few tenants with whom he exchanged greetings revealed nothing but despair. There, but for the grace of God, Peller shivered at Fate's whimsy.

He added the current date:

> July 23. The unending carousel ride would revolve yet again, another inescapable circle. Another long, stinking day inspecting tenements.

Peller shuddered. "It's just a job," he reminded himself. He flipped through the handwritten notes and found the one where he'd started to describe some of the characters with whom he was dealing.

> 1. The Immigrants. Isaac Fink—Orthodox—long black and white beard, peyes, yarmulke. Lvs. work Fri. afts. Yiddishisms: "*Zoy gesint*—you should be healthy!" Deep pockets. Made money in retail biz manufacturing men's suits. Retired and invests in R.E. (apts., shopping

ctrs.), stock market. Shimon Gould—Holocaust survivor. Came to NYC after WWII; 6 kids. Started drugstore on Lower East Side; now fastest-growing reg. chain in Northeast. 2. Next Generation. Dave Sloan—all-American. Wheeler-dealer type. Inherited money fr. family, keeps it growing through broad R.E. investments thru NYC, Long Island, and Conn. Syndicates deals in Bronx and Brooklyn with cronies just like him. Fully assimilated.

He scribbled a few more notes to jog his memory when he got back to the office.

Get Pollock to focus on workout deal. Pollock too worried about foreclosure or downside of bankruptcy. Finalize terms today—Amie avoids foreclosure and $8 million loss on Pollock's 32 prop'ties.

Peller looked up distractedly as his driver tapped on the window with a plastic container of half-and-half. As Peller rolled down the window, Tommy sang out, "Here's your order, Louie. Eat up! You'eh lookin' a little thin."

"You don't need to sound like my mother, Tommy," Peller joked as he unwrapped the warm, oniony bialy and licked his lips. "I moved away from home at eighteen to escape that broken record.

"Lana's bad enough: 'Eat right, Louis. Don't nosh all day. Sit down like a human being and eat a meal. I hate when you pick,'" he mimicked.

Tommy laughed. "I relate. Nothin' worse 'an a Jewish mama, 'cept an Italian one. That's why I don' need no wife to tell me what to do."

"A man should only have one mother," Peller agreed. "So what if I *am* getting a little broad around the middle? At forty, I've earned it, haven't I?" he asked rhetorically, pinching the love handles above his belted slacks. Although he looked much younger with his handsome baby face and thick, dark hair, Peller was indeed turning forty in the fall.

"Fa' be it from me, Louie," replied the fullback-sized driver, himself a man of indeterminable age.

For the duration, they consumed their bagels silently. Peller gazed out the windows at the urban peoplescape and wondered what new character material he might glean after the meeting with Pollock.

Tommy left Peller off at 58th and Madison Avenue. Tommy would go off on his own to engage in God only knows what quasi-illegal activities. The native New Yorker had been most generous in showing Peller some of the seamier—and more bizarre—highlights of the city, sights not native to suburban dwellers. These weren't the kinds of places featured on the Grayline Bus Tour, and Peller tried not to divulge their true nature to Lana. He didn't think she would appreciate the broad vistas he sometimes admired.

Peller stepped into the office elevator and, ignoring the congregation of commuters getting on and off as they reached their office temples, idly watched the floors tick off until he reached forty-eight.

I've got to bring my kids here, if only to experience the sheer heights of Manhattan, he mused. *New York. What a town.* In Washington, architecture was zoned to soar no higher than the dome of the Capitol, a wonder of federal design, but no match for the Empire State. The low-rise scale was a major selling point for Washington in Peller's book, not so closed in and oppressive as New York.

Striding down the hall, Peller swung the glass doors wide to the marbled reception area of Amie Mae's New York office. Of course, only the front office could really be called imposing. The rest of the suite was blocked off in impersonal cubicles, "work-stations" according to the nineties vernacular, surrounded by a few large, windowed offices reserved for the dedicated attorneys who labored until all hours. Those hardworking, upright defenders of corporate greed and red tape, who were afforded every perk to keep them from jumping ship and spilling dark corporate secrets, were able to peer out enviously each night at five thirty when a kaleidoscope of head and taillights unraveled like ribbons up and down Madison Avenue, and swarms of scurrying shadows trudged down to the subway, all of them wending their way home from work. No rest for the wicked or their advocates in the halls of justice. Their work was lonely, but at least they did rate office windows.

Peller stepped into the spacious square-with-a-view of his friend and colleague, Steve Shapiro, giving him a friendly punch in the arm.

"Hey, Steve-O," he called out. "How're your briefs? Or are they jockeys?" he joked, punching Steve again. "Haw, haw, haw."

Steve groaned at Peller's adolescent humor. "Spending too much time with the kids, Lou?"

Peller and lawyers enjoyed a love–hate relationship of sorts. Peller had survived law school and trudged diligently for an unhappy twelve months at a medium-sized Washington real estate law firm before he was courted by a developer who subsequently went bust, then the workout business. In the process, he developed a thorough distaste for lawyers. He'd only gone into the legal profession to make his dad, a member of the old school and one stern authoritarian, proud.

"What's important," his father would say to him, "is you should have a good profession. I don't know from real estate, and I don't know from marketing. Law. Better yet, medicine. That's a profession."

His father lived long enough to see Louis join the law firm. But in the end, Peller and the partners at the firm had never quite seen things eye to eye, and he'd quit—or they'd ousted him; Peller was not quite clear about the sequence of events. Thankfully, by then Peller had no need to impress his dad. The old man, puffed up like a peacock at his son's apparent success, had passed away.

Though the practice of law hadn't become an abiding passion, argumentation had. Something about legal training that compelled lawyers ever after to argue both sides of every issue simultaneously, no matter whether it be in debate with themselves or with able sparring partners. Louis Peller had a single-mindedness about him that could knock out many an able debater in fewer than five rounds. And he argued to win. Peller's adversarial zeal drove Lana nuts.

Now Steve, he was a typical New York litigator, a tenacious son of a bitch who hammered borrowers until they submitted. Divorced and alone in the city of strangers, he developed a fervor for winning that deterred the less passionate. He worked hard, played equally hard, and hated to lose at anything. With his black hair constantly falling across his black eyes and a tanned, muscular frame, he looked the part of the tough guy, a role he relished. King of the roost was the game he played. Steve loved nothing more than to sit back, feet up on his desk, brandishing his cigarette, to argue for argument's sake, and to win the contest. Peller, the lawyer basher, liked to take guys like Steve down a notch or two and could spend hours at the art of verbal repartee.

The two often sparred over late-night drinks, capping the office tradition of entertaining visitors from the home office *en masse*. Long after their colleagues had called it a night, the duo would celebrate their verbal victories at one of New York's infamous table dancing bars, where the women were hot, dancing topless "in yo' face." At such moments, they remained appreciatively silent, admiring a living, breathing Aphrodite, savoring the exquisite beauty of the female form. The two things they shared, love of the game and beautiful women, somehow provided a basis for a solid male bond.

"What's up, Steve?" greeted his friend.

"Louis, you are going to love this one," Steve announced, an unlit cigarette in one hand and his coded legal file folder in the other. "And I'll bet it's going to end up in your court. We've got this building up in Washington Heights. Amie Mae made a loan to some Persian named Assad in '89 for two million dollars. Guy hasn't paid on the loan in two years. Two years, can you imagine? Trouble is, today the place would be appraised for far less than two million dollars. We've been letting the borrower slide on his payments, but now the piper needs paying."

Peller waved away the warning. "Steve, don't worry me with penny-ante shit like that. Let's talk about the business at hand. I've got old Al Pollock coming in at ten fifteen. We're ready to foreclose on one of Honest Al's properties in the Bronx, with thirty-one to go. But I really don't believe he's been presented with every option. Do you realize this could be the biggest workout deal Amie Mae has ever closed? I say, let's give Pollock a chance to bring his loans current by forking over twenty-five thousand dollars a month for five years to work off the arrears. I'll bet he'd jump at the chance, especially if he understands the alternative is that no bank in town will ever deal with him, let alone lend to him, again. I feel it is my mission, should I decide to accept it, to work out a good deal for Al and the fine people at Pollock Properties. He's been a decent landlord, and besides, what's Amie Mae going to do with thirty-two rundown, foreclosed properties in New York's worst ghetto?"

Steve grinned. "Okay, pal, go right ahead and gloat. Just don't come groaning to me when you get handed this Washington Heights deal on a platter. I'll only say, 'I told you so.' As they used to say in the old country, 'What a *mishigas*!'"

Steve was one of three Jews in the New York office. When he wasn't impersonating the all-American, hotshot attorney for all-American Amie Mae, Steve Shapiro could offer a great impersonation of a *Yiddishe kopf*. Steve and Peller often speculated on how it must kill those good Anglo-Saxons in the home office to be forced to admit these Jewish "heathens" to their all-gentile, white men's club, but that was the price of doing business in New York.

At that moment, Pollock entered wearing the traditional black felt hat and wool suit of Hasidic custom. Peller wondered how Pollock could dress in that fashion in the radiant ninety-degree Manhattan July without sweltering. With his long, salt-and-pepper beard and side locks, Al Pollock looked like an old man directly out of the Eastern European ghettos of the nineteenth century. And, Peller speculated to himself, the man couldn't be fifty. He still had young children at home and was already a grandfather. So it could be with a family of ten.

Both men greeted the borrower, then Peller escorted Pollock to the company's marble and mahogany conference room to negotiate terms for a quick resolution of his delinquent loans. The tension he carried heavily between his shoulders was the only giveaway that Peller felt nervous.

"Mr. Pollock, my friend, how's business?" began Peller respectfully.

"Louis," Pollock sighed, "things could be better, a lot better."

After the inevitable haggling over terms for a deal that was, basically, Pollock's only financially viable option, Peller turned his newfound leverage to the subject of making sorely needed repairs posthaste: new boiler before winter, painting inside and out, repairing rusting fire escapes, and replacing the roof. "You have left me with nothing, Louis," exclaimed Pollock. "Under these terms, I will be working for Amie Mae for the next five years."

"Which would you rather lose, Mr. Pollock: five years of profit or thirty-two buildings?"

The two men shook hands to seal the agreement at eleven thirty, and Peller ushered his borrower into the reception area. Relaxed now, they lingered a moment, trading amicable banter.

"We can finalize the details next week when I get back into town. Meantime, I'll have Steve draw up a draft agreement," Peller stated.

"Mr. Peller," intoned Alvin Pollock, stroking his beard nervously. "You had me over a barrel on this workout. All my funding will dry up if I don't get out of this mess in a way you consider kosher. But don't underestimate my staying power. My company will be back doing deals … and I want Amie Mae to know I'm a good risk."

"You have my word on it, Mr. Pollock. Your credit will be good with us."

Peller escorted Pollock to the elevators. Though he managed to keep his cool, Peller was bursting with delight. He'd avoided foreclosing and just gotten the best workout deal in company history against one of its toughest customers. He smiled. He was feeling well satisfied with his astute reading of Pollock and their deal. The chiefs in Virginia would be pleased, even that stick-in-the-mud boss of his, Joe Vallardo. Mission accomplished.

Peller decided on impulse to call his old college buddy, Paul Chase, who brokered big, commercial real estate deals for a large New York firm. Maybe the two friends could meet in the coffee shop downstairs to celebrate over sandwiches before Tommy got back to escort Peller to his next boxing match.

"Paul Chase, drop everything and come meet your old roommate before I have to trek into the wilds of the Upper West Side of New York. Do you have time for a quick bite?" Peller was supremely confident in his ability to persuade anyone, but especially his friends, to bend to his will.

"Louis, couldn't you at least give a little warning before you're in town?" Paul protested. "I'm waiting for an important call and—"

"Cut the carping, my friend," Peller goaded him. "Turn on your beeper and come to lunch; the tab's on me. I just closed a deal of my own that's worth the expense. Meet you at the coffee shop downstairs in fifteen."

Whenever Peller got to New York, he tried to at least talk to Paul, who was struggling to fill all that commercial real estate amid New York's worst-ever corporate defections and a bust in office deals. Paul Chase was one of Louis Peller's oldest and most trusted comrades. He was a slim man, tall, patrician looking.

He dressed in khakis and blue blazers when he wasn't wearing finely tailored business suits and came from a family where the blood ran blue. His round, tortoise-shell glasses framed pale blue eyes in an otherwise colorless face. Serious and detached, he didn't have Peller's zest for mixing it up, but he spent much time observing and admiring the skill of his former college roommate. Peller and Paul had roomed together through four inspiring, and occasionally academically enlightening, years at Syracuse University. An unlikely pair, yet they had stayed in contact. By the time Peller moved to DC for law school, Paul had already been in Washington for a few years, marrying Sherry Burton, his college sweetheart. Paul too had studied the law, but he wavered in his decision to join one of the old-line, prestigious Washington firms as his family had urged him. Deciding he needed more stimulation than staid, sit-behind-the-desk contract law, Paul rebelled and went to work for the Central Intelligence Agency, after which he would disappear regularly. Peller was never sure what Paul did in those days or where he would go on his long junkets abroad.

It was hard on Paul's marriage.

For a long time, Peller and his bride, Lana, would try to have Sherry over whenever Paul got called out of the country, but the secret life of the CIA wife was too tough for such a social butterfly. After a while, Sherry became fed up with Paul's long, mysterious absences, and they divorced. It was amicable, but what a shame, Peller thought. He himself had suffered a terrible crush on Sherry during college and envied his old roomie for snaring such a beautiful temptress.

The divorce hit Paul like a brick. Other things about the Agency were wearing on him too. Finally, in the early eighties, Paul saw the light, or perhaps the darkness, of his duties and left the Agency for reasons, Peller guessed in hindsight, probably having something to do with the advent of Iran-Contra. Peller did his best to help Paul through those tough times, surfacing with Orioles tickets on summer evenings, organizing the occasional fall camping trip to the Shenandoah's, inviting him home for dinner, where Lana and the kids showered "Uncle Paul" with home-cooked dinners and much-deserved affection. Lana tried to fix Paul up with some of her more eligible friends.

It was Peller's long conversations with him about real estate that finally inspired Paul to venture back into private life without a government safety net … or snare. That's when Paul, a born-again capitalist, embraced commercial real estate as his salvation, during heady times. "Better rich than dead" was his newly-minted philosophy. He eventually made his way to New York, still seeking excitement, where he made money hand over fist until the recession hit. The only leasing boom in these bleak days was being created in the wake of the bombing of the World Trade Towers. "Relocating Peter to pay Paul," Peller had joked in macabre tones. Many firms working in those ungodly skyscrapers were moving to the amply empty and bargain-basement-priced office space of midtown Manhattan.

Now the hands and fists of real estate brokers like Paul all over the northeastern United States, once busy signing leases and grasping money as fast as it would flow, were clenched in rapidly emptying pockets. The radically altered marketplace worked to Peller's advantage in his role as mortgage lender to the formerly high-and-mighty. But the Paul Chases of the world were left clutching an empty bag.

Peller tried to be understanding in the face of his friend's downward turn of fortune, particularly since he felt himself partly responsible for Paul's choice of profession, never mind the unforeseen timing of the market plunge. But the fact was that Paul's misfortune was Peller's bread and butter. So here he was, basking in success and being jostled by patrons squeezing in and out of their seats, hassled by a hurried waitress, and waiting impatiently for Paul to show up so he could brag about his latest success.

By the time Paul slipped into the busy coffee shop, it was close to noon. He was wearing his customary blue pin-striped suit and blue button-down shirt with conservative yellow tie, jacket tossed carelessly over his shoulder. He carried himself with the grace and knowledge of a man who, by birthright, belonged to "the club," a place where Peller felt conspicuous. Peller noticed that his friend still appeared trim and youthful, although his hairline had receded rather dramatically over the past few years. As he approached, Peller could detect a slight shine on Paul's forehead on this sultry July day, the only sign of suffering from the heat in a city where forests of buildings magnified the sun's rays and furnaces of fumes erupted from dank subway tunnels, amplifying the thermostat to wilt even the heartiest souls.

Peller was sweating like a pig in the sun-drenched storefront coffee shop. He unconsciously ran a hand through his hair to smooth back his unruly waves.

"It's too damned hot out there, Louis," Paul muttered as he slumped into the chair opposite his friend. "Don't they have air-conditioning in this place?"

"C'mon, Paul," Peller admonished. "You've escaped jungle hot spots pursued by guerilla fighters out for your hide without sweating a drop. No complaints about summer in the city. Come, have a quick corned beef on rye with me before Tommy comes to pick me up. It's been too long, my friend."

Looking happily at his friend, Peller marveled at how, in his own way, Paul's habits of dress and behavior marked him a Wasp as distinctly as the black derby hat marked Al Pollock a Hasid.

"Ya been following the Mets this summer, Louis?" Paul asked, picking up his menu while the surly waitress came over for the fourth time to check on Peller.

"Yeah, maybe you can take me to a game next time I'm in town, Paul. 'Member the last time we took in that doubleheader?"

The waitress harrumphed impatiently.

"Hiya, Mabel," winked Peller. "How we doin' now? Got your orders under control?" Obviously he'd been working on a conversation with this waitress before Paul's arrival.

"Ya know, this ain't the Ritz, pal. Gimme your order and let me turn this table," she bellowed. As the two men ordered, she yelled out to the kitchen over her shoulder, grabbing their menus to give to the next two top, a couple of perky young secretaries just sitting down.

"You sure pick 'em, friend. Service with a smile," Paul observed, chuckling at Peller's futile attempts to charm.

"Hummph. Mr. Chase, New York is *your* town. I take no credit," Peller retorted.

"So, what's the big deal we're celebrating?" asked Paul, grabbing a pickle from the silver bowl on the table.

"Money in the bank, my friend. I just negotiated the biggest workout in Amie Mae's history and saved some poor slumlord the horrors of foreclosure. Guy's worth millions that are tied up in properties whose values are plunging like Niagara Falls, but you wouldn't know it to hear him talk, says he's a '*bissle* strapped for cash' right now. Anyway, I just made him see the light of day. 'Pay up, or we'll start the foreclosure process and take all your real estate.' If we foreclose, it could be a long time before Al Pollock gets financing for any other business venture in this town. And he knows that means the slow squeeze until ..." he wrung a napkin in his hands and uttered an ugly crushing sound, "financial ruin," Louis concluded with a boyish grin.

"Well, Scrooge finally heard me with that, and ya know what? I think I may have succeeded in pulling his ass out of the whirlpool and getting him to fix things up to save his miserable tenants from suffering through a chilling winter with heatless radiators. Although, as far as those tenants are concerned, I'm not so sure being kicked into the street is their worst option. Still," Peller sighed melodramatically, "if I've helped them somehow ..."

"You always did enjoy putting the screws to the rich to help the poor. What is this Robin Hoodism you practice? I have a few clients to whom I've leased and sold real estate over the years in this town who would make prime candidates for your form of socialism."

"No, Paul. In spite of everything, I'm a capitalist all the way. I figure these apartment moguls have a service to provide. As long as they're the only people who can find a way to offer shelter for the poor and still make money on the deal, I'll keep supporting their efforts to try."

"You know, Lou," munched Paul thoughtfully. "I think I'd like to try my hand as a property owner. I always thought I'd make a pretty decent landlord. And, what with your understanding of the business and my access to distressed real estate at rock-bottom prices, I think we could rake it in."

"I love you, Paul. We're on the same wavelength. In fact, I think I could probably turn you on to some owners whose buildings are near foreclosure who are willing to deal."

"I'm not sure being a slumlord is exactly my line, Lou. Although, I do think providing access to reasonably priced housing is a vital economic enterprise. The question is, can you deliver good quality and maintain it while still making a profit?"

"Tax credits, Paul. That's the ticket. You can trust me on that one."

Peller stopped talking as Mabel unceremoniously slid plates in front of them with the wrong orders on them. He observed archly to this unheeding waitress that he'd asked for turkey on wheat, not tuna on white. She gave Peller the fish-eye, picked up the plate officiously, and offered it to the secretaries at the next table.

"So ya can wait a minute more? They'll probably leave a better tip than you anyway, Mr. Wise Guy," she observed drily. Peller managed a sly wink at the women next to them before snarling again at Mabel hospitality.

"Peller," Paul intervened, embarrassed, expecting a war of words.

Before he could launch into his tirade on service and quality, Peller spied Tommy's burley frame in the door of the coffee shop. He felt the knot tighten in his stomach again.

"Uh-oh, Paul. Hate to run without eating, but here's my date. I'll have to pass on this next waltz." Peller rose to leave.

Paul sighed. "Louis, remind me next time you call not to have lunch with you. We haven't even gotten our food, and already you've given me indigestion. Don't forget, you pay at the door—"

"Cinderella, wrap mine up to go, and present my friend over here with the bill. Take good care of him, though," he winked with a smile.

To Paul, he explained his sudden rush. "Gotta get to the slums before the drug dealers come out to play."

Peller dribbled a pocketful of change on the table for the waitress, grabbed his sandwich from her in a flurry, and sprinted to meet Tommy at the front door, leaving chaos in his wake. "See you next time I'm in Paris, Paul."

****

Meanwhile, forty-eight floors overhead, there was tumult of a different sort. Amie Mae's receptionist, Julie Hudson, gripped the phone. A fresh, feisty young woman with a smart mouth, Julie was far from worldly. In fact, she had never been farther from Manhattan than Brooklyn or the Jersey Shore.

Julie looked ashen-faced under her artfully applied makeup, and panicky. Without turning around in her desk, she shouted in a loud voice, "Help me. This cawler's lookin' fa' Louis and sayin' somethin' about a fire in one of Amie Mae's buildings. Wha'?"

Steve, who happened to be returning from his lunchtime workout at the health club, pried the phone from her frozen grip.

"This is Steve Shapiro, Louis Peller's colleague. How can I help you?" he asked in as calm a voice as he could muster. He was frantically scratching out a note for Julie—*call the cops now*—pointing to a phone on a nearby desk while encouraging the anonymous caller.

"You say you're at Broadway and West 137th? Yes, that's our property. You live there?"

Victoria Fortash, or Vicki, as she liked to be called, the only other attorney in the New York office, silently picked up the line on a desk opposite the receptionist's to jot down the gist of the conversation and her impressions of the caller.

"I understand you've just left the building," Steve prodded the caller. "Is there anyone there who knows what's going on?"

Vicki waved to Steve to keep the caller talking.

Steve, nervous, was taking deep drags on his cigarette as he listened. He tamped the dying butt into the ashtray on Julie's desk and immediately knocked another one out of the pack, forgetting about his oft-repeated pledge to cut back.

Caller is agitated, Victoria noted on the pink phone pad, the only paper handy at Julie's desk. *Sounds black, deep voice. Male—no name given. Says he doesn't know the woman who claims she set boiler room on fire to screw over landlord. She's talking to reporters. Hispanic woman. She's been living in the bldg 2 years—nothing ever gets fixed. Caller on pay phone across 137th.*

Steve listened intently. He tried to reassure the obviously agitated caller as Julie reported to the area police precinct what she knew of the incident.

"Sergeant Brown here. You say you have some guy on the phone reporting a fire? He thinks it may have been set by one of the tenants? Keep him talking. We're alerting fire and rescue. We'll get a patrol unit to check out the scene. West 137th and Broadway, yes, we'll have someone there within two minutes." The officer started barking orders to someone nearby. Sgt. Brown came back on the line with Julie. "That neighborhood's been having lots of problems lately, but this report is unusual. If there's been an arson, why would anyone notify the mortgage company? You say the owner of the building hasn't been payin' on his mortgage? I'll lay money on the fact that his insurance is all paid up. We have a patrol car on the way. We'll check it out."

Julie hung up and motioned to Steve to let the caller off the line. "What was that all about?" Julie asked.

"The police are on their way," Steve mumbled, reassuring the caller before he hung up.

"There," Steve sighed. He looked around blankly, first at Julie, then at Vicki, extinguishing another cigarette in frustration. "Got me. Guy sounded panicky. Someone apparently lit a fire in the trash compactor room in the basement, and the place immediately filled with smoke. Anyway, the woman who they think may have started the fire, a tenant, has been standing on the sidewalk in front of the building giving interviews to some radio and TV crews that showed up." Steve looked over Vicki's notes. "This lady must be pretty PO'd. Says she's sick and tired of living in a building with no hot water, cracks in the walls and ceiling, and only intermittent heat in the winter. By the way, he mentioned she's a real looker and doesn't have too many clothes on. We've got to get out there fast. Maybe I ought to handle it myself."

"Steve, you are such a classic SOB. Everything boils down to S-E-X. Typical," Vicki chuckled. "You should have your head examined. This sounds like one for Oprah: Today, sexy tenants set blazes to smoke out derelict landlords."

For Vicki, now thirty-four and the mother of three-year-old twins, the same Vicki who had always regretted not going to work for the district attorney's office fresh out of law school, this scenario offered the perfect opening. Criminal law had always been her forte, but in the end, a big paycheck from the corporation and regular hours had outweighed her desires for a career in the courtroom. Still, a case like this could revive her dream.

"Vick, let's do our homework. Pull the file on that place." Steve was now all business. "Who owns it?"

Feeling a rush of adrenaline, Vicki moved into high gear. "There'll be a hot time in the old town today," she observed excitedly. "And it sure beats proofreading contracts."

"C'mon," Steve warned. "This is no joking matter. We've got to take this case seriously. Think of the negative press for the company if we handle it wrong. Think of our careers going down the sewer while this woman tangos through the living rooms of New York carrying on about rats in the building and children sleeping in stairwells. Someone around there obviously knows Amie holds the mortgage, or they wouldn't have bothered to contact us. And that same somebody might just see fit to give us trouble by talking to reporters. I mean, how would the company look if we're accused by the press of lending money to landlords we know milk the buildings?"

Steve looked up suddenly. "Julie, where was Louis going this afternoon?"

They exchanged horrified glances. "225 West 137th …"

Julie went back to the front desk to manage the phone, which had suddenly begun ringing off the hook.

Vicki was sorting through the loan files on the building. "Lucky it's not a big building, but it hasn't been maintained either, according to this inspection report. This incident could be the kiss of death on a building like that. A fire here, a rent strike there, and the borrower's cash flow dries up. And where does that leave Amie Mae? We'll have to wait for an eyewitness report from the scene. Louis and Tommy can get the real scoop on the property, up close and personal, as they say."

She slowly walked back toward her office, studying the details.

Steve followed. "What's the dirt on this place?" he asked.

"Here's the loan documentation. Sixty-unit building in Spanish Harlem, purchased in 1987 by Bud Epstein, made four payments in the past twelve months. A one-point-four million dollar loan currently under a defaulted agreement, and I think Louis was supposed to do an inspection there this afternoon. Boy, is he going to have something to check out now. Sounds like this one's right up Louis's alley: arson … beautiful naked woman …" Vicki was now chattering on, though Steve ignored her excitement and pulled the file out of her hand.

Steve gave Vicki a warning look. "Oh yeah? You don't know

Peller like I do. He won't be thrilled about this. You can't imagine how vile these buildings are. When was the last time you had to maneuver an obstacle course around hungry rats and putrefying garbage?"

"You forget, I've inspected condemned buildings in the South Bronx, wise ass. Look, Steve. I'll be serious," Vicki dropped all pretense of sarcasm. "Last week, when we were discussing the property, Louis mentioned something about a prostitution ring, just something he'd heard from one or two of the tenants last time he was up there. In fact, here's a handwritten note he must have thrown in as a reminder." She held up a sheet torn from Peller's famous yellow legal pad.

Steve considered this new evidence. "Prostitution, eh? Our little arsonist may be a livewire. Then Epstein will have a problem. And if she's got as big a mouth as it sounds, so will Amie Mae."

He hesitated, then added, "If anyone might know anything about a prostitution ring, it would be Romano; he's got the lowdown on all those joints. That would really be the icing on this cake, wouldn't it? Prostitutes setting fire to the place … We ought to try to warn them what's coming down. I'll try to get a hold of Louis," Steve suggested. "Julie, page Peller for me right away. Sing out as soon as he calls in."

Chapter 2
Ascent into Harlem

Tommy cursed as he and Peller dashed around the corner to the car stationed illegally in front of a fire hydrant, emergency lights flashing. "You're in there shootin' the shit with your goddamn fratahnity brother, and New York's finest are out ticketin' and towin'. I thought we understood each other, Lou. You say twelve thirty, and that means twelve twenty-nine, not twelve forty-five. In Washington, you might have time for your three martinis, but New York ain't no place for power lunches."

"Quit complaining, Tom," Peller interjected. "I said I'm sorry. I take care of the tickets anyway, not you."

"And I'm sick of meetin' up with punk hoodlums in these stinkin' neighborhoods where you like to house hunt." Tommy ignored Peller's interruption. "Shit. Copper's about to put another fifty-dollar fine on the windshield. I knew it."

They turned the corner to see a policeman tuck the ticket beneath the wiper. Tommy approached apologetically to weasel out of the penalty in his most charmingly persuasive manner. The cop just shook his head. "S-O-L, bub." Shit outta luck.

"Let's move it along, Tommy," Peller said, sliding in on

the passenger's side. "We've got worlds to conquer before three o'clock."

"Fa'gedaboutit," Tommy croaked in exasperation. They streaked their way across and uptown, weaving from lane to lane, outwitting the taxi drivers at their own game as the Impala boogied up to the Harlem apartment building that was next on Peller's workout list. The air conditioning wasn't working and, even with windows wide open and making all haste, there was no breath of air to break up that insufferably stale heat from the baking tarred streets and cracking sidewalks of the urban oven.

"Why can't you take on propahties in Scawsdale for a change?" Tommy demanded. "That's where these high-rollin' landlords live, ain't it? You shouldn't be hangin' around these glamorous parts of town, Louie. You're an easy mark."

"Unfortunately, Tom, Scarsdale doesn't have many low-income apartment buildings. It wouldn't be Scarsdale if it did."

Peller felt the beeper vibrate on his belt; he had the sound turned off. "I hate these damn things," he complained, checking the number. "They're calling from downtown. Probably Steve playing a joke on me again," he added, alluding to his colleague's occasional attempts to entertain him with off-color stories and practical jokes, distracting Peller even as he engaged in delicate negotiations. "Well, this time the joke will be on him. Steve will have to wait to hear from me."

As they wove through the crowded streets of New York, the character of the pedestrians on the Upper West Side gradually changed from affluent and predominantly white office workers to a more interesting and diverse ethnic population. Far uptown, sidewalks presented citizens of the world: three generations of ebony African women strolling to the neighborhood market and thirty-something grandmothers holding the hands of their teenage daughters, while the younger women wheeled their baby buggies in the time-honored barrio tradition. Bronze and black and yellow and white children playing hide-and-seek, running through the legs of their mothers who, in turn, were knotted in chattering groups in front of neighborhood bodegas, carrying bags toppling over with packages of beans and rice and a cornucopia of fruits and vegetables. Men, young and old, singly or in pairs, just hangin' in the 'hood, their faces sullen, while tweens and teenagers gathered excitedly around new gold Cadillacs inching ostentatiously down the crowded streets, skippered by young men eager to show off their newfound affluence from trafficking drugs.

The character of the neighborhoods changed too. Where flowerboxes once graced the outsides of buildings near Columbus Circle, there were now bricked-in windows around the "battle zone." Clean, white shutters and pastel print Roman shades gave way to yellow, red, and green striped kente cloth to curtain off what windows still survived the twin urban terrors of poverty and chronic unemployment.

Around 125th and Broadway, they entered the quarter known as Spanish Harlem. Here, close to Columbia University, a plethora of pale, studious university students emerged silently from the smoky gloom of the subway, dressed down so as to disappear into the scenery, in vapid contrast to the boldly colored dress of the Hispanic and African-American citizenry teeming on the streets. These mostly affluent students knew the rule: do not look anyone in the eye. In this part of town, "lookin'" at someone meant looking for a fight. And everyone in the 'hood loved a fight, anything to break life's wanton desperation.

Peller felt the pager vibrating again and, in annoyance, turned the damned thing off.

"Pull over here." Peller pointed to a corner of West 137th Street lined with decrepit apartment buildings, one more rundown than the next. On a building wall, here and there, were more of those murals—tombstones, they were—offering graphic, wrenching tribute to a young man or woman gunned down, a casualty of ghetto life. All these brightly painted brick walls illustrated different themes: religious symbols, a portrait of the victim, a serene scene far from this urban violence. What they all had in common were the names and dates of the dead, with the slogan "rest in peace." A monument and a reminder to the living that life was only the hell you passed through until you could die and go to heaven.

"This is the street. One of your better addresses, I might add." Tommy pulled over to the west side of Broadway to let Peller out and told him he would circle around the labyrinth of one-way streets to meet Peller as near as possible to 225 West 137th, where he would hook up with landlord and super. As Peller disembarked, he instructed the driver to hang close by, keep his eyes and ears open in case of trouble, and maintain a low profile. "And make sure you're ready to leave for the airport by two forty-five," Peller advised. "I'll have a good hour and a half now before this neighborhood wakes up to boom boxes blasting when the damned gangs get out of what passes for school here." Tommy sped away without a backward glance.

Peller walked quickly to greet Bud Epstein, another Jewish landlord holding properties in what used to be an all-Jewish neighborhood. Jews had fled these buildings long ago, leaving them to be inhabited by blacks then Hispanics until now, when the only place most Jews still visited were the cemeteries where their ancestors were buried. Unless they, like Epstein, owned property there.

Willie Johnson, the building's superintendent, was a black man who had grown up in Spanish Harlem when it was mainly tenanted by a solidly black, middle-class constituency. He stayed and raised his own family there. But the neighborhood had changed, becoming predominantly Latino, including many illegal aliens. Fortunately, Johnson spoke Spanish. He'd learned it in high school and in the neighborhood as a teenager, a matter of survival.

What a world, Peller thought, amazed, as always, at the odd conglomeration of nationalities and cultures cohabiting just a few square blocks. Within every borough of New York, a myriad of communities existed side by side, from Little Italy to Little

Haiti to the new Russian Pale. The neighbors lived separate lives, side by side, yet never crossing a certain street without fear. Far from a melting pot, New York was a boiling caldron waiting to bubble over.

But here and there, uneasy economic alliances existed. Only in New York could you find Jews and Turks, Greeks and Italians entering into volatile partnerships, relying on African-American middlemen to keep illegal Latinos in line. It was indeed ironic. Peller never ceased to be amazed at the off-beat bedfellows of business. This multiethnic business coalition was at the heart of many of his borrowers' problems. Landlords, who didn't speak Spanish, hired black or Latino superintendents who feigned not to speak English. *How is it suddenly my job to defuse the Mideast conflict and implement NAFTA in the middle of Manhattan?* he mused. He surmised it might be a relief to work with more traditional, upright, white-bread real estate developers from, say, Nebraska for a change. At least relations would seem civil.

It was a surprise that, by the time Peller spotted them, landlord and super had stationed themselves well down the block from their property and that they were walking quickly to the corner to intercept Peller, arguing vehemently all the while. As they caught sight of him, both men forced complicitous smiles for their lender. What could be wrong? Looking beyond them, Peller glimpsed a curious crowd gathering near what should have been Epstein's apartment building. He peered down the block suspiciously and noticed a fat finger of black smoke marring an otherwise spotless sky, then he saw the flash of red police lights in front.

Peller and company had been scheduled to explore the bowels of the building at West 137th, to examine the roof and stairs for structural and mechanical problems, then to begin another negotiation on resolving the debt. Now it looked as if a new set of circumstances might command their attention.

As Peller came closer to the building, he could hear agitated onlookers shouting indistinct obscenities. He listened for a sense of what was happening, but even though he was unable to make out the epithets, people were clearly worked up. As the urgency of the situation grew on him, he picked up his pace, sprinting past his borrower and shouting, "Did anyone call the fire department? What the fuck's going on here anyway?"

Bud Epstein strained to match Peller's stride while explaining the predicament, but running was simply too much exertion on a sixty-two-year-old body.

"Louis, slow down," gasped the winded landlord. "You should understand; there's been a small fire. The girl who set it—it was arson!" Epstein collapsed onto a stoop in front of a building a half block from his own, panting and waiting for Peller to turn around so the hapless landlord could outline his unbelievable story.

Peller halted and turned but didn't walk back to the stoop where Epstein finally flopped to catch his breath. He was impatient with Epstein's stories and excuses.

"I tried to call you at your office, but you were already on the way here, and they said you weren't answering your page," the older man explained between gasps. "The suspect is a tenant. We doused the flames quickly, before the fire trucks even arrived. I swear, I don't know much more than that. The woman doesn't speak much English. Johnson here knows her, thinks she's up to no good. She hasn't paid her rent in six months, and now there'll be trouble for this mess. I think she's crazy, and I'm guessing she has loose lips. She was talking to some reporter when we got here a few minutes ago; fractured English, mind you, but you know newspaper attention could mean trouble. Not that a reporter's gonna believe the likes of her. But frankly, Louis, I'm worried about what this little situation might do to my negotiations with Amie Mae."

Reporters. That was all they needed. Bud Epstein would not look too good in the light of a television camera if his building was a shambles and his tenants were burning it down for attention. And Amie Mae might get its butt kicked in the halls of justice for not putting a firm grip on its borrower's scrawny neck to maintain the place. Worse yet, Amie might have to take the building back in foreclosure and pay a small fortune to fix it up. Money down the toilet. Still, Peller was puzzled by Epstein's panic. "She's crazy, so what? Since when does your tenant's mental state concern us? You have legal means to recoup the rent or evict her. Her psychological and criminal status should not be our concern."

Willie Johnson had been walking back to the scene of the crime slowly, in no hurry to deal with the fallout, and just now caught up with the two men. "Let me try to explain, Mr. Peller," asserted the usually unassuming black man. "Miss Angel Sanchez up there, she's in apartment 617. She has been running a … um … shall we say, house of ill repute out of her apartment. There's guys jabberin' away outside, all hours of the day and night. *Yo hablo* Spanish, so I hear them talkin' about … talkin' to Angel. Well, she's mad with me, 'cause with her pipes cracking and her apartment's in bad shape. She's losin' customers. She claims that me and Mr. Epstein here ain't doin' our jobs, fixin' the leaks in her bathroom and kitchen and so on. But she ain't payin' the rent."

Peller looked levelly from the worried black man to his steely eyed boss. Maybe Johnson was on the up-and-up, he thought. The super had seemed like a good, honest man. But the landlord, he was another story. Peller wouldn't put anything past Epstein. That man was one slippery fish, and he was partner in one of the most successful real estate companies in the City of New York. This scene was undoubtedly one of Epstein's tactics to try to extract himself from his financial problems with Amie Mae … or collect the insurance money, he guessed cynically.

"I want to check out the woman's story. You say her name is Angel? I'd like to hear it from the horse's mouth," Peller announced, to Johnson's obvious dismay. Peller didn't miss the sudden glint in Epstein's eye as the older man silently watched Peller stride, Sherlock Holmes-like, to the scene.

Peller intercepted a police officer just as Angel Sanchez was being unceremoniously shoe horned into a patrol car. He admired her unabashed strutting, the proud sway and swerve of her hips. Her sleeveless gold lamé tunic descended only mid-thigh. Her brassy red hair was stiff as a skyscraper, teased to a height Peller hadn't observed in polite society since the beehives of the sixties. As Peller approached, the cop was waving away reporters seeking comments.

"Does this woman have legal counsel, officer?" Peller intervened.

"Not my problem. You her lawyer? If you are, best get crackin'. Not only can we book her on arson, but there's more'n ample evidence to hold her for prostitution," the officer stated gruffly, all business. Peller could see him locking handcuffs around her wrists.

"What evidence?"

"Oh, there's witnesses from one end of this block to the other." He motioned to the lineup of men leering at Angel beyond the patrol-car windows. Meanwhile, Angel was busy cooing and cajoling the patrolman at the wheel of the car. The first officer nodded over at Epstein. "Including her landlord over there."

Peller was immediately suspicious. "Could I speak with her, officer? I think she may need some good legal advice. I am an attorney," Peller used his most solicitous tones.

The policeman looked skeptically at this obviously well-heeled white man who had just happened along on the street to offer legal counsel to this woman who so obviously was not used to working day shifts. Oh well, he figured. Whitey wasn't his problem.

"I guess you can have a couple of minutes with her." Peller shook the policeman's hand gratefully. Motioning Peller aside, the officer confided, "Listen, man, this floozy ain't no angel. She don't give away nothin', 'cept for cold, hard cash. You want my personal opinion, this Sanchez girl is one fucked up chick. You speak Spanish? She's been jabbering away, can't speak enough English to save her soul … or won't."

Peller stooped down to talk to Angel through the open window of the patrol car. Her dark eyes were ringed with eyeliner, making them appear enormous. Her legs were curled kitten-like on the seat, and her gold strappy shoes with high spiked heels looked new. Peller could see this "angel" was quite composed and in control. He took note of the heavy makeup masking an otherwise unremarkable face and the dress that barely concealed her curvaceous frame and appreciated that this foxy lady would probably love nothing more than to make a splash across the pages of *Playboy*. He caught her eye.

"Ms. Sanchez, my name is Louis Peller." He heard himself speaking loudly, thinking she might understand his English better that way. "I work for Amie Mae, the company that loaned Bud Epstein the money to buy this building. They tell me you set fire to it."

The woman looked around her disapprovingly. "Mr. Peller," she announced conspiratorially. "Many things you need to know about that man." She nodded toward Epstein. "He's the crook here. He screwed me more ways than one."

"Do you have a lawyer?"

"No. I don't trust no one, especially lawyers. They just rip you off." To his surprise, the mysterious Angel spoke English fairly well, with only a hint of an accent, contrary to Epstein's allegations. Maybe her fluency was selective, and she spoke English only to the people she deemed helpful. She was clearly educated but undoubtedly chose to disguise that fact around the police. "I think you are different," she told him peering entrancingly into his eyes.

Peller felt sorry for her. She struck him as down but not out. Anyway, he couldn't resist helping a damsel in distress, especially if he thought he could somehow benefit.

He smiled earnestly. "Ms. Sanchez, I'll talk to someone about finding good legal representation for you. Meanwhile, don't tell the police anything. Just keep yourself calm and wait until the attorney comes. Have they read you your rights?"

She nodded.

"Good. Now if you can just play it cool, I'll see if I can help you." Peller, having offered that advice, could see that she knew this routine far better than he. Obviously, this was not her first brush with the law. He backed away from the patrol car as the first policeman entered. The crowd had been dispersed. Now only Epstein and Johnson remained to survey the scene. "Good luck," he murmured.

"Good luck you too, Mr. Peller," she said in a clear voice, calculated to be heard by these lingering witnesses. "Maybe I help you sometime too." Flashing a voluptuous, collaborative smile, Angel rolled away like a high school princess to a prom.

Now there goes one helluva dame, Peller thought as he turned back to his borrower.

Bud Epstein looked amused. "I didn't know you had such a way with women, Lou. She pretended not to speak English with me."

"She's clearly quite troubled," Peller responded, not biting on Epstein's bantering bait. "I wanted to make sure she wasn't hurt. No need for a personal injury suit to add the insult. Now, shall we proceed? I have an early plane to catch."

They entered the decrepit edifice single file: first Peller, then Epstein. Willie Johnson reluctantly brought up the rear. Peller anxiously stabbed the elevator button. As the three men waited for the slow, gray, scarred, urine-smelling service elevator to open out on the basement, Peller joked about hearing rats through the walls. Epstein's chilling laugh echoed through the empty hallway as he intoned proudly, "The only rat you'll see in my building is the one staring back in the mirror if you insist on foreclosure."

Willie Johnson looked away to avoid Epstein's asking glance.

The elevator shuddered to a halt to unveil a typical building's typical rathskeller, vintage 1945, six stories of red brick. The building had been constructed to house a cement underground bomb shelter in which the yellow and black fallout signs were still posted. In post-Cold War, current drug war New York City, however, the place also held remnants of a different culture that offered a far more destructive danger than any nuclear bomb. Evidence of drugs, Peller knew, had been erased for his benefit, but he still espied one or two empty crack vials swept away in corners. Where there was prostitution, there were usually drugs, and vice versa. Cobwebs loomed high in the rafters. Asbestos insulation covered the piping. Still, the boiler and burner looked well-tended for the old relics that they were.

The smell of smoke clung to cracking walls, and soot and ashes still drifted down from the small conflagration whose whereabouts had been the compactor room. The place was a dusty, sooty deathtrap. Both Peller and Johnson were dressed in worn, sturdy shoes, casual slacks and shirt sleeves, clothes befitting their task. Epstein, on the other hand, appeared attentively tailored. The little man looked elegantly out of place.

"Glad I wore my old shoes," grumbled the landlord as he carefully inched his way through the cellar in his hand sewn, Italian leather moccasins. Grease puddles made a trail to the old boiler. Epstein carefully removed his dark jacket to avoid dusting the fine silk and linen tailoring with the inch-thick powder that coated storage crates and walls.

"Listen, man, I told you this ain't the place to be tryin' out no glass slippers," the super goaded him.

Peller was already making notes about the conditions around him. The basement was relatively free of debris, and miraculously, he didn't notice any common well-fed rodents scampering across the floors at their approach, although he was as certain of their presence as he was of the owner's false pleas of due diligence and impending poverty.

"Exterminators come every month," the super offered, "because I despise pests. I try to run a clean operation, but I can't control everyone's bad habits. Some of the tenants don't take the time to put garbage down the chutes. They leave it in the hallway or throw it out their windows into the alley."

Peller stared at his borrower, unconvinced by Willie Johnson's weak defense. "Clean, huh, Bud? How clean is Angel Sanchez's place?"

"Listen, Louis," Epstein asserted, "this morning's events aside, you won't find the problems here you might in some of Amie Mae's other properties. I can turn a profit and maintain the building without endangering my tenants' health and safety. You guys just have to cut me a little slack until I'm back on my feet financially."

Peller scrutinized his borrower dispassionately. Bud Epstein was a small, slim man. His stooped, halting gait belied a surprising strength and vitality. He didn't necessarily look the part of the wealthy landlord. And he didn't look impoverished, as evidenced by his hand-tailored clothing, neatly trimmed beard, and manicured nails. Epstein was as street-smart as he was well-groomed. A survivor, not just of the streets of New York, but also of the unspeakable horrors of Holocaust Germany. Bud Epstein was one of New York's assimilated Jews, speaking without accent or costume that might hint of the Old World. Although his parents had instilled a deep faith in him from the time he was ready for school and had hoped and prayed that he would go to the yeshiva to learn Hebrew and study Torah, it was not meant to be. He had embraced their faith then been carted off in a boxcar with them, had suffered with them in the concentration camps while they prayed for the deliverance of their children if not themselves, and had watched his God-fearing parents herded off to gas chambers to die. His sorrow and mourning over their brutal death at such a young age had hardened his young soul and turned his mind to disbelief. So when, as a young boy, he had been liberated from Auschwitz with an older brother and their baby sister, having stayed alive by a combination of wits, luck, and determination, he could no longer pray. Even in his parents' memory, he could not intone the mourner's *kaddish*, for, to him, those words were empty.

After the liberation, the three children had travelled alone to

New York to be raised by an uncle with his own four children, growing up in the Lower East Side in what was then the Jewish neighborhood. Later, as a scrappy and independent teenager, Epstein made it his goal to earn lots of money, to blend in with the then-prevalent Waspy high society and get out of the old neighborhood as fast as he could, as soon as he scraped together enough to buy new shoes without holes and a dark-blue suit. He never looked back. Quietly, he was a big giver to Jewish charities and a big fish in the Jewish community, but more out of a commitment to the community than any feeling of spiritual union. Even though his wife, Sarah, had been committed to the ideals of communism when they first met, had shown the fire and spark of a zealot, and just as passionately, had embraced Orthodox Judaism and even Zionism after seeing the righteous flames of communism cool to dark embers, he remained aloof from the nostrums of religion. He held onto his own conviction: there is no God. From the time of Sarah's religious rebirth, when she donned a somber scarf to cover her flaming red hair and long sleeves and heavy stockings to hide her freckled arms and legs, even in the heat of summer, he had mentally bowed out of her life.

Bud Epstein tolerated Sarah's conversion to Orthodoxy with bitter resignation and retreated from her world, a professed agnostic. The loss of their only son during the Vietnam War, a son who wanted to resist that war on philosophical grounds but who acceded to his authoritarian father's demand that he fulfill his patriotic duty—only to be killed in friendly fire—hardened Epstein's heart to stone and turned his mind to gold, a love that grew to exclude all else.

Now, the negotiator, Louis Peller, was trying to speak Epstein's language: money. "Bud, we've been through this before. I can give you only so much leeway. But you've got to follow through on our original workout agreement and not play any more games with Amie Mae. You owe us one hundred seventy-six thousand dollars on back payments and legal bills. I'd like to give you a break, but frankly, you don't seem too poverty stricken these days to me," Peller observed wryly. "I haven't seen you trading in your new Mercedes for a used VW Beetle yet." Peller caught sight around the corner of a locked, chain-linked storage area that Willie had obviously not intended him to see, where mounds of half-empty boxes mottled with dust balls holding who knows what contraband had been kicked hastily aside. Peller made a few notes and said nothing more, but he caught an angry glance between borrower and super. They continued on their inspection.

I'll have to have a private chat with Mr. Johnson, thought Peller, making a mental note of it. *He's got something on Epstein, and I want to know what it is.*

Chapter 3
The Home Office

Hanging up the phone with a small grin of satisfaction, Joe Vallardo swiveled around in his chair and put his feet up on the mahogany credenza by the window behind his desk. *There are certainly advantages to being part of the management team at Amie Mae*, he thought idly, doodling with his Mont Blanc fountain pen on company letterhead. Like a corner office with an expansive view of the wooded park surrounding the building. Like this rather impressive office furniture. Like status for managing a good-sized staff and rescuing the company from loans gone bad. Like a nice salary well into six figures. In the corporate world, he had indeed arrived.

Finally, thought the manager of asset resolution, king of foreclosures. Expanding his horizons beyond the company was a dream within sight. And that last phone call confirmed he was on his way. Vallardo's financial advisor was now transferring twenty-five thousand dollars from his savings to buy into a New York investment partnership that had paid out a 20 percent annual return for the past four years, buying up apartment buildings (many of which held Amie Mae loans). The investment partnership was beginning to diversify into shopping centers and mortgage-lending services. If everything went according to the investors' plans, the corporation would go public within eighteen months. With such a burst of growth and aggressive management, the partners estimated the return on their investments would eventually reach 150 percent over five years.

Nice little payback on the dime, he thought. It didn't bother Vallardo at all that he'd been tipped off to the opportunity by one of his Amie Mae borrowers, or that, based on that little bit of insider's advice, he'd actually given the borrower a major break on the terms of his workout. After all, the settlement had been fair to everyone: Amie Mae recovered seventy cents on the dollar for the loan, and Vincent Cinoletti gained a new investment partner on the side. With a little extra incentive for Vallardo, perhaps.

Meanwhile, Vallardo's investment, he had been assured, would not be used in any of the properties purchased with Amie Mae financing. Cinoletti would personally see to that. *No conflict in taking advantage of a good opportunity outside the company*, Vallardo mused. And besides, he was the most silent of partners. Even his wife didn't know where he was putting this money since it didn't come from either their joint account or their secure but conservative mutual funds. Wouldn't she be surprised when he drove home in that little red-hot Mercedes she had been begging for for so long.

Maybe then, finally, he could count on her unconditional love. His wife's only measure of success was a fat paycheck. For Andrea, love was an asset that could go to the highest bidder. But Vallardo was determined to build his own fortune, providing them the lifestyle his wife expected. He had sold Andrea on his ambitions and married her in a whirlwind after a three-month courtship founded on half-revealed truths and fantasy. Now the pressure to deliver on his grand promises was a vise squeezing his heart little by little, threatening to crush his aspirations … and her expectations.

And so his only option, he deduced, was to invest in the only thing he understood: real estate. Though the strategy was risky, it permitted him to stretch his grasp a little closer to the brass ring. Joe could sleep easier at night. He wouldn't end up like his dad, whose jobs on the railroad and the assembly line in upstate New York factories that eventually went bust barely fed the seven of them, much less afforded new clothes or nice cars. For uneducated "wops," the world offered few opportunities. Vallardo had been embarrassed for his dad and sorry for his mama, who had gone years working the second shift so the family could keep up the rent. He himself was determined never to live their life of tattered souls and faded dreams.

Leaving the farm, escaping to College Station, Texas, far from his mother's rosaries and homemade ziti and his father's weary excuses about opportunity lost, he'd attended Texas A&M for four years on a football scholarship. There he met Andrea, Texas to a tee and head cheerleader who was seduced by his dark good looks. They married. She settled into a lifetime passion for shopping, and he took a job doing real estate workouts. Then the housing market in Texas rebounded, and things looked uneasy. She didn't want to leave home. Finally, his tales of golden opportunities to be had back east unbounded by the vagaries of oil wells running dry, and his vows to make reams of money seduced her.

From Vallardo 's new vantage point on this ladder of success, he swiveled his chair around to study the family photo on his desk. Even though his parents were only in their late fifties, they looked old and worn. Profit felt good. Now Vallardo would be able to buy his folks a little condo near an ocean and let them retire with grace and dignity. In Washington, he would scale the corporate heights. To fit in, he shed his Italian upbringing like dead skin.

And he would show Andrea and everyone else just what he could do. He didn't want to be stuck on the middle rungs of the corporate ladder for long. He had higher ambitions. Standing up, he adjusted the sleeves on his six-hundred-dollar Italian wool suit and brushed off some lint from his lapel. All those kids he'd grown up with had laughed at him for wearing well-patched, misfit hand-me-downs. All those "friends" he'd had through college had driven hot-looking cars and could entice voluptuous young women out on the town. The Aggie crowd. Only his status on the school's winning football team had given him any real entree to them. And he'd been ashamed to reveal the truth, that it was only the football scholarship that allowed him to attend college at all, to the kids in the fast lane he liked to run with. No more. Look out world—now was Vallardo's time to shine.

****

Joe Vallardo made his daily rounds among the workout specialists in the office. He liked to show them that he was involved in their work, an integral part of the team. In fact, in Vallardo's mind, managing his small group was a lot like coaching football: bring the guys together for frequent pep talks, build team spirit, and keep them busy so they'll stay out of trouble—that spelled success. And never give away your final game plan, not even to your players. Sports became the metaphor for success in Vallardo's life.

So it gave him a lot of satisfaction to see his team buzzing along, in sync with one another and with his game. After all, Vallardo was young—thirty-two, ambitious, and, after spending his early career as an itinerant workout specialist himself, finally at home with his life and his wife and new baby. McLean, Virginia, was just a stone's throw from the nation's capital. Perhaps, he occasionally mused, he would go for the brass ring; what he might accomplish as a young Turk in the halls of Congress or as appointee to run one of the low-income housing programs administered by HUD. Public service was the accepted path to power in this town. Any doubts in his winning charm and ingratiating manners in allying himself with the powers that be, the doubts that plagued him growing up, never resurfaced.

For Vallardo fit right into Amie Mae's corporate culture. The company had been chartered by Congress in 1970 to buy mortgage loans from banks and savings and loans. Amie Mae purchased the loans, packaged them into securities, and sold them on Wall Street. That, in turn, left money available to the banks to make more loans for mortgages. The workout business where Vallardo led the troops was concentrated in low-income areas where the company had purchased a large number of mortgages. Not surprisingly, many of these loans, with an overabundance in New York City's worst neighborhoods, had soured and created a nagging drain on the corporation's profits. The resulting work, renegotiating bad loans at a loss to the company or foreclosing on properties, was just a sideline for the financial giant, one that it couldn't escape. The company's charter described a corporation with a conscience, designed to "preserve decent, affordable rental housing, consistent with sound business principles." In other words, it existed to make a profit for its investors by providing lucrative returns on housing finance and, incidentally, to make mortgage loans available to those less fortunate.

Corporate offices were situated amid booming suburban sprawl, which, ten years earlier, had been a secluded and remote part of Northern Virginia. Although official Washington legislated and debated just ten minutes as the crow flew, Amie Mae operated in a replica of suburban anywhere, USA. At the crossroads of a busy thoroughfare, the wealthy community was well hidden by trees. Huge tracts of farmland had been chopped up into prosperous subdivisions and upscale shopping centers.

McLean, Virginia, though, differed from Shaker Heights, Ohio, or Orange County, California, in this way: it was a community also home to the CIA, off the toll road on the way to Dulles International Airport, a place where foreign delegations proceeded on their way to the White House, where the politicos departed for junkets around the world, where influence peddling comprised a growth industry.

Company business took place in a contemporary glass and concrete structure with ample open spaces. Inside, white-walled corridors concealed secondary hallways that snaked into a labyrinth of small, impersonal cubicles. The bullpen-like offices were functional but devoid of any human touch, even with human beings inhabiting the cubes in each three-quarter-walled square. Everything was white and spare, and the place had a rather Spartan feeling. The company's taste in art, including what it purchased for its public spaces, was expensive yet conservative.

In such an environment, where good taste was programmed, creativity did not flourish. Walking around the offices here and there, a visitor might catch an inconspicuous family photograph on an employee's desk and, amazingly, the odd treasured artwork of a child. But cold conformity was the rule.

It was these antiseptic environs that housed the workout team run by Joe Vallardo, where his team was expected to flourish. The higher-ups in the company didn't recognize the need for a more relaxed atmosphere for this band of highwaymen and women, didn't recognize that their line of business was entirely different from Amie Mae's bread-and-butter industry. Ironically for Vallardo and most of his workers, the job they performed daily involved the disposition of buildings as filthy and forlorn as this one was sterile and secure.

Meanwhile, on this typical July Friday, Vallardo was strolling from cubicle to cubicle, chatting up his people and checking on the status of various deals. Most of the specialists continuously conversed over the phone with borrowers, and since the office was fashioned in open workspaces, he could listen unobtrusively to their phone conversations. To accomplish his harmless sleuthing, the six-foot three-inch former college football hero, who had even seen a short but sweet professional experience with the New York Giants, during which he had all but destroyed the ligaments in his left knee, could move with surprising stealth.

In Vallardo's mind, this open workspace was ideal. There was a real advantage in being able to hear each specialist in action. Their styles were all different, but he could determine who was effective from the tone and direction of their conversations. Of the seven people working for him to handle apartment loan defaults in the Northeastern United States (mostly New York City), six were men. Three of those men he had brought on board himself from his previous workout gig in Texas, good men. Two people had been with the company when Vallardo was hired, steady workers, good producers. One person had come on board with Derek, Vallardo's boss, and the management duo had recruited one together: Peller.

Peller had joined their team only six months earlier and was already upsetting the game plan. Vallardo kicked himself whenever he thought about it. Hiring Peller had been a huge mistake. Not that Peller wasn't good at what he did—in fact, he excelled. Shined so brightly that he dulled the accomplishments of the rest of the team, including Vallardo himself. Trouble was, Peller was too good. Vallardo didn't believe in stars, no sir. A good, solid team playing to each other's strengths was worth all the Joe Theismanns in the world in Vallardo's book. Besides, a quarterback shouldn't be coaching the team.

Unfortunately for Vallardo, Peller the quarterback was a natural leader. Peller was close to forty and didn't like taking direction, Vallardo knew, from "pipsqueaks" like himself—younger, less experienced, still wet behind the ears. In fact, Peller was downright cocky in his dealings with his superior. To Vallardo, the organization deserved its employees' unquestioning loyalty and dedication. So the question became how do you keep a guy like Peller in line?

Luckily, Vallardo also knew that the organization didn't take kindly to Peller's kind of attitude, and it would not be rewarded. Take, for instance, the question of compensation. Okay, Peller had taken a big salary cut when he joined up. Times were tough in the real estate biz, and it remained a buyer's market for employers like Amie Mae. Everyone in the group had sacrificed. Well, maybe not everyone; Vallardo had done okay coming to Amie Mae, so had Derek. They were management. But Peller was not in a position to command six figures here. Still, their stellar employee had taken on a self-initiated crusade not only to try to increase his own base wage and bonus package, already higher than his colleagues, but to bring all the other workout specialists up on par with him.

Maybe it wasn't fair that some of Vallardo's people made less money for doing the same job; that merely reflected their inexperience and poor negotiating skills. But Peller had talked to the human resources folks and gotten personnel in line to support increases across the board so everyone would be in the same salary ballpark. Particularly Ellie, the lone woman in the group who had been making some ten grand less than Peller. She'd been okay with it until Peller put a bug in her ear about "fairness." She would never have taken up the flag without Peller's goading. Well, she'd won her fairness battle with Peller's assistance, and that was that.

Now, as a result, upper management was looking at Vallardo's department as a greater financial drain to the organization. Didn't Peller realize that he was only making waves for Vallardo and Derek with the higher-ups? Hell, he even wanted hazardous duty pay for working up in the slums of New York. Well, shit, that was the job. Vallardo couldn't coddle this guy. Times were tough and due to get tougher. Of course, Vallardo took some satisfaction in knowing that Peller had only been awarded a 3 percent salary increase, despite his crusade. Vallardo had seen to that. Served him right for making waves.

Vallardo continued on his rounds. "How's it goin' there, Bill?" he asked one of his people with a slap on the back as he passed by. "You worked out the details on the Yonkers deal yet? We need to have that proposal in to the investment committee for consideration by their Friday meeting, you know."

"Joe, I'm working it through," replied Bill Worthmore: white, all-American boy and heir to the Worthmore retailing fortune. "I may need a little more time to get my borrower to come around to some of the fine print. But we can work on that right up to the meeting. I think we'll be fine."

"That's good news, Bill. What I like to hear," exclaimed Vallardo as he slapped Bill on the back and turned to listen in on Ellie's phone conversation. He knew she was supposed to be working with a borrower who had recently declared bankruptcy. Ellie had waged an uphill battle to get the borrower to pay off the loan. She didn't have much legal leverage. This deal amounted to a big loss to the company.

"Okay, Barbara. Call me back as soon as you've checked his temperature. I'll call the doctor to make an appointment for him today." Ellie hung up the phone dejectedly, idly fingering her Rolodex to find the pediatrician's phone number, unaware that her boss had been listening.

"Marty's sick?" asked Vallardo sympathetically. After all, he was a new dad too.

Ellie turned around, startled. "My babysitter thinks he's got a fever. He's been crying all morning and acting cranky. That's not like him, poor guy." Marty was seven months old, a big bundle of baby who was his parents' pride and joy. They had tried to conceive for seven years before he came along.

"He seems like such a happy baby," Vallardo agreed. On the surface, he showed concern, but in actuality, he was annoyed to have her distracted by family matters, thinking she was overreacting to a little fever.

I knew having a woman work for me was going to spell trouble, he reproached himself silently. He was nothing if not cynical about the role of the fairer sex in the office. Luckily, Ellie hadn't asked for more than the minimum maternity leave when Marty was born. Vallardo was perennially too shorthanded and underbudgeted to afford a long absence by any of his people. He would have denied any sexism in practice or philosophy, but Vallardo made it clear that he would frown on any requests for extended leave. Truth was, all the men in the office were afraid of being stigmatized by taking paternity leave, all except maybe Peller, who simply didn't care about anyone else's opinion. Meanwhile, Vallardo hoped Ellie was through having kids. Thanks to the new federal family leave rules, he wouldn't be able to limit her to six weeks any more, although he could probably make her life pretty miserable should she ask for more time.

"Listen, Ellie, I know how these kid things can be. If you need to take the baby to the doctor's, go for it. But try to make the appointment for the end of the day if you can. We've got too much stuff going on this week, critical deadlines. We've got to stick to the game plan, you know? I'd hate for us to fall behind." Vallardo gave her his most meaningful "Look, I'm sorry, but ..." glance, turned on his heels, and headed back to his office.

Ellie sighed. She knew that behind Vallardo's words and gestures was your basic, unreconstructed male chauvinist boss whose wife had quit work with their first, and only, child. Vallardo wouldn't ever have to take the baby to the doctor or worry about babysitters who one day just decided not to show up. "He doesn't have a clue, the jerk," she mumbled under her breath, half hoping Vallardo would hear her complaint as she punched out the office number for her doctor.

****

"Vallardo," Joe answered as he picked up the blinking line. His secretary, Mildred, who had been at Amie forever and knew everything that went on inside the office and out, had waved him to the phone as he rounded the corner. "Emergency," she mouthed, and then, as her boss picked up, she stayed on the line.

"Joe, this is Steve in New York. Listen, we have a situation up here you guys need to be aware of. It may involve Peller, and I'm worried that this is the kind of crisis that could blow up right in our faces."

In the space of time it took to soak in those words, Vallardo's adrenalin was already flowing. Peller. Trouble. Again.

"What's up, Steve?" he asked, trying to sound cool. A newly nagging worry clouded his otherwise unlined face.

"You know the property Louis came up to look at today on West 137th in Spanish Harlem? He's on his way there with Tommy right now. Well, our boy doesn't know it yet, but he's going to be greeted by cop cars and fire trucks. We haven't been able to reach him by page, and no one's answering at the superintendent's apartment." Steve's voice was wild.

"Look, Steve, I don't know what's going on up there," Vallardo interjected loudly, hoping to jar the lawyer back to reason. "You're making no sense here. You mean the building's on fire?"

"Nothing too bad, although there are some tenants who may be pretty fired up about this, not to mention our Mr. Epstein. He's probably out there pouring gas on the flames. Although, at least if it burned down, Amie could be reasonably certain of collecting the insurance money as payment on this loser." Steve's attempt at gallows humor was lost on the impatient Vallardo.

"So what's the deal here, Steve? Is Peller safe?" Joe began pacing the floor in front of his dark mahogany executive-style desk.

There was a pause on the other end of the line. "Steve?"

"Listen, Joe, gotta go. Tommy's on the other line." Steve abruptly hung up, leaving Vallardo standing in front of his desk with the phone to his ear and exasperation clouding his face.

Peller had waded into turbulent waters again, it would seem. "Don't panic yet," recited Vallardo like a mantra. "This could all be just your basic New York City hard-luck story." But then again, one crisis like this could undo Vallardo's budding career.

His bum knee ached, and his brain pounded at the threat of

impending doom. In the office anteroom, Mildred's muffled voice was the only evidence that she was already telegraphing the news to her counterparts across the company: Peller, the troublemaker, is playing with fire. "Why me," sighed Vallardo.

Chapter 4
Got to Escape This Madness

Tommy Romano was getting restless. As he sat in his car outside Epstein's apartment building, he kept checking his watch nervously. The streets were ominously quiet at this hour.

"C'mon, Pelleh," he grumbled aloud to the sooty, crumbling brick and concrete walls. "Let's get movin'. Harlem afteh three ain't a pretty sight." It was close to three already. "Not that it's so sweet before three—not today."

Tommy had reluctantly called in to Amie Mae, on Peller's orders, to report to Steve what little he knew about the apartment fire. Tommy, in fact, despised Steve, who always complained that the driver spent too much time talking and too little time figuring out how to get places quickly. Steve frequently berated Tommy for incompetence and never apologized for misinstructing the driver in usually abortive shortcuts through the city.

Yesiree, thought Tommy. Steve could be a real bastard, and his abuse of everyone was not his best attribute. It was always "fuck you" and the "fucking landlords" and the "friggin' assholes living in these crappy condemned buildings." Although Tommy had grown up in an Italian neighborhood in Brooklyn where every third word was an obscenity, he liked to think of himself as more refined.

Still, Tommy basically agreed with Steve that life in New York's slums constituted a blight on society. He hated every minute wasted on the streets of Washington Heights or Harlem. The incident earlier in the day with the Angel woman, melodramatic though it was, had been a prime illustration of all that was wrong with this part of town—drugs, prostitution, violence, corruption. The same cop who arrested Angel was probably knocking her up and promising to look the other way when it came to any prostitution rap. Harlem was like that: corrupt and filthy, rotten to the core.

Which could, in fact, account for its own perverse charm. In Harlem, you could indulge in any and every sin imaginable, anonymous and absolved from penance. God and the law weren't watching what went down in Harlem or the Bronx or Washington Heights, he was convinced. Tommy was not wholly immune to some of the carnal pleasures that the big city offered. He allowed himself a moment to muse about his morning's activities—the "ladies of the evening" plied their trade anytime of the day in New York, and Tommy knew some who were really sweet and nubile, albeit in the Bronx, that hell on earth, but certainly a better part of town than this godforsaken slum.

"Mmmm, hmm." He licked his lips, remembering. Hunts Point was mainly industrial, row after row of warehouses, with a few decayed-looking little ramblers and house trailers dotting the landscape, if you could call that wasteland a landscape. There, girls not older than sixteen or seventeen, prancing and strutting their budding bodies, parading up and down the streets wearing men's extra-large T-shirts (and little else), seeking out truck drivers who could afford to part with their bonus pay after they made their deliveries. Their prices were reasonable enough; the girls usually started out asking for twenty dollars a trick but came down rapidly to fifteen or ten dollars if they saw they wouldn't score otherwise. These girls were desperate; they had men to support, and babies. One girl Tommy knew strutted around with her infant, advertising, "I got something you ain't tasted in a long time." A combination prostitute and wet nurse. Even Tommy was appalled at this pitiful promotion.

Tommy indulged in such sweet sins every once in a while—pleasure, not pain, to be sure. Tommy didn't want any part of those plague-like sexually transmitted diseases off the street. He'd seen other guys brought down by their weakness for cheap sex. Tommy preferred methods that precluded any possibility of infection.

There are other ways to enjoy the talents of a professional, he thought, smacking his lips again.

Tommy heard the sounds of a boom box, rap music getting louder and more distinct amid the usual cacophony of street sounds that made up Spanish Harlem. It was time to get the hell out of here. However, Tommy didn't consider himself a likely target for the street gangs in this part of town—his huge bulk and menacing scowl from under black, bridging eyebrows were intimidating enough, not to mention his skill in the martial arts. But Tommy knew that the pale-faced desk jockeys he protected were sitting ducks in this part of town—particularly Peller who naively considered himself impervious to assault.

Time to split, but no Peller in sight. The bodyguard decided to track down his client so they could avoid trouble.

Tommy entered the decrepit apartment building through the front hallway, stopping momentarily to speculate where Mr. Peller and company might have gone on their tour, then decided to hike up the stairway for easier reconnaissance. Tommy generally tried to stay out of these stinking buildings; you never knew what you would find inside. When he, Tommy Romano, had to inspect buildings, he made it a point to be in and out before seven in the morning and to *never* speak to anyone. Peller was different; he seemed to somehow enjoy mixing it up with the full-a-shit landlords and their lousy tenants.

Listening through the walls, he trekked up, stopping at each floor for a quick look. The stairwells were stained with piss and smelled like hell. The heavy smoke hung like a storm cloud. There were spiderwebs decorating every corner of the stairway, and Tommy barely missed stepping on what appeared to be a rat's nest—vacant though it was at the moment.

"Gawd, I've got to get me a better line of work," he grumbled. Finally, on the fourth floor, he found Peller walking out of a vacant apartment suffering from a serious water leak through the ceiling, a busted pipe upstairs. Tommy noticed Peller's trademark legal pad on the floor in the hall, dog-eared and wrinkled, scrawled with notes about the problems he'd found.

Tommy glowered at Peller and started to cuss him out for dragging his heels until he noticed Bud Epstein shuffling out behind Peller, making noisy excuses for not fixing up the place sooner.

Shit, how Tommy hated these fucking landlords. He thought most of these bastards were just plain weird, and he couldn't believe they actually made money from these rat-infested stink holes they called apartments, at least, not on the up-and-up. They all had something going on the side, Tommy was convinced. Especially the ultra-Orthodox Jews. They were nothing but crooks—rich crooks at that, and double-crossing. It was the Jews moving out of his nice, quiet neighborhood in Brooklyn, selling out to the damned blacks that ruined the streets, bringing out the wrong element, and with them, drugs, gangs, and guns. The Jews had left a fucking curse on his neighborhood, moving out. Well, to hell with them.

Jews were suspect. Tommy didn't mind Peller; Peller was a different sort of Jew, not crazy like these New York Shylocks. But the pushy ultra-Orthodox … secretive, calculating, and driven; they couldn't be trusted.

He watched Epstein maneuver, holding his tongue. When Willie Johnson walked out behind his boss, a mean glint in the black man's dark eyes despite his seeming agreeability, Tommy sneered. There was another one. They thought they owned the world, these blacks. Tommy, with a curse and a prayer, tried jealously to figure out how bastards like Bud Epstein could deal with these damn "African Americans with an attitude" so successfully.

"Sawry, boys. Time's up," Tommy intruded contentiously. "The plane's about to leave the hangar, and Mr. Peller needs to be on it." The joint was getting too hot to hang out any longer.

Waving to Tommy without turning around, Peller fixed a searing eye first on Epstein, then on Johnson, as if to pin them in place. One could not be too careful in dealing with this crowd, Peller knew from experience. Unwritten rule of the trade: never trust the borrower, or his super.

But Peller could also play their game. Charming to a fault. "Gentlemen, thanks for your time and attention. I want to review the insurance adjuster's damage report. Until I understand how much money is involved in repairs, I won't be able to suggest final terms for the agreement," Peller oozed sincerely.

Epstein smiled. "As usual, Louis, we'll certainly take care of any repairs and put this building in tip-top condition. You have my word on it."

Willie Johnson, who had been locking up the apartment, shot his boss a skeptical look that Peller did not miss; he too doubted the landlord's sincerity. A leopard does not change its spots overnight, frowned Peller cynically.

"Well, I'm out of here. Bud, we'll be in touch. Sorry about your shoes, by the way," Peller said in mock dismay, looking at the fragile tan moccasins, now black with soot and scuffs. "I'll stop by K-Mart before I come up next time and buy you work boots for our inspection."

The irony, of course, was that a man as wealthy as Bud Epstein, who could afford as many pairs of shoes as Imelda Marcos, stubbornly refused to wear anything but the best. Because, in the Jewish ghetto of the Lower East Side growing up, he had seen his cousins and sister and brother grow up with second-hand shoes with newspaper substituting soles. Because, when he was taken to Auschwitz, he had been forced to pile his shoes with all the others', until there were mounds of Jews' shoes to match the mounds of Jews' bodies. He wouldn't wear cheap, sensible shoes to walk through the filthy buildings he owned in the new New York ghettos.

"Size ten D?" Peller quipped.

"Louis, I hope to God you and I are looking at our last inspection together for a while," announced his borrower bitterly. "They say the market's about to turn around." Epstein sighed the sigh of a man who had heard it all before. "I keep waiting to see the rewards of this economic recovery everyone's talking about. The fortune I've lost ..."

"Ah, c'mon, Bud. Don't give me any of that crap," Peller began, feeling himself being pushed in the back by his driver.

Tommy had maneuvered himself to Peller's side and was propelling him to the elevator for a speedy departure, knowing his only chance for haste with the shit piled on this thick depended on either shoving Peller out of the muck or waiting an eternity until the two sides exhausted their bitching.

As the graffiti-graced elevator door screeched open, Tommy firmly pushed Peller inside, even as his rider seemed to think of one more warning to add.

"Oh, and about that problem with Ms. Sanchez and her fire," Peller started again, resisting Tommy's urgency. "I'll call you on that one," he finished with a suspicious grin, the elevator door closing, but not before Peller saw the landlord's face flush.

Finally, Peller and Tommy were going to depart, descending in the cranky, stuffy old lift.

"Listen, Louie," growled Tommy. "How many times I gotta be aksing you to get outta here? This ain't no place to be hangin' around afteh three. Whattaya think this is, Disney World? Fa'gedaboutit! The gang kids are stahtin' to get outta school, and if you ain't had enough excitement for today, just try a run-in with the Crips or the Bloods—makin' deals on the street and lookin' for trouble with theah pagehs and theah crack and theah weapons." Tommy continually looked left and right as he directed Peller boldly toward the Impala, checking for mutts, strays, punks, and other unwelcome passersby.

"I catch your drift, Tommy. We're going, okay?" Peller was annoyed with his driver's insistent tone, even though Tommy was clearly looking out for Peller's best interests. They marched quickly to the car, past storefront evangelical churches and rolled barbed wire fences around the public school playground, a menacing sight, and barren. The basketball nets had been ripped from the hoops long ago.

Peller, trying to look inconspicuous, spied kids standing in bunches outside the playground looking annoyed and hardened, the seats of their jeans comically sagging to their knees; who knew what was hidden in their pants' baggy folds. The kids called out dares to one another, boasting, taunting, doing the nines.

A white stretch limousine had pulled up and double-parked alongside the Impala. There were more teenage boys decked out in chains and garish gold rings glaring at it. They all sported that ubiquitous pager, clipped to the hip, some with rope, others with heavy gold chains. Drug money bought lots of stuff up here, tough stuff. But Peller needed to ignore it all, for at this moment, he was a man with a mission: get home, fast.

"We're outta here, Tommy. I want to get home in time to have dinner with the family tonight."

Tommy edged the Impala nervously past the limo, ignoring the glare of its driver who was just waiting, probably thinking, *Go 'head and scratch my fender, mothafucka, so I can lay a bullet in you.*

Out of danger at last. Tommy's race to the airport was punctuated by perilous potholes dotting East River Drive and causing the big car to weave hazardously through heavy traffic on the Triborough Bridge.

During the ride, Peller dictated his recommendations and conclusions of the Epstein deal into a small Sony tape recorder. He would use these thoughts about the site inspection to augment his notes for the memos and agreements that inevitably accompanied every agreement.

"Great gadgets, these little recorders," Peller remarked to his disinterested driver who was steeped in his own thoughts. "Saves time, makes money," he continued, looking curiously at the sleek, hand-held model he now carried, pushing the off button for the final time. His endorsement sounded comically like an ad for the giant recording manufacturer. Still, the driver was silent, lost in thought, staring straight ahead.

In an effort to jog Tommy from whatever dark ruminations he was engaged in, Peller joked about the arson on West 137th in the most macabre tones.

"Now for New York's latest crime statistic," he announced in a mock-anchorman voice. "A featured attraction at one of the Upper West Side's poshest apartment buildings … Tommy," he interrupted his stand-up, "couldn't you just see the spectacular video footage of that old facade, with its dirty, bullet-pocked archway and the crumbling steps?" Peller laughed nervously. "Hey, maybe the TV crews could even hire a tenant—a teenage mother wearing hip-hop clothes and long, decal-painted nails, holding her pathetic baby—to pose under the arch. Hell, what could it cost them to exploit the hopeless anyway—five, ten bucks? Helluva photo op." Peller laughed at his own cynical humor.

Apparently, Tommy was not amused. He scowled at Peller and shrugged, then looked down and fished a baloney sandwich out of a brown paper sack under the front seat and began to chew noisily. But Peller, whose turkey on wheat remained untouched and wrapped on the seat beside him, couldn't eat. The job, and Tommy's gluttony, made him feel sick.

They arrived at La Guardia with just enough time for Peller to hurry down to Gate 18 to meet the four o'clock Washington shuttle. At the curb checking in, Peller found out the plane would be delayed a half hour for repairs. His luck.

"Want me to wait, Lou?" asked the driver unconcernedly, stuffing a second baloney sandwich in his mouth.

Peller turned to Tommy and grinned again. "Leave now, Mr. Romano, and go enjoy a little golf at the country club before you call it a day," Peller joked to his city-born, street-bred driver, knowing golf was the farthest thing from Tommy's reality.

Tommy looked at Peller as if he was from outer space. Then, he too grinned. "Fa'gedaboutit," he joshed. The heavy curtain of tension finally parted, Tommy saluted Peller as he pulled the Impala out of the in-bound lane, where arriving and departing taxicabs disgorged their impatient passengers before the yellow hacks were swallowed back into the city's anonymity.

****

As the plane circled Washington's National Airport, making its quick but dramatic descent via the customary path, sweeping the Potomac River with its magnificent view of the monuments and the Capitol, Peller reflected on the experiences of his afternoon and thanked God, not for the first time, for the blessings in his life. He had a beautiful, if sometimes stubborn, wife; a happy, healthy family; a steady job; and a nice home in suburbs far from the obscenities of Spanish Harlem or Washington Heights or even Southeast Washington. He could not ask for more. No, nothing really. Except maybe better pay and more recognition for his work and … but no, thought Peller, he couldn't complain.

Driving home through the dusty July serenity of Washington's Rock Creek Park, Peller stared out the window at the creek bed, dry but for a midsummer's trickle. Sweating joggers, helmeted bikers, and dogs tugging at their masters' sluggish pace peopled the bike path. Peller didn't often travel this way, preferring a speedier passage up the George Washington Parkway to the world-famous gridlock of the Washington Beltway, but today he felt an urge to enjoy a little denser greenery and the pristine rustle of the creek, anything to counter the concrete-and-steel jungle that was New

York. Ah, yes, this was the relief he needed to decompress, to forget about the sights and sounds of an hysterical prostitute making a scene by torching the trash room to make public her demands for decent housing, albeit for her own peculiar motives: liability insurance for her burgeoning, non-IRS-compliant profession.

Here in Rock Creek Park, Peller knew things were not so rustic as the crawling creek might suggest, but at least the view offered a quick escape from the horrors of Gotham. Lost in thought, he drove slowly along the winding road and out to Sixteenth Street, wending his way up past downtown Silver Spring until he turned into the neighborhood then pulled into his driveway. Honing in on his arrival with their own instinctive radar, Peller's children rushed out to greet their daddy jubilantly with kisses and hugs, telling new jokes they'd made up and giggling uncontrollably at their own cleverness.

Life is good, he thought again, extricating himself from the kids' exuberant welcome to enter the coolness of a pristine, climate-controlled castle.

It was almost time for the Sabbath. The Pellers' babysitter, Sofia, formerly from Peru and now a sometime college student studying English, had scrubbed the children and helped them change into clean clothes for the family's weekly celebration to welcome the day of rest. Sofia was like family. She kept track of everyone's comings and goings and kept the household running. She informed Peller that Lana had called before she left work and would be home momentarily. Lana was a newspaper reporter working on a regional suburban daily, and though she often had deadlines that delayed her, her early Friday departures were sacred. Peller thanked the sitter affectionately for her help and sent her home.

While he was upstairs changing into shorts and a polo shirt, he could hear Lana's station wagon pull into the driveway. Manny, the schnauzer, sounded enthusiastic greetings at the front door.

That dog sure loves his mistress, reflected Peller happily, glancing out the bedroom window at Lana, watching the swing of her rich brown and golden hair in the sun. She glanced up and smiled at him, clutching her battered briefcase in two hands and carrying her newspapers, including today's final edition, under her arms. Inside, she swept through the obstacle course posed by dog and children, greeting everyone cheerfully and sorting carefully through the day's accumulated junk.

By the time she was organized, the older children were already engrossed in their favorite video and could barely be bothered to greet their mother. Lana came tromping up the stairs, stewing in feigned annoyance at the latest calamity to befall her.

"I can't believe they assigned me to cover these council hearings over the county's low-income housing policies. I know you really get off on this stuff, but frankly, Louis, it bores me to tears to hear about the rate of loan defaults in the area and these fat-cat real estate developers pleading poverty. I know the recession's been tough, but you can't tell me that these guys who were buying yachts and Mercedes a few years ago don't have just a little bit of collateral stashed away to keep from going belly-up. The only real story here is how these same people who live in the county's richest neighborhoods have blocked affordable housing from coming into their own communities." She paced the floor in irritation. "These old, knee-jerk liberals have the same 'not in my backyard' mentality that the conservatives do; they just lie through their teeth about their commitment. I mean, since when is one hundred eighty thousand dollars affordable?"

Peller planted a wet kiss smack on her pouting lips. "Bad day, honey?"

"Louis," she answered in surprise at this greeting. Lana's pretty face was flushed with the heat, enhanced by the fervor of her rectitude.

"This one beats all," she rejoined, not diverted from her cause. She began peeling the stockings off her shapely, tanned legs, not unaware that Peller was watching her every move intently. Stripped to her lacy-pale lingerie, she sashayed to the clothes hamper to deposit her dirty work clothes.

Peller laid back on the bed, hands behind his head, amused at his wife's tirade—and more than a little aroused to watch her undress this way. He loved seeing her when she was perched on one of her soapboxes, anger flashing from those passionate blue-green eyes, tousled hair falling from the casual coif she had to fix up, on a "bad hair day," at least five times. Peller whistled appreciatively.

Fury spent, Lana laughed. She had one of those magical faces that transformed puttylike into a hundred different expressions at will. Now it morphed from fury to delight.

"You're pretty sexy yourself," she called back. "How was your day, *mon cher*?"

"Come with me to New York sometime, my sweet, if you want to see how the other two thirds really live. A tenant set fire to my borrower's building in Spanish Harlem this afternoon. Now there's a story for you," Peller responded baitingly.

But Lana was already listening to something else. She could hear the children beginning to argue. Something about "you did and I didn't and I'll tell Mom and nanny-nanny-boo-boo." The usual.

"Well, of course, Louis, I'd love to hear about your latest conquests in the world of high-powered mediation with thieves and gangsters," she said, a hint sarcastic, brushing out her hair slowly, deliberately languorous in her movements. "But I hear restless natives, so I'm afraid it may have to wait until later this evening ... that is," she winked with a flirtatious pout, "if you're still interested in talking, you brave boy." She was teasing, now.

Peller studied her, trying to appear indifferent, but with the customary wolflike glint in his eyes. Lana laughed, knowing that Louis would always be ... well, Louis. Meanwhile, the level of commotion downstairs was escalating.

"Let's go down and have a nice Shabbat supper before the kids kill each other. We'll have our own little *mitzvah* later, once they're in bed." She quickly slipped into a cool, colorful sundress, checked her face and hair, and pulled Peller to his feet for a quick kiss—suggestive of more to come—before leading him downstairs.

****

In the kitchen, Peller helped Lana cut the *challah* and pour the wine, recounting a story about what had been on Al Pollock's mind at the conclusion of their negotiations.

"So this guy, in all his bearded glory, asks, 'Mr. Peller, are you a devout Jew?' Imagine him, nervous, constantly fingering the fringes of his prayer shawl under his heavy coat, pulling on his beard. And I say, 'Well, I probably don't go to synagogue as often as I should.' He goes, 'Mr. Peller, you know in this world there are only two kinds of Jews: those who believe and those who are about to believe.'

"Now get this, Lana—this is the best part. He gets up like a rabbi on the pulpit with his arms raised to the sky and says, 'As it is written in the Good Book, when the *Meshiach*, our Rabbi Schneerson, returns to the Holy Land, all doubters will become believers.'"

Lana glared into the bowl where she was trying to toss a quick salad.

"Sure, that's enough to make a true believer out of all of us," she quipped. "If this guy's so certain Schneerson's the messiah, a man who hands out dollar bills from his doorstep and whose followers replicate their good rabbi's dilapidated, red-brick apartment building in Brooklyn down to the plumbing on a kibbutz in the desert in Israel, I say, God bless them all. Frankly, I think they're all a little *meshuganah*! But imagine, Louis, how much fun you'd have negotiating a workout on that 'Brooklyn in the Negev' when Schneerson can't pay the mortgage and blames his 'landlord' on the loan default." Lana shook her head and raised her arms toward the heavens. "Wonder if he has air-conditioning over there," she said, somewhat distracted by this un-Godlike prospect.

Once dinner was ready, they rounded up the three children to assume their places at the white-clothed holiday table. There was Alison who was eight going on eighteen, a real little beauty and the spitting image of her mother, and Alexander, the five-and-a-half year old with dark hair and the face of an angel, who was obsessed with Legos, video games, and, to the delight of his like-minded father, tennis. As for the baby, the thirteen-month-old mophead, Ashley, with a tousle of auburn hair and a Milky Way of freckles on her Muppet face, she had just begun toddling about and getting herself into everything within reach. It was too early to tell what Ashley's fancy might spark. At any rate, thought Peller proudly, looking around the table, theirs was a handsome family, closely knit.

They each took a turn reciting the Sabbath prayers. As was the tradition, Lana lit the two slender white candles standing straight in glistening sterling holders, uttering the Hebrew words to usher in the new week. Alison joined her mother, while Peller and Alexander recited the blessing for the wine. Together, everyone took a slice of twisted egg bread and blessed it. Ashley gobbled down her *challah* and took a bite out of every piece in the basket in front of her as she mimicked the Hebrew prayers she heard all around her.

Sabbath. Quiet. Restful. Healing. Peller was not a devout Jew, but he believed strongly in the precepts his religion taught, and he wanted his children to have a good grounding in the teachings of God and the law, important values that would prepare them for life. Judaism's emphasis on family and on academic achievement had strengthened his own upbringing immeasurably. Lana, Peller knew, found her strength in the traditions of Judaism, drawing comfort from its familiar rituals. Her religion served more as a spiritual support than his. To Peller, Judaism was an obligation that he must shoulder for his family's well-being: respect for parents, continuity of the faith, and commitment to preserving the Jewish homeland, Eretz Yisrael.

As the prayers concluded, the children settled into their usual dinnertime routine, alternating between gluttony and disinterest in their food, taunting each other, and stealing scraps from the table to feed to the hovering dog who knew he would be well-provided for. Peller and Lana continued discussing their respective days, occasionally soliciting input from the two older kids who recounted the highlights of their lives in silly jokes, cracking each other up with their own version of "dirty" language, much to their parents' chagrin.

Peller purposely avoided telling Lana about his experience with Angel Sanchez during the meal, knowing that Alison would understand far too much and be fascinated and repelled by such a tale. The discussion might go in a direction he wasn't prepared to talk about, raising too many questions better left to a much later, more private conversation with her about the facts of life, not that Alison didn't already know most of those facts. With her curious mind and precocious nature, Lana had felt it the better part of wisdom to make sure she understood certain dos and don'ts from the get-go. But the implications of the afternoon's events and the motives of someone like Angel Sanchez were much more complex than just the birds and the bees. And Alex was certainly not ready to soak in such lessons. No, this material was X-rated as far as the children were concerned. But maybe if they could get the kids to bed early, a little embroidery on Angel's tale could serve as an exotic prelude to Lana and Peller's own nocturnal symphony, or so Peller dreamed.

In the meantime, Peller bestowed fresh bakery cookies on the children for dessert, the doughy kind with a dollop of chocolate icing on top, as Lana began to clean up around the "pie eaters" at the table. Chocolate hands and faces threatened to smear the white linen cloth on the table, not to mention clothes, hair, walls, dog. The long shadows now slanting through the dining room window heralded the onset of a lingering late-July dusk. Peller put on some coffee as the two older children headed outside to play energetically in the descending coolness. At long last, everyone could relax.

"So, Louis, what great deals did my desk warrior close today? And what's this about tenants torching buildings?" Lana asked baitingly.

"Honey, you would not believe my day," he jumped in, needing no prodding. "I want to save the best part of the story for later, but suffice it to say, it's a doozy. Meanwhile, this has to be a banner day for Louis Peller and Amie Mae. You remember what I told you about Alvin Pollock, how he'd outwitted Amie Mae for three years, even Joe Vallardo? Well, of course, they leave it to Peller to clean up the mess," observed Peller by way of self-congratulation. "Pollock now recognizes that if he leaves Amie hanging out there in the wind, he won't get a red cent from any other lender in the country. And believe me, he ain't gonna hang himself that way, not Pollock."

Lana continued clearing the table, conspicuously inattentive.

"I did good, honey," Peller prompted, looking for approval.

Lana looked up, suddenly aware her husband was waiting for her reaction.

"Well, I'm proud of you, Louis—I think," Lana said as approvingly as she could.

Peller settled for the half-hearted compliment with a disappointed grin.

At that moment, a baseball bounced off the dining room window as Alison slammed her first home run of the evening, giving vent to Peller's fury.

"You could have broken the window, damn it, Alison. That's it," he screamed out the window. "You kids can get ready for bed, *now*. How many times have I told you to hit away from the house?" Then, seeing their pale and stunned faces, he relented. "Sorry, guys. But we've talked about this at least ten times before."

"Eleven hundredy thousand," observed Alex.

Ashley toddled up and grabbed Peller's leg. "Da da mad." She started to cry. This melted Peller. Picking up the baby, he said reassuringly, "No, I'm not mad, Ashley. You go get lollipops from your momma for everyone, and I'll feel better."

"Pops," squealed a delighted little girl. She waddled into the kitchen as fast as her fat little legs could carry her.

Peller went out, scooped up his own mitt and an Orioles cap from the toy box on the porch, and yelled, "Now let's turn this outfield around and play ball."

Lana was glad to see the moment pass. He seemed more like the funny, sensitive boy of their courtship. Sometimes Peller's temper got the best of him, although that happened less of late than when they were first married. Her husband had quite intimidated her back in the early days of matrimony, his sudden furies reducing her to tears. Arguments over anything and everything had been quick to surface. Why couldn't she quit working and stay home? Why didn't she love to cook and clean house? Why didn't she listen to him? When would she be ready to have kids? He goaded her that they would never make a family because she was too selfish.

Peller was quite the traditionalist, a man with a mission, a throwback to those families of the fifties, of their respective childhoods, where roles were well-defined and never wavered. Louis Peller wanted the reassurance of the "good old days," that black-and-white certainty. Lana, in turn, liked the flexibility and openness of these times. They fought this battle at every turn, and ultimately, Lana managed to show him that the world was not lost because she was a working mom and the house was not a model of efficiency. In fact, for a while, it had been up to her to support the family when he left the law firm. He stayed home with the children, a treasured time for them.

Reactionary thoughts still captivated him, she knew. At moments, he forgot the "new" Peller, and began to fight the old battle. Usually, it would pass, but there were times when Lana would find herself drawn in by his rhetoric, to her own chagrin. Still, she thought, looking at him through the soft, pink glow of twilight, he was awfully cute with those thick black lashes framing the soft, brown puppy-dog eyes. How could she love him when she couldn't stand him, she would berate herself. And then he would do something foolish or playful or funny, and she would fall in love all over again. Contemplative by nature, she nonetheless loved to laugh; and how he could make her laugh.

Lana began to wash the dishes, analyzing the dynamics of their relationship for the umpteenth time. Why was Peller so unyielding? He was so demanding of himself and everyone around him—a perfectionist quick to criticize and unrelenting in his demands. He could make life so much easier for himself, and for them, if he would just be a little more flexible. Take this deal Peller had just concluded today. How different he would be acting tonight if he had not been successful. He would be kicking himself for not being able to rectify a situation even his own boss had been unable to fix.

Fortunately, this time things had worked out well. He could relax this weekend and enjoy his victory, and so could she.

Lana was, however, increasingly upset about Peller's dangerous duty in New York's worst slums and felt her husband ought to get the heck out of the business. *I don't plan on being a thirty-four-year-old widow with three kids to raise on my own.*

She shook her head slowly in somber reflection, watching a "Kodak moment" develop in the yard. *What would it take to get Louis to stop chasing danger?* she wondered.

In the drawing twilight, Peller pitched a slow ball to Alex while Lana stared steadily out the window, noticing the perfectly manicured lawn, the picket fence, and the perfect little family, laughing and playing happily. And she thought about how different her life might be but for the coincidence of their circumstances, and fate.

Dusk deepened quickly into night. A full harvest moon hovered low over the horizon. Frogs and crickets croaked their greetings. Peller was about to call the game for darkness, but he hesitated for a long moment to savor the fading July day with

Alison on third, Alex on first, and that round-cheeked, cherubic baby with the red lollipop picking flowers in the outfield.

Finally, even Peller had to acknowledge that he had something special, something worth hanging on to. "I've got to escape from this madness," he called out to the unending night.

Chapter 5
The Latest Assignment

Peller came to work on Monday morning, bright and early, buoyed by his victory and the repose of a weekend with his family, ready to take on all comers. With the exception of a late Friday night phone call from Vallardo coming, as it did, at a strategically inopportune moment in his marital relations, he had managed to put the whole Angel affair behind him. Now he was ready to reap psychological and, he could only hope, financial rewards from his colleagues and superiors for closing the biggest workout deal in Amie Mae's history. In reporting the story to Lana, Peller had practiced a few flourishes to his Al Pollock anecdotes, just for emphasis. Now he would try them out on his colleagues.

First in was Ellie, whom he cornered by the coffee pot. After the perfunctory "how was your weekend" greetings, Peller began to regale her with tales of Alvin Pollock, the golem from Brooklyn, replete with a vivid description of the pious man's long black wool coat, his blue and white embroidered *tallit,* his black hat and beady eyes shining out from behind the gray beard and *peyes*, and his button of Rabbi Schneerson, ringed by the words, "The *Meshiach* is on the Way."

Ellie was used to Peller's overblown descriptions and usually managed to discount his stories as about 50 percent bravado, so she settled down as he talked, sipping her coffee, occasionally feigning interest. Peller didn't notice her preoccupation.

"Uh huh, and what happened next?" she asked tonelessly, looking through the files she would need for her first meeting of the morning.

"Would you believe it," Peller replied, "the guy actually tried to weasel out of our deal at the last minute, said his lawyer wanted him to declare personal bankruptcy and take his chances in court. I half thought he might even take out his gold money clip and peel off a few large bills to get me to change my mind on the terms."

Bill wandered in during this exchange, and after his visit to the coffeepot, he pulled a chair into Ellie's cubicle, stretched out his long legs, and joined in listening. Bill liked hearing Peller's tales of heroism in dealing with New York's "sleaziest opportunists," especially because Bill fancied captivating the audience with his own successes. Guys recounting feats of conquest and adventure, drinking stale coffee under fluorescent light and shooting the bull seemed, however remotely, the urban equivalent of the Wild West: cowboys driving longhorns, a campfire under the moonlight, and rotgut coffee in hand, storytellers weaving tales of flood and famine, women won and lost. It all translated, in Bill's view, to the romance and adventure missing in modern life. This kind of work was a childhood fantasy come true. There they were, the loan rangers. Somehow, though, Bill's stories were never quite as colorful as Peller's. Of course, workouts in Rhode Island and Connecticut did not quite compare to New York, even in Bill's wildest imaginings.

"So, Lou, you think Vallardo might reward you financially for your success over Pollock?" he quipped, knowing Vallardo's legendary tight grip on the department's purse strings. "Sounds like you done good, old buddy. I've always thought we workout specialists ought to hold out for a percentage. Let's see ...

conservatively speaking, 1 percent of six hundred thousand dollars … six thousand dollars for a day's work. That ain't peanuts."

Peller smiled. "You are an enlightened man, Bill. I vote we overthrow the dictator and elect Bill boss. All in favor, say aye."

Ellie looked around impatiently. "I hate to break up this party here, boys," she announced, "but I have some time to make up for leaving early Friday to take the baby to the doctor. Oh, and thanks for asking. Marty's much better." She swiveled her chair around to answer the phone.

"I guess that's our cue, Bill," Peller responded, only slightly contrite. "I knew you all would want to hear about our company's good fortune first thing."

"Yeah, good work, Louis," Bill Worthmore remarked enthusiastically. "Well, I guess it is about time to start the day."

But Peller had not yet tired of telling his tale. He decided to hang out at the coffee maker a while longer for his next audience. To his misfortune, it was Derek, Vallardo's boss, another technocrat who had missed those B-school lessons on the finer points of managing people.

"Louis," he opened tersely. "I think we need to talk. Joe's told me about your trip last Friday, and although you did good work on the Pollock deal, I'm worried about this business with Epstein. I want you and Joe to come into my office at ten o'clock." Derek took his black coffee and four packets of sugar and strode away.

"Yes, Derek, I had a very nice weekend, thanks. How about you?" Peller muttered mockingly to the chief's disappearing back. "Nice chatting with you too. Glad you're proud of our work on the Pollock deal. I look forward to our meeting." The guy acted like such a jerk sometimes. Good at the business, yes, but somewhat lacking in the social graces.

Peller walked back to his cubicle, ready to begin chiseling away at the resolve of some other defaulting borrower. The advantage of this cozy little office arrangement, he reasoned, was that everything was within arm's reach. Swivel the chair forward to grab the phone. Swing around to the back, and the bookshelf is in easy reach. Turn another quarter, and the coat hook is positioned just so. He allowed himself one small poster hung surreptitiously under the hook: a yuppie-looking beagle wearing spectacles over the caption, "It's a dog's life." On Peller's desk wall, the sign read, "Trust No One, Cover Your Ass, Amie Mae Is No Charity," the group's golden rule. Half a rotation again, and there was the computer, although the printer was shared by five specialists and located close to the coffee machine. Couldn't ask for anything more, unless you suffered from claustrophobia, of course. Fortunately, Peller wasn't smothered by close spaces, otherwise he could never venture into the confines of the apartments he inspected in New York.

Peller picked up the phone and dialed while flipping nervously through his Rolodex. "Gotta help the Sanchez woman before I get into it with Joe and Derek. Maybe Paul can help me find a good legal aid attorney for her up there."

The line was picked up in New York. "Chase here."

"Paul," he whispered. "It's Peller. Listen, I need a favor. If you do this one for me, I'll treat you to a real meal next time I come up. We can dream about becoming real estate moguls. When I left you last Friday, I got involved in a three-alarm fire … literally. I can't go into it now, too many ears. Suffice it to say that I have a friend from that apartment building I went to inspect who's suspected for arson. Jail. No lawyer. I'm not sure if they've set bail, but for the record, she's broke. Do you know someone who might help her out?"

"Look, Louis, are you gonna get me into trouble here?" Paul Chase queried. "Because if this is what it sounds like … "

"Paul, I really don't have time to chat. Look, call me at home tonight, and I'll give you the whole scoop. It's kind of amusing really. Angel Sanchez. I think she has some dirt on one of my borrowers who's pleading poverty. First, we have to get her sprung, and it's not the kind of case Amie's lawyers would want to dirty their hands on. You see, old Angel is a professional, a lady of the evening so to speak. But I've got to gain her confidence before she'll tell me what I need to know."

"Listen, Lou, now I know I don't have time for this. But I know an attorney who might be able to help."

"Thanks, Paul. I knew I could count on you," Peller interrupted. "Have your attorney friend call me at home tonight too." Peller hung up abruptly as he heard the jingle of change and a familiar voice by his cubicle.

"Louis, let's discuss New York. I hear things have been heating up up there."

"Hello, Joe," Peller sang out, a little too loud. "Sorry we couldn't really talk Friday night. I just figured this one would hold 'til this morning. I spoke with Derek earlier. He wants to meet with us so I can bring you both up to speed."

"No, Peller. I want details before we go into that meeting. No surprises. What the hell's going on up there?" Vallardo meant business, there was no way around it.

Peller began, "First off—Pollock." Vallardo waved him off the subject. "Okay, the Epstein deal. I went up there to inspect his building as planned. But a funny thing happened on the way to Harlem." Peller laid out the scenario, adding that he had no idea what the Sanchez woman wanted except to get Epstein to fix up her apartment. "The whole thing escapes me," Peller concluded.

"Obviously she wants something big that she believes a little mischief and a lot of publicity can deliver," Vallardo observed. "Do you think it's money?"

"No, I doubt it. I think Epstein's trying to put the screws on her for some reason. She hasn't been paying her rent. Maybe she wants sympathy, or revenge. She was furious at Epstein and his super, Willie Johnson."

"Sympathy for what? A leaky pipe? Everybody in New York's got busted pipes. Seems revenge is the more likely cause. Revenge for what though?"

"Well, Joe, the other tidbit I heard is that she might be running a city-wide prostitution ring out of the apartment. If so, maybe our boy is allowing her to run the operation out of the building and taking a cut in the profits of her little cottage industry. I tell you, he was pretty upset that I stopped to chat with her before the police took her in. Epstein must have had some good reason to look the other way while all that shit was going on in her apartment. If she's done anything to cheat or betray him, he could screw her over in a big way by going to the police about her, shall we say, business dealings. I certainly wouldn't put it past Epstein."

Peller's phone rang. "It's Derek. He wants us in his office now."

****

Peller kidded with Joe as they walked into the anteroom of Derek's office. "Think of it like this, Joe. If you handle this crisis well, maybe soon this office and this job will be yours." Peller had Vallardo's number when it came to great expectations and Vallardo's not-so-well-concealed ambitions to rise in the ranks of the corp. Peller had often speculated on the relationship between Vallardo and the big boss since Derek had taken responsibility for Vallardo's career eight years ago when the younger man had started working for him in Texas. Was there more to this pair than met the eye?

Derek King had clearly had some lucky breaks early in his own career to insinuate himself so smoothly into the ranks of upper management. As far as Peller could determine, he did not possess any particular insight into business or the politics of a giant corporation, nor did he demonstrate much finesse, but he had a knack for knowing the technical details of every workout and an uncanny ability to produce results. Derek was small in stature with a penetrating stare and a voice that demonstrated authority. His subordinates thought him a terrible taskmaster since he was all business during meetings and rarely took time for personal pleasantries. His position in the company proved something of a mystery to those who worked for him.

Offering their homage to the formidable Elaina Rogers, who reduced them to clay with one beautifully haughty glance, they strolled into Derek's domain, Peller with his usual confidence and Joe looking a bit apologetic in advance of what he assumed would be Derek's verbal hailstorm.

Derek rose from behind his oak desk and gestured to the two men to sit in the easy chairs in front of him. His smooth face was inscrutable. "I heard you did well on the Pollock negotiations. Someday remind me, and we'll celebrate. In the meantime, I need to know exactly what happened when you went to call on Epstein. I've already heard from legal up there, and they are concerned. Steve and Vicki expected you to brief them in case Epstein decided to talk to reporters who might dig into the financing end of these tenements and point the finger at Amie. Who knows what that guy might do when his back is to the wall. Really, Louis, what were you thinking about, leaving without saying 'boo' to anyone about this affair? That aside, news reports that night on television didn't mention Epstein or anything other than a typical New York hysteric attempting to burn down her building. But I'm afraid those enterprising reporters at the *Daily News* might dig a little deeper and find something threatening to Amie's interests."

Peller nodded in solemn agreement, crossing his arms over his chest. It was true, Amie Mae was already in a lot of trouble with its shareholders, the press, and Congress for the vast number of overleveraged loans the company had underwritten and purchased in New York City. Wall Street didn't like to hear about Amie Mae's loans and continuing losses. That kind of news was sure to have a negative impact on the company's stock value.

Patiently, Peller repeated his story, omitting his call to Paul Chase soliciting help for Angel Sanchez. *Let this be an anonymous act of right versus might*, he thought. Peller also failed to mention his speculation that the good Mr. Epstein might be using Angel's "sex-for-sale" enterprise, with a take for Epstein on the side.

"So the police arrested her a few minutes after I got there, and Epstein and Johnson made some excuse about her not being able to pay her rent among other problems and probably setting fire to the place." Peller leaned toward Derek, giving Vallardo a conspiratorial glance. "But frankly, I don't buy it. Something about this deal smells. Epstein could be setting us up to prove that his tenants are screwing him out of the rent so he can't pay us. And he knows we couldn't sell that building for anything near what we loaned him. It's in terrible condition—cracks in apartment walls, rotting pipes, and water leakage just for starters—and it's loaded with drugs, prostitutes, and welfare tenants. Maybe he thinks we'll forgive the debt and walk away if he makes it enough trouble for us."

"What have you been smoking?" asked Derek. "It's an interesting theory but a bit far-fetched." Peller still couldn't tell if Derek was angry or merely perplexed by the situation. "You know, Louis, I think you're getting yourself too wound up in Epstein's woes. You need a break from him; he's a classic bullshit artist. Anyway, this matter shouldn't concern you any further." His tone verged on a reprimand; the look on his boss's face was tough. "I'm giving you a new assignment. We'll let the New York office worry over Epstein until this thing cools down."

"Sure, chief," Peller smiled, somewhat relieved he wouldn't have to worry about officially protecting the company's name at the same time he was unofficially trying to find out how deeply Epstein was involved. Nonetheless, Peller loved the intrigue. He often got wrapped up in the drama of his work, creating excitement where there was none, only to be reminded that his job was cut and dry: either work out the default or foreclose.

"Who's the lucky borrower this time?" he asked, curious.

Derek settled back in his chair, pulling a folder off his desk for Peller. "The company is Assad Enterprises. Omar Assad is our man. Borrowed two million from us in '89. Hasn't paid a nickel in eighteen months. Needless to say, the building's probably worth only a fraction of that today. We need to make a deal. We've already lost too much on this loan."

Peller took the folder thoughtfully, wondering why this particular borrower might be so special. It always seemed to be the same story in New York real estate: no one was paying off loans. "Where's the property?"

"Washington Heights."

Peller started to ask another question, but Vallardo cut him off. "I'll brief you this afternoon, Lou. This one's of distinct interest to the company. It's big." Joe knew how to get Peller's attention.

"Thanks for the report, Louis." Derek peremptorily stood up. "Joe, I need to discuss another loan. Stay here for a second. Peller, please don't confide anything about the Epstein incident to the group." Derek's dark eyes locked Peller's in shared confidence. "Remember, I owe you some champagne. Kudos on the Pollock deal."

The three men stood up and shook hands all around, as if to seal a pact. The bulky Vallardo slapped Peller on the back. "Good man," he cheered, looking at Derek for approval.

Peller ignored the patronizing pat. Preoccupied, puzzling out what had just happened, he left the room more than a little curious about the secrecy Derek had invoked. *Wonder what Derek's got on this*, he mused. Obviously, there was more to the scenario than met the eye. Peller was intrigued.

Sitting back in his stuffy cubbyhole, he opened the Assad file to sort through the documentation on the original loan. So this was the Assad loan Steve had mentioned last week in New York: 488 West 158th Street. Not the nicest neighborhood, but then, Peller had dealt with properties in Washington Heights before. He'd just have to follow the three o'clock rule he and Tommy had instituted.

Omar Assad had purchased the building in 1985 for half a million dollars in cash. Property values were on the rise during this period, and owners were riding high on their new-found prosperity. When Assad refinanced the property with Amie Mae in 1989, two million dollars had not been an unreasonable loan for the 105-unit property. Now it seemed obscene. An inspection report indicated this place was yet another decrepit shell stuffed with a couple of families per apartment, holes in the ceilings, and dust balls in the alcoves sheltering disease-carrying varmints of various shapes and sizes. Peller estimated the building's 1993 worth might be closer to the original five hundred thousand dollars, and he made a note to have an appraiser and engineer evaluate it next week when he was in the city again. Peller saw a yellow stickee attached to the loan agreement that noted in Derek's handwriting, "Doesn't want to sell. No payment in 18 months." The note was dated June 12, 1993. He rifled through some other papers for background.

The phone rang. It was Paul. "Listen, I have the name of an attorney for you to call. She comes highly recommended."

"Paul, you're a superstar. Shoot."

"Christine Boyer. A former Peace Corps volunteer. She and I used to play softball together down by the Lincoln Memorial. She's not bad at second base. Liberal, into helping the down and out. Big on women's rights. Does a lot of pro bono work. Call her at home. Mention me. You'll like her; she's real down-to-earth, no bullshit. Short on looks, long on brains."

"Paul, I didn't know you had any acquaintances in the Peace Corps. You know, it does my heart good to find out—"

"Love to chat, Louis, but there goes my other line. Remember, you owe me dinner."

"You make the reservations for Tuesday a-week, old buddy. I'll be starting work on a new assignment up there. Omar Assad, some Iranian multimillionaire mufti who claims he can't pay up on his grossly overleveraged investment. So what's new? Anyway, dinner's your choice. How about Tavern on the Green?"

"I'll make reservations, Louis. Say, how about them Mets?"

"Pennant fever, no doubt. See you at the Series," Peller hung up feeling good, fingering the number he had jotted down. Christine Boyer. Sounded perfect: do-good, Waspy, all-American girl to represent poor, downtrodden, immigrant victims of the underclass. He was pleased with Paul's choice. Peller made a note in his calendar to call her at home that evening.

On an impulse, he decided to place a discreet call to Willie Johnson for some additional intelligence about Bud Epstein and Angel Sanchez. Maybe he could talk with Johnson in New York before he met Ms. Boyer. The super, speaking hesitantly, reluctantly agreed to meet with Peller outside a little bodega owned by a friend, far from the apartment building he took care of. "By the way, Mr. Peller," Johnson added, as if this answered any question Peller might have, "the police released Angel Sanchez early this morning on a thousand dollar bail. One charge was arson, the other, prostitution. She was also ordered to see a court-appointed psychiatrist. I guess they think she's crazy." Obviously, so did Willie Johnson. They set a date to meet, then Peller reluctantly decided he needed to put Angel Sanchez behind him.

For now, Peller had some other fish to fry. Like putting the finishing touches on Pollock. Vallardo had barely mentioned it. Not that Peller held much stock in Vallardo's opinion; the guy was good at banking basics, but get him beyond rudimentary options to work out a loan or foreclose, and his eyes glazed over. It was frustrating to work for such a naive guy in such a sophisticated business. Now Derek, he was another story altogether: sly, with a mind like a computer. Peller was gratified that Derek had at least noticed his work on the deal this morning. Personal congratulations were not generally Derek King's style. He usually left that sort of thing to a perfunctory memo, a standard form that Elaina Rogers had developed, that would be posted somewhere near the men's room. Derek did everything secretively. Even kudos. What a ferret he was, reflected Peller as he dialed Steve to review the fine print on the Pollock loan agreement with him.

"Louis, I told you." Steve dispensed with niceties. "I knew Assad would be handed to you this week. You want my advice? Go for the balls on this guy. He's extremely suspicious. Downright dangerous, in fact."

"Sorry to disappoint you, Steve, but I have no time for your wit and wisdom on the estimable Omar Assad today, so save it. I need you to get the draft documents to Pollock. Oh yeah, Epstein; while I'm thinking about it, I have a list of repairs that Epstein agreed to that you need to translate into good legalese. We'll have to include the insurance adjuster's damage report in a final estimate on repairs. Steve, I have a sneaking suspicion we are close to getting Epstein."

"Hope you're right, Peller. Okay, we'll dot the i's and cross the t's on the Pollock deal and get that one out. What a coup, assuming, of course, the *meshuganah* follows through. That reminds me, Lou," Steve interposed, his curiosity up, "just what happened between you and that prostitute up in Spanish Harlem on Friday? You could've clued us in down here. She was all over the six o'clock news."

"Yeah, well, her timing was perfect. I think she cared more about making headlines than actually trying to burn the place down. I mean really, did you see the way she was dressed?""Did I ever. They had her beautiful mug—and some other nice features—on the news from down at the precinct house in Harlem, and I think half the cameramen in town were angling to get the, shall we say, appropriate exposure. She sure stood out from behind bars there. So what's her game?"

Desperate and dateless, that was poor Steve, pitied Peller. "Damned if I know, Steve. I just happened to show up at the wrong time. Anyway, I make it a point never to get involved in anything sordid. Hurts the old reputation, you know."

"Louis, Louis. This is Steve here. You know, the guy you slum around town with? You trying to tell me you didn't get the dope on this babe? And you were right there? Gimme a break. Besides, old Tommy must have been drooling all over himself trying to get close to her."

"Don't waste your fantasies on call girls, Steve-o. What you need is a serious romance to keep you from walking off the deep end."

Peller could imagine the scene if their positions had been reversed, Steve falling all over himself to brush up against a woman as raw and alluring as Angel Sanchez: her wild red hair flamed as fiery as her passion and her full red lips, so inviting. And that outfit. Strangely, though, Peller himself was not especially excited about her. She was too easy, and too cagey, for his tastes. A dangerous female.

"I swear, Steve. Tommy wasn't even near her. He let me off a few blocks away, because we were running late, and there was a lot of traffic. By the time Tommy came back around to Epstein's place, the cops had already taken Angel Sanchez away. Meanwhile, I was running, because I was afraid Epstein would hightail it out of there if I was even five minutes late for our appointment. You know, I just can't trust that guy. He's been trying to buy me. Did I tell you he even offered me a job with his company? Hinted at six figures, plus a 30 percent signing bonus. Is that obvious or what?"

"No kidding. Did you accept? Then you could have an excuse to get close to Angel Sanchez. Even your wife couldn't complain. What an opportunity. I'll bet Epstein would pay good money too. Better than old Amie here."

"Steve, I'd love to continue this scintillating conversation, but I'm afraid I actually have a lot of work to do. I'm out there fighting in the trenches, not like you corporate lawyer types up there, working in the lap of luxury. So just have those documents ready to send out to Epstein and Pollock by Friday. And don't forget copies for me this time. By the way, I'll probably try to schedule a meeting with Assad for late in the week or early next week, so I'm sure I'll be up there for a couple days minimum. I'll be in touch."

His phone rang again. It was Vallardo.

"I want to talk to you about the Assad loan. Let's meet over lunch. We can run over to Tyson's Corner Center for a bite at the food court." Tyson's was a glitzy, marble shopping mall, with high-priced boutiques and the best department stores. "I have to pick up an anniversary present for Andrea. I need your advice on what to get the woman who wants only the best of everything." If Vallardo didn't come home with something pretty, and pricey, for his lovely, indulged wife, he would be an awfully lonely man tonight.

"Sure, Joe. How about twelve thirty? I'd like to review this file a little before we talk." Why would Vallardo choose a shopping mall for their meeting? *I hate shopping*, Peller reflected. Well, at least Tysons would be better than the Amie Mae cafeteria, that was for damned sure, and away from Mildred's sonar. And Peller figured Vallardo was looking to bitch to him about the inconstancy of women: guy gossip they both indulged in.

He reached for the yellow legal pad covered with notes about New York's neighborhoods. There was the phone number of the real estate appraiser he had used for the last Washington Heights deal. Peller would have him do the appraisal first thing: ammunition for his negotiations with Assad. He remembered Steve's warning, "Assad is evasive, but be careful; even if you can catch him, he's a crazy fox."

And there, under the name "Jimenez," he found his impressions of Washington Heights:

> Mostly Hispanic pop. Dominican. 2–3 fams./apt. living in disrepair. No cops on streets—Dominicans hate police. Bands of kids selling drugs after school. Sidewalks crammed with unlicensed street vendors. Typical econ.—sm. mom and pop shops, high unemployment.

Bernardo Jimenez had held the only other loan Peller had worked on in that part of town. Not a bad guy; active in the community, he'd helped raise money to staff a neighborhood center for kids to hang out safely after school. Working for the American dream. But the tenants in that building. Many of the young people he'd seen milling around the Jimenez building wore the kind of menacing attitude you had to take seriously. Some of them undoubtedly carried concealed weapons. Self-preservation.

And Peller remembered Tommy's last warning about going into Washington Heights. "If I'm takin' you up to the Heights this time, Lou, it's 'cause I like you and want to see you come back alive. Don't even think about asking me to drive you theah again. Not even between ten and three. No special favors." That was after the second cabdriver was shot near the Jimenez apartments. "They don't go fo' no Italians up there … Jews neither." Well, that macho Italian would just have to swallow his paranoia again to drive Peller up for an inspection next week at the Assad building. Tommy could carry a knife if he was worried about his safety. Peller wasn't worried, not really. At least all his life insurance policies were up-to-date. He wasn't invincible, but he figured, if his time was up, there was not much he could do about it. Although he couldn't help but think maybe Lana was right; he did deserve hazardous-duty pay for going into a combat zone each and every week.

Peller thumbed through the file for Assad's phone number. Maybe he could arrange to meet with the borrower within the week. Peller insisted on inspecting buildings with his borrowers, usually to put them on notice that he wasn't afraid to check out their handiwork after the repairs were made.

****

Peller and Vallardo each went their separate ways in the food court at the tiny shopping mall at Tyson's Corner. Vallardo went for the big burger and fries, while Peller preferred a salad and a fruit shake.

Vallardo bought his meal fast and chose the first empty table he could find in the dining area, waving Peller across the room. Surrounded by a posse of strollers, toddlers, and hysterical parents laden with packages, Peller threaded his way warily across this shopper's mecca until he reached his boss. "At least it's nonsmoking," he ventured optimistically, looking for a chair to replace the one with a large wad of bubble gum freshly planted on the seat by some warring Ninja toddler.

"Come on, Louis," remarked Vallardo. "Surely you're used to this kind of anarchy."

"That's why I come to work every day, Joe. I want to spend my days somewhere that is sheltered from pint-size chaos," Peller sighed. "And I'm pretty sure you can do your own shopping. So why did you really bring us here?"

Vallardo sat up to the table, playing with the ketchup and frowning, bulging brown eyes under bushy brows. "I wanted to get you away from the office. Who can talk on the field without worrying about counterintelligence? Peller, you disappointed me Friday. I had to hear about this whole arson thing from Steve. You know I need to be kept informed about any play that might bomb like that." Vallardo stuffed a fistful of fries, dripping viscous red paste, into his mouth, chewing conspicuously.

"Joe, you don't understand. I had to get out of there before three o'clock. That neighborhood is crawling with drug runners. Besides, Epstein was hassling me again. He knows we are playing the endgame with him. We need to keep the pressure on, or he'll just keep toying with us. Trust me on this, Joe."

His boss patted his lips with a napkin advertising Western-style bagels. "Louis, you know my game plan. I don't want to tell you how to do your job. Play things out with him. If he can't pay on the loan, foreclose, and let's keep moving the ball down the field. Otherwise, it's not fair to the rest of the players." Vallardo hesitated uncomfortably.

"Look … I gotta tell you this, friend. On the Q.T., of course. Derek just gave me the heads up. New policy comin' down the pipe at Amie. Corporate profits have fallen off. Layoffs in the wind. Efficiency, that's the name of this game. Trading some of the bench players, big time. You're good, Lou; you're a superstar. But I have to say, if it comes to recommending who stays and who goes, I gotta go with those guys who hand off the ball to the open players."

Peller stopped his defense short, startled. Vallardo's voice echoed hollowly in his brain. Layoffs.

Joe continued. "Really, Louis, I can't keep guys around who run for the touchdown every time. Catch my meaning?"

Peller caught it in the gut.

"Now, I don't want you spreading the word around to anyone else in the group. When the time's right, we're gonna huddle on it, don't you worry. But for now, just hug this little ball close to your chest. Okay?"

Lecture over, Vallardo sat back, relaxed, ignoring Peller's bewilderment. "'Nough said." He bit into the thick, greasy burger, also coated with red goop. Peller's stomach was churning.

"Now, let's just forget about this little chat for a while, Louis. I need your advice on a present for Andrea. She's been ragging on me for weeks: 'I know you're going to forget our anniversary, so I'm just gonna go and pick something out for myself.' Well, I want to prove her wrong. What's some pretty bauble that she'll think is expensive? You know how my wife goes for the gold."

Andrea. Gold. Layoffs. Shit. Peller couldn't hear what Vallardo was saying. What was he implying with this unexpected news? What did it have to do with Peller? He couldn't think about it. He should press ahead with Assad, try to stay clean.

Unable to focus, Peller's eyes were dazed by the cosmopolitan crush of shoppers scrambling to and fro. Why did Peller suddenly feel so lost? Vallardo was warning him. Had his boss meant to distract him like this? Couldn't think about it. Not now. Change the subject. Stick to the game plan: Omar Assad.

"Joe, I thought we here to talk about the Assad workout. What's his story? Why would this guy want to hang on to a loser piece of property that could cost him more to repair than it would cost to bail out?"

"Don't sweat it, Louis; that's not our problem. Just concentrate on making this guy pay off the loan. But I'll warn you, he is some kind of snake. He has a heavy accent—I think he's from somewhere in the Mid-East. I'll bet he was even behind the scenes during Iran-Contra at some point. You know, 'FOA,' a 'Friend of the Ayatollah.' He's *that* cagey. And apparently, he's worked himself into the power structure here too. Contributes to the right members of Congress. Worked for the mayor raising money—quietly, you know. Doesn't do to have an Iranian making big campaign contributions if you're a Jewish New York pol, facts be known. We know he owns at least two other buildings in New York, privately financed. He came to Amie to refinance a building he bought for five hundred thousand dollars. He pocketed one-point-five million dollars in refinancing proceeds. Our underwriters back then thought the rents supported a two million dollar loan. Boy, were they ever bamboozled. That appraiser was later indicted for fraud, but no connection was made with Assad, and he got to keep our one-point-five million dollars." Vallardo knew this was just the kind of conjecture to hook a guy like Peller: a "big" deal, speculation, intrigue, confusion. The guy should have been a detective, he thought.

Peller filed this information in the back of his head. Iran-Contra … hmm … Maybe Paul would have some insights into this guy. "Sounds like a man of strong moral fiber," Peller observed wryly.

"I worked on the original loan. But now, with my administrative overload, I don't have time to deal with him anymore. Listen, I don't trust this guy for a minute, Louis. That's why I wanted you on this case. I know you're tenacious as a bulldog and won't let up on him. Am I right?"

Peller rose to the challenge. "You can bet on that. I've already scheduled a meeting with Assad for next Monday in New York." Peller couldn't wait to dig into this one. Sounded like he could test his wits against a real tiger. Just the kind of challenge he thrived on.

"Good," said Vallardo as he hastily swallowed the last half of his sandwich, wiping his mouth and rising. He looked at his watch. "Hurry and finish up that rabbit food. We have just about enough time to find Andrea's present." Vallardo watched Peller expectantly. "Well? You coming?"

Since the coach held the ball, and the car keys, Peller didn't really have much of a choice. He hadn't eaten during their conversation, and now he felt a rock sitting on his stomach. The greens on his plate suddenly looked slimy, rotted. Peller had been sidelined, taken out of the big game; of that he felt certain. But Peller was no benchwarmer. He wanted to bring Vallardo back around to discussing his future.

But Vallardo was already on his way out to the shops without a backward glance.

Chapter 6
The Eye of the Storm

When they got back to the office, Peller had nine messages in his voice mail. Three of them were from Lana: "When will you be home for dinner? Hope you're staying out of trouble;" "I miss you, Mr. Honey. It's a slow news day. Call me;" and "I forgot; can you take Alex to buy him new shoes this weekend? He likes you to help him pick them out. By the way, where the hell are you?" It was reassuring to hear her voice, even on mundane matters. One message was from Steve: "When did you say you expect to hear from the insurance adjusters on repairs Epstein needs to make to his building?" Three were from other borrowers he was working with. One was Pollock, asking when he'd have a draft of the final workout agreement to give to his attorney for review. And one was from Christine Boyer, Paul's lawyer friend.

He decided to call Lana first, but he didn't want to share Vallardo's warning about pending layoffs with her. No need to worry her yet. With a deep, Lurch-like voice, he announced, "You rang, my dear?"

Lana laughed. "Louis, you're incorrigible."

"I hope so." Then he whispered, "By the way, what's the 'I love you' for … trying to butter me up? Or are you just in the mood for love? Maybe tonight we can spoon beneath the sheets."

"Too late. I need you now."

"I can't talk long … too much going on here. But wait 'til I tell you about my meeting with Joe and Derek this morning. You're going to love this."

"Louis, I want you to tell me all about it, but promise me you'll be home early tonight to stay with the kids. We forgot to get groceries this weekend, and for once, I'd like to go to the grocery store alone, without three commercial-saturated children telling me which sugar-injected junk food we have to buy. Okay?"

"Honey, I'll try. I don't know if I can get home before seven thirty. I've got a lot of work to do to get ready for this new assignment. And I'll probably have to go up to New York for two nights next week. What a drag," Peller exclaimed.

Lana knew that Peller actually looked forward to his trips to the Big Apple. The big time. He was totally enthralled and totally repelled by the lights, the glamour, the decadence.

"C'mon, Louis. You promised me you'd be home on time tonight. Or, if you'd like, I'd be happy to let you do the shopping on your way home," Lana ventured generously, with mock consideration.

He again felt the rock pressing against his gut. First Vallardo, now Lana was provoking him. If only she knew the pressure he was under. They'd have to talk tonight. He could guess at the look on her pretty face, the pout to match her voice. Watch the kids. The idea that Lana would try to sweeten him up just to babysit for her annoyed Peller who felt he shouldn't have to check in like a child every time he had any plans to work late or catch a drink with a buddy.

"I'd really like to help, sweetie. But I just can't. I'm exhausted already, and it's only two o'clock. I promise, I'll make it up to you this weekend, honey bun. How about finding a sitter for dinner and a movie Saturday night?"

Sugar turned bitter. "Fine. But pick up some milk and eggs

on the way home. And your promise to go out Saturday night, just the two of us, better be real this time, or I'd advise you to be prepared for serious consequences." Lana hung up on a dare.

He ran his hand through his waves and sighed. He wanted to rant and rave, let off steam. He knew Lana was more than a little piqued at what she considered his shirking of familial responsibility. She usually reserved that angry tone for one of his more serious trespasses, like neglecting the to-do list for months on end or working late every night and then demanding to know why there was nothing for dinner (with characteristic timing, he usually managed to arrive after the main course had dried up in the oven) or all the above. Like he could control his workload. He realized that he *had* promised her he'd be home early, and that admission annoyed him; it made him even angrier that Lana was right. Again. He was working too much. Again. Could he help it if the "powers that be" had decided to load another messy loan onto his already full plate? Again. If he told her that layoffs might loom ahead, what would she make of that?

Reluctantly, Peller got back to work on some reports he'd been procrastinating over for two months. Each new loan he acquired had to be written up in full detail and reviewed by both Vallardo and Derek before being submitted to the investment committee and the auditors. The auditors were a cursed part of daily existence at Amie Mae and could, at any time, query the workout team for hours on the smallest technicalities until they were satisfied that the letter of the law was being carried out. He'd convinced his superiors that he could have the reports on their desks *yesterday*. Then, like any college freshman, he ignored the due date, figuring he'd burn the midnight oil if he had to. Anyway, he worked best under pressure.

He heard his stomach growl and ignored it. He surprised himself when, looking up from the final report, he noticed the cleaning crew noisily pushing around vacuum cleaners and making a pass with dust mop and broom. He glanced at his watch: eight thirty already. No wonder he was hungry. Time to leave and face the wrath of Lana.

He had one remaining mission: call Christine Boyer. He pulled out the number Paul had dictated and dialed it. After five rings, a toneless voice answered, "Yes?"

"Yes, Christine Boyer, please," Peller said.

"This is she. Who's calling?" She sounded very formal, considering he'd reached her at home after hours.

"I'm a friend of Paul Chase. Name's Louis Peller."

"Oh, Mr. Peller. Paul mentioned you might be calling. But you've picked a most inopportune time. I'm in the middle of something very important right now, so you'll have to be brief. How can I help you?"

What else had Paul mentioned about the case that had this woman sounding so irritated, Peller wondered.

"Well, it's a rather long story. But to keep it to the point, you might have seen some news reports on TV last week about an Hispanic woman who set fire to an apartment building in Spanish Harlem?" She murmured, distracted, in the affirmative.

"Well, she's sort of a friend of mine. Angel Sanchez. Anyway, she lives in one of the buildings my company holds the mortgage on. I happened to be there when she pulled off her little charade, and I saw the police take her away. She's out on bail now."

"It seems this woman is no innocent. Arson is a serious offense. So what's your point, Mr. Peller?"

"My point is this; she has some information that could be very useful to my company. She indicated as much to me when we chatted briefly at the scene. It may even be that Mr. Epstein, her landlord, put her up to this ugly act to justify his failure to pay my company. I'm interested in helping her so I can find out what she—"

"I'm not in the habit of representing companies to protect their corporate interests, Mr. Peller. Besides, you must have a cavernous conference room full of corporate attorneys at Amie

Mae to help you," Christine Boyer replied, cutting off his explanation.

"Please, call me Louis." This advocate seemed to be motivated more by principle than logic, thought Peller. He'd have to find her hot button. "Of course, I understand your position. But I also understand you are interested in protecting the rights of women who have been victimized by the system. Ms. Sanchez claims she was being raped and blackmailed by this landlord who also happens to be my borrower." It could've happened that way, Peller justified. "Anyway, I think you'll find her case compelling, Ms. Boyer," Peller replied provocatively. "And Amie Mae wants to keep its distance." He paused to gauge her reaction.

"Amie Mae must have access to some fine criminal attorneys," she pointed out.

"The company is not in the business of defending tenants. First of all, Amie's attorneys are not criminal lawyers. Second of all, our advocates are about as button-down as you can get."

"So what's the point, Louis?"

God, how he hated lawyers. So adversarial. "Amie Mae is not going to want to defend some two-bit floozy who claims her landlord's hitting on her. But I tell you, this woman deserves a zealous defense. If you were to meet my borrower, Epstein … Please, just hear me out."

"Okay, Louis, I'll meet with you. But I must tell you, my caseload is full right now. It's going to be difficult for me to take on any new cases. Let me talk to her first, and I'll get back to you. You'd better tell me where to reach Angel Sanchez so I can get her story before we meet."

"Thanks," said Peller warmly. "You won't be sorry you took this on, Ms. Boyer. I promise."

"I think I'm sorry already," she answered, echoing Paul, and hung up the phone.

****

"Monday, August 2—Manhattan," began the notation on his well-worn legal pad. "Assad meeting."

Once again, Peller was riding into New York City, this time in a yellow cab. Tommy was busy ferrying Derek and Vallardo to a Brooklyn site for yet another building inspection. It seemed everyone was running around looking at bad properties these days, even the chiefs. Even though Vallardo was easing out of hands-on loan management and Derek rarely got his hands dirty in that stuff anymore, they were short staffed these days, and the big guns were forced to pitch in.

This cabdriver was taking the scenic route via Outer Mongolia, Peller observed with chagrin. Obviously a recent Russian émigré (as Peller could tell by seeing the name Nicholas Czernik posted on the back seat), he barely spoke five words of English. Despite Peller's directions to take the Triborough Bridge, the driver had gotten on the Brooklyn–Queens Expressway. Either he misunderstood, or it was the only route the guy knew. The whole thing amounted to a huge fiasco that set Peller's teeth on edge, more so after watching row after row of depressing old two-story duplexes passing out the windows while Peller's watch and the meter ticked relentlessly on. Peller tapped his foot impatiently, wondering how to convey his haste to this thick-skulled Russian.

"Look, I'm in a real hurry. Can't you step on it a little?" Peller pleaded, not for the first time. The driver, oblivious to Peller's obvious distress, cut off the Parkway, taking a seesawing detour through Long Island City, with some delight in pointing out the little brick apartment building where his sister lived with her family. "My sister, she marry rich American," he beamed. "Big, happy family. Own apartment."

In the end, the cab ended up in a long line of traffic at the 59th Street Bridge—the only bridge into the city that didn't require a toll—waiting behind every other dumb schmuck who wanted to get into Manhattan gratis. "No vorry, misterrr. I get you to city," insisted the driver. Somehow this was not how Peller preferred to "take Manhattan." The detour had added, by Peller's computations, at least forty minutes to an already interminable ride.

Finally, the midtown skyscrapers were looming grandly above their heads. Peller was glad he hadn't scheduled the meeting with Assad too early, or he would have had further reason to panic.

As the cab slowed to a halt outside the office, the meter showed $20.50. Peller peeled off twenty-one dollars to pay for the ride and stepped around to the trunk to grab his suit bag. He couldn't tip this guy. Peller growled as he slipped the driver the bills then hurried inside and disappeared into a waiting elevator before the driver had a chance to complain.

"Why, if it ain't the infamous Louis Peller," Julie confronted him mockingly. "I thought you might bring that Angel you met on your last visit here, to introduce us—or more to the point—Steve. He has been dying to meet her. And I must say, I'm a little curious myself."

"Sorry to disappoint you this time, Jules," he replied evenly. "But Angel's out of commission for awhile. Where is old Shapiro this bright and beautiful morning?"

"Unfortunately, he's out of the office, or I'm sure he'd want to rub your nose in it. I understand you're meeting with the mysterious Omar Assad."

"Right. Our meeting is supposed to be set for the conference room at eleven fifteen. Let me know when he gets here. I'll be in Steve's office in the meantime."

Peller wanted to be armed with the cost estimates of existing repairs and deferred maintenance in addition to the amount of payments Assad failed to remit over the past eighteen months. Typically, he would also review the borrower's personal financial statement, but Assad had never sent one in. "Understand the property and maintenance costs, the cash flow, and the borrower's financial resources. That is the key to making a loan work." Amie Mae Policy 001. Peller stowed his bag and briefcase behind Steve's desk.

But before he got started, he would check in with the businesslike Christine Boyer to confirm their meeting.

"Ms. Boyer? Louis Peller here. Yes, I'm in New York now. I'm between meetings at the moment. Are we still on for four thirty? Good. Yes, I'll come to your office. Have you spoken to Angel Sanchez? Frankly, I'm not surprised she wouldn't say anything to you. She seems to be suspicious of everyone. I think I can help on that score. For some reason, she seems to think I'm okay, so—"

The office intercom intruded with a staccato beep. "Mr. Peller? Mr. Assad is here to see you."

"Ms. Boyer, my eleven fifteen meeting has just arrived, so I'll have to go. See you at four thirty. Oh, and thanks again for taking this case."

****

Peller was seated at the head of the long conference table when Julie escorted Omar Assad into the room. Louis Peller wanted to establish the psychological advantage from the outset of this game, although he doubted such a ploy would have any effect on this cagey business mogul. Peller was surprised at what he saw. Omar Assad, rugged and swarthy looking, exuded a dynamism that filled the room. Somehow he fulfilled all of Hollywood's conflicting stereotypes to form the composite of a modern-day Arabian sheik: tall and lanky; a swarthy, taut face; coolly mysterious; somehow primitive, yet urbane; ageless, yet showing the lines of a certain age; commanding an aura of enigma. Omar Assad, imagined Peller, went home to a smoky harem of voluptuous and solicitous wives lolling indolently in wait for their master. Peller noticed a glint in his black eyes that telegraphed that this guy was as shrewd as his reputation made him out to be. Louis Peller was immediately on his guard.

"Thank you, Miss Hudson, for all your assistance," said the borrower courteously. He spoke in that precise British clip, Oxford, no doubt. Peller noted that Julie was acting in a far more circumspect manner than her usual "bull in a china shop" habit. Trapped by his charm, no doubt. *If she isn't careful, she could get herself wrapped up in his silky web*, Peller thought warily. But then, maybe that was the point.

"Mr. Peller." Assad extended his hand, flashing a thick gold ring that looked like a coiled snake inset with a diamond eye. The two men shook hands in an apparently amicable greeting. "So good to meet you at last. I've heard quite a bit about you from your colleagues, and I look forward to working with you. I admire you, Mr. Peller. You understand the problems of borrowers like me. Your understanding will go a long way in fixing my loan."

So he's done his homework too, Peller thought. *Well, this ought to be interesting.* "The pleasure is all mine," Peller replied. The two men stared each other briefly in the eye. "I hope we'll be able to work through this little problem together without too much trouble. Amie Mae would hate to lose your business."

"Mr. Peller, I think you'll find me extremely amenable to any deal your company has to offer, as long as we all understand one thing at the outset: I won't give up this property under any terms." Assad's lips curled like Whistler's Mother, undeniably unreadable.

Peller grinned back cautiously. "I think we may be able to work things out to our mutual satisfaction." He showed Assad the seat across from his and sat down. Assad set his black eelskin briefcase on the table next to him with great deliberation.

"Mr. Assad," Peller began. "Your reputation for financial acumen is widely known and respected in our company. So you'll pardon me if I ask you a rather personal question, one that's got me a bit confused." *Open slow. Start with the positive Peller, old boy.*

"You're far too kind, Mr. Peller. I understand you too have the respect of your colleagues for your fine insight. Fortunately for me, I've never had to test my skills in this workout arena … until now. Maybe you can help guide me through the process." Assad flashed his white teeth and settled back, signaling he had all the time in the world for Peller's questions.

Peller reminded himself to have patience. You didn't just start punching away at these Middle Easterners the way you did New Yorkers. No, the game was played far more subtly than that. Still, Peller thought, it seemed time to finish posturing.

"Well, for starters, one doesn't borrow two million dollars and renege on one's commitment." Peller was rummaging through the papers in his file. "According to our records, you haven't paid Amie Mae a nickel since … when was your last payment?"

"June of 1991, Mr. Peller," volunteered Omar Assad. "And you're wondering why I haven't made any payments since then, isn't that right?"

"Well, my question ran somewhere along those lines. Suppose we talk about it." Peller sat back too. He was beginning to think he might enjoy this game.

"I've had something of a temporary financial setback, Mr. Peller. You've heard, perhaps, that this country's been going through a recession and that the real estate industry, particularly in New York City, has been a bit slow. Well, despite the rumors about my alleged millions, Assad Enterprises has been hard-hit by this economy, and we're suffering too."

"Since I owe my job to this unusual set of circumstances, Mr. Assad, I'm well aware of what the recession might be doing to your business. But no, what I'm curious about is this: we clearly lent you too much money on this building. You and I both know that, at today's value, 488 West 158th Street is worth far less than the current loan amount of two million dollars, probably even less than a million. Amie Mae loaned you that amount on a bad bet, on the strength of your original investment and the assumption that property values in this town would continue to rise indefinitely. We both lost." In fact, Peller had learned from the appraiser that the building's current value was more like a quarter of a million, but he wasn't about to show his hand.

A quarter-million—how Vallardo and Derek had shuddered at the vast loss the company had incurred in loaning so much money on such a terrible property. But that pattern was the norm for the 1980s. Amie Mae wasn't the only mortgage company that had lost, nor was Omar Assad the sole loser among real estate investors.

But the high cost of the improvements required to restore this building was worrisome—more worrisome than most. Peller had pored over the appraiser's report, analyzing the status of the building on West 158th. An engineering study now showed the building had serious structural problems. An underground stream was causing the building's foundation to shift and crack. Because of the shifting, floors in apartments and hallways throughout the building were bowing. Pipes had cracked, and the water leakage was substantial. Door frames were tilted. Cracks in the bricks outside the building began at the ground and climbed in zigzag fashion, uninterrupted, to the roof.

Peller would make Assad aware of just enough of the analysis to let his borrower know he was prepared. "You know, Omar," he insinuated confidentially, leaning across the table toward his borrower, "it would probably take at least a million more just to fix the place up to meet New York building codes. And given the property's current finances, why don't you just let us take the building off your hands for you? We could put in a receiver within a week and repair the building fairly quickly. Bankruptcy won't work for you, because Amie is grossly undersecured."

"I see you are far too smart to believe my sob story, Mr. Peller," said Assad smoothly. "So let me tell you the truth. This building has far more worth to me than any value your appraisers might assign. You see, this was my first investment in the United States. It is like a child to me. You have children, Mr. Peller; would you sell them, no matter how poorly they were living up to your expectations?"

Peller shook his head slightly, wondering what Assad had in mind.

"I'm willing to give my baby another chance here. We both know that whatever Amie Mae might be able to recoup, it wouldn't come near your two-million-dollar loan. And unlike

Amie, I am not a corporation. I run a small family business. For purely sentimental reasons, I am willing to pay off the loan right now for, say, eight hundred thousand dollars. Cash. Half at the time of sale, and the other half in smaller installments over the next twelve months, your terms. What do you say?"

Peller was astonished at this proposal. He'd been prepared for a lot of hemming and hawing by Assad. Maybe a "let me contact my very rich and powerful friends in Teheran and get back to you in a week" stall tactic. But nothing as stupid as this. Why would a guy be willing to pay eight hundred thousand dollars cash on a building worth one quarter that amount? And where would he then find the million bucks or more he would need to outfit his "baby" to meet New York building code and pass inspection? Sentimental attachment. That was a new one, and he thought he'd heard them all. But what a windfall for Amie. A short payoff for four times the building's appraised value? Peller would be a hero.

Try to stay cool, he cautioned himself. *There must be a hitch in this deal somewhere.*

Louis Peller stifled a grin and assumed a serious look, tapping his pen on the table as if deep in thought. "To tell you the truth, Mr. Assad, I am not authorized to agree to a short payoff of your loan at this time. We have a credit committee that looks at any and all proposals to determine the best course for the borrower and the company. I'll have to present your offer to the committee and get back to you. And it may take a while. They're swamped right now."

"I appreciate the fact that you have other problems to contend with, Mr. Peller. My offer will stand for thirty days. After that, we will see what other paths we might need to cross. But remember, I intend to keep my property."

Peller could barely contain his jubilance. He summoned up his most official airs. "You realize, of course, we'll have to inspect the property and have it appraised during that time.

I'll commission a more in-depth engineering report to assess solutions to the structural damage."

Assad closed his briefcase thoughtfully, uncrossing his long legs slowly as he stood. "Call me next week to arrange a time to walk through it. And I hope we might conclude this transaction quickly—I may need to go back to Teheran on business in a couple of weeks for an indefinite period."

Peller stood up, remaining at the head of the table, appearing to command more presence than his five-foot, six-inch stature might normally permit. "Mr. Assad, I can't tell you how pleased I would be to wrap this up quickly. I am working on fifty-seven other troubled loans. I appreciate your understanding. Let's speak again within the week."

Assad stretched out his hand. "Goodbye, Mr. Peller. I hope to see you soon." The dark-skinned man had a secretive air about him. Peller could not tell whether or not he was serious. He even wondered whether there was a smirk underneath that suave mask. Assad slipped out, pulling the door softly behind him.

Peller stared at the door. "What the hell was that all about?" he asked himself aloud.

A moment later, the door opened with a bang, and Steve Shapiro, looking wild in his disarray, barged in. "I hear I missed the Great Assad. How'd it go?"

Peller jumped with a start, absently shuffling papers back into his briefcase, lost in speculation.

"Steve, don't you ever knock?"

Steve flashed a grin.

"Listen, you wouldn't believe this guy Assad." Peller was dying to tell someone about his experience with the "sheik" of real estate. "He 'can't pay the mortgage,' right? Hasn't given us a nickel in two years, while good old Amie Mae conveniently looks the other way. We've just been too busy to look after this one little borrower, I guess." Peller, perplexed, looked at Steve for confirmation. "Well, today he comes in here, slick as oil, and offers me eight hundred thousand dollars cash to take the bad debt off of good old Amie's hands."

"Eight hundred grand? He's got to know the building's only worth a fraction of that," Steve said in astonishment.

"Mr. Assad doesn't know it yet, but I've already gotten back the appraisal. Are you ready … 235 K. That's it. The property is down to one eighth the original value of our loan. Meanwhile, this guy's no dummy. He's got to know he's carrying a white elephant."

"Hard to ignore a white elephant. So what's his angle?"

"Says he's 'sentimentally attached' to this property. It was his first investment in America. You know, 'sweet land of liberty' and all that hogwash. But I think there's more here than meets the eye, Steve. I don't know what it is yet. But I smell trouble." Peller was getting really worked up.

"Louis, I see a dangerous glow in your eyes. Don't jump in over your head on this deal. You've already made news with the voluptuous Angel Sanchez. Do yourself a favor; do a workout, foreclose, or give the guy the short payoff at eight hundred thousand dollars. Give this deal the K.I.S.S.—keep it simple stupid. By the way, do you think you could introduce me to your Angel?" Steve asked jokingly, fumbling through his pockets for a cigarette.

Peller ignored the bait. "Steve, we're talkin' *major* shady deal here. I think he might be trying to bribe me. Assume he knows the building's only worth a quarter million. He knows that, I know that. He's not saying it out loud, but I think he's telling me to give Amie the two hundred thirty-five thousand dollars and pocket the change. Imagine, I skim five hundred sixty-five thousand dollars off the top—that's serious payola."

Steve thought about this a moment as he pulled a lighter out of his jacket pocket. Lighting his cigarette with a mischievous glint in his eye, Steve sized up Peller who was clearly feeling his oats. "Louis, I know you. You would never do anything illegal like that." Steve took a puff and blew smoke into Peller's face, as if to clear the fog from his colleague's eyes. "Relax. This is a win-win deal. Bring in the eight hundred thousand dollars to the company, and you're a hero—again. We've never had a settlement that big. It's a no-brainer, pal." He paused. "All the luck," he swore under his breath.

Peller detected the note of jealousy in Steve's congratulations. "Maybe you're right, and I'm overreacting. Anyway, I told him I needed time to let our 'committee' review the deal. I want to hear what Vallardo and Derek think about this one first. And maybe ask around town, a few questions about the enigmatic Assad, just out of curiosity."

Steve gave him a skeptical look and grumbled, "You and your curiosity. It'll buy you trouble, mark my words. Just remember who warned you." Then Steve thought better of lecturing and grinned. "Not to change the subject, but wanna do lunch, Mr. Rainmaker?" Steve asked, putting the issue aside for now.

"Sure. Your treat. I'm famished. But we need to make it short. I have to meet with another borrower uptown at two o'clock." Peller didn't want to reveal to Steve that he was talking with Willie Johnson about Epstein and Angel.

The two men headed to the Star Deli on Lexington Avenue. The place had glass-encased food displays that were to die for. The restaurant was run by a Lebanese family, but it had the best knishes in town. Their favorite neighborhood deli, it was short on service, but long on taste.

****

Lunch over, Peller mentally prepared an agenda. He felt like a spy. Here he was, venturing into who knew what kind of perils to meet with a man who worked for his borrower, for Christ's sake, and expecting to get the lowdown. Willie Johnson was in a tight spot. For all he knew, Willie Johnson could be ready to rat to Epstein that Amie Mae was digging where they had no business. A scene that could blow up in his face, he thought, restraining himself. Maybe he should have been the one to join the CIA, not Paul. Even the Agency was getting into business espionage these days.

Johnson was waiting nervously in the back office of a little neighborhood bodega on the Upper West Side. When Peller arrived in the front of the market, a beautiful young woman with cocoa skin and dark chocolate eyes, a West Indian to judge from her accent, greeted him in the manner of an old friend, and hurriedly, though seemingly without hurry, ushered him into the back room. "So good to see you again, Mr. Peller." Peller had never met the woman before, but he presumed this was part of a ruse to protect Willie Johnson. He played along, smiling. "I'll get you some tea," she said for the benefit of any eavesdroppers. Then, more quietly, "Please have a seat. Mr. Johnson's waiting." She smiled briefly, and disappeared.

Johnson came in as if on cue from some back entrance Peller could not discern and motioned Peller to sit at a small, red-check-clothed table.

"You have excellent taste in women, Mr. Johnson," Peller commented appreciatively after the young woman took her leave.

"She's the manager and the daughter of one of my dearest friends. She and her father live right next door here." Johnson seemed nervous. He picked up a salt shaker from the table and shifted it from hand to hand. "The Salvadoran people who own this market pretty much give her carte blanche to run it as she sees fit, and she makes a handsome profit for them. I visit a lot, so it's not unusual for me to be seen here. We've helped each other out many times in the past. Like family," he noted, peering suspiciously at Peller.

"I know what you mean. Families are important—especially extended families." As his eyes adjusted to the dingy light, he could see that the room was not only an office but a small warehouse. Boxes and crates were neatly stacked in the cool, dry storage room. There were several old refrigerators lining the walls.

Exotic spices and herbs mingled curiously, wafting through the air. Peller closed his eyes and breathed deeply, trying to divine the unusual blend playing on his nose.

Willie Johnson clasped his hands together, squeezing the salt shaker tightly. "What can I do for you, Mr. Peller?" His weathered face was creased in a frown.

"Of course. Forgive me, Mr. Johnson. I wanted to savor this wonderful breath of paradise." Peller smiled, hoping to get Johnson to relax. He needed the black man's cooperation to find out what was really going on in Epstein's building.

Johnson didn't budge, his back ramrod straight.

"I'm interested in knowing what kind of a boss Bud Epstein is. You've worked for him for eleven years now. In that time, how has he dealt with you?"

"Before we go into that, Mr. Peller, I'd like to know where this interrogation is leadin'. 'Cause I need to keep my job. I have four kids still at home, hoping to go to college, and I don't need you to destroy their dreams." He set the salt down emphatically as he spoke. "Jus' why should I pour my heart out to you?"

Peller could see Johnson's hedging could delay their conversation interminably. "I understand your skepticism. You don't know me, why should you trust me? But I got the distinct impression that if I read the situation correctly after the little incident with Angel Sanchez last week, all is not as it seems in your neck of the woods, Mr. Johnson. I need Bud Epstein to follow through on his commitments, and if I'm not mistaken, you need him to let you do your job and run that building on the straight and narrow. Close enough?"

Willie Johnson closed his eyes and sighed. "You're a good judge of character, Mr. Peller. Okay I'll take a gamble on you bein' straight with me." He looked Peller dead in the eyes. "But what I say is strictly off the record." Peller nodded. "I'm tired of dealin' with this shit alone. This ain't been no easy job. Not since *she* moved in, that is."

"I assume you mean Angel?"

"Yes. She's bad news, trouble with a capital P if you see my meanin'. In fact, I was the one who called your office from the street when the fire was first discovered. I was in the boiler room when I smelled something. She disabled the smoke alarm, so it took a few minutes before someone knew there was a fire. We had to run through the halls and warn the tenants to evacuate. There were lots of folks home that day.

"After that incident, I finally decided this was one tenant I couldn't handle alone. And I certainly couldn't talk to Epstein about her. Ever since she came here a year an' a half ago, things have been mighty dicey. Mr. Epstein has gotten in too deep for his own good. She seduced him with sex and introduced him to drugs. Next he's bendin' every rule in the book to keep he' happy. Meanwhile, she's got several hookers comin' and goin', all right out of these apartments. Where there's hookers, there's dope."

"Is that all?"

"That's all Epstein's problem. My problem is the othe' tenants are beginnin' to get a little, well, upset, if you know what I mean. They not gettin' their apartments fixed, and believe me, there's a good deal needs fixin'. They seein' these evil characters hangin' around all hours. And their kids are in more danger than ever. And who do you think they complain to?"

"So what do you tell them?"

"I tell 'em I'll do what I can, but until the landlord fixes *his* problem, there ain't much I can do about everyone else's. Everyone sees what's goin' on.

"Anyway, Angel Sanchez has been talkin' to me about Epstein. I tried to avoid her, but, well, she's gettin' no more free ride. Now he's tol' her to pay back rent, with interest, pronto, or she's out on the street."

Willie paused, started to speak again, then shut his mouth. "I've said too much, Louis. I knew I shouldn't've come today."

Sensing that this was enough for one day, Peller didn't press the man to continue. He desperately wanted to know whether Epstein was getting something more than sexual favors from

Angel. He watched as the furrow returned to the older man's brow. *Save it for another day*, Peller advised himself.

"Don't worry, Willie. You've been very helpful. I think I can help us both. And rest assured, this little conversation will go no further."

Again the suspicious glare. "I hope so, Louis. I sho' hope so."

****

It was four forty-five, and Christine Boyer was standing impatiently looking down eight stories out of the one window in her lonely office to watch for Louis Peller. As if she would know what Louis Peller looked like even if she could see him from here. She glanced across the street at New York's majestic City Hall, the old, white-columned edifice—neo-Classical topped with contemporary, an interesting blend of architectural style. New Amsterdam, the letters spelled out. New York. At the top of the building was a gold cupola. The street corner, boxed in between tall buildings, was a reminder of what New York used to be from its days as a Dutch colony through the bosses of Tammany and what it was today: a rich patchwork.

She sat down on the edge of her desk, feeling vaguely frustrated. If it weren't for this appointment, she probably would have gone home early today. Chris slid her tortoiseshell glasses off her turned-up nose and rubbed her temples in small, circular motions, hoping to alleviate the growing pressure in back of her eyeballs. Paul had asked her to take on this new cause, one which she was reluctant to champion; the details sounded so convoluted.

No, she was doing this for him, for Paul. Out of a sense of debt and gratitude and maybe a deeper commitment, she would talk to his one-time roommate and try to do good. She certainly didn't want to be counselor by proxy for a corporate monarchy like Amie Mae, no matter how noble its purpose. And she wasn't sure she could advocate the cause of this woman who, far from being manipulated by her landlord, seemed intent on manipulating him. Why should she take up the banner for Louis Peller? She was tired of causes. Chris had been involved in causes since high school, when she'd been a leader in her church youth group: Episcopal, of course. That had been fun and socially rewarding. But as she got older, the rewards of charity for divine salvation faded. She even began to question whether there was a God, much less one who could offer to save humanity. In college, she'd woken up to the religion of rebellion. She became active in the anti-Vietnam movement and a pacifist. She burned the draft cards of her "brothers" in the peace, love, dove movement and, in the throes of her first true love and under the inspiration of President Kennedy, joined the Peace Corps—along with her new love, of course. They'd gone to Somalia together, lived in shacks, and tried to help the locals. Her job was teaching. His had been farming. They led a beatific, fulfilled life together for a while, doing good and, in their own small way, improving the lot of others. Until the squabbling began. He was hanging out with natives, she with expats. He decided to shack up with a beautiful young Somali woman. They had a major split. Prince Charming turned out to be a first-class, dope-smoking, two-timing jerk. After denouncing Chris as an unreformed, capitalist pig, he ran off with the native woman, professing to go native himself.

With the fading of her first love came the fading of the Peace Corps experience. Though exciting at first, it had ultimately been disillusioning; there was still famine, still illiteracy, still corrupt warlords. The virtuous Americans devoting themselves to bettering the world, American style, couldn't really make such a difference after all.

After completing the requisite two years, she returned to the States and made a beeline to Washington, hoping to make a political, if not a social, difference at home. That's when, luckily for Chris, Paul Chase arrived on the scene. She had been devastated by the break up: dumped by her once-true love. In her despair, no other white knight had ridden by to take up the banner with her. She was lonely and wavering in her mission to save the world. Paul offered her a shoulder to cry on. Such a nice guy. He was in law school, looking for his calling, searching, "finding" himself, he told her. He'd been dating someone at college, but he wasn't sure she was the one and wasn't ready to make a commitment. He didn't know what he wanted to do with himself. Meanwhile, he thought the nation's capital sounded like a promising place for an ambitious young man to make his way, he and all the other bright-eyed young people then streaming into Washington on the wave of the civil rights and antiwar movements.

Chris and Paul became friends. They would eat together and talk politics, philosophy, and, ultimately, romance. They slept together once, decided it made things too complicated between them, and agreed their friendship was too important to muddle it up with sex. Besides, Paul had begun to realize how much he missed Sherry. And Chris realized, well, that the physical attraction just wasn't there.

But Chris and Paul remained close, even after he graduated from law school, married Sherry, and joined the CIA, something of which Chris heartily disapproved. She couldn't bear the thought of him plotting to overthrow Communist regimes while shoring up right-wing dictators in two-bit, sleepy island nations caught in a shooting match between the Soviet Union and the United States.

Still drawn to the public interest, Chris went to New York and got her law degree at Columbia University, thinking she would one day return to DC. Columbia, at the time, was part of the social experiment: live with "the brothers" in Harlem, fight with them and for them. Young white people wanted to purge the guilt of their parents' systematic oppression of "colored" people. She once again embraced the cause, then felt herself getting lost in it. She knew she would need to leave again. Then, in an about-face, she decided to stay when she met a young, articulate law student, Arthur Johnston. He was editor of the Law Review. She too was on Law Review. It was love at first sight. Both of them were passionate in their embrace of the law as a means to right social wrongs. And they fell into each other's lonely, intellectually passionate embrace.

They eloped across the river in New Jersey right after their last finals. It seemed the perfect climax to a brilliant law school career. Chris's mother was disappointed; she'd dreamed of a fairy-tale country club wedding as the social event of the season. But with a silent sigh, she said she was happy if her daughter was happy. Chris joined the New York District Attorney's office. Arthur went into a big Wall Street firm. Somewhere along the way, greed got the best of him, much to Chris's disgust. Ultimately, they found themselves arguing opposing sides, not in court but at home. The divorce came less than a year after their breathless nuptials.

She called Paul on a whim to see if he might still offer a strong shoulder. Paul was steady and sure. As fate would have it, he and Sherry had just split too. The saucy, social Sherry couldn't stand the secrecy, the long separations, the anxiety over Paul's safety. Knowing the CIA was gnawing at his personal life, eroding his moral fiber, and taking a physical toll at the same time, Paul had decided to leave the Agency. Paul and Chris leaned on each other long distance. Ultimately, Chris convinced Paul to come explore business opportunities in New York. They took up just where they had left off. Their friendship was easy and reassuring—sometimes maddeningly safe. Chris often thought it might be nice to turn on a little romance, try it again. But Paul never took the lead, and each time she got up the nerve to initiate something, she would change her mind at the last minute. Then she would sit and mope or start an argument, never telling him what was really on her mind, only letting him guess at what caused her moodiness.

Even so, he was her best friend. Now, as Paul had so often helped her, she felt she owed it to him to meet with his friend Peller, the famous Louis Peller.

Chapter 7
Meeting of the Minds

Peller hurried down Broadway to the West Street building across from City Hall, late to his meeting with Paul's lawyer friend, Christine Boyer. Peller didn't even have a chance to return to the office. His meeting with Johnson had run on longer than expected. Though cautious, the black man had offered some revealing information Peller was eager to share with the attorney.

To focus his thoughts, he decided to walk downtown to Chris's office. He glanced at his watch and lengthened his stride. The walk was longer than he had anticipated, so once again, he was rushing, finally breaking into a steady run, his feet pounding the pavement heavily. He hoped his knees wouldn't begin to ache again as they had lately. He hated to put his running days behind him—a routine that he attributed to keeping himself fit and youthful. Oh well, he could always break down and hail a cab. After all, there were hundreds of them crawling down Broadway, popping their horns, idling in front of office buildings.

Peller wondered what Christine Boyer might look like. Paul had never mentioned her before, so he could only imagine. His only clue was the frosty impression he had gotten on the phone. If she was as uptight as she sounded, he pictured her a straightlaced, stiff-necked, overzealous female attorney, a man hater who had no thought for anything but the law—and public service law at that, so she surely was not wealthy. Christine Boyer, a pale-skinned brunette with a plain face and wan, colorless eyes unassisted by makeup. Of course, she would have a philosophical aversion to makeup, he decided. Hardened and tough, he concluded. Oh well, all the better for Angel Sanchez, he supposed, whose appearance was anything but bland.

He finally reached her building and, without looking for the elevators, sprinted, then walked once that sharp pain in his knee began, up the eight flights of stairs to the floor where Christine Boyer had her office. He strode down the long hallway, looking carefully at the office numbers and painted signs on wooden doors with frosted glass windows until he found Suite 806 at the end of the deserted hallway. He knocked on the door: "Christine Boyer, Attorney-at-Law." Just like the office of those private eyes you always saw in old B movies on TNT, a small front office and dusty, old-fashioned venetian blinds. All that was missing was the lovely young widow waiting in the front office, whose innocent husband had been shot by mobsters during a bank robbery, seeking protection and banking on a substantial life insurance policy to keep her in style for life. But then, for all he knew, such a widow, or someone like her, might be one of Christine Boyer's clients. The door was locked. He knocked. The secret code, he mused. "What's the password?" he growled aloud, just to hear how it would sound.

At that moment, a woman of indeterminate age opened the door. A dishwater blond with a slim face and tortoiseshell glasses looked at him askance. "Password?" she repeated. The woman facing him wore a blue Bloomingdale's off-the-rack suit and a white frilly shirt. Her face was unlined, and her long hair was brushed back into a simple ponytail and tucked under in an attempt at style. Her generous, soft-lipped smile animated the soft blue eyes, enlivening the moonlit face, warming up her pale visage. Sweet. Innocent looking somehow. This woman had the appearance of a serious college student momentarily distracted from studying for finals, not a seasoned attorney who'd defended hardened criminals. So naturally, Peller assumed he was addressing the receptionist.

"I'm Louis Peller, here to see Ms. Boyer. I think I'm a little late."

"Mr. Peller, I am Christine Boyer," announced the advocate, extending a firm handshake. "Please, call me Chris. I was beginning to think you weren't coming."

Paul had warned him not to expect much on looks, but Peller had been expecting someone who looked a little less like a schoolgirl and more like a forty-something professional. The woman who had sounded so brusque on the telephone couldn't be the same as this meek-looking mouse in front of him. Still, she had a firm handshake and a steel-like quality to her that he couldn't quite define. "Excuse me, Chris, but I thought—"

"I share a conference room and a secretary with the other tenants on this floor," she interrupted, sensing, perhaps, his assumption that her little operation might resemble one of Amie Mae's high-priced uptown firms. She took his coat and hooked it on the coat tree near the door, showing him into her small, austerely furnished office. "The secretary leaves at five."

She turned and stared at Louis Peller, frankly surprised. This man was nothing like she'd expected. From the way Paul described him, Peller was some sort of bullying giant-killer, not the unassuming man she saw before her.

Chris Boyer walked into her office and sat down behind her old, beaten-up wooden desk. "Now what can I do for you, Louis?" she asked bluntly, motioning to him to sit in one of the red plastic-covered seats opposite her desk.

Peller sat. "Really, I hope I can turn this whole Angel Sanchez matter over to you and get myself uninvolved. Angel Sanchez lives in one of my buildings in Spanish Harlem. I met her last week. She's been in the building for two years. She's clearly not a woman of means, or I'm sure she wouldn't stay in that rat's nest, and wherever she gets her limited income, I'm equally certain it's not through legal means. The landlord, my borrower, has been milking that property for years. He has, quite frankly, run it into the ground. He's apparently also been diverting income from the buildings, using our money to support his unusual lifestyle and Ms. Sanchez's little enterprise—a prostitution service—on the side. Of course, there are drugs involved. At least, that's what I suspect. I've just finished meeting with Willie Johnson, the building's superintendent, who corroborates some of my suspicions. Johnson's scared, but he's madder than he is scared, so he might be a good source. By the way, I promised him anything he told me would be kept confidential; that's the only way he'd talk. But I think he might be willing to open up some more, under the right conditions, if you know what I mean. He wants the drugs and prostitutes out of his building. He's got kids and doesn't want to become a victim in this whole mess.

"All this time, the other tenants have been complaining, and finally, Angel is one of them. You see, Epstein's little infatuation with her and her so-called business prowess finally went sour for whatever reasons. She's been accustomed to free room and board; part of the condition of their relationship was that she not pay rent, nor would any of her so-called employees. He wants her to pay back rent immediately, with interest. So now, Angel's getting her revenge against Bud Epstein. If we want this guy to agree to our terms for repaying Amie Mae the money he has failed to pay us over the past two years, I think she might have useful information. Leverage for me, shall we say. But as long as she's in legal hot water, she won't talk. So you see, my motives aren't altruistic, no matter what Paul told you."

"I'm not terribly interested in your motives, Louis, although Paul mentioned you tend to spend a lot of time tilting at windmills. In fact, I'm tempted not to take this case at all. You want me to make a case for this woman against an abusive landlord? No thanks. I don't need to defend another hostile client, especially one who, by your own account, is no stranger to depravity herself."

Chris was all business. Peller could feel he was losing her interest. If only he knew what she did get excited about, maybe he could convince her that this case would be good for her career. Reputation-making publicity was usually a strong temptation, even to the purveyors of truth, justice, and the American way, a club to which Chris seemed to belong. It was worth a shot.

"Chris, let's talk straight. This case could be a career maker for you. Think of the publicity: Attorney Links South Harlem Arson to Landlord's Scorn. Perfect *Daily News* material. New Yorkers will go nuts over that one. Of course, you'll want to talk to Mr. Johnson and maybe some of the tenants who've begun to complain about the unusual late-night traffic and Mr. Epstein's once frequent comings and goings."

"Not a winner, Louis," she said coolly, playing with a pencil. "I know you bureaucrats in Washington think scandal and corruption are big news. But in New York, that's very ho-hum stuff. Corruption here is a way of life."

Peller sat silent as she swiveled her chair around and stared out the window. Another tall building loomed across the alleyway. She appeared to be lost in thought.

"Really, Chris—" he began.

She interrupted him without turning around. "No. The only defense could be in this poor, downtrodden woman's valiant struggle to succeed in the only way she knows how, selling her body. It's that kind of world, you know, for someone with no money, no education, no hope. Prostitution is probably Angel's only financial recourse. I doubt if she has the skills or training to make any honest money—and the landlord kept her until he got tired of her."

Peller could feel she was slowly warming to her subject. "Yep. I think you're right there, Chris."

She turned around and frowned at him from behind her studious glasses. "You think I'm right? Damned straight. Hers is an old story. How can she say no when he holds all the cards? It isn't fair. But as long as men still call the shots in this country, there will always be victims like Angel Sanchez."

Here we go now, he thought, listening with only one ear to Chris's diatribe. Peller knew only too well how the Angel's of the world succeeded at business. *Sounds like Chris might be talking herself into it*, he speculated, *for reasons that have nothing to do with this case.* He couldn't argue with this upper middle class white feminist about the fact that some women, whether of the Third World or the First, chose to ally themselves with rich and powerful men in order to screw those men out of some of that wealth and power. That fact was not, strictly speaking, politically correct thinking. Well, whatever her reasoning, at least he'd found Ms. Boyer's hot button.

"No, Louis, if I take this case, it's because Angel Sanchez can convince me that she's a woman who's trying her best to stand on her own against a system that silently promotes this kind of abuse against women and rewards the perpetrators. Your Mr. Epstein stood to gain sexual favors at his whim and fancy from their little arrangement, and he didn't hesitate to put the screws on her as soon as she tried to stand up for her rights. Now she's retaliated in the best way she knows how. And she's on the verge of being kicked out onto the heartless streets of New York City. I don't give a damn about whether she can help you blackmail your borrower."

Suddenly, Peller felt tired. Life was such a struggle. Convincing this woman to defend her own cause was a struggle. Women were a struggle, exhausting, in fact. There was no question that Chris would be a zealous advocate for Angel. And with that, maybe he could bow out of this strange case. After all, what did he care what Angel Sanchez's story was? She was just another whore. He had now fulfilled his promise to help her. He could let it go.

"So you'll take Angel's case on?"

"Reluctantly," she nodded.

"Fine with me. Just take care of Angel so I can wash my

hands of this mess. I've got another sob story unraveling this week." Peller dropped Assad's name to see if there was any flicker of recognition by the lawyer. After all, she had worked for the DA. If Assad did have any fishy deals or connections in this city, the DA's office might offer some clues. He watched her serious face carefully for reaction.

Chris was thoughtful for a moment. "Assad, you say? Is he involved in any way with the squad that bombed the World Trade Center Towers last spring?"

Peller shook his head.

"Must be someone else I'm thinking of. The name does sound familiar, but I couldn't tell you why. Oh well, it will probably come to me in the middle of the night." Chris finally looked relaxed. Pretty, even, in an earthy way. "That's usually when I'm thinking clearest. If it does, I'll call you." She smiled a mischievous smile.

"No thanks. That's when I'm sleeping clearest. Anyway, I must get back to my hotel. I'm meeting one of my borrowers there for a drink."

He stood and picked up his suit jacket. "Thanks again for your help. I'll be in touch. And good luck," he said, grasping her hand firmly.

Chris rose from behind her desk. She walked Peller to the door, feeling vaguely manipulated. Somehow Chris sensed instinctively to get involved with Louis Peller was to get stuck in the snares of an industrious spider who could weave ever more complex patterns to lure unsuspecting creatures into his web. Still, she couldn't resist his persuasive charm. She'd take on the case and do her best, of course, that much she owed Paul. Her head resumed its pounding now, a full-fledged migraine brought on by stress and compounded by the *chutzpa* of Louis Peller, whose middle name must be trouble with a capital T.

"Goodbye, Louis."

****

With the shadows now looming longer on New York's tightly hemmed-in avenues, Peller hailed a yellow cab for the return trip uptown. He'd go get his bags out of Steve's office and check into a hotel room at the New York Hilton. He felt himself well rid of Angel as long as Chris was on the case. Now he could turn his attention to matters at hand.

Driving over Seventh Avenue past 42nd Street, he could feel New York pulsating with life. He marveled yet again at the variety of the city's amusements: adult XXX peep shows flashed their come-ons just around the corner from Broadway's most elegant theatres. On the spur of the moment, he tapped the cabdriver on the shoulder. What the hell, he deserved to indulge himself in a little adventure in this city of sin. He couldn't resist. Neon-framed clubs, bars, strip joints, and sex houses blinked their welcome. Any form of perversion imaginable was for sale in this town. And although Peller made it a policy never to taste these forbidden pleasures, that didn't preclude window shopping. No indulging, just investigating. It was rather like researching a term paper for Masters and Johnson. He suddenly forgot how tired he was.

Peller hailed the cabby, a Muslim Indian who averted his eyes from the sex-for-sale symbols lining 42nd Street, apparently disapproving of such blatant signs of pornography all around. With a frown, he dropped his customer off in this particularly raw part of town. *Such duplicity*, thought Peller. *This Muslim's religious aversion to sex didn't keep him from treating women as chattel*, he averred. *His kind of abuse is the worst*, rationalized Peller, *certainly more offensive than a little adult entertainment of the kind that could only be produced in New York*. To Peller's mind, bringing sex out of the closet was healthy. God made men to want to procreate, and He made women alluring to men for that reason. Why be secretive about it? Lana, barely better than a modern-day Hester Prynne, abhorred such displays, saying it showed what a sick society they lived in. Knowing her sermon on this subject, Peller didn't share with her the results of his research into the subject matter. He preferred not to be lectured.

As usual, he took his trek solo from Eighth Avenue along 42nd to Times Square. Most of Peller's colleagues professed to be as prudish as Lana, so he didn't exactly advertise his pastime at the office. Of course, he and Steve did occasionally paint the town red together, but even then, they generally partook in tamer activities. Steve's stomach for freak shows was not as strong as Peller's. To take full advantage of these uninhibited adventures, they both liked to get themselves soused: the better to enjoy the trance of bright lights and the smoky, sweaty lairs they visited. Tonight, Peller stopped first at a local watering hole—a typical yuppie fern bar filled with nine to fivers, easing out of their uptight ties and stiletto heels—rather a sober joint by New York standards. He sat at the bar alone and watched the seductive tango initiated by those poor, lonely New Yorkers seeking sexual partners of either gender and every ethnic group (condom in hand) to ease their solitude, a game so far removed from Peller's party pick-up experiences of the seventies as to require a whole new pedigree for sexual partners, tests for diseases and past exposures. When he had been part of the singles scene, by custom, a man would grab a barstool next to an attractive woman and try to guess her sign of the zodiac. Free love, unfettered. Times had really changed, he thought. Maybe not for the best.

As he sipped his bourbon, imbibing the bar's unnatural noise and false familiarity, the strain of the day faded into a distant memory, and his mood lightened considerably. After all, Peller thought, the life led by the Angels and the Epsteins of the world was not his life. He motioned to the bartender for a second drink as he chanced to observe some new mating rituals, at least to him: the mating ritual of a fifty-something man and a young guy still wet behind the ears. How had matches like this emerged to become a commonplace part of life not just practiced in privacy or with discretion at recognized gay nightclubs? Homosexuality frightened and repelled Peller: no need for discretion in this day and age, just let it all hang out. Well, that promiscuous lifestyle was not for him. Hastily, he decided to depart, leaving twenty dollars on the table, forget the change.

Blinking against the harsh glare of bright lights in Times Square, Peller detoured over to Eighth Avenue to sample the Eros Theater, a cinema for the sexually searching. He had read about places like this and, after two drinks, let his curiosity lead him. "Wanton Sex Wanted" was how the marquis ought to read, he mused. He felt compelled to explore, to experience the many exciting possibilities of life in a city that knew no bounds, ready to test the tacky, the tasteless, and the tactile pleasures of the flesh. He entered, fully expecting the reputation of the place to exceed its reality. Publicity had a way of distorting truth. In this case, there was no distortion. There, in the dark and flickering anonymity of adults-only movies, there were couples coupling. No adolescent petting or innocent smooching, but actual sex, couples in various stages of undress, trying partners on for size. Sex with "the girl ya brung," and sex with your neighbor. He watched in open amazement and fascination even though he had imagined himself immune to shock. No one else there even noticed his bald curiosity. He wondered if anyone would approach him with a touch or a stroke. Although he was resolved to follow his "look, don't touch" policy (more from fear of AIDS than out of any moral compunction), the sounds of furtive and passionate love-making from the sea of seats surrounding him aroused him like no cheap porno film would. It was New York at its worst, and unwittingly, he reveled in the fantasy. He left after about twenty-five minutes of this prurient peep show without so much as a proposition, although a rude pair of lovebirds practically fell over him in their haste to get at their recreation. *What a show*, he thought sadly as he slunk out, suffering decidedly mixed feelings: arousal and disgust, shock and dejection.

He ducked into a dive next door. The noisy bar-cum-runway was filled by this hour of the night with drunks and prowlers; bums or bankers by day, they were all wastrels drowning their sorrows in drink, drugs, and promiscuous abandon by night. The showgirls parading there looked used up, unhealthy, past their prime. This was where they came after their debuts as topless dancers were toppled by younger, more supple Venuses.

Amidst the crowds and clouds of smoke in the room, Peller found a small, concealed table near the kitchen and knocked down another bourbon to blot out his distress and dilute his unstated appetite for mischief. He stared but barely registered the flirtatious dancers shimmying for cash.

By midnight, even in his semi-inebriated stupor, Peller had suffered just about enough of such trash. He hailed the first cab he saw to return him to the New York Hilton. In his drunken haze, he remembered he'd left his overnight bag stowed in Steve's office. Well, he could buy a razor and a clean shirt in the morning. His head began to ache dully as they bounced up the rutted avenue. Louis Peller was moving slow. When he got out to pay the driver, it was only with great concentration that he managed to reach inside his jacket pocket for his wallet. Much to Peller's astonishment, the pocket was empty. No wallet. He felt inside his pants pockets just to make sure he hadn't slipped it there. He had been pickpocketed.

"Shit." He pulled out his pockets in the Little Tramp's gesture for empty. The cabdriver showed no mercy. An imposing black man who had passed the ride complaining ruefully that, after surviving the worst tribal treacheries in his native Nigeria, he came to America only to be stiffed for cab fare by rich American corporate executives. The driver slid from his cab and pulled himself up to his full six foot something, towering over Peller. As Peller's head began to clear from its alcoholic fog, his nerves were suddenly on edge. This was not a man he wanted to mess with.

"Look, I know this looks bad. I've been robbed. I have no cash to pay you at the moment. I'm sorry." Peller's head was throbbing. "I'm really not trying to stiff you. If you wait right here, I'll just run inside quickly and call American Express, and I think we'll be able to clear this whole thing up immediately."

The Nigerian came in close to Peller and began poking a

finger in his chest. "I need $5.50 from you. Now. And the meter's still runnin'."

Peller looked wistfully over toward the door of the hotel and back to the driver. No doorman in sight. No one who could lend him a sou or give a damn. Outside this hotel, the city that never sleeps was a lonely shell. And this guy was not in the mood to let Peller escape from sight, much less wait for American Express to open, that much was apparent.

"I don't have no patience for guys like you. Find a way to get me my money now, or you'll be even sorrier in the morning." The driver gave him a slow, menacing smile, revealing a broken front tooth.

Peller was thinking sluggishly. "Then drive me to Columbus Circle. I have a friend who lives there who will lend me the dough." In a pinch, Steve Shapiro would have to forgive Peller's unexpected visit. After all, Peller would do the same for him.

"You sure this friend's gonna pay? 'Cause I ain't stoppin' the meter while you jump around town looking for cash. And that will be another three, four bucks."

"If you won't let me call him, how can I know for sure? Don't you have a phone in this cab?"

"Not yet. They're thinkin' about givin' 'em to all the drivers but can't figure out how to keep us all from bein' ripped off. After that last driver was killed in Washington Heights—lunatics out there—driven off the road and shot, no reason. Anyway, if you're doin' the callin', I'm comin' with you."

With that, the burly man with the smooth ebony skin and massive forearms began walking into the hotel without a backward glance, making it clear that he expected his rider to follow. Peller balked. "But I have no quarters," he protested uncertainly. He didn't want to antagonize this guy, but it was true, his cash was gone. He'd heard that some cabdrivers routinely kept a gun inside their cars, and he sure wasn't anxious to find out if this was one.

"I'll loan you twenty-five cents. Let's call it a good investment." He grabbed Peller gruffly by the arm and escorted him unceremoniously into the hotel lobby. At the phone, Peller fumbled in his pockets for the address book carrying Steve's number, praying it was still there. Lucky he'd brought the book with him; Steve kept his phone unlisted—too many nutcases in New York, he often said. Peller breathed a long sigh of relief when he heard his friend's sleepy voice at the other end.

"Steve, can I come over? I know you're not gonna believe this, but I just got robbed. My wallet's gone. Some pickpocket around Times Square must've got me. And this cabdriver here needs to be paid. It's not much, a measly five bucks or so."

At the other end of the line, he heard his colleague explode in a long string of epithets. "Louis, you son of a bitch. You wake me up. You expect me to pay your cab. I warned you about going into those sex joints alone, but you wouldn't believe me. It's goddamn one in the morning, and I have to meet with some other cagey son-of-a-bitch borrower at seven thirty in the Bronx. Jesus."

"Listen, Steve," Peller said quietly, willing his friend to help him out, while the big black man stared at him angrily in the middle of the luxurious lobby of a hotel he couldn't enjoy tonight. "I now owe you big time. I'll make it up to you. I promise. Please, bail me out."

Steve sighed deeply. "Okay, Louis. But don't make a habit of this. I'm not the Good Samaritan type."

As he hung up, Peller nodded to the cabdriver who walked him back to his cab for a short spin past Lincoln Center to Steve's very humble abode. No doorman in his shabby building. Steve buzzed them into the well of the walk-up apartment and ran down six flights wearing only white-and-green-striped running shorts, which he had hastily put on in the dim of the night. Steve's putty-colored, muscular chest took on an other-worldly appearance under the glare of the dangling globe-shaped fixture in the hall. Luckily, it was cool for August, otherwise Steve would have broken a sweat from his quick sprint. This building had no central air-conditioning.

Steve took one look at his friend and whistled softly. Peller looked a sight: rumpled and pale, eyes rimmed with red. He reeked of smoke and alcohol, although he obviously wasn't inebriated now.

Steve paid off the driver, with an extra tip for his trouble, and punched his friend in the arm. "What'd you do? Get ripped off in a strip joint?" he asked mockingly. "Ya shoulda stuck around for the Grayline Bus Tour like all those other horny out-of-towners lookin' for a little action."

Peller thought Steve might be just the slightest bit envious. Peller knew that Steve had been required to attend a meeting at the Staten Island borough president's chambers that evening and assumed he'd gotten home early and alone. Neither man was one to enjoy the clubby chatter and kissing up that characterized those corporate political events.

Steve's apartment felt stale and musty. The smell of smoke clung to the couch Steve had "straightened" for him to sleep on, and to Peller too.

"Shut up and don't give me any grief. I'm tired. I feel like shit. I have to cancel all my credit cards and stop my checks and borrow enough money for cab fares, so I hope you have some cash floating around. I'm out two hundred bucks and all my credit cards. Meantime, I was planning to drop in at my newest high-brow uptown address in Washington Heights to pay a little informal visit to the rats, the four-legged variety. And who knows, Assad might be there too." The sarcasm dripped out of Peller's mouth. "And you think you have it tough? Just go back to sleep and leave me to my self-pity."

Chapter 8
The Neighborhood

Peller hadn't been this hungover since college. He'd finally dozed off at about two, getting a fitful four hours of sleep before he heard a sound. When Peller first squinted awake in the slate gray dawn, it was a struggle to remember where he was and what had happened the night before. He heard the coughing whir of an old window air-conditioner from somewhere close by. His tongue tasted the cotton balls that stuffed his cerebellum. He awoke with his clothes on: a wrinkled shirt smelling of tobacco and booze and an unknotted necktie stained with ketchup. He didn't remember eating anything with ketchup. He was laying uncomfortably on top of the brown and tan couch in what passed for Steve's living room. There was a green wool army blanket tangled uselessly around his feet.

Steve the runner rose at the crack of dawn. "What the hell happened last night?" Peller mumbled, his head pounding, as Steve walked through the room outfitted in designer running gear. It was an irony of life that Steve the smoker was actually a fitness nut who sweated and panted his way daily through pristine Central Park West at the crack of dawn.

"I'm not sure, buddy. All I know is you look like hell today."

Steve set the timer on the coffee machine in his kitchen to make a quick cup of java before he got back.

"Thanks for your helpful observation, Steve, old pal. Last I remember, the cabdriver was taking me to my hotel." Peller gazed blankly into the mirror in the bathroom and noticed, to his chagrin, he did look somewhat the worse for wear.

Steve was grinning as he walked back into the living room. "Lucky for you, your old friend Steve here had a few bucks lying around to pay off that cab ride. You got ripped off big time in some downtown joint last night. Remember? You called me from your hotel to bail you out with that cabby. By the way, your suitcase is locked up in my office, so I don't know what you were planning to do for clean clothes this morning."

A slice of memory cut through the muffling insulating his brain. The cab ride. The Hilton. No money. He spied an open phone book flung over the back of the couch and the portable phone on the floor next to him. Anxiety swept over him.

"Shit. It's true. I was hoping it was just a nightmare."

"Last I heard, before I got back to sleep at about one fifteen, you were frantically making calls to cancel your credit cards," Steve reminded him. "Look, I've gotta run now so I can get back in time for my first meeting. Here's some cash," he said, flinging some bills out of his wallet, "and a clean shirt and socks.

"What I do for my friends," Steve sighed mockingly. "There's a new toothbrush in the bathroom and a clean towel on top of the radiator. You'd better get yourself cleaned up before you go to Washington Heights this morning. Or on second thought, go as you are. You'd fit right in in the 'hood." Steve laughed, and Peller began to grin until the muscles in the corners of his mouth met his throbbing temples. He rubbed his fingers gingerly over his forehead to ease the pressure.

"Oh, God. I can't go through with a visit to Washington Heights. Not this morning," Peller groaned. "Do you have any aspirin?" He laid back down on the couch, hoping his headache would disappear. He wanted to think, but it hurt too much.

"Judging by the way you look, you're gonna need some hair of the dog to take some of the jabs out of that pincushion," Steve commented, walking back to his medicine cabinet for the white tablets.

"Oh, my God …" Peller sat up again with a start. He suddenly felt nauseated. "Lana. I'd better warn her not to use the credit cards today. She's gonna be pissed. Maybe I can tell her I got mugged walking through the park. Everyone else does. Think she'll believe me?"

"Lana knows you too well, Louis. You'd better dream up a better story than that. Or you might try the truth. It could go a long way to rebuilding trust in your marriage." He threw two pills over to Peller.

"Listen to you. Mister Sincere himself giving advice to the lovelorn. When was the last time you had a successful relationship?" Steve ignored Peller's insult as he began his warm ups. Taking a quick breath, Peller downed the aspirin without water. The pills caught in his throat. He began to choke, his eyes tearing. He looked over at Steve in a panic.

"There's springwater in the fridge," Steve smiled snidely as he sprinted to the door. "I've gotta get moving. Oh, if you're staying tonight, you'd better make sure your reservation's still good at the Hilton."

Before Peller could choke out a reply, Steve was gone. He slowly, excruciatingly, dialed his own phone number. Luckily, Lana had already left home when he called and wasn't yet in her office, so he left a cryptic voice mail message for her not to charge anything or use the checkbook before he could talk to her. "I'm not anywhere you can reach me 'til about seven tonight," he ended. "I'll call you at home. I love you." That ought to tide her over for the day until he could get a better handle on things. The "I love you" was calculated to soften her up. He used it on rare occasions when she was likely to be upset with him for something. He knew that she knew it was a ploy, but what the hell, it usually worked.

Peller felt a little better after his shower. He stole a cup of Steve's coffee—high-test, fortunately—just as it stopped brewing and got ready to face the day. And what a day it promised to be.

****

Tommy drove up Broadway in a gloomy silence. Peller had recounted the mishap of the previous evening as soon as his driver pulled up at Steve's. Tommy shook his head and clucked without so much as an "I told you so." He had warned Peller from day one that it wasn't safe for him to gallivant around New York on his own at night, especially in the "badder parts" of town. Since most of New York at night constituted a badder part, that effectively put the kibosh on any nightlife, unless, of course, Tommy was along.

Mostly, Tommy was happy to oblige Peller in his strange nocturnal wanderings. This mama's boy was lonely for male friends, and Peller was about as close as he came. Tommy was puzzled about why, for some unknown reason, Peller hadn't bothered to request his company last night. *Maybe this would teach him a lesson*, thought Tommy. Frankly, it was a good thing that only a pickpocket had slipped his hand down Peller's pants, given the kinds of places Peller had sampled. Much worse could have transpired; stabbings, muggings, and robbery headed the list. Apparently Peller was just waiting to fall into criminal hands.

Having confessed his sins to Tommy, Peller felt a little better. Steve's coffee had also helped calm him—a paradox he couldn't really explain. Nothing worse could happen. With this pleasant delusion in mind, Peller decided to ignore Tommy's tongue lashing. He did, however, resolve to include a friend the next time he ventured out into New York's lonely night.

Peller and Tommy rolled forward for Peller's surprise inspection of Omar Assad's Washington Heights apartments. Peller wanted to get a flavor for the place in its authentic state, before Assad had a chance to make cosmetic changes that might put Peller off the scent of details such as water leaks and poor maintenance. Bathtubs sinking through floors, inoperable elevators, and chipping lead paint could not be easily covered up. Such disasters were commonplace in sixty-year-old buildings like Assad's, not to mention the one-bedroom apartments inhabited by a young couple, their grandparents, and four or five children. Thinking about another inspection with an inevitable plethora of problems left Peller with a feeling of despair.

As they drove north, the streets grew more and more congested, sidewalks teeming with people of all sizes and shapes and colors. Peller often felt that visiting the length and breadth of the twenty-four-mile island of Manhattan offered the curious visitor a veritable rainbow tour, a slice of every color, every tongue, every nationality on Earth. Uptown this far, the one common denominator among the inhabitants was poverty. An uplifting experience, it was not.

He stared out the window. Few trees lined the great "broad way" so far uptown; no flower boxes hung from the bricked and barred windows. Instead, street vendors sprouted in every doorway, practically accosting people in their efforts to sell their schlocky wares, and ragamuffin children scampered, unattended, dangerously close to the streets. Finally, as they moved out of Harlem and into the Heights, living conditions plunged to those of the most primitive, desperate, and deprived Third World countries. There was no joy to be found amid this squalor. No one smiled on the street. People moved as if encased in glass frames, eyes downcast, ignoring their neighbors, denying their relations.

Peller was glad for the heavy, clunky car shielding him from the streets and ardently wished the windshield was bulletproof. Who cared that the airless interior felt stifling? Windows up, they were safe. Tommy joked grimly about putting on his flak jacket as they pulled up in front of 488 West 158th Street and double parked, leaving the Impala's emergency lights flashing.

Peller stayed frozen in his seat. The storefront on the ground floor of the building housed a beauty parlor, complete with pictures of the latest African twists. There was a steel gate locking the door and rolled razor wire edging the top of the shop. A place so armored wasn't terribly inviting.

"Are you buyin' today or just lookin'?" Tommy asked his rider.

Despite the tension in the street and the ringing in his head, Peller knew he needed to get out of the "big white machine" to chat up some of the tenants who might offer some insights into Assad. He tried to muster his friendliest, most nonthreatening manner.

"Buying, I guess." Peller still looked a little tentative. "Want to come along, just for laughs?" he queried Tommy.

Tommy Romano never left his car. "Fa'gedaboutit. I think I'll stay right he'yah if you don't mind. I only wanna eat my baloney sandwich and be left alone. I'll try to keep an eye out in case anything happens on the street. But you try to keep your nose clean, Pelleh, and stay out of dark and dirty places so's I don't have to pull you out in a body bag. Got it?"

"Sure," replied a currently compliant Peller. "I'll just stay in lit hallways and elevators—if any are working, that is. And I won't be gone long, say fifteen–twenty minutes?"

"Whateveh you say, boss. Just make sure you're out of theah before—"

"I know, three o'clock," Peller finished the warning. "I don't plan to make this a day trip. It's only ten fifteen now."

"Yeah, but I seen you operate before, and I know you love to schmooze. So keep it sweet and simple today. We don't need nothin' else to happen to you this trip. And turn your beeper on this time. I'll use that pay phone on the corna' to signal you if I think things are gettin' outta hand." Tommy pointed to the phone at the busy intersection of 158th and Broadway.

Peller emerged from the car, apprehensive, still feeling vulnerable from last night's adventure. Looking at his building from the side, he noticed another of those wall murals penned by some anonymous street poet; "Rest in Peace, Marcus Brown, Taken Young and Free, Dreams Shot Down," this one read, with another portrait of a black youth, wide-eyed and smiling serenely. A white lily, wilting now, was laid on the ground against the wall. There was a crucifix painted on one side and a Nation of Islam symbol on the other, the dates painted in red on the bottom: 1978–1993. No matter how jaded Peller became doing these inspections, he could never get used to this. Senseless killing. Random violence. A boy robbed of his whole life. Even if that life was one of deprivation, this kid deserved to live it through to manhood, to make his own choices. Peller stood staring at the mural commemorating mort, death, defeat, despair, feeling dispirited and powerless.

Tommy was watching him carefully. Why did Louie always take these risks, he wondered, shaking his head. Didn't he know to get outta the street where he was an easy mark—the only white guy for twenty square blocks. Tommy was about to roll down his window and shout at Peller to go inside when a big black boy walked up and tapped Peller on the shoulder.

Mechanically, Peller turned to look at him. Then he glanced up at the portrait again. Same face.

Seeing Peller's defenselessness, Tommy ran across the street to break up the anticipated fight.

"That's my brutha', man," the teenager was saying to Peller. "You got a problem wid'at?"

Tommy hurriedly moved in front of Peller, between him and the kid. "We gotta go, chief," he yelled.

"It's okay, Tom. We were just talking," explained Peller reasonably.

"Yeah. You got a problem wid'at?" the boy threatened Tommy, narrowing his brown eyes, his attitude showing.

Tommy glared at the kid, taking in his baggy jeans and one hundred twenty dollar "pumps" and trying to determine whether the kid was armed. "Louis," he said again, more forcefully this time. "I think we oughta be movin' along."

But Peller ignored Tommy. He was looking at this boy who seemed tough and, at the same time, vulnerable. The kid had just lost his brother, after all. Peller felt sorry for him.

"Look, kid," said Peller. "I don't mean any disrespect to your brother's memory. I'm real sorry," he began.

The boy came closer, one hand outstretched, palm up, the other in his pocket. "So, man, you can help me out ..."

Suddenly, Tommy pushed Peller out of the way and yelled into his ear, "You gonna be sorrier if you don' get the hell out of heah—now."

A bunch of kids moved in phalanx up the street toward their pal: kids with attitude. Seeing their menacing faces, Peller finally ran around and ducked into the stone-arched doorway of the building.

After Peller closed the door behind him, Tommy looked around grimly, showing the glinting blade of the knife he had pulled from his pocket when he saw the gang approaching. The band of kids had disappeared. Apparently they weren't interested in waiting around for Peller's return, at least not as long as Tommy was around. He got back into the Impala, locked the door, and buried his nose in *The Racing Form* to wait out Peller's latest foray into the wilds of Washington Heights.

Peller really had every intention of making this a brief stay, especially after opening the door. The stench that greeted him mingled mildew, urine, and cats marking their turf. So much for any "sentimental value" Assad assigned to the place. The hallway was lit by one dim, naked bulb suspended from the ceiling. Peller saw signs that, once upon a time, there had been a larger, grander lighting fixture in its place. Walking through the dusky hallway, Peller's practiced eye noted common signs of disrepair: chipped and cracking plaster adorned one elevator wall where the up button should have been, as if someone, in a fit of rage, had tried to put a fist through it. The hall ceiling was stained—water rot, Peller speculated—undoubtedly from some outside leak.

He decided to make the rounds, to talk to anyone who might

be willing to complain, off the record or on. The first person he passed was a small, plump, Hispanic-looking woman taking her emptied waste baskets back down the hall from the overflowing trash room. Peller caught the corner of her eye and smiled.

She barely acknowledged his approach.

"Hello, my name is Louis Peller. I'm inspecting this building for the bank. I wonder if you have any problems in your apartment I ought to know about."

She peered at him. "Problems, you want? Problems I got. Marguerita Fernandez. I'm in 2C. I been complaining to the super for months about leaks under the sink and in the ceiling of my apartment, and he's done nothing about it. I have a hard enough time keeping water off my floors as it is. These buckets that catch the drip are always full. You don't know how hard it is, with all the other problems around here: dealers on the streets and users in the hallways. I'm trying to keep my kids honest. I don't want to raise them clean to be killed by a bullet from one of these punk's guns." Clearly Peller's simple question had unharnessed a torrent of troubles. "I hope you're serious. Does this mean we will finally get some help?" Marguerita opened wide her plaintive eyes, lifting her hands in the age-old gesture of supplication.

Peller didn't expect the overpowering gust of her complaint, not right off the bat. "I can't promise anything, Ms. Fernandez," Peller replied solemnly. "I need to document as many problems as I can so Omar Assad will fix them. May I come look in your apartment?"

She stared at him hard, as if to judge whether he could be trusted. Marguerita had been an open soul before moving to Washington Heights from San Juan two years ago. In that short time, she had learned not to rely on anyone, not after her apartment had been ransacked and her television and stereo stolen a short month after she arrived, not after her young children reported seeing large sums of money changing hands between sixth-grade neighbors and teenagers from another neighborhood in their gated, fenced-in schoolyard, not after she had received enough obscene and threatening phone calls by harassing con men in the wee hours of the night to request an unlisted number.

But as she scrutinized his serious, open face, she decided Louis Peller did not look as if he would take advantage of her. He was clearly not from the neighborhood, nor was he used to life in the barrio. He had an honest countenance and a gracious manner. Perhaps this was someone she could trust. Perhaps now she could dare to hope again. She opened the four locks to her apartment and motioned him in quickly.

The wood around the door frame was deteriorating, he noted in passing.

As Peller entered the narrow flat, he was immediately impressed at how clean and cozy she had made it. It was hung with bright, festive pictures, some obviously designed by her children, others posters of the French Impressionists. She had lamps in every corner, taking the place of windows, brightly lighting the darkest spots. The few windows toward the rear of the apartment were barred. He noticed a crucifix and a small statuette of the Madonna nestled in an alcove next to the kitchen. In the living room, which also served as a dining area, she pointed out a large plastic bucket catching occasional drips leaking from a light fixture. Peller circled around it, checking the ceiling with a critical eye. "Anyone above you with floor problems?"

"It would not surprise me. No one ever in there during the day, but at night I have heard voices, talking quiet. Usually men. Lots of footsteps, I hear too. Coffee, Mr. Peller?"

"No, thank you." As he walked around the one-bedroom apartment, he jotted notes on his trusty legal pad. "I have several other tenants I want to meet with this morning too. I'll make a note of this, Ms. Fernandez. And when I make up my list for Mr. Assad, I'll let you know what he says." Peller extended his hand. "I would like to make sure he takes care of your place. I can see you're a good tenant. I'll be back to see you again."

"I would like that. Oh, and my friends call me Marguerita. As a friend, I want you to know, please be careful when you come around. For your own safety, Mr. Peller. The gangs around here are out for drugs and blood money and won't let anyone get in their way."

"Call me Louis. Let me ask you this, Marguerita. How difficult is it for you to raise your children in a place like this, where you must live with so much fear?" It was a question that had long been bothering him.

"Luis, you cannot know what it's like. Your world must be so different. You might hear about the danger, but it is not real. When you live in this place, danger is very real. We do what we can. I would like my kids to grow up to be law-abiding, decent boys. They don't have no one to look up to, no one in their lives gives a damn, not their father, wherever he is, not their teachers, not their friends. No one except me. I have to always be strong for them."

He gave her his card. "Call me if you need anything," he said earnestly. "If you think I can help."

She studied the card. "Amie Mae," she read. "Who is that?"

"It's a what, not a who," Peller replied. "I work for a company that lends money to people to buy homes and apartment buildings."

She walked him slowly to the door, thinking.

"So you gave Mr. Assad the money to buy this building?"

"That's right."

"And he still owes you money?"

"You've got the picture now."

"Then you can help us screw this bastard right back? " Marguerita spoke low, with sudden malice.

"I'm not sure about that. That's not my job."

She sized him up with a new glint in her eyes. "Luis, I think we could be very good friends. We will work together to get Mr. Assad to be a good landlord, no?" She smiled a conspiratorial smile.

"Yes. We will work together."

"And I will have a place to raise my boys to be good, safe."

He smiled reassuringly. She had it tough. There was such strength in her, marveled Peller, such determination. There but for the grace of God, as they say. Although, thought Peller, I would sooner lie, cheat, and steal to get out of a pit like this than raise my family here.

****

Tommy opened one eye and glanced quizzically at his watch, roused by the sound of a siren passing somewhere down busy Broadway. He had fallen asleep parked outside the building. It was past noon. Luckily the street was pretty empty this time of day. Two hours after Tommy watched him go in through the archway, the driver finally saw Peller emerge from the dingy building, looking pale and grimy. Even Tommy Romano, the tough guy, felt a little sorry for this fool Peller who misguidedly thought he could help the godforsaken souls imprisoned in a place like this. They didn't want help, not these people, not Peller's help or anyone's. *Do 'em a favor, and they pull out their weapons.* Tommy got out of the car to chastise Louis Peller.

Peller was dazed by sunlight. Spending time in that place could make you forget the sun shone anywhere. He squinted, then put his hand over his eyes to see.

Tommy was lumbering toward him on his massive frame, glaring at him, determined to hurry him along.

"Louie. Where ya been, man? Why didn't ya get out of the way before, when that kid was preparing to hit ya up for money? Haven't you lost enough cash in the past twenty-four hours in this town to suitja?" Tommy ribbed him.

Peller just kept walking straight ahead, not listening. Despite Peller's best intentions to stay only a short while, his curiosity had gotten the better of him. He felt guilty.

"I got a good snooze in the car while you were touring the joint. I got a little bet in too. Hunnert bucks on Way to Go to win in the t'oid race, and what happens? Damn pony came in second. Another damned loss. Hey, what happened to the short visit? Why should I be surprised you took so long?"

"Tommy …"

Tommy gave up his nagging, resigned to this character flaw in Peller. He continued grumbling under his breath.

Peller frowned. Why did he have to justify himself to his driver, of all people? Tommy was being well paid to wait around. He hated being nagged, so he changed the subject. "I thought you were done with off-track betting, Tom," observed Peller. "After all, you dropped twelve grand last year on the ponies. Does your mama know you've broken your promise to her? You'll break her heart yet."

"Louis, you better not start on my case. I got a lot of stuff I could throw in your face, in case you don't remember. I think Lana might be interested in the details of your adventure last night, for instance. Don't be moralizing against me now," growled Tommy defensively.

"Okay, all right," Peller conceded with a grin. "I won't mention it again. Forget about it, Tom."

They had been walking slowly toward the car while they argued. As soon as Tommy closed and locked the doors, Peller pulled out the legal pad and the ubiquitous Sony to elaborate with details of his visit.

"Met four good tenants in Assad's building.

"Grandma Eva Jones, fiftyish, black, raising three grandchildren while her high school dropout daughter tries to find a job. No visible source of income. Apartment 2G, one bedroom, ceiling shows water damage from apartment upstairs, H_2O rot in the ceiling. Filth in the hallway outside her door and burnt-out lights.

"Elevator not working. Empty crack vials on stairs, and piss on walls. Stench is awful. Tenants so accustomed, don't notice.

"Samuel Leiter, eighty-year-old widower alone in 2F, home of thirty-five years. Uses walker, increasingly incapacitated. Difficult to get out. Daughter in California hasn't visited in ten years, but calls and sends money. Too proud to ask for help.

"5B, two bedroom, subdivided living room. Cordova brothers from Dominican Republic. Nine people there, including four small kids. H_2O dripping from faucets and can't be turned off 'cause knobs rusted, bath tiles missing, tub sinking, window panes cracked.

"Twenty-fiveish Hispanic woman, Marguerita Fernandez, three young children. Apartment 2B, one bedroom. Part-time receptionist in Midtown. Sis takes care of her baby when she's at work. Marguerita has energy. Outspoken. Tenant organizer: petitioned Assad for basic repairs and maintenance.

"Marguerita Fernandez," Peller repeated, cheered somewhat. Peller had taken an immediate liking to this straightforward and determined young woman. Marguerita could be an ally. In fact, Marguerita was the one bright spot in this whole scenario, he ruminated as they drove back toward civilization. How desperate, the lives of these people. He wanted to do something but felt helpless. He could pressure Assad into repairing the building so his tenants could live like human beings. He could puzzle out a strategy for that later. Right now, he was too exhausted to worry about it. What *he* needed desperately was a cold shower, room service, and a cable movie. What he *wanted* was to go home.

Tommy pulled up to Amie Mae's midtown office, leaving the car idling illegally at the curb. He left Peller wearily watching for cops while the he fetched Peller's bags. Tommy was anxious to get home himself and wouldn't give Peller the chance to go inside and start talking. Just let Peller and Steve get started—maybe it was something about Jews that they felt compelled to talk, talk, talk, talk, talk. Let Peller continue to pour his thoughts into that damned tape recorder—at least he could carry it with him and not waste any more of Tommy's time.

Tommy was in and out of Amie Mae quickly, now crawling back up through traffic to the Hilton over 51st Street, that congested thoroughfare blaring with horns and sirens, a rush of pedestrians and frenzied sightseers.

Driving up to the hotel, the driver dropped his worn-out passenger safely with the doorman and could head back to his humble home in Brooklyn to feed the pigeons. Flocks of pigeons. He raised them to race, for money naturally, part of his gambling habit. Pigeons were just one of Tommy's little idiosyncrasies.

Peller trudged up to the check-in desk, feeling grubby and tired and doubly defeated. New York was getting to him more and more as time wore on. And now, to top off every other unnatural disaster he'd encountered in this dreaded metropolis, he'd been ripped off, boldly and brazenly, in the dead of midnight. It was all greater than he could bear to think about at the moment. The clerk at the reservation desk gave him his key and two pink message slips. One was the predictable urgent call from Lana. He guessed he'd have to deal with her at some point. The second was from Paul, confirming dinner.

Christ almighty, thought Peller. He'd forgotten all about his dinner date with Paul. Tavern on the Green was about the last place he wanted to be tonight. He'd have to put on a suit and shave for that, and he just wasn't up to donning his corporate uniform at the moment. He rubbed his stubbled chin. Maybe he could talk Paul into something casual. At least with Paul, he wouldn't have to make scintillating small talk. Maybe Peller could even confide some of his recent anxieties to him; that wasn't something he could often do, being much too self-protective to let his real emotions show through to his colleagues or to Lana. Although, come to think of it, Lana could usually guess when something was wrong. She had a good sense for his worries, and Peller knew he could let down his hair with her. His relationship with Paul was like that too. Thank goodness for old friends.

In the dim afternoon light of his room, Peller dialed Paul. "Mind if we forego suits this evening and take in some good eats somewhere *cazh*?"

"You're not trying to weasel out of your end of the bargain, are you, Louis? Don't forget, I know how you operate."

"C'mon, Paul. You know I never welch on my promises. It's just that this has been a pretty harrowing trip so far, and I'd prefer to keep dinner low-key. I'm really looking forward to talking too. I need to tell someone about all the shit I've been through in the past thirty-six hours. Now, if this is a problem …"

Paul sighed. How typical of Peller to change the ground rules at the last minute. "No problem, Louis. How does nouvelle cuisine sound? Not touristy stuff, but an authentic French bistro. I know just the place." If Peller was trying to get out of paying for uptown cooking, he would be surprised by the restaurant Paul had in mind. Paul smiled. Le Vieux Grenier in Greenwich Village was definitely a neighborhood kind of gathering place, but it was also definitely pricey. A blue jeans and champagne kind of place. The dining, from Tarte a l'Oignon to Framboises en Creme, was glorious.

"Just lead me there. I'm at your service tonight, Paul."

"Great. Say eight o'clock, then? I'll come to your hotel and we can venture out."

"I'll be waiting. Oh, and Paul, there's just one other thing …"

Paul drew an expectant breath.

"It's like this, I got mugged last night, and well, you'll need to pay."

"Louis, what the hell?"

"Thanks a lot Paul. I'll explain when I see you. And I'll write you a check as soon as I get home. Really."

Paul slammed the phone in anger. Just like Peller. "If I wasn't such a nice guy, what wouldn't I do?" Paul cursed the phone. "Maybe I won't even show up." He considered for a moment, then smiled. "Or maybe I'll just have a little fun with Lou." And he picked up the receiver again.

****

Peller was hanging out in the lobby. eyeing the "local talent" when Paul arrived promptly at eight. As requested, Paul was in casual attire, albeit the casual attire of a perennial preppie: khakis and blue blazer, pink polo shirt, open at the neck, no tie.

"Isn't this city wonderful, Paul?" Peller asked, eyes following a particularly nubile female guest to the registration desk. "A 'ten,' I'd say." Peller was freshly shaven and combed. He'd had time for a catnap, and his eyes looked less red rimmed.

Following his friend's gaze in the direction of a stunning, leggy blond, Paul replied, "Louis, you're incorrigible. You have a beautiful wife and a terrific family. When are you going to quit your search for 'the perfect woman'?"

"Why give up on a fascinating anthropological study? Some people watch birds; I watch women. What's the difference? As they say, 'beauty is in the eye of the beholder.' Besides, Lana kind of expects it of me by now. If I stopped looking, she'd probably think I was having an affair or something."

"You're going to get yourself into serious trouble someday with that attitude, my friend. But I guess it's not my problem. Anyway, I'm starved. Let's go eat. I got us reservations at Le Vieux Grenier in the South Village.

The two men walked outside and hopped into a waiting cab. On their way downtown, Peller shared his impressions about Christine Boyer.

"I think your lawyer friend'll be good. She's obviously impassioned about what she sees as the chronic underclass status of women, and her seriousness can counterbalance Angel Sanchez's obvious character flaws—or, um, assets, depending on your point of view. Anyway, I can't thank you enough for putting me on to her, Paul."

"Chris is first rate. And a true friend. Try not to rub her the wrong way, Lou. She's sensitive, and genuine. No phony airs."

"Paul, if I didn't know you better, I'd think you might be carrying a little torch for Chris."

"Well, I do care for an old friend, just like I care for you, though God knows why. So don't take advantage of Chris—or me, for that matter—with any of your cockamamie plans to save the downtrodden. What I still can't understand is why you'd bother to get involved in this affair at all. Whoever lives in the building is not your responsibility or your company's. And the landlord—what'd you say his name was? Epstein? Epstein's private affairs are his own doing, as long as they're not costing you anything."

"That's just it, Paul. I think they are costing us. I'm willing to bet that part of the reason this loan isn't being paid back has nothing to do with Epstein's alleged business problems. I've been talking to the building superintendent, off the record, of course, and he says it's common knowledge: Bud Epstein's attention to his real estate investments has dipped to zero since he became involved with this glorified hooker. Look at it this way, the old codger was probably worried he couldn't even get it up anymore until she started giving him the time of day. He fell head over heels for this chicky and gave her free rent on three separate units for the past eighteen months in return for her attentions, and now he considers himself a lucky man. I mean, who wouldn't at his age? To heighten her power over him, she probably turned him on to drugs. Johnson says the dealers are hanging around that neighborhood night and day. Of course, it's fairly safe to say, where sex is for sale, so is dope.

"Anyway, up to now, no one's noticed how distracted Epstein has become. Hard times, sure. Amie Mae's giving everyone a break. But he needs more, and the place is still a dump. If the rent money's not going into repairs and debt service, whose pocket is it lining?" Peller looked at Paul for a reaction. Seeing none, he continued, "I think Angel is ready to talk. According to the super, Angel must have double-crossed Epstein somewhere along the line, because now he's strangling her financially. Epstein has started to turn off her free ride, and she wants revenge. My theory is, if I help Angel, she may be willing to provide evidence that her landlord's diverting Amie Mae's money into drugs or some other misuse of funds or taking a share of her ill-gotten gains to subsidize his mortgage payments."

Paul looked at Peller curiously. "What the hell difference does all this make to your company, Louis?"

"The company's made deal after deal to get him to pay off his loan. But he's a slippery fish, and he keeps finding ways out of it. I say, there's clearly more here than meets the eye. He's not maintaining the property, he's not paying on his loan, and he's pleading poverty. But his clothes are Savile Row and the new Mercedes, well, need I say more? We don't want to foreclose and take title to the property, because we think the problems are too great. There's lead paint and friable asbestos in the building. It would create a huge liability for us if we owned it. Forget about the property's street value. We want Epstein to keep it and pay off the loan. If I can get the scoop on him quietly, he'll have to stick with our deal, or he'll find himself in even bigger trouble."

"*Trouble*. Louis, your common sense has flown out the window for good this time. Either that, or I've underestimated your appetite for danger. Listen, Indiana Jones, don't ask for my help anymore. It's none of my business, and I don't think I want any more to do with this. And if you want my advice, neither should you. This situation sounds like something that's much bigger than you or me. My advice is, let Chris help your Angel Sanchez on the prostitution charge, and you leave bad enough alone."

Peller turned away from Paul, unwilling to listen to his friend's advice—the same advice he'd been given numerous times by Lana, by Vallardo, by Derek, even by Tommy.

He changed the subject, aware of Paul's disapproval, afraid of his silence. "Hey, buddy, remember that little investment idea you had? You know, low-income housing tax credits? I've got a line on some great property in Arlington, Virginia. One of my borrowers owns several apartment buildings that need major rehab. He's looking to sell."

Paul thought he ought to nurse Peller's guilt a little further.

The guy had been such a cad lately. He stared out the cab window for a long moment, until curiosity got the better of him.

"You've seen it then?"

Peller smiled despite his anxiety. "I think it's got our names written all over it, partner."

"Partner? I'm not sure it would work out for both of us, Lou."

"Look, Paul, I haven't been the best friend lately, I'll admit. But haven't we been together longer than any duo since Robin Hood and Little John? C'mon, it'll give us a chance to collaborate, help out people who really need it, and make a little money."

Paul had to laugh. "I guess so."

Peller stuck out his hand. "Partners?"

Paul slapped it, nodding. "Partners."

The two men got out of the cab at a tucked-away townhouse replete with green-and-white-striped awning, flower boxes planted with vining geraniums, and a few white wrought iron tables lit with candles on the sidewalk out front. "It's trendy, but I think you'll like it," Paul commented, courteous. He held the door open for Peller and followed him down the steps. Inside, the dark cellar gave off a blast of cool, refreshing air. Peller took a deep breath. Ahh, cool and clean.

Paul gave the maître d' his name and murmured something Peller couldn't understand about the table. As the host escorted them to a back room through a chic crowd of haughty, incurious diners, Peller loudly continued his soliloquy, lamenting the horrors of working for a huge bureaucracy, lambasting his borrowers, until he noticed they were being ushered into a private room with an intimate table set for three. Paul had been listening idly to Peller's tirade, and now, noticing his friend's sudden halt, Paul looked over at his preoccupied pal and grinned.

"Surprise! Louis, I've asked a dear friend to join us. I think you'll enjoy her. I've told her you're one of my oldest friends and very generous. She's thrilled to meet this wealthy pal who's taking us all out for dinner and dancing this evening."

At that moment, before he could protest this obvious chicanery, Peller heard a chipper female voice whispering behind them. "Cuckoo, Paul!"

Turning around with a smile, Paul gallantly took the hand of a vivacious female bundle of energy. She looked to be all of twenty. "Jerri! Thanks for joining us on such short notice. I've been wanting you to meet Louis for the longest time," he added, kissing the dazzling woman on both cheeks.

"Paul's told us how thrilled he was that you had to stay over unexpectedly and how you offered to take us out for a night on the town," Jerri bubbled breathlessly. Fashionably sculpted, she was his "trophy:" a sparkling but hollow adornment for the successful male on the fast track. "It's been so long since we've had dinner at such a boffo place … and dancing. You don't know how exciting this is for a poor working girl."

Company, especially company as demanding as this livewire, was the last thing Peller wanted to endure. "Paul, why didn't you tell me?" Peller said aloud in a bristling voice, more than a little surprised. "No, I mean *really*," he whispered in Paul's ear as Paul tried to brush his question aside. "You knew I couldn't pay for—"

The realization that Paul had decided not to listen to his pal's woes this evening dawned slowly on Peller, like a bad joke. He'd been dwelling far too much on his own *tsouris* and not paying attention to Paul, he could concede that. But just when he needed Paul's ear most, his pal had short-circuited him.

"Oh well, joke's on me," he mumbled, embarrassed. "I guess I asked for this."

Small talk dominated the intimate evening *à trois*, but Peller's mind remained fixated on Washington Heights. Paul accepted Peller's wincing IOU, a disappointed handshake, for the $198 dinner date.

After dinner, Peller stood at the curb with the sparkling couple, Paul hailing a taxi.

"Come dancing with us, Louis?" gushed Jerri.

He was worn out. "I've got a meeting with the Queens Borough president and a tenants' group tomorrow morning, and I think I ought to hit the sack early tonight.

"Too bad," she sighed, a little coy, Peller thought.

In the end, Peller went back to the hotel alone after watching Paul and his "bracelet" pack merrily into a cab headed for dancing under the stars at the Rainbow Room. Rain check courtesy of Louis Peller. As he got into his own cab to head uptown, Peller realized he was vaguely frustrated that Paul had denied him the luxury of reciting the legend, man to man, about how he'd been mugged and violated and his subsequent chase around town in search of cab fare, of being threatened by that menacing kid that afternoon, of disillusionment and despair. He retreated, moody and disappointed and deprived of his only sounding board.

II.
Good Morning

Good morning, daddy!
I was born here, he said,
watched Harlem grow
until colored folks spread
from river to river
across the middle of Manhattan
out of Penn Station
dark tenth of a nation,
planes from Puerto Rico,
and hold of boats, chico,
up from Cuba Haiti Jamaica,
in buses marked New York
from Georgia Florida Louisiana
to Harlem Brooklyn the Bronx
but most of all to Harlem
dusky sash across Manhattan
I've seen them come dark
    wondering
    wide-eyed
    dreaming
out of Penn Station—
but the trains are late.
The gates open—
Yet there're bars
at each gate.
    What happens
    to a dream deferred?
Daddy, ain't you heard?

—Langston Hughes

Chapter 9
Obsessed with Assad

At nine forty-five, weary, Peller's eyes were still riveted wide. He kept flashing back to the scene where he must have been ripped off the night before: the crowded, drunken, alcohol-drenched club where he had been jostled by jumbles of men, mostly drooling over the surgically-enhanced bodies on runways, shimmying mechanically over the voyeurs' chemical cocktails until they suffered the inevitable groping hand all for a stiff, green bill under their g-string. His brain shuttled on fast-forward to a picture of Assad's Washington Heights building. He scanned honest, suffering faces in rapid succession: Marguerita Fernandez, Samuel Leiter, Eva Jones. Then he heard Johnson's voice in his ear, "They seein' these evil characters hangin' around all hours. And their kids are in more danger than ever." Then the face of the black boy looking up at his dead brother's portrait. Threats masking fear. After fifteen minutes of tossing and turning, he gave up the ghost, got out of bed, and lit all the lights.

But his body felt too heavy to move, so he laid down once more. He tried again to clamp his eyes shut, to let his conscious mind float away to a more pristine place. That same nickelodeon replayed relentlessly in his mind. Finally, sirens and clacking horns on the street brought him back, eyes wide, to New York. He was chilled, though the room was warm.

What was causing him to react so violently? It couldn't be just the stolen wallet. No. Nor the black kid posturing. The terror of temptation was picking at his brain: Assad's bribe. He hoped he was wrong, but there was no avoiding the facts. Omar Assad was hoping that Louis Peller would be seduced by half a million dollars in good U.S. greenbacks. He would buy Peller's silence and rein in an adversary. Assad was crooked and smart, just like Epstein. He had everything to hide and nothing to gain by letting Amie Mae force him into bankruptcy. Some family man. What illegitimate "baby," holding such sentimental value, was he hiding at 488 West 158th Street, Washington Heights? Somehow Peller must find out.

But tonight, he wanted only to rechannel the river of suspicion flowing in his brain. He turned on the television, flicking channels in the way of a seasoned surfer, and realized that this waking nightmare was one he witnessed on the tube every night, though usually from the safety and comfort of his own suburban castle. Every image he switched on advertised decay or corruption: CNN or MTV, fact or fantasy. The specter of drugs, sex, violence, and danger lurked in deep shadows. He couldn't escape. He decided to postpone tomorrow morning's tenants meeting with the Queens Borough president until his nerves were less taut. He would take the early morning shuttle back to sanity.

Even with this comforting decision, Peller couldn't sleep, his brain abuzz. The fireworks sparked behind his eyelids whenever he tried to jam them shut. He snuck down to the lobby and purchased every innocent, wholesome magazine on the rack, from celebrity gossip to fashion to automobile mechanics, embracing the newsstand copies as if determined to soak up what was inside, to erase the terror from his brain. He needed to divert his thoughts from their destructive course, from contemplating the evil Epsteins and Assads or risk falling into their well-baited traps. Assad's money could not tempt him. He couldn't become one of them. He wouldn't betray his principles. Let everyone else give in to the expedient, the devil's demands. Not Louis Peller.

Returning to his room and securing every lock, a "Do Not Disturb" sign suspended outside the door, he passed the night reading gossip, or pretending to read, red-eyed and uncomprehending. He drifted off.

And then he heard it. The explosion. He saw the sky light up with rockets dripping hot, hot flames too close to the spectators watching from the ground. He felt chunks of brick and concrete blasted from the roof of the building grazing his head, his back, his hands. And he began to run, trying to look back as he sprinted away, back at the disintegrating facade and searching, at the same time, for someplace to hide. He was panting, trying to catch his breath, trying to keep from stumbling, but there was no place to go … no place to hide.

Louis Peller awoke in a sweat, his heart racing. "It's just a dream, Louis," he told himself, trying to be calm. "Just a dream."

****

"What are you doing back so early, Louis? We didn't expect you in today. Thought you would be in that meeting with the Queens Borough president on the co-op deal," Vallardo remarked, a crease furrowing his forehead. Peller was sitting at his desk, feet up, staring vaguely at a blank computer screen.

"Had to come back early, Joe," Peller droned. "I was mugged Monday night. Borrowed some cash from Steve to make it through the day yesterday. Thank God for Steve. The only productive part of this trip was visiting 488 West 158th—you know, Assad's baby—in the morning. Boy, is that ever a depressing place. Anyway, by last night, it really got to me. I just couldn't take another day in that pressure cooker. If I hadn't gotten the shuttle back here first thing this morning, I don't know what I would have done."

"C'mon, Louis, it's not worth it. You're getting too involved in this thing. Look, I admire your sentiments. You want to see the best team win. So do I. So let me say it again, our game plan is to work out a deal with the borrower, not get sidelined. You haven't been sanctioned to fix anyone's life. And no one's elected you to legislate housing policy in New York City. So let's get on with it."

"I know, Joe. I know. I have a tendency to get carried away sometimes, that's all. I'll be okay."

"So what did Assad say?"

"You're not going to believe this. He wants to buy the building. Eight hundred grand, cold cash. Half now, half in installments over twelve months. Can you believe it? The appraiser valued the place at 235 thou, no more. And according to my estimates, it could easily cost him another million bucks to bring the place up to code." Peller gazed curiously at his boss.

"You kidding? That's great. Go for the touchdown before he changes his play. How fast can we get an agreement drawn up?"

"Wait a minute, Joe. Don't you see? I think he's trying to pull something over on us. Either he's incredibly stupid, or there's more here than meets the eye. And he ain't stupid."

"Louis, I think you've been working too hard. It's not our job to read into our borrowers' motives. Wrap this deal up, and I'll tell you what, I'll talk to Derek about giving you a few days off. Take a long weekend with Lana, and go to the country. Whaddaya say?"

Peller scowled at the computer again. "Don't you think it's the least bit suspicious that he told me his price before he even asked what Amie's value was? I think he knows what the place is worth and expects to buy me off on this deal. Why would he want to buy me off? A quarter million or so for Amie, a half million or so for Peller. Plus, here's the rub, he told me he might have to go to Teheran soon, so he wants the ink dry on the deal before he heads home. Does Assad pick up the cash in Ayatollah country?"

"Okay, let's suppose for a minute you're right, and there's more to this deal than meets the eye. Number one, you're not for sale, right? Witness you even told me about your suspicions. Number two, what if he does get his money from Teheran? Who cares? We have no reason to suspect dirty money. Number three, maybe he is being foolish, or maybe he's so filthy rich, he doesn't care if he loses money on this deal. After all, he might need the loss for tax purposes. I say, let's do this deal before he changes his mind."

"You're right, Joe. I know you're right. But look, I feel this company has a responsibility to preserve decent housing, especially in New York City. These slums—there's no other name for them—offer the only homes some people might ever have. We—Amie Mae, that is—have to ensure that these people have someplace to call home. And I don't trust Assad to be true to that spirit. I went into his building. I saw how he's milking it. People are living in conditions not fit for animals. If we sell to Assad outright, we lose any leverage we have to see these people get treated with dignity." Peller was just getting warmed up. His eyes were shining now. Vallardo noted the early warning signals.

"Louis, I admire your attitude. I really do. I feel for these people too. But we're in the business of getting rid of bad loans for the company. This is a bad loan. If we sell to this guy, and by the way, I don't know how he's gonna come up with the cash if he's been complaining for eighteen months now that he can't pay back the loan, we're getting a big liability off the books and making a lot more in the bargain than anyone would ever bet. So stop second-guessing, and let's run with this thing."

Peller had a stubborn look on his face.

"If it makes you feel any better, we'll ask Assad to bring the building up to code as part of the agreement," Vallardo offered.

"I'll make sure we get the most out of Assad, Joe," Peller replied. "You can bet on it."

Something of a Don Quixote in his lonely crusade to help the downtrodden, Peller strongly believed in keeping these entrepreneurial slumlords in business. They were a different breed. After all, they were the only ones willing and able to make such risky investments in the inner city. Big real estate companies thumbed their noses at such opportunities. The city and state of New York and the United States government couldn't do it; in fact, every time government got involved, it screwed things up.

And here was the real crux of the matter: these property owners were tuned in to the art of economic survival in New York. That was their business. They knew how to keep drug dealers out of their buildings, they had figured out how to make a profit under rent control, and they could outmaneuver New York City's excessive regulations. They weren't threatened by hoodlums or manipulated by pathetic tenants. So the deal had to go to Assad. But at least Peller could use Amie Mae's financial leverage over Assad one last time to make sure he would provide Marguerita Fernandez and his tenants a clean, decent place to live.

****

Paul was seated on the brown plaid loveseat in Chris's office, his face scrunched into a speculative scowl. "To be honest, Chris, I don't know what's gotten into him."

Chris had presented her take on Peller's meeting with her from day before.

"When I met him for dinner last night, he was terribly shaken. Damned fool was hanging out around Eighth Avenue looking for thrills and got mugged. Crazy." Paul nodded his head in dismay.

"Frankly, your friend wasn't any too rational when he came to see me, either," Chris interjected. "Either that or he really is on a soapbox. What's he care about this woman and her little escapade anyway? Seems to me, if he wants to foreclose on his borrower, there's ample grounds to do that, hooker or no."

"All I know is Louis has always been there for me, and now I can return the favor. Besides, we're discussing working together to become big real estate moguls," laughed Paul. "We rehab apartment buildings in tough areas and sell the tax credits to major corporations in need of relief. Really, Chris, isn't America great?"

"I commend you for your vision, both of you, Paul. But Louis has got to know when to stay out of other people's problems," Chris lectured.

"You don't know Louis like I do, Chris. He's got a kind heart. He wants, no, he *needs* to do good. He could've closed this guy out a year ago, but he wanted to give him a chance. Says 'the Epsteins of the world are the only people who can provide—'"

"'Decent housing for the poor and still make a buck.' Spare me the histrionics, Paul."

"C'mon and humor him a little," Paul urged as he rose and walked around behind Chris's desk. He picked up her hand gently, giving her a meaningful look, his eyes shining out from behind the studied glasses. "Please. For me."

Chris had been feeling lonely and out of sorts all day. Not only was Louis Peller dragging her deep into some hapless plan to save the unredeemable, but her one little attempt at romance—an ISO ad in the *Village Voice*—had met with disaster. The supposedly "sensitive, intellectual DWM looking for literary discourse and evenings at the Met" had proved another fiftyish, barrel-chested, married man on the make. A perfect little rendezvous at a quiet espresso bar had gone bitter when he let slip that his wife was at their beach house in the Hamptons for the summer. His lame, "Oh, the divorce papers are as good as sealed," was her cue to scram. It seemed there were no decent men left.

So frankly, she'd begun thinking about Paul again. After all, they were the best of friends. They knew each other's secrets and fears. They always rallied to the other's need through thick and, maybe this time, Peller. Paul was quite adorable, Lord only knew, and brilliant. And like her, Paul was all alone in this crowded, empty city. Why not try again, she reasoned. So when he took her hand, so warm and sure, she melted.

"Paul, I'm only doing it for you," she sighed, meeting his luminous eyes. "Not for that so-called friend of yours, that's for sure. And if I were you, I'd want to have a heart-to-heart with Louis to make sure his head's still screwed on straight."

"You're right, Chris. I've been having doubts myself lately. But you might like to know that he and I are planning to undertake a little joint venture. Something to provide long-term economic stability and maybe an opportunity to blow the big city for a quiet rural retreat. How about a walk through Little Italy so I can regale you with our vision. I'll treat you to some cannoli and caffe latte." He smiled.

Taking Paul's proffered arm, Chris shed her irritation and her loneliness, eager to be persuaded that she was missing something in her analysis. But she really didn't think so.

****

Into August, Peller worked hard to get his mind off Assad's apparent deception. It was none of his business what other kinds of business Assad was involved in or where his money came from. Peller was determined not to get ulcers worrying about it.

Thinking they might rediscover romance during this concerted effort to bow out of landlord–tenant politics, Peller took Lana to a show at the Kennedy Center, a gesture that satisfied Lana's passion for theatre and gave them both a much-needed respite from life. There was champagne and the plush, hushed splendor of the white building overlooking the river, with its perfect vista of ornamental Washington and the inspiration of mauve and orange sunsets reflecting in Potomac's placid waters. At intermission, captured by the passion of *The Phantom of the Opera* and Lana's watercolor eyes, Peller stole a kiss from his wife and picked up her warm, willing hand to pull her into his embrace. She melted at this unpredictable gesture. Later, still caught in the spell, these onetime and future lovers meandered home driving along the still Rock Creek, pulling off to listen to the strumming chorus of crickets. They necked, teenagers again on their lovers' lane, to the rise and fall of late summer's sonorous serenade.

Calmer, life went on. While Peller was still revved up at the office, his colleagues were either on vacation or thinking about it during those dog days when the sun sweltered and the sidewalks sizzled. Peller tried to take it a little slow too, electing for some long weekends just to putter around the house and take the kids to the pool. In the evenings, he wrote a little in his journal, exorcising demons, developing ideas. But mostly he sat in front of the television, surfing through sixty channels from news to sports to comedy to oldies, seeing nothing. When he let himself be roused from this luxurious lethargy, it was to challenge Alison to a tennis match.

One night, after the kids were in bed, he registered his state of mind on the yellow pad:

> I'm trying to forget about Assad and just enjoy the family. It's not working. Marguerita keeps popping into my head, "Help us." Going through the motions at work ain't enough. I can do a mitzvah here.

Lana was involved in a special series of articles at the newspaper, so she was wrapped up in her own affairs. She really wasn't too attuned to his state of mind, apart from knowing that her husband was launched, once again, on one of his crusades. He hadn't shared much with her about the latest crisis in New York since the mugger incident had pretty much superseded everything else. She did notice that Peller seemed to be taking more time with the children, and she was relieved. Kids and playtime—key ingredients that relaxed Louis Peller far better and quicker than anything else Lana could divine.

Chapter 10
The Battle of 158th Street

The dog days of August passed quickly, and Peller felt renewed. With September, he resumed his commute to the city. Peller was back. It was his first trip to New York in over a month. He flew up on September 12 to inspect a six-apartment building in Borough Park, owned by a nice Jewish man, Henry Katzenbaum, somewhere in age between eighty and death, complete with the requisite salt-and-pepper beard, black hat, and fringes.

This Brooklyn neighborhood was solidly Jewish, Orthodox, in fact. Every business, from the butcher to the undertaker, was owned by a member of the tribe. It was a completely self-contained ghetto, an island of yarmulkes within the Diaspora. There were yeshivas on every third street corner. Serious school boys walked the streets without looking left or right, never smiling. The cars parked on the curbs all sported bumper stickers advertising the return of the Messiah; "Rabbi Schneerson is the *Moshiach*," they announced. Shop windows showed posters with the good rebbe's face, a shrine every bit as intimidating as other religious icons, from Moses on the Mount to Khomeini. The apartment buildings in this part of town were all brownstone or brick, and while they weren't in immaculate condition, they were a far cry from the decay of comparable buildings a few blocks in any direction.

Katzenbaum. Poor old guy couldn't meet the mortgage payments. Peller knew from the engineering reports that the place was in reasonable condition structurally. But for the second time in four months, one of Katzenbaum's tenants, a sweet Jewish widow, had passed on, may she rest in peace. Now, with two apartments vacant, the remaining rents didn't generate enough to cover Katzenbaum's mortgage payments. On the phone, old-man Katzenbaum had complained that he was advertising in the Yiddish newspaper to get some new people in, "the right kind people." No luck.

But Peller needed to inspect the place and negotiate terms so the guy could pay on his note, or foreclose. He'd probably have to take over this one, like indenturing one of the family. And there in Brooklyn, but for the grace of God and his father's industriousness, Peller's family would have remained if it hadn't been for his father attending medical school in rural Pennsylvania and settling there.

Really, Peller didn't know why he even bothered with these inspections; it was always the same story. This time, Peller found the sightseeing rather amusing. Driving through Brooklyn's Hasidic neighborhood, he felt transported back into the Polish ghetto. The Brooklyn *shtetl* today, a haven for these Jews, was a hive of activity. Women in wigs and kerchiefs towing a brood of children; boys on their way home from yeshiva playing chase, the fringes on their prayer shawls flying in the wind, and their hair twisted in side locks; old men with their long beards standing eye to eye, arguing intently, fingers pointing at each other's bony noses in fierce religious debate. It was a place just barely containing a lot of passion and fervor. The same place that had erupted tragically in violence when several Jewish boys were gunned down by an Arab Muslim, retribution for the massacre of scores of praying Palestinians at the Temple Mount in Jerusalem by a right-wing Israeli religious fanatic. Like the Holy Land, peace among Arabs and Jews in New York was a tenuous arrangement that could flare into ferocious flames at any moment.

After his visit to the new "old country," Peller decided to call on the manager of 488 West 158th Street. It was, for Peller, a pro forma call. On his arrival, he noticed an unusual cluster of people outside the super's apartment, sitting silently on the dingy carpet or standing in knots of two and three in animated conversation, as if prepared to wait a long time. These men—they were all men, mostly Hispanic, Peller deduced from the few Spanish words he could understand, tenants perhaps—did not look as if they tolerated outsiders kindly. Not outsiders like Peller, anyway, *quien no habla español.*

Passing by the others nervously, he knocked cautiously on the door.

"*Un momento, por favor,*" someone inside shouted in irritation. The young black man who cracked the door ajar wore a colorful crocheted hat covering a rat's nest of dreadlocks. A small gold hoop adorned his nose, and an elaborate silver earring dangled from his right ear, just under a small diamond solitaire in the same ear.

Even as the door opened ajar, the crowd in the hall seemed to mobilize, ignoring Peller as they shouted out complaints and God only knew what else to the super in Spanish. Carlos de Leon ignored their angry yells and peered curiously at the strange *gringo* standing calmly in front of him.

He quickly arranged his irritation into an ingratiating smile. "*Hola, Señor,*" he said, slower now. "Can I help you?"

Peller frowned. "Perhaps," he answered, noncommittal, immediately on guard. He didn't like the way this young man apparently did business.

"Are you Carlos de Leon?" asked Peller. When the wiry man nodded, Peller resumed. "My name is Louis Peller. I'm from the bank that holds the note on this building for Mr. Assad. I'll be looking around, and I wanted to let you know. Mr. Assad suggested I drop by to introduce myself." Peller wasn't sure how much English this super understood.

Carlos opened the door a little wider to meet his guest and slapped Peller on the back congenially. "Oh, the *banco*. Of course."

Peering inside past Carlos, Peller could see the narrow, ground-floor flat was dim, any outside light shrouded by drawn green-, orange-, and yellow-striped blinds. Peller thought he could discern the faint scent of incense. Light glowed yellow from a low-hanging ceiling lamp covered with a bell-shaped, scratched metal shade swinging low over the old Formica-topped kitchen table cluttered with papers, books, and erotic-looking primitives to grace the space.

"Does Seńor Assad know you are here? I'm sure he can show you apartments better than me," offered the super as his official visitor stood impatiently outside the door.

"No, Mr. Assad couldn't join me today. He asked me to see you," Peller lied.

Carlos pulled Peller in quickly and closed the door behind him, even as a waiting supplicant tried to push his way up to see him. "I want to show you something. Stay here," he told Peller. He reappeared with the "fix-up list" for the building while knocking continued at the door. "What can I do?" Carlos asked, nodding toward the clamor. "They keep complaining to me." He showed Peller a rather long list of problems, dismissing most of them with an air of puzzlement.

"What do people expect with the rents they pay in this place? This ain't no sugar plantation. Half the tenants in this building have missed more than one rent payment, so why should I run to fix their apartments?"

"But you do have to make sure you pass the building code inspection," Peller insisted. "Did you know the engineering report on this building mentions a problem with asbestos and lead paint, Mr. de Leon?"

"I repair the minimum to pass: boss's orders. You know, he

can't exactly pay me, or you, if he don't get paid." Carlos grinned. "And I don't work cheap either."

Peller would have to file that information away for later analysis. Meanwhile, he was taking a surreptitious glance around the dark, cluttered apartment, haphazardly decorated with what Peller assumed to be native crafts and artifacts from the Dominican Republic. It reminded him of his first apartment in college, when he'd roomed with a bunch of guys off campus and frequented local "head" shops to outfit their "pad." Carlos's radio blared out tunes for aging rockers, symbolic of Peller's youth, music that inexplicably triggered passionate memories: smoking marijuana at a peace rally; angering his father by bad-mouthing "Tricky Dick" Nixon; having sex with a girl for the first time, an "older" woman of nineteen; streaking. This particular song, "Wild in the Streets," was a rocker's mantra that seemed oddly in tune with his life today: "Wild in the streets, we're running mad / Wild in the streets, rebellious child / We're out to save the earth / For us to give rebirth / Wild in the streets." The lyrics reverberating in his head seemed incongruous in this twenty-five-year-old Latino's apartment. Peller tried to remember the year it was first released; around '71, he thought. Why, this kid wouldn't even have been born yet. He fingered a crude straw picture frame, the portrait of a defiant teen he assumed to be Carlos.

Noticing Peller's attention, Carlos grinned eagerly. "My family's all in the Dominican Republic. They went there from Haiti when I was two. They send me things to remind me of home, want me to move back." He picked up a photograph. "Here are my brothers and their children. Handsome family, no?"

He looked into Carlos's foolish face, then down at his picture. Peller quickly counted four brothers and at least nine of their children from infancy up through young adulthood. The men had light skin and black hair, slicked back or in dreadlocks. The men and teenage boys all had the same small, wiry build; the girls were ebony skinned and round. They looked like a tough group. The family was lined up formally in front of a tumbledown shack made of tin with a roof of corrugated metal. Roosters and hens appeared equally at home in front of the shack. Peller assumed it belonged to one of the brothers.

"They don't have too much to live on. I send money home every month for food and clothes. It's too hard to live there. No work," Carlos continued, setting down the picture next to a pile of junk on his vintage 1950s kitchen table.

Carlos de Leon was a cultural hybrid. Light of skin and conversant in both Spanish and Creole, he spoke passable English in his unique, colorful patois. Born in Haiti of once-affluent multiracial parents, the family fled with baby Carlos to Santo Domingo after the political ascension of Jean-Claude "Baby Doc" Duvalier in order to escape political and economic repression under that pseudopopulist regime. They left everything when they fled. Still, Carlos himself had never known the brutal political repression in Haiti and considered himself a Dominican to the core. At eighteen, Carlos left for New York to join its significant Dominican community.

So now, he was under the employ of one Omar Assad, working as a building superintendent in New York's Washington Heights and face-to-face with Louis Peller.

"These people in my building have it good," Carlos told Peller, pointing to his own apartment to show the contrast between home and his building here. "It doesn't usually rain through cracks in the roof, and the plumbing is indoors."

Peller spoke impatiently. "It doesn't seem to be a fair comparison. What exactly has Omar Assad instructed you to do with this repair list?"

There was another insistent rap on the door. On the Tuesday afternoon of Peller's visit, the stream of tenants waiting to see the super were ostensibly there to complain about bad plumbing, no hot water, or faulty wiring.

Carlos shrugged. "Now I think that should be a question you ask Mr. Assad, not me, Mr. Peller. I just do what he says." Carlos sat down, stretching his legs under the table and motioned to Peller to sit.

Peller shook his head. Other unusual paraphernalia was scattered about the living room. One corner, in particular, was curious, for it had been furnished with what seemed to be an alter, complete with ritual pictures of saints and incense. The nest of hand-crafted gourds in wild designs, masks, and unlit candles caught his eye. Carlos noticed his interest.

"These are the crafts they make on Hispaniola, Mr. Peller. You know these? We use them for religious ceremonies."

Peller shook his head. "I'm Jewish," he explained. "I'm afraid I'm not familiar with your religion."

"You have heard of the religion voodoo? *Vodun*, we call it. Some people say it is black magic, but we use it for good, not evil. We have our own saints, like the Roman Catholics, demanding their own sacrifices." Carlos walked over to the alter and picked up a picture of a black "saint" dressed in white robes, with an intense, otherworldly face. "For example, this is our St. Patrick. As you know, Patrick is the patron saint of Ireland who scared all the snakes away from his island. In *Vodun*, he represents Father Dambala, the most powerful of our spirits or *mysteres*. His symbol is also the snake. To us, though, he is more like your Moses." Next, he picked up a carved wooden snake. "Like Moses in front of Pharaoh," he grinned, "Dambala throws down his rod, and it turns into a snake." Carlos obligingly threw down the carved snake. "He picks it up," here Carlos thrust the snake into the air, "and it turns back into the rod of the shepherd. Both saints have a certain … magic, no? So you see, in our worship, Mr. Peller, we have much in common," concluded the wiry man with a conspiratorial smile.

"I think there may be a few important differences between my religion and yours," observed Peller wryly. "Especially in your idea of spirits and magic," Peller said, returning Carlos's grin. Looking at the wall again, he noticed a clock. He'd far overstayed this visit with the super.

"I'd love to discuss this with you someday, but I've got to be going, Mr. de Leon," he said. "I still need some time to look around, I have a plane to catch, and I need to meet my driver shortly. But I do hope we can talk again sometime."

Taking his leave, Peller speculated briefly about the somewhat exotic ambiance in Carlos' place but chalked it up to cultural convergence in the Americas. He completed a perfunctory inspection of the hallways and elevator and then went outside to look over the exterior. A more detailed review would have to wait for a later date.

Once outside the building, it took Peller a moment to adjust to the bright glare of midafternoon. The sky looked white, either overcast or polluted, he couldn't decide which. Cracked sidewalks still radiated the heat of midday. Either way, based on the obviously heightened adolescent activity outside, it was apparent he had just violated the three o'clock rule. Noticing Tommy scowling as he leaned against his car a few yards away, a frown that would soon be directed at Peller, he beat a hasty retreat down the front stairs.

But before Peller even reached the sidewalk, he was stunned by piercing, high-pitched noises like the screaming of banshees. The sharp scrape of gunshots scattered across the busy street. Tommy dove for the car as a stray bullet ricocheted off the hood. With a growl of the engine and a screech of rubber, Tommy took off down the block, and Peller, crisis dawning dimly on his shattered consciousness, shrank clumsily behind the metal garbage cans on the curb nearby and knocked them over nervously. He was shaking, but his mind was a blank. The incident hadn't quite registered in his head. From Peller's hiding place, he heard Tommy blow the car horn, and assuming that was the all-clear signal, he rose hesitantly, hugging the buildings for cover, then sprinted down the street to rendezvous with Tommy as his driver backed up to meet him. His legs were rubber.

"What the hell kind of reception was that," Peller yelled at his obviously agitated driver.

Tommy yelled right back. "Louie, this time they was shootin' at me. You know why? I was the only white man on the block. Because I'd been sittin' there, mindin' my own business and waitin' for you to get your ass outta there. They thought I was a cop. A cop! So *they* shoot first, before the 'cop' can blow 'em away. They don' cotton to no cops around here. Cops ruin the drug trade, fo' Chrissakes. And I'm tellin' you, I don' cotton to hangin' around this joint while you piss away time socializin'. You know our deal: in after ten, out before three. Now you seen why first hand." He drove ten or more blocks before he spoke again, calmer this time.

"Let's just make sure nothing like this happens again," warned Tommy, wearing a grim expression. "I need a bulletproof van if you guys are gonna keep sendin' me into the war zone."

The rest of the uneasy drive to La Guardia passed in stony silence.

****

Peller finally spied the silvery ribbon of the Potomac River beneath the wings of the 727. Only then could he permit himself to unclench his fists and untense his back. He had been on edge the entire flight, certain that, as things were going, the plane too would prove unsteady and crash into the cemetery (how fitting) whose tombstones lined the flight path, row after eternal row, at take off. Or perhaps the airplane would plummet in a fireball, struck in midair by an inbound aircraft. He realized his mind was playing tricks on him and wondered if, in fact, he had some kind of subconscious death wish, anything to take him away from the unrelenting pressure of his work. It would take him weeks to unwind from this latest series of disasters.

As the plane touched down gently on the runway at National, pulling up to Gate 18 at the old terminal, Peller was grateful to be home, no matter that Washington DC, in his own front yard, was known as the murder capital of the world. The murders that took place routinely in drug-infested Northeast Washington were far from his reality, even as the insanity of New York's poorest, most dangerous neighborhoods was becoming all too familiar. Even though the George Washington Parkway, where his car now crept through the rush hour crawl, was within view of the slums of DC, he was home, and he felt safe. He was in a hurry to get to his house, in a hurry to tell Lana about his day.

Panic turned to frustration, then anger. Never one to suffer the insanity of rush hour silently, today's quotient of tolerance was depleted even before Peller reached the Beltway, as traffic screeched to a halt. It was bumper to bumper.

"Oh, this is just perfect," he said aloud sarcastically. "Just what I needed to cap off a terrific day."

He flicked on the radio to listen to the traffic reports: "There is a tractor-trailer jackknifed on Interstate 495 at the I-270 spur. All but the far right lane are blocked on the inner loop, and 495 traffic is being diverted at River Road. At the scene, traffic is slowed to a crawl in both directions as cars on the outer loop pull over to allow emergency vehicles through."

He could hear the whirling blades of the traffic copter circling low overhead.

"It appears that the HazMat team is on the way, although I don't see evidence of any spills or leaks. Oh—I can see smoke coming from a car that apparently rear-ended the tractor-trailer when it careened out of its lane."

Well, at least he wouldn't have to worry about an oil spill or chemical waste dump. But smoke? If there was a fire, it could tie up the Beltway for hours. And Peller wasn't in the mood just now to deal with the infamous Washington Beltway.

There was a momentary breakup on the traffic reporter's radio, one could hear mumbled "ten-fours" and "Roger" as his chopper communicated with someone on another frequency. "We now have confirmation that the Maryland Shock Trauma team is flying to the scene to take the driver involved in the accident to a nearby hospital. According to reports from the scene, driver and passenger may have suffered serious injuries. Drivers are urged to consider alternate routes. "

"Too late for that now," Peller screamed at the radio. "God, I hate this." He quickly flipped through the FM stations, listening out for some bluegrass or soft oldies to soothe his jagged nerves. Better figure on at least an hour in this rat's maze, he realized with irritation. "Damn it all," shouted Peller at the drivers parked all around him on what should have been an expressway. Not even a car phone to call Lana.

****

Lana had been monitoring the road conditions since four fifty-seven when word first came over the newswires about a truck jackknifed at the spur. Fortunately, she didn't have to use the Beltway or I-270—hated both with a passion, in fact—but she realized Peller would probably be coming home that way. She had tried to page him and warn him about the situation before he left the airport, but to no avail. By now, she figured, noting it was already close to five forty-five, he'd be dead smack in the middle of that mess on the Beltway and grouchy as hell about it.

Lana called as she left the office to let Sofia know she would be a little late; traffic on the side roads would be predictably heavy because of the accident. She wanted to make sure all was well on the home front. Even though she didn't look forward to the prospect of fighting rush hour, she wasn't really thinking about it; her mind was on other matters.

Lana was feeling pretty good. After ten years of paying her dues at the newspaper, first writing obits, next covering the County Council, then as a general assignment reporter, she could sense some positive currents in the air. Her editor had been dropping hints lately about giving her a chance at the editor's desk, as assistant news editor. It would be the perfect promotion—more money, more responsibility, no more ridiculous assignments or insane deadlines. She couldn't wait to tell Peller her news.

She climbed into the station wagon and headed for home, purposely taking the most indirect routes to avoid traffic jams. Here she was at last, Lana Baer Peller, ace reporter, about to be kicked upstairs. It was a plum promotion for someone who had always considered herself to be pretty average in most ways: hard worker, decent writer. As for looks, she was of average height, although she had a petite frame. Her hair was now a golden brown, and she wore it styled for "wash and wear," to suit her frenzied routine. Last year, at age thirty-five, in a step toward reclaiming waning youth, she added highlights, shooting for "provocative." It took a long time before Peller noticed the highlights, signaled by the charge on their credit card more than any revelation of eternal youth or special beauty. His response at the time, as she remembered it, was, "One hundred fifteen dollars! Whaddaya think we're made of?" before conceding that he really thought the sunny streaks made her look sexy. She liked herself this way, so she kept on coloring it. Men stared at her from time to time, and her mother-in-law insisted she thought Lana was beautiful, but with three children and a husband demanding as much as her full time job and no time to take care of herself, she really felt, well, ordinary.

Driving home, thinking about her pending elevation to the ranks of news editor, there was high color to her tanned cheeks and a sparkle in her aquamarine eyes. She was excited and aware how excitement heightened sensuality. At least to Peller, she would be alluring, and that's what counted at this moment. His attitude about her career had changed from highly negative to studied neutrality, and it was important for her to seduce him to the possibilities of what this promotion could do for her … for them. Frankly, she knew Peller would still prefer she stay at home and be full-time wife and mother, something that was not even a remote possibility in her mind. So it became more important, as she climbed the ladder, for her to keep low negatives in public opinion (read: Peller) polls about her new job prospects. It was never too early to start campaigning.

As she pulled into the driveway, she had a strategy fully mapped out in her mind. Seduce first, break the news later.

"Hi, everyone. I'm home," she shouted over the television, the baby's tears, and the "rat-a-tat-tat" and "pow" of Alexander playing video games with his buddy from next door.

"Mom, can we play Scrabble?" called Alison from the kitchen. "You did promise we could play, remember?"

"Not this minute, Allie," she replied. "Maybe later, if you take an early bath and help your brother and sister get ready for bed."

"Yippee," shouted Alison. "You hear that, Alexander? I have to take a bath first tonight so I can play with Mama."

Sofia walked out carrying Ashley who was still sniffing back a few tears, mostly for effect.

"She fell down in the family room, but I think she's okay," Sofia explained. "We washed off the boo-boo, didn't we, honey?"

"Thanks, Sofia," Lana said, taking the baby into her arms. "I appreciate your waiting around. Sorry I got here late."

"No problem. I'll see you tomorrow," Sofia called back as she opened the screen door. "Oh, I fed the kids already. They were hungry."

Thank God for Sofia, thought Lana as she followed the baby attentively, Ashley climbing slowly up the stairs on short, fat legs. Lana wanted to change into something a little more comfortable. The turquoise silk sheath skirt with its complimenting fuchsia bolero jacket had been one of her little "finds" when she went up to New York last spring with Peller. She had opted for bargain hunting on the Lower East Side while he inspected buildings across the Brooklyn Bridge. Pulling on her pink leggings under a cool pink, crocheted sweater, she reminisced about their afternoon dim sum in Chinatown and a romantic evening out on the town. It all seemed far away.

Now Lana would pull out tonight's less exotic repast: leftover lasagna. Every once in a while, she would try to introduce her family to something new but not too adventurous, clipping a tasty recipe from one of her parenting magazines. But it was useless. "Why eat interesting sauces and salmon pies when God made hotdogs?" quoth her progeny. So she rarely took the time to create a chef d'oeuvre anymore, much to Peller's consternation.

After piling her plate full of lasagna, she nuked it in the microwave and threw together a quick salad for her and Peller to munch. Lana figured she would eat now since Peller would probably be in gridlock for another hour, judging by TV news updates on the Beltway traffic situation. The kids streaked outside to play with the neighborhood children, tauntingly comparing notes on computer games, in-line skates, television shows, and a reasonably comfortable life on the Planet Earth in the 1990s. It was a comfortingly predictable sound.

Finally, around eight fifteen, just as dusk was gathering and the children were filing in for their baths, Peller arrived home. Lana and the kids were already upstairs as he stomped in the front door, cursing loudly. Even the dog was intimidated and refrained from taking his usual running leap for his master's chest.

Lana called down, "Hi, honey. I've got your dinner waiting for you. You just need to put it in the microwave for two minutes. The salad's on the counter. I'll be down in a few minutes." Judging from the tenor of his arrival, now was not the time to broach her possible promotion.

He stomped into the kitchen. "Shit, not lasagna again." This was a customary refrain; he didn't like any of her casseroles the second day around. He poured Frosted Flakes and milk into a bowl and turned on the television for another *Star Trek* rerun, defensively tuning out his own world to one of science fiction, where every crisis in the universe could be resolved within an hour.

"Daddy's home," yelled Alexander, dripping bathwater head to toe as he dashed down the stairs, a towel flying cape-like from behind his naked little body. He ran and jumped onto his father's lap while Peller tried hard to block the little tackler.

"Dad, Mommy won't play Scrabble with me," Alison

complained from the top of the stairs. "And she really promised me."

"Come back here, Ashley," he heard Lana call as the littlest Peller made her slippery escape from the tub and toddled into the hall. "We have to rinse the shampoo out of your hair."

Another evening of domestic tranquility at the Peller home. He sighed and pushed Alexander firmly off his lap. The boy was the spitting image of his father: thick, dark, wavy hair, dark complexion, thick eyebrows—minus the moustache, of course. "Can't you let me eat my dinner, such as it is, in peace, you little bugger? Lana!"

"Come back up here, Alex," Lana commanded, "unless you don't want a bedtime story."

"Story time! Can we have *Alexander and the Terrible, Horrible, No Good, Very Bad Day*?" inquired the kindergartner, proud that there was a book named after him.

"If you hurry," said his mother. "One … two … two and a half …"

Up scrambled the miniature Peller knockoff without a backward glance. Halfway up the stairs, he remembered what he'd been after. "Forgot our goodnight kiss, Daddy." His father was only too happy to throw his son the proffered kiss from afar.

"Dad, what about Scrabble?" queried Alison for the third time.

"I'm afraid not tonight, sweetheart. I just got home, and I had a really rotten day. Maybe tomorrow. Goodnight, honey. I love you."

"That's what you always say," Alison muttered, disappointed.

Finally, after much shuffling and bustling and demands for water and "one more story"—the usual stall tactics—Lana quieted the lights, kissed three angelic heads, and dragged cautiously down the stairs.

Before she could ask Peller about grinding gears around the Beltway for the past three hours, she absorbed his ashen, worried face. This was more than a case of gridlock nerves. "What happened to you?" she asked. "You look like you lost a shootout at the O.K. Corral."

"Lana, you don't know how close you are to the truth. Would you believe we got shot at today?" His voice was strained. His throat sounded tight with tension.

"Shot at? That's it. I want you to resign tomorrow. I'll help you write the letter. I don't plan on being a thirty-six-year-old widow with three kids to raise on my own."

"Thanks for the sympathy. Did you even stop to think about how *I* might be feeling?" On Peller's face was something close to sheer panic.

She looked at him again in alarm, then softened as she saw his fear. "If I were to guess, I'd say 'scared shitless' just about sums it up. Wanna tell me what the hell happened?" She came close, putting a gentle hand on his, training those sympathetic eyes on her man.

As Peller recounted his tribulations in shorthand, she could see his shoulders and face relax just a bit as he transferred some of his anxiety to her. She turned away in outrage at this latest example of corporate exploitation. How could they be so heartless? How could he? The plan to convince him about the benefits of her job opportunity flew out of her head, shaken by rage.

"If they're going to send you into the battle zone, they need to give you special protection," she fumed. "Tommy or no Tommy, there are not enough bodyguards in all the world to satisfy me that you're taking adequate precautions. At the very least, you ought to be getting combat pay. I don't see Joe or Derek venturing into Washington Heights, and they're paid a hell of a lot more than you. If you're not going to insist on a special deal, I am. Just give me Derek's phone number, and I'll give him a piece of my mind. "

Weary as he was, Peller looked panicked at the thought of Lana lighting into his bosses. He hadn't anticipated this vehement reaction from her; he was looking for a little sympathy. But her interference in his job would spell professional doom, that was for sure. And despite its serious flaws, there was too much he liked about this job to have her jeopardize it. He tried to appease her.

"Look, Lana, these guys know what's going on. They wouldn't send me in if they weren't sure things were pretty much okay. And frankly, I would refuse to go if I thought it was all that dangerous. This thing today was unusual, a fluke."

"I'm not satisfied with that explanation. Either you talk to them again, or I will. Or better yet, you remember what you told me last week? You know, the brewing scandal over how your company has refused to purchase any more loans in New York City, despite its Congressional mandate to finance affordable housing in the inner city? How they're rejecting all the deals the New York office recommends? I think that's just the sort of grist for the mill my editors would love—it has a certain appeal to our readers: senators, cabinet members, judges. You know, a series on how a major national investment company engages in real estate redlining in New York? I'll suggest a two- or three-part exposé to my editors."

"Relax, Lana. Don't try to run my job the way you try to run my life. I'll talk to them again if it'll make you feel better. Let me see what I can do."

"This time, no namby-pamby excuses. You *insist* they do something."

"I will. Meantime, I've just got to keep plugging away at this stuff. Look, I wish there were other real estate jobs up for grabs these days, but there aren't. So I have to hold onto this one for now. You and I both know this job isn't going to last forever. For the time being, though, I want to squeeze it for all it's worth."

Lana gave him a skeptical look and said grimly, "I'll buy the excuse for now, but things better change around here, or I'll follow through on my threat."

Peller resumed his frown. "Why can't you just listen and let me complain without creating more stress for me for once?"

In general, Lana tried to be supportive but was often stymied about how to support her husband. Peller was stubborn. He wore blinders, saw only one way up. So demanding of himself and all those around him, a perfectionist quick to criticize and unrelenting in what he wanted from life. No matter how good things were, they were never good enough, an annoying attitude he inherited from his father. Sam Peller had been a product of Lower East Side immigrant poverty and the Depression who had bootstrapped to become a doctor and a self-made millionaire in a small Pennsylvania town. In the process, Sam left his parents and sister in the same old Bronx apartment their family had inhabited for fifteen years when they migrated uptown from New York's Lower East Side, where it remained a religious Jewish enclave in a turbulent sea of poverty. Though he sent them checks on the holidays, Sam Peller appeared eager to distance himself from his parents' old-country ways and stubborn steadfastness to the *shtetl* mentality. Sam had rarely talked about the hard times growing up to his children and buried the past in pious silence, a fact that wrapped his offspring in the ignorance of privilege.

But expectations were hard to ignore. Peller stepped obligingly into Dad's self-reliant boots. The son, like his father, had a volatile mix of temperament: intolerant and inflammatory, stubborn and opinionated. The Peller household, with young Louis and *père*, must have smoldered continuously with conflict, considered Lana.

Lana herself, while she always did her best, refused to take problems too seriously, because from her perspective, life was difficult enough without berating yourself for events that spun out of your control. At this moment, Lana was, however, extremely lathered over this dangerous duty in New York for reasons she felt were obvious. Lana's position: Peller ought to get the fuck out of this slumlord business.

Tonight, however, Lana swallowed her anger to respond to her husband's needs. Arising lightly from her chair, she stepped in back of him and began a massage, kneading the knots from his neck, even as she could feel them tightening at the nape of her own. Teeth gritted, she mindfully commenced humming some mysterious mantra, soothing, allaying, assaying his fears.

Moments later, bullets blotted temporarily from his memory, tension melting away, Peller's hand grasped Lana's tenderly, and with a suggestive grin that reflected his lightening mood, he led her up the stairs.

They made love with deliberate care and a desperate fear. The secure world they had hoped to create for one other and their children was an illusion, fast slipping away. Just yesterday, they had both felt so sure that world was rock solid. But today, the rock was crumbling.

They were scared. Fear heightened their intimacy and bred a passion they had forgotten. Peller touched Lana tenderly over various parts of her body, caressing, caressing, caressing her until she begged him to stop touching, to keep touching, and returned touch for touch, arousing him to intense sensations of intimacy. For the first time in years of making love together, Peller and Lana climaxed simultaneously. Lana cried softly, joyously, and felt Peller's tears as her fingers softly traced the smile on his lips. They held each other close for a long, long time: he, to keep the nightmares—those of the day and those of the night—at bay and she, to make sure he remained, at least for the moment, safe in her arms.

Nonetheless, "the dream" managed to slip between the cracks of their love. Lana heard him muttering, felt his body tense. They were so close now, she could feel his heart racing. He moaned. She held him tight, stroking his back tenderly, hoping her rhythmic motions might exorcise his demons.

Chapter 11
A Prescription for Burnout

As promised, Peller dutifully went to his bosses—first to Vallardo, then to Derek—to report his latest crisis in Washington Heights, as much to ease his own anxieties as Lana's. As expected, both had offered the company line, which boiled down to, "Gee, I'm really sorry, but it's not Amie Mae's policy to offer any special treatment for any employee. Even the chairman does his New York business without a bulletproof vest." And Peller strenuously pointed out that the chairman didn't visit 488 West 158th Street when he made his trips to the city. His pleas fell on deaf ears.

Peller walked away grumbling about a company that didn't value his hard work under adverse circumstances or the fact that he was the highest producer in the department, that none of his experience or education, not to mention what he contributed directly to the bottom line, mattered.

Vallardo and Derek, in turn, grumbled that here was Peller causing trouble again. But they couldn't deny his effectiveness. They would eventually have to address his concerns if they wanted to keep Peller focused and productive, but not now. Please, not now when the company was talking about reengineering, a nineties euphemism for downsizing and streamlining and improving productivity—all corporate buzzwords for firing people to add to profitability—again.

Over a defiant three-hour lunch with Ellie and Bill, Peller repeated his Washington Heights experience without flourishes. The trio, demoralized and disgusted with management's response, plotted and schemed to take this matter to the highest levels of the organization if necessary. By the time each drained a third cup of coffee, Peller and Ellie and Bill were all keyed up and ready to march directly into the executive suites to bring attention to the deplorable lack of security given to the team whose job it was to investigate desperate, defaulting borrowers in dangerous urban battle zones all to the same end: to clean up the company's portfolio of bad loans. Fortunately for their livelihoods, by the time they returned to their cubicles, the caffeine buzz had subsided enough for them to reevaluate the wisdom of that plan.

As that week drew to a close, and then the next and the next, a nagging annoyance settled over Peller. He reluctantly realized that things were not going to improve. He became more and more irritated with his bosses. Where did they get off dictating that kind of insensitive policy? They were clearly good technicians, but just as clearly, they were not "people" people to whom personal loyalty held any value. Their management style, "knowledge is power," meant they withheld often-vital information about company policy from their employees. It drove Peller crazy.

The constant politicking was wearing Peller down. He hated office politics. He wasn't cut out for the diversions of petty bureaucrats. And now that he was trying to keep his nose out of the minutiae of the Assad and Epstein cases, work had become rather tedious. He talked on the telephone with borrowers all day long, nonstop. Just for diversion, once in a while he would call Alvin Pollock to hear the latest updates on events in the Hasidic community. Word was that the revered Rabbi Schneerson had suffered a stroke, and members of his sect were holding a round-the-clock prayer vigil outside his hospital room. There had been weeping on the streets of Brooklyn at the news that he was in a coma.

Pollock invited Peller to attend a service at his synagogue and join in the prayers for the Messiah. "He will be healed by the power of our prayer, Louis," Pollock proclaimed. "Besides, I want you to hear our cantor. He's from Guatemala. What a voice that man has. He can enchant the angels. Anyway, he's from a very wealthy family, and he has a little money to invest. I think he may want to finance some property through your company. I'll introduce you. What a *shiddoch*."

After the updates, it was back to the drudgery. Peller had no secretary, so he had to file all his own papers, type up all his reports, prepare business plans for each property, generate spread sheets, fill out expense forms every week, and write reams of cover-your-ass memos. Peller's world was now painted a dull shade of monochrome.

For in the final analysis, it was the face-to-face stuff that intrigued Peller. Most of his borrowers were really pretty decent—landlords with one or two small properties, a cooperative here and there in Brooklyn and Queens—people he could easily help out by negotiating new mortgages with lower interest rates.

He loved the variety and color and culture of his borrowers: a cornucopia of ethnicity. Aside from the Hasidic Jews and a Persian, one borrower was Greek American, another Indian American. And his experience was indication of how times had changed. Today's immigrants came by airplane, boat, and car, looking for visions, ubiquitous in even the remotest parts of the world, of an America painted prosperous on televisions or on the silver screen. Today's hyphenate Americans would always retain their ethnicity, refusing to relinquish the mother tongue and wearing their differences as a stripe of distinction. The poor and uneducated who reached U.S. shores with no chance of leaving the barrio were manipulated by bald-faced opportunists, often newcomers themselves, landlords who considered themselves outside the law and were determined to succeed at any price.

Peller liked the feeling of helping the newest generation of immigrants gain a foothold in the American dream. But dealing with discord and cultural conflict had a way of wearing down the heartiest of souls.

Now that September ushered in shorter days, and the older children had started back to school, Peller usually found the household in a state of chaos by the time he got home at about seven thirty: bathtub bubbling over, children running in every direction, clothes flying, screaming, giggling, crying. And Lana, an island of calm in this turbulent sea, patted dry hair and arms and legs on various bodies, read stories and sang songs, packed lunchboxes and cleaned the dishes from dinner. Numb from the humdrumery, Peller barely seemed to notice.

"I can't believe they've got me doing all this filing," he announced loudly to Lana from the kitchen. "Do you realize that if they paid one secretary to do the clerical work for two or three of us, we could each be one third more productive. Really, I'm too high priced to be a clerk. And frankly, they're not paying me enough to do the job they hired me for." Under his breath, he observed, "Such assholes."

"Awww," Alison piped up. "Daddy said a bad word." The ears of the house never missed a note, unless it was about homework or picking up. Children were keen observers of the really "important" stuff.

Lana was upstairs trying to dry the baby, without much luck. A slippery fish, Ashley was running down the hall, sliding down the stairs and creeping up again, laughing. "Nudey nudey. Nudey nudey."

"What's for dinner?" Peller called without bothering to help round up the littlest whirling dervish. "I'm starved. Haven't had anything to eat since this morning."

"Gotcha," Lana called triumphantly from the head of the stairs, finally getting a secure arm around the squirming Ashley. "There's some turkey casserole in the oven and carrots on the stove," she told him. "You might need to heat up the carrots." Ashley wiggled free again.

By eight thirty, everyone was finally snug in bed, lights off. Little whispers continued, punctuated by occasional guffaws as Alison told Alex her latest silly joke. Only the baby slept peacefully.

Lana came down to read the newspaper. Bedtime was about the only time she could catch up with the news, except what she caught on the radio on her way to or home from work. She sat down at the kitchen table across from her frazzled-looking spouse. She still had not found the moment to break the news about her promotion.

"I've really got to spend more time with the kids," pronounced Peller, helping himself to seconds on the casserole. "This job is getting to be a real pain. I think Joe would like to get rid of me. He's mad because he knows he can't. I'm his biggest producer. But he's on my case all the time. And this business of going up to New York, every week, the same thing. Up at five thirty to catch the shuttle. The drone of the city. Rush, rush, rush. Back to the shuttle. It's really getting to me. I can't sleep at night. My stomach always hurts. And I've probably put on a good five pounds since I started."

"Well, if you'd put something *healthy* in your stomach during the day, you'd probably feel a heck of a lot better. And you wouldn't be so ravenous by the time you got home," Lana observed. Peller was now rummaging through the dessert cabinet for cookies. Even though he denied eating sweets during the day, she usually found an empty box or two of Good and Plenty in his car. And the kids always complained about Daddy eating their popsicles, "all gone."

"C'mon, honey, you know I try not to eat junk," he said, pulling out a jar of jellybeans. "You and I need to eat healthy foods to set a good example for the kids. By the way, I hope you're not letting them eat candy every night."

Lana ignored this broken record. She'd been hearing the same song since Alison was born. Peller was nothing if not repetitious. She paged through the *Washington Post*, concentrating on the local "Metro" news coverage to check out her journalistic competition before turning to the all-important "Style" section for the best gossip of the day. In the back of her mind, she was mulling over whether she should risk his wrath and spill her own good news.

He turned on the TV, flicking impatiently from channel to channel.

"Listen to this, Louis," she chirped, a sarcastic edge to her voice. "Here's a story on burnout. They even quote the psychologist who coined the term after he counseled a bunch of potheads back in the sixties. Evidently, that's where he first encountered the burned out syndrome."

"I know what you're going to say, and I am not burned-out." He picked up the remote control yet again, popping a few more jellybeans in his mouth.

She glared at him, then continued, "Here are the symptoms: 'inability to pay attention or concentrate, a sense of forgetting, a heightened sense of suspiciousness or guardedness.' Oh, and get this, 'on the physical level, there's weight gain, chest pains, sleeplessness.'"

"Okay, so maybe I am feeling a little stress," he said, putting his hand against his chest as he remembered the constrictive pain he had complained of earlier. "You get stressed out too," he shot back defensively.

Again, she ignored him. "'Emotionally, there's impulsiveness, a tendency to behave irrationally, to become increasingly cynical, to feel empty and suspicious of other people's motives.' Gee, honey, that does sound familiar."

"C'mon, Lana. Let's drop it, okay?" Peller was sorry he'd left himself open to this evaluation—he was the one who usually did the analyzing. But this time, he had brought it on himself. "I'll try to stop working so hard. You've been working a lot lately, too. Maybe we should both take a vacation. Why don't we plan a little getaway, just the two of us to, say, Maui?"

"There's nothing I'd like more, Louis. Haven't I been begging you for us to go away by ourselves for years? It could be two nights at a bed and breakfast in Annapolis for all I care. But knowing you, it won't happen. You can't tear yourself away. You know what this psychologist says about why people work so hard that they burn out?"

"Stop. You're hurting me," he mocked.

She heard him groan, but Lana was kind of enjoying validating everything she'd been telling Peller for years. She continued, "'Perfectionism, a need to be liked, trying to prove yourself to the degree that you believe that no one else can do your job. You're not a good delegator.'" She shot a look at him and saw that, for once, he had no rebuttal. She'd hit the mark. "Ha ha," she concluded in triumph. "I rest my case."

Peller got a stubborn look on his face. "I'm going to bed," he announced, turned off the TV, and tromped defiantly up the stairs.

And so it went. Day in, day out: work, work, work. At home, he increasingly tuned out the family and lost himself in the mindlessness of the boob tube. He simply existed; he didn't feel alive anymore. Even writing in the journal was losing its therapeutic powers.

And Lana, knowing she was impotent to change his course, now turned a deaf ear to his complaints without so much as an "I told you so."

****

Peller, Vallardo, and Derek had decided to wait Assad out. They wouldn't take his first offer, no matter how good it sounded. They were going to play with him. If Assad was as eager as he sounded, he'd come back with an even better offer. Peller's first target was to hold out for full payment of the loan, in cash. No time or credit. They'd been burned by borrowers like this before.

Peller called Omar Assad to offer him the verdict: cash on the barrelhead, a full pay off of the loan, or no deal.

"Mr. Peller, frankly I don't understand how you think you might get a better offer from anyone else, but I'm willing to bide my time." Time was on Assad's side. Peller would not foreclose with all the liability hanging over his property. "You know," he continued, "I'm a very patient person. I usually get what I want. As I may have mentioned, I'll be going to Teheran next week on business, and I may be gone for some time. Perhaps we can reconsider or discuss this when I get back. Then, in case you wish you'd made that deal, I'll be sure to bring my checkbook."

Peller sat back in his cube, feeling slightly baffled. He was fairly certain, even after the rejection of his offer, Assad would come back. Peller could afford to wait in this high-stakes poker game. But would Assad sweeten the deal? Perhaps his wealthy connections in the Middle East would come through with the necessary cash.

For now, a little vacation from Washington Heights might be just what the doctor ordered.

Chapter 12
Marguerita's Alarm

It was Friday afternoon. In Washington Heights, the few sickly trees dotting the concrete landscape in this urban desert looked even more bedraggled as autumn crumpled their leaves and stole their scanty cover.

Inside 488 West 158th Street, Marguerita was finally having some success enlisting her neighbors, Eva Jones and Samuel Leiter, in her fight for decent maintenance of their building. Although these two had been reluctant to make any noise, they were among those "good" tenants who might have the clout to force the landlord's hand. The crusading trio had circulated a petition among the residents, and 113 of 200 tenants had signed on. Now they were meeting, unannounced, with Carlos de Leon to demand certain improvements, including uninterrupted heat in the winter, better-lit halls, clean stairwells, security to keep crack users out of the stairwell, a working elevator, repairs to roof leaks and broken plumbing, and new paint to the interior of the building—all long overdue. Marguerita had consulted with Saunders Freeman, a lawyer with the Legal Aid Society and a landlord–tenant specialist, about organizing a tenant's association.

Marguerita arrived in Carlos's apartment armed with all kinds of rules and regulations on tenant's rights, landlord's responsibilities, and a legal mumbo jumbo of threats if Carlos didn't comply with their demands. The 113 tenants were prepared to start decreasing rent payments, at Marguerita's suggestion, until the repairs were made. She knew that the very real risk of a rent strike could be enough to get the landlord to do something—or send Carlos packing.

"What's this pile of paper here?" inquired Carlos suspiciously, as first Marguerita then Eva and Samuel came forward to drop their petition, copies of New York City rent codes, and a list of building code violations onto his already-groaning table. "What kind of problems are you bringing to me this time?" Carlos asked Marguerita, knowing full well that this tenant was capable of making his life miserable.

"I'm sick and tired of your trying to bullshit me, Carlos," Marguerita replied. "So I've been talking to my lawyer." She looked him directly in the eye to see how he would react to the news that she was consulting an attorney.

He didn't flinch. Walking into his living room and motioning them to follow, Carlos said, "I'm a reasonable human being, *Señora* Fernandez. Why don't we sit down and talk about this problem." He motioned her to a chair, smiling first at the implacable Marguerita then at Eva and Samuel who, in turn, nodded back uncomfortably.

Marguerita adamantly refused to sit. Instead, she crossed her arms intently in front of her and shifted her weight impatiently from one foot to the other. Following her cue, Eva and Samuel also remained standing, looking slightly abashed.

"I won't let you sweet-talk me again, Carlos," Marguerita exclaimed. "I'm tired of complaining with no results. I've told you the problems. The place is falling down. The paint is peeling in the hallway outside my apartment. And Miss Jones, too. Mr. Leiter, ditto. My ceiling's leaking, and the plumbing, well, we've got constant drips. The heat goes on and off during the day. Last week, Miss Jones's sink backed up, and five other apartments had toilets out of commission. Everyone started using their bathtubs for toilets, for the love of Jesus. The trash isn't being taken out, and the whole place is starting to stink. Who knows how many big fat rats are scampering between the walls? There's not enough hot water. The elevator hasn't worked in almost a month. The steps to the outside are crumbling. Have I missed anything?" she queried her companions. "Oh yes, worst of all, drugs are ruining the street, and you're doing nothing about it. Well, if you aren't, we are, right?" As she stared them down, her cronies signaled their tepid agreement. Marguerita handed Carlos the petition along with a repair list. "Now this is only the beginning."

Looking suddenly nervous, he glanced over the petition, thinking he might be able to buy off most of them. The majority of the names scrawled on her page were not exactly sterling tenants, and as long as they had something to hide, they could be silenced. But there were enough of the "good" tenants signed on to mean he might have a real problem if he didn't respond. Rent strikes were not uncommon around here. Noting that Marguerita was obviously the ringleader in this unlikely band of musketeers, the wiry super tried to assuage her rage. He needed to buy some time. If he could appease Marguerita, her two timid backups here would obviously also back down.

"Okay, you win. I'll talk to Mr. Assad about helping you. Just as soon as he gets back in the country." Carlos promised to do something about the list right away and made a date to meet with them again after he talked with the landlord. He was fidgeting now, backing them toward his front door.

"I will take you at your word this time, Mr. de Leon," Marguerita promised, scowling as Carlos smiled his most charming smile. Marguerita followed the super, her gaze wandering curiously around the cramped, cluttered room. She looked twice at Carlos's kitchen table. Glimpsing something out of the ordinary, she surreptitiously turned to talk to her comrades, a ruse to get a better look. Thinking she'd better not mention it aloud, she nodded to Eva to make sure the older woman got a good glimpse as she too walked by.

A ledger open on the table read "De Leon Ventures." There were entries noting sums of money and, next to the ledger and almost concealed under de Leon's jacket, small plastic bags filled with white powder. It wasn't laundry detergent, that much she knew. It was obvious that de Leon was careless, or if not, he had tried hastily to hide the goods when they barged into his apartment.

Marguerita shot a sharp look at Carlos. He was obviously in a hurry to show his guests out.

"Thank you for bringing this to my attention. Rest assured, I will do my best to help."

Silent for a moment, Marguerita fixed her steadiest eye on Carlos. "Make sure that promise means something real this time."

Walking down the hall, she congratulated Eva and Samuel for their brave support. "Finally, I think something will happen." And to herself, she added resolutely, "I'll make sure of it."

Marguerita decided to contact her lawyer first thing on Monday morning. Back in her apartment, on an impulse, she dialed the phone number on Peller's card. Collect.

****

It was another hellacious day in Virginia. Peller's telephone, hot from constant use, was growing out of his ear. From eight thirty that morning until now, he had barely set down the receiver. The clutter on his desk was cloning itself until it threatened to overtake him. The minutiae were swallowing him up.

At long last, it was lunch time. He was taking Ellie out for a light bite. Both of them were fast approaching their fortieth year, and both of them felt glum about the prospects. Peller had imagined himself a developer at this stage, building shopping centers, and here and there a townhouse community. Ellie had been certain she would have reached the director level at Amie. This was her fourth year with the company, and she was still stuck in the trenches with the other grunts.

His phone rang again. "Ready?" asked a friendly voice. "Where do you want to eat?"

"Boy, am I ever ready. What a day. You name the place, Ellie. I'll drive," Peller announced with relish.

"Just let me clean up this pro forma on my latest borrower. I'm almost done. I'll meet you at your cube in five," she said.

Peller hung up and gulped down the dregs of his coffee for a final caffeine lift. The phone—there it was again. He stared, frowning. *Let it go*, he thought. *I'm out to lunch.* A second time. Once more, and it would go over to voice mail. What if it's a borrower, he pondered. He ought to answer. *One less phone call to return after lunch*, he reasoned, still staring at the phone. It was Peller's practice to always return calls the same day. Just as the phone began its third trill, he grabbed it.

"Peller here."

"Luis, this is Marguerita Fernandez. Remember you said if I ever needed your help, I should call you?"

"Marguerita, can I call you back? I'm just about to go to lunch with a colleague to discuss some pressing business."

"Oh, of course. Please excuse me, Luis." There was disappointment in her voice. "I'm sorry to bother you. It seems it's something important, but you call me back when you can. That's okay."

A prick at his heart. He *had* promised. "It's okay, Marguerita. I would like to help. What's up?"

"It's something urgent we need to talk about. I think de Leon's the problem, the main reason nothing ever gets fixed around here." He could hear children quarreling in the background, sirens from the open window screaming echoes of New York's mean streets, the sounds of rap music once more shattering the insular calm of his life.

"Luis, I didn't know whether to call you about this right

away or not. But I think something's wrong. I was just in de Leon's apartment with Mr. Leiter and Miss Jones to talk about this petition we wrote up that we got so many other tenants to sign about fixing up the building." With pride in her voice, she announced, "One hundred thirteen signatures. Anyway, when we went to see Carlos, he seemed nervous during the whole conversation, and so we spoke quickly and agreed to meet again after he could talk to Mr. Assad. But as we were leaving, I noticed a book with the name 'De Leon Ventures' on his table, showing tens of thousands of dollars. I know it was a business ledger, and next to the ledger, under his jacket, there were many small plastic bags filled with something white. It looked like white powder. I made sure Miss Jones noticed, and she thinks it was cocaine like I do. Not just a little, Mr. Peller."

Peller thought about his own interview with the irreverent Carlos. "Okay, Marguerita, I wouldn't panic. Maybe he runs a legitimate business on the side. That's not uncommon for someone like him: young, ambitious. And as for the powder, you know he's into all that weird 'voodoo' stuff. Maybe it's some damn herb or spice he uses in his religious rites. I don't really think Carlos would keep cocaine in plain view in his apartment, too many people come through, like me and New York City building inspectors and Assad himself."

He stopped to weigh his defense of this wiry little eccentric man. "Marguerita, I really wouldn't jump to any conclusions. I've seen Carlos's apartment, and I know he has a wild collection of black magic. Nothing illegal about that, as far as I know. I couldn't help you anyway if there were drugs. You yourself told me that it was unavoidable in that neighborhood."

"You don't understand," Marguerita interrupted. "It's not voodoo. That stuff he keeps in that little corner he's got fixed up like a shrine. Listen, Luis, I understand Carlos. I understand black magic; we have these rituals in my country too. Everyone knows about the candles and the skulls and the animal sacrifices.

No, what I saw was not voodoo, Luis. I think our super is selling drugs."

"What makes you so sure, Marguerita?"

"Miss Jones reminded me of the—how you say?—lowlifes hanging out in front of his apartment every day. And there were many people who laughed at my petition and said I could never get everyone to sign. Now I think I understand. I want to talk to a lawyer on Monday to see what to do."

Peller considered briefly, "If I report illegal activity on that scale to Assad, I'm not sure it would matter to him. I wonder if he even suspects his super could be selling drugs to the tenants and ruining his building while he's losing his shirt on that place."

Marguerita was silent while Peller did his thinking out loud. She didn't really care whether the landlord suspected anything.

"Marguerita, I want you to keep this conversation between us. Don't mention what you know to anyone, not even your attorney. I want to check on a few things. I'll call you back sometime next week after I do a little homework."

"If you're sure, Luis."

"I'm sure I can't help you if you repeat what you know to the wrong ears. Let's keep this between us for now. I promise I'll tell you if my, shall we say, research doesn't bear fruit."

"Okay, if you're sure. *Hasta luego,* Luis. *Vaya con Dios,*" whispered his friend.

"Goodbye, Marguerita."

He held the phone for a long moment before he hung up, worried anew whether Assad would change his terms if he was award of Carlos's illegal enterprise. Maybe he ought to keep quiet about it. Or maybe not.

"What's with you, Louis?" a mocking voice rang outside his cubicle. He looked around and saw Ellie espying him curiously. "Just see a ghost?"

"No ghosts: snow. Cocaine in Washington Heights. More trouble in paradise this morning," he sighed.

"No. I'm shocked. A tenement in New York City awash in

illicit drugs? Batman—to Gotham." Her mocking made him laugh.

"C'mon, let's get out of here before someone realizes I'm off the phone and decides to call me just to punish me for my multitudinous sins of the past thirty-nine years."

"Ready, Robin? To the Batmobile," he announced, playful again. The phone rang … again. He looked at the phone, he looked at Ellie, and they groaned in unison and walked away.

****

After satiating themselves on fresh shrimp and crab cakes at The Crabby Shanty, a nearby family seafood dive, they returned reluctantly to the office. "Back into the slavehold," as Ellie put it sarcastically. As expected, Peller's message light blinked, indicating calls on his voice mail. Standing up at his desk to try to digest the greasy lunch, he picked up the phone. This time, only three messages. The first, of course, was Lana; she would be working late that night, covering a Board of Education meeting. At least this story was on a subject near and dear to her heart. She loved tuning into the perennial debate over schools, and once in a while, she would attend a meeting wearing her "mother" hat if the subject was one meriting her input. Otherwise, her journalistic creed kept her from joining the fray. Second, Vallardo left a message that Peller still owed him a report on the Pollock settlement. "Damn," he thought. "This guy's relentless." Vallardo had been on Peller's back for two weeks about that report, even though Peller knew his boss didn't actually need it until the end of the month. Well, a few days more wouldn't kill him. He had other things to think about at the moment, a fact of which Vallardo was well aware, since he had assigned Peller three new cases this month, in addition to the ongoing Assad discussions and the back burner Epstein negotiations. The third message was a bit more cryptic. Chris Boyer wanted to bring him up to date. Something about a new wrinkle in Angel Sanchez's defense. Peller dialed Chris up immediately.

"Louis, she'll get off light on the arson charge: first offense. The judge will consider the fact that the landlord was screwing her in a number of ways. Look at the precedent these days—I mean, for attempted rape, she practically could have murdered Epstein and gotten away with it. Compared to Lorena Bobbitt, her sad little fire looks like child's play. And frankly, despite the publicity after the fire and her rather brazen behavior in front of the cameras, the evidence against her on solicitation is pretty weak. I think we can come to some agreement with the DA's office to reduce or even drop the charge before it reaches court."

"Thanks, Chris. That's good news. Best I've had all week, in fact."

"But that's not why I'm calling. Remember when you came to see me, you mentioned someone named Assad, a borrower you'd been assigned to negotiate a deal with?"

"Yeah, of course. I'm trying to deal with the guy now. A pretty slick character, if you know the type."

"No, I don't, but it would appear that Angel Sanchez might. She told me she felt she owed you a warning about him. Something about Assad and Epstein both being in bed together … with her."

Angel? In bed with Assad? And Epstein? What could Angel know about Assad? How was Epstein involved? And how could Angel know that Peller cared?

"What's she know about Assad being in bed with anyone?"

"I haven't asked her," Chris responded tartly. "It's not germane to our case."

"Well, ask her, then," Peller commanded.

"I beg your pardon, Mr. Peller," Chris responded sarcastically, offended at his imperious tone, "but I wasn't aware you were paying a retainer for my services."

Chris Boyer could sure be one heck of a hard-nosed attorney. But, supposed Peller, maybe that's what people paid her for.

"I'm sorry, Chris," Peller apologized, changing his tone. "It's just that you took me by surprise. I would love to know what aces she's holding, this Angel," Peller continued, perplexed.

"I'm sure I don't have a clue, Louis," Chris answered, only slightly appeased by his conciliatory tone.

Recognizing how much he was imposing on Chris, Peller made a note to himself to send her a big bouquet of flowers. And a box of chocolates for what he was about to ask.

"Chris, one last favor—for Paul," began Peller. "Please see if you can get anything out of her. Please?"

Chris Boyer sighed. Paul had warned her about Peller and his favors. But she knew what persistence meant: the guy wouldn't get off her back until she gave him something. "Well, okay, Louis. I'll try. Are you planning to come up here anytime soon?"

"I'm sure I'll be in New York soon," he responded.

"Stop by when you can. I'll approach Angel in the meantime. But this is the last favor, Louis Peller," she said with finality.

"Hell to pay," Peller muttered. "Well, thanks for calling Chris … I think." With that, Peller hung up the phone and rocked back on his heels, trying to work this latest odd-shaped piece into the big puzzle before him.

First, Marguerita's scoop on Carlos dealing coke from the his apartment. Why not? Maybe this would be the next twist in the mayor's "legalize drugs" campaign: "Get drugs off the street; let your super do the dealing." Anyway, that might explain the incense burning in Carlos's creepy apartment. Peller wondered morosely how many tenants there were clients of De Leon Ventures. It would figure that this offbeat, jovial young man delved into weirder things than the native crafts of Hispaniola. Sending money home every week to support his poor mother and brothers required cash from somewhere, and Peller knew Carlos wasn't exactly well remunerated for running Assad's place. Still, this kind of information was hardly relevant to Peller's discussions with Assad. "My job," Peller reminded himself for the umpteenth time, as if reciting the Boy Scout pledge, "is to get Assad to pay off his loan and get Amie Mae out of this building."

But this latest intelligence from Angel; she knew Assad. *In the biblical sense?* he wondered. Not knowing her real motives, it was hard to know just what to believe. Willie Johnson's buzz about Epstein and her was just about as much as Peller could handle. What if Assad had also crossed Angel's path? That path was probably littered with men's bodies. If she really ran a prostitution ring, he wouldn't put it past her to have her finger on the city's rich and powerful. He remembered those come-hither reddish-brown eyes.

The damned phone: one ring. It had to be someone at Amie calling. Outside calls rang twice.

"This is Louis," he answered.

"Louis, it's Joe. I've gotta see you this afternoon, in my office. Can you meet at three thirty?"

"I'm waiting for a borrower to call me back about three," Peller said, looking at his watch. It was two twenty-eight. "I think we'll be done before that. Listen, Joe, if it's about that report …"

"That's part of it. Just make sure you're here." His tone was serious. "There are a few things I want to discuss with you."

Peller sighed. Now he would be in trouble for turning in a late report and who knew what else. He briefly imagined standing in front of his boss's desk, hearing Vallardo's Rule #317: "You know about procedures, Lou? It's all spelled out in the rule book. Take the time to read it." It was all so juvenile. Well, he'd play by Vallardo's rules from now on anyway. He couldn't afford to be out of a job.

Peller made his way to Vallardo's office at precisely three thirty. "He can't accuse me of being late." The boss was on the phone standing behind his desk, but he motioned Peller to sit down. For pep talks, Vallardo would step out from behind his fort and sit companionably on the cushiony, tweed couch where Peller was now uncomfortably perched.

"Louis, I've asked you not to get involved in any matters that aren't strictly related to Amie business. Lately, I've been hearing through the rumor mill that you're nosing around Assad's building, asking all sorts of people questions. I do not see how that pertains to our negotiations."

"Joe, I just know there's more to this mystery man than meets the eye. I mean, why is he so anxious to pay off his loan for four times the value of the property? Where's he suddenly getting the money to pay off the loan if, for two years, he said he couldn't even pay on the mortgage? Something about this situation isn't right, and I just intended to check it out. You know I met with his super, Carlos de Leon? He's a very suspicious character himself, always has a seedy group of stragglers hanging around his apartment. Why? He's not doing any maintenance. I checked that out from some reliable sources and—"

Vallardo raised his hand halting his litany. "I really don't buy the conspiracy theory. I just want you to do your job. No one else gets involved with the tenants' problems. How many times I gotta tell you: we are not social workers?"

"But …" Peller began, thinking he might add Marguerita's latest intelligence. Then he caught himself. Best not to get Vallardo involved. "Of course. You're right as usual, Joe. I'll keep my nose out of it."

"Fine. Since you understand the problem now, I'll tell you how I see the solution. You're off the Assad case. I'm assigning it to Bill."

"Worthmore? But surely you wouldn't let someone whose closest brush with Washington Heights is occasionally reading *The New York Times* "Metropolitan" section take over a case as problematic as this one is? Come on, Joe, let me keep it. I promise I'll behave. One more chance?" God, how he hated to beg. But he couldn't give this case to that white-bread aristocrat Worthmore to fuck up, not when he was this close to the deal of the decade.

Vallardo looked thoughtful. Inside he was laughing with

glee. To reduce the pompous Peller to pleading. It was such fun. He'd let him keep the case, couldn't afford not to. There was no one else on his staff who could play hardball like Peller. Not with Assad.

Chapter 13
The Deal

The caller didn't identify himself over the crackling international line. It was about six in the morning Teheran time. "We have a problem." The urgency of the speaker disoriented him; it had been weeks since he'd spoken anything but Farsi. Most Iranians thought the Western tongue was a tool of the infidels, defilers of the Prophet. His business partner here, for example, detested America and shunned all things Western … except capital.

Omar Assad had been awake for hours, negotiating eye-to-eye with this mullah who wanted quicker returns on his investment. Assad needed more time. Investments weren't yielding big profits, he kept explaining. His white-swaddled partner refused to understand. And now this.

Assad rubbed his stubbled chin, thinking quickly, the sting in his eyes reminding him of his need to sleep.

"So kind of you to ring me here," he bluffed into the phone, aware that his partner was scrutinizing every word. "I'm glad to hear things are returning to normal."

"I think the bank is investigating a little deeper than we were led to believe," the caller replied, a coded message to deter the "ears" that might be tapping the line. "San Juan has been contacted and may be on our trail."

"I will take it under advisement, my friend," replied Assad. "Perhaps we can buy something meaningful to send to San Juan." His partner had stooped over the low hammered-tin table to sample his tea.

"I agree. Some flowers perhaps, an aromatic scent."

"And my attorney might be interested in this deal."

"The American woman? What does she know?"

"Russell is quite well versed in my investment strategies and has been most useful in that regard. Meanwhile, send my regards to our friend at the bank. I would hate to miss him again."

"Of course. I will see to it. Adios."

"More tea, Omar?" asked his partner in the Queen's English, an inscrutable emotion in his partner's inscrutable eyes.

As Assad hung up the phone, he detected that penetrating stare with alarm. "I would be honored," he responded in Farsi.

****

It was midway into October when Peller was surprised by a phone call from his "sentimental" borrower. Hard to imagine Omar Assad had been away so long. Of course, for a week or so, Peller had really believed Vallardo had tossed him off the case. Vallardo even set up a meeting for Peller to brief Bill Worthmore on the background and turn over his case files. By the time Peller finally called the bluff, he'd already detached himself emotionally from the *Sturm und Drang* of Omar Assad. In any case, he vowed to let it go.

In the meantime, he was having fun: playing a weekly tennis match with a neighbor, coaching Allie's soccer team, foiling plans for his surprise fortieth birthday party by calling all the guests to invite them himself ("Don't tell me, it's a surprise."), taking Alex hiking up in the Shenandoah's. He even researched Lana's suggestion for a little weekend trek, just the two of them, borrowing a book on historic inns from their newlywed neighbors, Bruce and Pam, who were footloose and fancy free. They advised him on a few of their favorite retreats in the Shenandoah's. Characteristically, Peller ignored their advice and settled on a visit to the Catskills, a place he felt he ought to show Lana for the unembarrassed "Jewishness" of it all: the Concord, with its kosher cuisine of matzo balls, ersatz chopped liver, and pot roast, all equally tasteless, boiled to blandness, and prepared without seasonings for those on special diets, and the characters who frequented the place, *meshuganas* like his borrowers, providing local color. Besides, he could write the whole thing off as a business expense, "research" on the culture of his borrowers. Living in comfortable, assimilated Maryland and working in Virginia with country gentry, it was difficult to get a handle on the cultural variations at play in his dealings with borrowers. Lana, who had grown up in the Midwest, could never even remotely imagine life and leisure in the Catskills. It would be a positive learning experience for both of them, he justified.

He planned to surprise Lana by kidnapping her later in the month for their tenth anniversary. She would revel in the retreat he envisioned: russet leaves falling in lazy luxury at the resort, a throwback to the early 1900s, an age of innocence for a closed society of Jewish families from New York and New Jersey who could summer with their closest friends and relatives.

These days, Jewish singles and couples of a certain age danced the foxtrot in the superstore-size ballroom, and aging yentas made matches for their friends' divorced grandchildren. Tennis for the geriatric set, and bingo for grandmothers and their toddler grandchildren went hand in hand. There were even *shabbos* services Friday night, and hundreds of Jewish families, assimilated and otherwise, assumed their place in the circle of faith. The Concord was no Greenbriar, but it offered a slice of Jewish life that Peller wanted to introduce to Lana. Yes, they would really go this time, he promised himself. Soon.

Autumn cycled in lazily on its long slope toward winter,

carrying with it a crisp, invigorating respite, with apple picking and hayrides reserved for country weekends with the kids. Until this one velvety voice carried calamity crashing back.

"What's your decision, Mr. Peller? Have you reconsidered?"

"I'm afraid we're firm, Mr. Assad. Unless, that is, you have some new terms to offer?"

"I just might be able to sweeten the pot at that, Mr. Peller. Can we take up the matter next time you're in New York?"

Peller pondered the question. "I do plan to come up next Tuesday."

"Good, then it's settled. Shall we say, ten o'clock? Your offices?"

Peller felt Assad's coercive charm pulling him, curiosity melting his resolve. What the heck, he thought. It's worth talking to the guy. Any way you looked at it, he had nothing to lose and an awful lot to gain.

"You're on. Ten o'clock on the forty-eighth floor at Amie Mae, Mr. Assad. I'll see you then." Let the chips fall where they may, he challenged silently.

"I think you may like what I have to show you. I know you won't be sorry, Mr. Peller." Assad rang off.

Peller's heart resumed pumping after a month of concerted relaxation. This could be the deal of the decade: eight hundred thousand dollars cash for a property worth one fourth that amount. Royal flush, jokers wild.

The rest of the week returned to its old pace, preparing for these new negotiations. Peller wanted to make sure he was prepared for this meeting: no surprises. There was suddenly a relentless staccato to his days. Any minute not on the phone, he spent with the lawyers and his bosses, hammering out every eventuality that Assad might dream up. It was clear, at this stage, that all parties were ready to make a deal. Plans left some leeway for Peller to negotiate a payoff schedule not to exceed six months, as long as there were hard-and-fast payment dates and a consent to receivership in the event of a late payment. He called Steve

Shapiro to make sure the attorney would be in the office Tuesday, just in case Peller had any last minute conferring to do during the negotiations.

As Peller boarded the shuttle under a cool, cloud-streaked, gray-and-white sky that late October day, he was more than a little nervous. After all, this could be one of the most profitable payoffs in Amie Mae history. This time, he didn't want Assad to weasel his way out of a commitment.

It was windy and unseasonably cold that morning in New York, and by force of habit, Peller craved a large, hot cup of fresh-brewed coffee en route. No such luck today. He rubbed his hands together to warm them. Whether they felt clammy from nerves or the cold, he couldn't tell. His stomach growled. He hadn't had time to grab any breakfast before leaving the house. He wished he'd instructed Tommy to carry out breakfast. But today, Tommy Romano would waste no time stopping for bagels or selecting stimulating detours past salacious street shows.

They headed straight for the office, from La Guardia via the Triborough and down FDR Drive, cutting across on 53rd Street. The view of the East River from the FDR inspired Peller: energetic joggers and bikers pumping down the path along the river, passing spike after spike of iron-gated trail, leaves turning hues of gold and orange and red, and just beyond them, the river itself, silvery smooth out to the sun-peaked white caps, churned from the wake of the slow-moving barges and tugs. Two helicopters landed on pads between the drive and the river. The view energized him. Typical of New York, people drove through this spectacle in a trance, insulated from each other and the sights and sounds of Manhattan, preoccupied with their personal woes. Their expressions reminded Peller of the walking dead. It was safer to look dead than alive in the city.

Tommy pulled up to the cold, imposing stone-and-glass-faced edifice on Madison Avenue at precisely nine forty-five. "When do you need me next, chief?" asked the driver.

"With any luck, I'll be done with this deal by noon. I may

meet with someone downtown afterward, depending. Then I'll be ready to turn back around and go home. I don't intend to spend any more time in town today than I have to."

"Ain't no place like home," Tommy quipped. "I'll come up to getcha 'round twelve. Break a leg, Louie." The driver darted out into the Madison Avenue snarl.

Peller sped upstairs. "Good morning, Julie," he said crisply, summoning a stiff, nervous smile, as much for himself as for the receptionist. "Anyone here yet?" he asked, nodding toward the conference room.

"Nobody heah but us chickens. And Shapiro, of cou'se. He's waitin' fa you in his awffice." Julie's New York accent was pronounced.

Peller noticed that Julie had donned a form-fitting, fire-engine-red knit minidress. Red, three-inch heels accentuated her stubby legs. She wore a touch more makeup than usual, and her pouting lips were also painted red. Her long hair was swept back in a French braid. She smelled of gardenias.

"Thanks, Jules," he smiled, genuinely this time. "Lookin' gorgeous today."

She gave him a withering look. "Not fa you, sweetheart."

Peller feigned disappointment.

"You want me to send Omar in when he gets here?"

"Yeah, I'll wait in the conference room." Peller walked back into the suite of offices. Vicki was sitting in Steve's office when Peller looked in. The two attorneys had been speculating over how the deal would go. "My, don't *we* look like the cats who just swallowed the canary," Peller quipped. "You guys gossiping about me, again?"

"Would we really do such a thing, Louis?" Steve demanded. "Come on. There are many more interesting things to talk about."

Vicki got up. "Gentlemen, I'll leave you to your strategy session before Assad the Iranian snake shows up. I myself have work to do," she grinned. "Good luck, boys."

Peller looked at his watch. Almost ten. He would have to settle himself in the conference room right away. "Sorry, can't stay to chat. I must prepare for my meeting with destiny." Those last words, uttered in jest, took on the ponderous weight of Moses on Mount Sinai as Peller walked solemnly out of Steve's office. Steve tagged along, pretending to be helpful.

"Make sure you get him into the corner, then keep punching away. First, a quick, one-two punch. Then, a verbal cross, followed by a hard right. Keep going for the head, Lou. That's what it takes. And if you can't corner him, call me. I'll distract him for you. Together, the mighty workout duo will wear down Sheik Assad." Steve assumed a fighter's stance, dancing around, fists clenched close to his face, looking like a high-strung monkey.

Peller laughed nervously.

"Remember to protect your face," Steve winked.

Peller staked out his place at the head of the long table. He deliberately spread out his papers. Remembering how Assad had set out his eelskin briefcase to establish his space, Peller opened his heavy, camel-colored, worn leather portfolio and pushed it toward the center of the table. He may not be rich, but he had presence, mused the workout *artiste*.

He looked at his watch: 10:05. Good, he was all set.

He picked up the phone and pushed the intercom to the front desk. "Is he here yet, Julie?" Peller asked.

"No, Louis. You bet I'll bring him right back though. Want some cawffee fa your meeting?"

"Great idea, Jules. Would you mind?"

"Whatsa matta wit' you? Your arms don't work so good today?" asked Julie. "Making cawffee for the boss went out with dictation."

"Just this once, Julie?" he pleaded. She gave a grunt. "You're fantastic. Thanks." Peller sat back down to review his papers.

Julie wobbled in on her too-high heels five minutes later to fix up the Mr. Coffee. "Look, Louis, I'm not pourin' out," she said, setting down two Amie Mae mugs, sweetener, and stirrers.

"Think you can handle it from here?" she asked, pouring a premeasured packet of grounds into the brown plastic basket.

"I can handle it, Ms. Smartass."

She laughed her screeching, high-pitched squeal, chalk on a blackboard.

Peller completed his review of the file for the last time and snuck the first cup of coffee as the machine strained the last drips into the pot. Mmmm, caffeine sharpened the mind. He gratefully quaffed the black brew; the perfect pick-me-up, he thought. Peller looked down again at his watch: ten twenty-one. Although borrowers were frequently tardy to meetings, Peller took this tardiness as an ominous sign. He had a bad feeling in his gut about this Assad. Maybe now the guy had second thoughts about his original offer.

He rose and began pacing along the back of the conference room, making tracks in front of the table where Julie had set up the coffee maker, cups, napkins, and other niceties for conducting his meeting. The long, narrow room was a sophisticated mahogany-paneled, Carrera-marbled space designed to impress its occupants as the embodiment of success. It featured state of the art technology, discreet, recessed, dimmable lighting, and a beveled wood cabinet filled with audio/visual gear to dazzle the big guys on Wall Street. Still, the room had a cramped feel to it. No windows. Oversized, formal chairs lined up like stuffed soldiers around the table. Even the sumptuous carpet, a tapestry of red roses on a bed of forest green, crowded the room. A narrow edge of dark, stained hardwood floor framed the rug. With Peller's nerves on edge, he felt the room overpowering him. He drained his coffee dry and poured a refill. Again, he picked up the phone. "Steve. Peller here. Assad hasn't shown. Think he's standing me up?"

"Don't lose your cool yet, Louis," Steve said calmly. "Could be the traffic. Or it could be the sheik is trying to get you ruffled. In any case, calm is the key."

"He's not a sheik, you idiot. And if you called him that, he'd probably kill you. The Iranians despise the Arabs." Peller sat down again. Keep calm. How should he do that? If he looked at these papers anymore, he would forget what was in them. Never the master of patience, Peller stood up and began to pace again. Without thinking about what he was doing, he emptied his cup a third time. His nerves were getting a little more frayed. He waited. And watched. And paced. Now ten twenty-eight. The phone rang. Peller jumped out of his skin.

"What is it?"

"Mr. Peller, Mr. Assad is here to see you." Julie's voice took on those honey-sweet tones she reserved for the truly rich, the truly famous, or the truly gorgeous.

Her familiar, unctuous inflections broke his tension momentarily. Despite Peller's anger at being kept waiting by his high-and-mighty borrower, despite the trick the caffeine was playing on his nerves, Peller had to laugh. "You're a piece of work, you know that, Julie? Show him in please."

Julie, beaming her sweetest smile, escorted the elegant Assad into the room with unusual reserve, for her. The two men shook hands, while Julie made a great fuss about the emptied coffee pot.

Peller asked his visitor to sit down and prepared to begin when, to his surprise, Omar Assad put up a well-manicured hand to stop him as he looked toward the door of the conference room. On cue, in swept a stunning woman with thick waves of black hair and full red lips. "Mr. Peller, I'd like you to meet my attorney, Leslie Russell." Assad made the introduction as if her arrival was expected.

Peller was startled. She moved like a dancer, fluid in her azure swing coat, unbuttoned to reveal a tailored, cream-colored blouse, a short, straight, cream linen skirt, and the loveliest, longest legs Peller had ever seen. The woman extended her hand in a firm, businesslike clasp. Peller hovered at arm's length, unsure of what her presence portended.

Although he had never met her, Peller was acquainted with

the indomitable Leslie Russell's reputation as a tough, take-no-prisoners New York trial attorney. He hadn't realized she handled real estate law too. He was caught by surprise. Well Peller, for one, was determined that he wouldn't let himself be taken in by smooth talk and the granite-chiseled face of a Greek goddess. He decided immediately on his tactics: ignore the diversion and plow full-furrow ahead. Peller nodded briefly as Assad explained that Ms. Russell would be representing him in this negotiation. Peller briefly spelled out the company's position: payment-in-full, cash, to the tune of eight hundred thousand dollars, due immediately. In exchange, Amie would release Assad from any personal recourse and discharge the note and mortgage. Assad listened, glancing at his attorney for her take on the subject. Russell had no visible reaction but read quickly through the draft agreement penning notes in the margins.

How anyone could detect holes in this proposal was beyond Peller. The beauty of this plan was its simplicity: pay Amie Mae eight hundred thousand dollars, and take title to the property, free of Amie's first lien. As straightforward as they come. As Peller finished his presentation, he smiled tepidly and looked around the room to gauge the response. He was met with Assad's preoccupied silence. Russell was tapping her Mont Blanc pen absently on the table. Otherwise, the room was still.

A long moment passed. Peller wondered whether to break the hush but forced himself to remain silent. He tried to peek at his watch. It was close to eleven thirty. He wondered irrelevantly whether Tommy had returned. He nervously tapped his foot under the table, knowing the game they must be playing. In the Middle East, to do business, one must have patience. The game was to see who could wait the longest. Peller imagined a clock ticking its inexorable passage, hearing his heartbeat thundering in his ears.

The good lawyer, Russell, was writing something again, something Peller couldn't read upside down from across the conference table, and Assad seemed to be thumbing through the agreement for the fifth time. Peller could wait.

Suddenly, without his conscious knowledge, Peller's mouth opened, and he heard words flowing out of it. "Mr. Assad, I think it's time to get our house in order. Can we work together on this, or should I proceed with the foreclosure?"

"Mr. Peller, I thought I was here to make a proposal to you," Assad interjected finally. In his nervousness, Peller had almost forgotten that the borrower had, indeed, called the meeting.

Peller hemmed, wondering what to do next.

Russell looked up sharply from her note taking, scrutinizing Peller. "If you don't mind, Mr. Peller, I would like to confer with my client privately." Her voice was low and throaty. Her brilliant black eyes had assumed a shiny glaze that was not altogether pleasant.

Peller, who had taken an immediate dislike to this brazen attorney, stole out of the conference room none too graciously. He could feel Assad and Russell awaiting his retreat as he pushed through the door. He closed it discreetly.

Embarrassed, Peller slumped over to Steve's hideout to caucus. "You were right about his being a pugnacious bastard, Steve. Assad's trying to bluff on this one. Did you notice, he even brought in Leslie Russell to represent him? If Assad is going to outflank me, then I'm going to harden my position," Peller exclaimed.

"Leslie Russell? You mean the trial lawyer?" asked Steve.

Peller nodded, frowning.

"Ohhh—that may be bad news. We'd better start drafting the foreclosure documents and receivership order just in case," noted Amie Mae's attorney with foreboding, rolling up his sleeves. "I'll talk to the home office while you're meeting with them." Steve fished around on his desk for a cigarette, gathering his papers and his thoughts as Peller simply stared out the window.

"C'mon, Louis, don't come unglued," urged his comrade. "Assad's merely pulled a diversionary tactic on you, that's all. You still have the upper hand, because we've thought out this deal every which way. Even Leslie Russell will have to admit you're prepared for them. Now buck up, partner. I think I hear the enemy ready to outline the terms of their surrender." Indeed, the two conferees were exiting the conference room.

Steve and Peller both rose as Assad and Russell walked into the office. Again, Peller was struck by the force of Leslie Russell's presence, the simple grandeur of her habile poise. Omar Assad motioned for Steve to remain, then sat down at the small round table across from Steve's desk. The two attorneys and the workout specialist remained standing.

"Mr. Peller," Assad began, "my attorney and I have conferred, and we agree that we ought to be able to work with you immediately to bring our negotiation to the best conclusion. I have asked Ms. Russell to work with you on details. Your proposal is not satisfactory. I don't have eight hundred thousand dollars on hand to pay you back all at once." He glanced at Leslie Russell, whose expression was Sphinx-like.

Assad stood up slowly. "We'll be in touch," he said, smiling discreetly. Then the borrower looked at each of them in turn, his Mediterranean eyes penetrating their thoughts, as if he could see into their heads. He hesitated, awaiting their response.

Steve and Peller glanced at each other in undisguised shock. They hadn't anticipated any of this, not Assad's long-delayed arrival, not the appearance of his lawyer, not his abdicating control of the negotiations. After all, Omar Assad was renowned for his clever negotiating skills and the pride he took in manipulating his opponents like marionettes. What could this stall tactic forebode?

Seeing his adversaries off balance, Assad apparently decided to press his advantage. He started for the door, graciously thanking Russell for her advice and noting silently that the Amie duo was, for once, at a loss for words. He passed into the hallway and marched toward the reception area, followed by Leslie Russell. Steve and Peller, off-guard as they were, brought up the rear.

Completely absorbed in this improvised recessional, it slowly dawned on Peller that he had forfeited his advantage. Assad now held Peller in check. Out of the corner of his eye, Peller could see Julie running in circles to help, in a swoon over Assad and, at the same time, casting evil glances at Russell.

Russell, adieux to her client completed, turned her full attention to Peller.

"Mr. Peller, I look forward to working with you. Soon. My client is in serious financial trouble, but he *will not* lose this building. He has some interested investors who may be able to participate, but Omar needs time to bring them up to speed on the property. In the meantime, there are some changes to your proposal that we would like you to consider. I'll be talking to you about them." She turned, preparing to leave. Then she paused and looked back at Peller.

"That does suit you?" she asked in peremptory fashion, holding Peller's warm brown eyes in lock with her marble black eyes.

He nodded, speechless.

"Here's my card," she concluded haughtily. She scrawled something on the back, then handed him the card, looking up suddenly with a playful sparkle in her eye. "Give me a call soon. Maybe next time you're in New York, I might take you to lunch. We can finalize this deal."

Before Peller had time to respond, she waltzed grandly out the door.

Again, Steve and Peller exchanged dismayed glances. Despite their thorough planning, no one had expected to emerge from the day's meeting with nothing, not even a firm date for a follow-up. Peller glanced at Russell's card. Leslie Russell, attorney-at-law, it said. Strawbridge, Watts, Barker, and Harleiter, one of the most prestigious firms in New York. Turning it over, he noticed she had scrawled another phone number with the notation, "Call me at home. I have news that might interest you." What the hell?

He was completely done in by the hit-and-run maneuver Assad had sprung on him. It was only twelve fifteen, but to Peller, it felt late. He'd set himself up to close this deal today. Instead, he felt defeat. Knowing he couldn't sustain Assad's cat and mouse game, Peller instructed Steve to file a motion to put a receiver in the building and proceed with foreclosure. Leslie Russell be damned.

"Louis," admonished Steve, "whatever happened to the bold crusader, that champion of truth and goodness?" Steve was a dragon slayer par excellence. "You're not gonna let a little delaying tactic deter you, are you?"

"Steve, I'm worn out. I've spent at least fifty hours jawboning this guy, we've been working on the details of a quick payoff for months, and we're no closer now than we were in the beginning. I give up."

Steve sighed. "Listen, Louis. I hate to see you admit defeat. And to a sleaze ball like Omar Assad. Sometimes you have to slacken the reins a little to drive the horse; don't you know that? Tell you what I'm gonna do. I plan to come to Washington next Monday anyway, to meet with a law firm that wants Amie's business. Another dog and pony show. Anyway, let's sleep on this over the weekend. We'll get together late Monday and see if we can develop a strategy to get Assad to fish or cut bait. Let's go for the jugular and get it over with. And never mind about Leslie Russell. I can handle her."

Peller did not look relieved. "I don't know what to think anymore, Steve. I want to go home." He thought about the quiet balm of his own house, his affectionate kids, his loyal schnauzer … and Lana. He suddenly wanted to pour his heart out to her, for her to make it all better. "I'll check in with you Monday," he told Steve grimly.

Peller had planned to get together with Chris Boyer to talk about Angel's "intelligence." But now, well, there was no sense in it. His stomach ached from disappointment. That, along with the headaches, the tension, the dreams, maybe he ought to undergo a physical. It had been five or six years since his last one, and he was fast-approaching forty.

Chapter 14
New Wrinkles

Louis Peller took a few days off to decompress. The long weekend passed slowly. Physically, he was present and accounted for at all those family activities, ballet recitals, birthday parties, and religious schools that passed for leisure time in the lives of baby boom parents. Mentally, he was hundreds of miles away in New York, replaying Tuesday's encounter with Assad. He agonized. What's gonna bring this guy to the closing table cash in hand? He had to make it work. Driving to work bright and early on Monday, he set out on a new strategy: get Assad.

Peller deliberately tapped out his to-do list on the computer:

1. Verify probability of Assad filing for bankruptcy protection.
2. Research Assad's other assets.
3. Brief Vallardo on meeting with Assad and Russell.
4. Check NYC agencies for record or registration of a "De Leon Ventures."
5. Ask Tommy to note any suspicious activity at the building on West 158th Street.

To Peller, there was nothing as satisfying as laying out the day's plan, except, perhaps, checking off those activities that he had successfully completed. Of course, Peller had experienced far too many of those other days recently, the days where nothing ever got crossed off and the list kept on growing. But he decided those days of frustration were over. He promised himself solemnly that his luck would change.

He got on the horn. "Steve, it's Louis. Start the foreclosure on West 158th. We can discuss it further when we meet. I'll treat you to lunch."

"What's the occasion, oh frugal one?" Steve mocked. He was hiding out in the luxurious offices of the Amie legal department at headquarters for the day.

"It's the new me—true only to the bottom line but generous to a fault. Anyway, I owe you."

Steve laughed. "I'll believe it when I see it. Anyway, I'll come to your cube after this presentation. Another high-power legal eager beaver."

"There's no place to work in my 'fat man's misery.' See if you can get an office or conference room in legal. Besides, we'll also need computer access to some databases for an asset search. I'll come to you," Peller commanded.

Well, that was easy, Peller thought. Time for some research that would allow Peller to move the wrecking ball over the Assad empire. He speed dialed Tommy Romano at home.

"Tommy, I know it's not in the job description, but I've got a very important assignment for you."

"Louie, get a life. I'm at home. Today's my day off—the one day of the week I can spend wid'da pigeons. I ain't been able to race 'em in over a week, and I gotta keep at it regular, or they won't be in top form. I got some serious money riding on this with my buddy next door. And I promised my ma I'd go ovah to spend some time wid her. 'I ain't raised my son right,' she complains. I don't need that guilt. I'm not even Jewish, but I gotta listen to the 'Jewish motheh' thing, 'cause Italian mamas are pretty good at guilt too. Anyway, I gotta go see he' today."

"Tommy, take the day; it's yours. But I need you to spend

some time at the Washington Heights building, the one on West 158th. Just record who's going in, who's coming out, that kind of thing. You know, anything out of the ordinary, you tell me." Peller had to try the soft sell. Tommy was too stubborn to buy into any other approach.

"Lou, I like you, man, but you're crazy. I hate that place. I been shot at. I been kicked around theah. And I don't take to that kind of attitude in the 'hood.' Those kids are lunatics. I ain't spending time theah—not fa you, not fa nobody. Get y'self anotheh watchdog. I'm busy with my pigeons, an' I'm stayin' right here to race 'em." Tommy was making noises that the conversation was at an end.

"Tommy, don't hang up yet. Okay. On the up-and-up." *Think fast, Peller.* "This is a very important project to the company. Remember how I told you last Tuesday that Assad is putting a wrench in this deal? Brought in a heavy-hitting attorney? It's costing the company time—and money, big money. It's so critical that this deal be brought to a conclusion soon that Derek's okayed a special 20 percent bonus for you while you're on assignment for me. Just keep track of the number of hours you spend in Washington Heights, send me an invoice, and I'll get the check cut for you pronto."

You have to take on the overtime, big dumb mutt, Peller prayed, *I need you.* Then, hearing Tommy considering the offer on the other end, he had a flash of anxiety: *how the hell am I gonna get a goddamn bonus approved?* Amie Mae would never go for that expense.

Well, he'd pay for it out of his own pocket if he had to. This job just had to get done. Besides, if he bagged the kind of shark he had his eye on, Tommy's overtime would seem like loose change.

"Well, I d'know, Louie." Tommy was wavering. "How long do you need me?"

"It'll be a couple weeks at most, enough time to get the scoop on this guy Assad screwing everyone over. That's all I need. If it takes less than that, you'll be off sooner, you've got my word on it. And listen, I think I can get you a coupla good tickets to the Knicks, besides." Tommy Romano was an incurable basketball fanatic, as only New Yorkers could be. He and Peller shared a love for hoops, although college was more Peller's sport.

"Okay, okay. I'll give it a shot. But remembeh, you owe me. I don' let my chits off easy," warned Tommy.

"My word is my bond, Tom," Peller replied. "I won't let you down, man." He hung up, relieved. Tommy Romano would be on the watch to check out what might be coming down in Washington Heights. Louis Peller wouldn't be outmaneuvered by the likes of Omar Assad and Leslie Russell again.

"Okay," he thought aloud. "What's next?" Peller was really ticking now. He called Mildred in Vallardo's office to set up a time to brief his boss on the Tuesday meeting with Assad. Earliest they could meet would be Wednesday afternoon. Well, that suited Peller just fine. He would have some more time to prepare the story for his boss's ears. Wait until Vallardo heard about Leslie Russell horning in on Peller's act. He'd blow a fuse.

In the meantime, he could plow ahead with his program to bring Assad around. Maybe he could even confirm Marguerita's suspicions about Carlos, one way or another, and make sure he got her some assistance.

And there were still unanswered questions to be resolved. Just how deep was Assad? Did Assad own other properties that he had not revealed? How much cash did he really have available for this deal? Did he have partners? Who were they?

Peller decided to begin the process of researching real estate apartment transactions for New York City from 1986 through 1992. He would need help on that one. It could take a squadron of lawyers weeks to comb through the city's land records and sort through the maze of partnerships and corporations involved in those transactions. He would have to solicit Steve's help and trust him to take it seriously. Maybe Vicki could pitch in too, especially if Peller held out the temptation of litigation to her;

she would love to see some courtroom action, he knew. Assad's case offered just the right kind of temptation to propel a paper-pushing would-be litigator like Vicki to go the distance.

Peller was also curious to learn what Carlos de Leon was hiding. What if the evidence Marguerita had observed boded more than suspicion: long lines at his door, day and night, cocaine stashed in the apartment. If Assad only knew what his super was dishing out. But wait, what if Assad did know? That possibility slapped Peller with such a jolt that, inadvertently, he raised his hand to rub the sting away.

He picked up the phone again, this time to call Chris Boyer. He needed to see her, and maybe Angel, too. What *was* Angel's bombshell? Did she really have something to do with Assad? Could Assad and Epstein really be partners? What a stinging nest of hornets.

What if Angel … what if Bud … what if Assad? No. He couldn't speculate. Such prospects stunned even Louis Peller.

Chapter 15
Sundaes and Sympathies

Steve and Peller dropped in at Clyde's, a fern bar for the middle aged in Tyson's Corner, which, as it happened, was definitely short on live ferns (silk being the greenery of choice at this establishment), for a bite. But the food was decent, and the surroundings were comfortable, all brass and brick and booths. The place looked shopworn but homey. Etched glass windows evoked Washington landmarks, and scuffed wood floors marked innumerable drinkers whetting their whistles of an evening. There was even a smoking section, one of Steve's prerequisites for fine dining. Not too many Amie Mae people patronized the place, so they could speak freely.

"There was this *look* on Leslie Russell's face when she handed you her card, Louis: 'Take me, I'm yours.' You lucky S.O.B." Steve inhaled his bacon cheeseburger in that panicky way that children who are very hungry will devour anything that doesn't moo. Steve's perennial lack of female companionship stoked his hunger, deduced Peller sympathetically, watching his lunch companion's primitive, cannibalistic performance, repelled yet fascinated. Peller avoided red meat out of principle and trepidation over the three Cs: chemicals, cholesterol, and carcinogens. Peller stared disinterestedly at his own tuna on toasted cardboard. To make matters worse, they were sitting in the smoking section to accommodate Steve's dirty little habit, and breathing in the smoky air made Peller's throat bristly. His appetite seemed to vanish.

"Anyway, I don't know why she couldn't talk to me. After all, I am better looking than you and, God knows, very eligible," Steve continued, unaware of his lapse in table manners as he licked his greasy lips.

"I don't know, Steve. I can't see what you find so attractive about her. She's nothing to write home about."

"Louis, you don't know this woman like I do. I mean, I don't really know her like I'd want to either. She's not only sexy as hell, but she has negotiated some of the shrewdest and most complicated business deals in New York. I mean, she represents a bunch of white collar moguls—a Boesky-esque clientele—and as I hear it, when she's in front of a jury, she can paint these guys as some kinda saints led astray by temptation. Fascinating psychology. It wins. And afterward, on television. The way she uses the medium is incredible. She's made for TV. She holds a news conference, and the camera just eats her up. Very subtle, very restrained. But it's her performance that really knocks 'em dead. She won't take any credit for winning, humble as pie. She insists these cases win themselves on the merit. 'Anyone could have done it,' she mugs for the cameras. But if you notice that certain glint in her eye, you know … she's in this game for her pound of flesh. No one should ever underestimate Leslie Russell. No sir."

"Steve, I think you've been single too long. If she's as cunning as you say, how can she carry off the sweet *ingenue* routine she showed us the other day with Assad?" Steve's description was at odds with the Leslie Russell Peller had met, although, of course, he always suspected appearances and presumed Russell was not what she seemed. Steve had suddenly piqued Peller's interest.

Peller, champion of the Socratic method, was always analyzing, curious to find logic in human behavior.

Steve laughed. "I hear she studied acting in New York. They say she was in class with star pupil and man about Europe, Roberto Valencio. She had him eating out of her hand. Anyway, rumor has it she decided there was no money in starving off Broadway while she waited to be discovered, so she went into trial law, the next best thing to Broadway. And a helluva lot more lucrative. And what an act she brings to the courtroom. Then she saw the big bucks being made in real estate and changed her venue. What a woman."

Steve was clearly starstruck, thought Peller in dismay. Peller almost laughed aloud at his friend, just to wake him to his folly. Steve's starry-eyed predisposition would not help Amie Mae in its negotiations. Peller would have to make sure Steve Shapiro was far away from any discussions with Leslie Russell about Assad's property, he recognized as he watched his pal making a fool of himself. Too bad Peller had to pop his balloon. Steve's unabashed crush was pretty amusing.

The conversation hit a momentary lull while the waitress cleared off their table, and Steve ordered a hot fudge sundae with extra whipped cream and a bunch of those juicy maraschino cherries that, years ago, the manufacturers had loaded with cancerous red dye. Peller swallowed at his friend's gluttony, undoubtedly brought on by an excess of male hormones; at least, that's what Lana would say.

"Listen, pal. Leslie Russell or no, we've got to get cracking on Assad. I want to pursue a two-pronged strategy with him. I'll keep the negotiations going in good faith, and I want you to get a receiver in the building ASAP. And move ahead on the foreclosure. Keep the pressure on. As soon as he hears that a receiver is taking possession of his property, he'll go ballistic. If he wants to hold on, he'll have to stop jerking us around and come up with the cash."

As Peller talked, he stared Steve straight in the eye, as if to say, "Pay attention now, my friend. It'll be your hide if you don't help me seal this deal." Steve had never before seen Peller so calculating.

"Hey, this is just a workout, Louis. Ease up, huh?" Steve said, lighting up over coffee. "Don't get so revved up."

"Just a workout? Steve, don't you see that we could be heroes if we play our cards right here? I don't want to put a receiver in that building. I don't want to foreclose on old Omar. Amie Mae doesn't need that Washington Heights disaster in its inventory. We want out of this property and all that liability, right? We want cash. And I'm going to get it. This company's gonna sing our praises from here to the Bronk's Farm if we manage to sell this turkey."

Sensing Peller the crusader stepping up on his soapbox yet again, Steve attempted an end run.

"Yeah, yeah, I know. We have to make sure the poor have places to live in New York. You've sung me this chorus before, remember?"

It was too late. Peller was winding up for an impassioned delivery. "Look, what are we gonna do with another rundown property on our hands? Sell it to another slumlord who'll screw us all over again? Worse yet, what's gonna happen to the Marguerita Fernandezes and the Eva Joneses of this world if we don't keep these buildings in the hands of the Assads and Pollocks and Epsteins? How many times ..."

Closing his eyes in frustration, Steve could imagine Peller speaking at a large political rally on the Fourth of July, stars and stripes flying briskly behind his back, his hand raised in salute, and "God Bless America" playing in the background. He would be the perfect Libertarian candidate for Congress. Just corny enough to command the crowd.

"Bravo. I get the picture, Lou," Steve interrupted impatiently. "We'll do it; don't worry. But I still don't think it's fair you monopolize Russell. How 'bout getting me her home number? She and I should be collaborating on this loan, you know, lawyer to lawyer," Steve finished, barely able to contain his enthusiasm. "Don't you want to see me happy, Lou?"

"Happy? With Leslie Russell? Why don't you just look her up in the phone book if you're so determined to see her after hours?" Peller queried.

"She's unlisted. I already tried. And she won't return my phone calls at the office." Steve's grin masked the pain of loneliness. "No, for some reason, she wants you."

Peller was tiring of his friend's one-track talk. He picked up the check quickly and stood. Steve made no attempt to grab it away from him.

"I'll consider giving you her private number if you can make some headway on an assets search on Assad. I need to know everything he owns and every deal he has made in the past five years—every piece of property he's bought in New York. I have a hunch that our friend's not quite the sentimental character he'd like us to believe. But I need proof. I think that if we can track down his other assets, we'll know better whether he's jerking us around." Peller was not yet ready to tell Steve about Angel's allusion to a connection between Assad and herself, and perhaps, speculated Peller, Bud Epstein too.

"You want a complete assets search? That could take weeks. Our database covers only properties or assets in his name. What if he's involved in partnerships? Or corporations? Those deals aren't listed by partners' names. Come on, Louis, give it a rest." Steve grabbed his coat and hurried to match Peller's swiftening stride. "I've got other cases pending. Epstein's still in arrears, and we've got hundreds of other borrowers begging us to negotiate new terms on their loans. I'm so backlogged."

"I don't really care, Steve. We've got a sweet opportunity here to unload a sour property and come out way ahead. And you're either with me on this one or against me. I'm telling you, I smell something rotten here. Leslie Russell's trying to pull something over on us, and I think Assad is still calling all the shots and using her as an intermediary. She may be the devil incarnate, but she doesn't know who she's dealing with yet. After all, they don't call me 'Bad Louis' up in the Bronx for nothing. I'm going to keep squeezing. If you don't want to work with me, I'll recruit Vicki. Besides, I think we might even see some court action by the time we're through, if my hunch is correct, or if Omar doesn't come through with his end of the bargain."

Steve sighed. Once Louis Peller had focused on his goal, he looked neither left nor right. There was no talking to him rationally.

"Louis, you've got me. I'll talk to Vicki too, see if she can spare some time for you. But you've got to realize we're all under pressure to produce here, and anyway, this is just another loan payoff. Make the best deal you can with Omar, and let's move on."

Peller knew only too well that there were other deals waiting for his attention. But he could not let go his obsession. Angel's little hint about Assad and Epstein was burning him up. It was just too coincidental. Something strange was going on, and he, Louis Peller, was determined to find out about it.

****

Joe Vallardo was sick of meeting with mortgage bankers. After all, he was involved only on the periphery of the business of making loans to borrowers, and he hated the endless speeches on the "implications of rising interest rates" delivered with inflated pomposity by economists who could no more predict the nation's economic tides than weather forecasters the snow or expert seminars on mundane matters like the money supply that bankers found endlessly fascinating. Fortunately, the meeting, which took place over two days in a warren of conference rooms at the cavernous Washington Hilton, was afloat in yellow ties and charcoal-gray suits. Vallardo could easily lose himself in that tide; no one would ever miss him.

The crisp, cool October day was inviting. As Joe Vallardo

ascended the escalator to the hotel's main lobby, he decided to take a little stroll up Connecticut Avenue toward the nearby National Zoo to clear his head of the morning's cobwebs so he could return for his scheduled late afternoon meetings with renewed commitment. He started out briskly.

Vallardo had been to the National Zoo only once before, on the first birthday of his son, Little Joe. It was one of the rare occasions when he and his wife had paused to sightsee in Washington. Since the zoo was laid out on a long hill descending from the heights of Connecticut Avenue to Rock Creek far below, the path leading past the exhibits sloped endlessly downward. Vallardo and Andrea had tired early of pushing the stroller containing their busy little boy whose major interest had been throwing popcorn to the ever-present sparrows and pigeons. The farther down they strolled, the farther uphill their trek back, with Joey crying to get out of the stroller, to climb back in, to be carried, to eat, to drink. Andrea decided she'd rather go shopping, an activity of which she never tired. So they headed back to the Watergate, with its chic and pricey boutiques, where she could shop to her heart's content. Vallardo strolled over to the boathouse across Rock Creek Parkway, where he could watch sailboats and sightseers cruise the Potomac River with his fascinated baby.

As a result, Vallardo now considered this his best opportunity to visit the seals and panda bears he had missed on the first visit.

Vallardo loved zoos. He'd always enjoyed visiting the small petting zoo in his home town. One of his fondest childhood memories was of a warm Sunday afternoon after church spent there with his grandmother when he was about four or five, feeding hungry goats peanuts out of his own hand, petting a strange-looking llama, and chasing quacking ducks around a small, lily-choked pond—just the two of them. Such a rare treat for the youngest of seven.

But today's stroll was important to Vallardo for more than psychic satisfaction. He urgently wanted to puzzle out the next step in how to make more money from his recent financial investment. The partnership was ready to go public and promised to bring in a windfall, as advertised. Just Sunday afternoon, Vallardo had gotten a call from Cinoletti, one of the managing partners in the deal, offering him a final opportunity to increase his investment before the public offering. The potential as mapped out by Cinoletti was limitless, and Vallardo was quite excited by this sudden prospect for bushels of profit. Cinoletti painted glowing pictures of the potential to branch out into areas besides real estate, including investment in the Mexican Stock Exchange on the strength of the North American Free Trade Agreement, oil-drilling ventures, or the purchase of a South African shipping company. Cinoletti said the deals were being cooked up by a family of silent investors with some foreign-sounding surname and offices in Mexico and somewhere in the Middle East, but it was all based on good-old, honest American entrepreneurialism. To Vallardo, anxious to make a fast fortune and finally convince Andrea he was as good as he claimed to be, it all sounded too good to be true.

The wide avenue was crowded this afternoon. Young couples, seemingly having nothing pressing to do, strolled hand in hand past the zoo's impressive wrought iron gates; past street vendors selling balloons and buttons, peanuts and popcorn; past parents trying to keep order among the young children running circles around them; past kids pausing in their play only briefly to squeal at the antics of some engaging animal. A few joggers flew by, sporting running shorts and earphones, their autumn-pale legs pounding the bricked walk. Not many self-important Washingtonians ventured this far uptown during a Monday when Congress was in session; there were too many braying members of congress and their hawk-eyed staff to be lobbied, too many lawyers scurrying around with five-hundred-dollar brief cases filled with pressing motions to be filed, too many monkey business scandals for enterprising reporters to uncover for workaholic Washington to while away lazy hours at the zoo.

In short, it was a lovely day to be freed from his own cage—and good for some creative thinking. In Vallardo's mind, as he paced past the panda's habitat and mused over the many exotic birds, he was formulating an aggressive strategy for investment and already spending all that money he was about to make. Another quick twenty-five thousand dollars slipped into the partnership before the deal went public, and his return would be at least double that. A Lexus sounded nice to him; Andrea would want her little red Mercedes two seater. Maybe they could buy a beach house in Rehoboth or Bethany Beach, Delaware. Any self-respecting person of means in the Washington area had a little hideout on the nearby Delaware shore. He could envision it already: a quiet summer getaway, a quaint little gingerbread cottage near a resort where they could play tennis and golf, maybe get in some fishing. Vallardo would call his broker after the meeting adjourned that very afternoon and tell him to pull out all the stops.

He stopped at the seal tank to admire the dolphins streaking through the cold pool and arching gracefully in and out of the water. True to form, there were the sea lions, those comically mustachioed clowns, basking on the concrete deck surrounding the pool, their wet, black hides glistening in the sun. Vallardo smiled at their sloth; what a life these creatures enjoyed, so un-Washington. One of the seals lifted his head lazily and seemed to stare Vallardo directly in the eye. The sea lion shrieked and dove back into the pool with a plop.

"That slippery fellow reminds me of Stan Sponzelli," Vallardo mused. Stan, his black hair slicked back with gel, a handlebar moustache, and penetrating black eyes, was a hometown pal. They were two Italian kids from the wrong side of the tracks making it big in Washington. They used to caddy together at *the* country club back home. Now Stan was a lawyer in a Congressional office. The guy was always working, or so it seemed to Vallardo who didn't get a chance to hang out with his friend too often anymore. Still, Vallardo had so few real friends, so few people he trusted enough to be himself. Even Andrea expected him to be what he was not. Stan was an anchor in a sea of deception and a role model of success.

As Vallardo stared at the slapstick seal now surfacing in front of him, he had an inspiration. Stan had helped so often while Vallardo was struggling, why not make it up to him? Cutting Stan in on the "investment deal of the century" would go a long way in repaying the debt Vallardo owed him. He stopped at a pay phone near a kiosk with animal-fronted t-shirts hanging from hooks in the ceiling and draped with "Friend of the National Zoo" bumper stickers. He listened as his quarter dropped and dialed his friend's direct line.

"Stan, you won't believe this, but I'm strolling through the National Zoo, and I get a brainstorm. How would you like to get in on the ground floor of a big opportunity?"

"Are you kidding me, Joe?" his buddy replied. "I have no time for Amway or NuSkin or whatever the latest pyramid scheme might be. I'm under a lot of pressure with this new job. They kicked me over to a committee that's investigating the insurance industry. Here are all these Congressmen callin' me, PACs lobbying, and I'm about to lose my job, because I'm not finished researching the legal precedent for some fucking legislation that's up for a vote this week. My wife hates me, because I forgot to pick up the kids from daycare yesterday, and I've got six thousand dollars ridin' on my Visa at 21 percent interest, and you're asking me if I wanna make some money? Sure. But make it fast. What's the scam?"

Vallardo hadn't known about his friend's new job. He felt a slight twinge of jealousy; Stan was moving ahead while Vallardo was treading water. *Oh well*, he consoled himself. *Keep your sights focused on the bottom line: investment opportunity.*

"One of my borrowers turned me on to an unbelievable deal last month. He started a vulture fund in the form of a real estate partnership a few years ago. The partnership purchased quite a number of properties at the bottom of the market when banks were desperate to unload bad assets. Some were purchased at tax sales and from the RTC. And he's got some big-time investors." Vallardo paused to get Stan's reaction.

"Yeah, what about it?"

"This guy wants to spread the wealth, get into other things besides real estate. Like I said, I know he's got a good track record, 'cause Amie's financed him on three or four properties, and they're all run like he lives there. Never any problem getting him to pay."

"No can do bank properties, good buddy. You know where that's gotten some of our most entrenched politicos over the past ten years."

"That's just it, Stan. They want to diversify. It'll be a whole separate venture. They're thinking about international markets now. They're looking into foreign oil ventures and a shipping company in South Africa. They invited me in—I put up ten thousand dollars—and asked me if I knew anyone else who might want to invest. I thought about you immediately. Now they're about to go public. I talked to the managing partner yesterday, and he thinks I can double my investment inside of six months. I'm thinking of chipping in another twenty-five thou. How 'bout it, Stan? This could be the mother lode."

"Let me think about it, Joe," Stan replied as his line signaled a call waiting. "I can't tell you this week. I'm swamped."

But Vallardo was suddenly determined that his friend share in his good fortune. "Stan, think about it. But don't miss out. Opportunities like this don't come up every day. Picture this, we hit it big and take the wives for a long, well-earned sabbatical in the Cayman's. Just you and me and Andrea and Jean, some deep-sea fishing and some great golfing."

"I said I'll think on it, Joe. Call me next week when we're in recess. I've got Marino on the line here from New Mexico. Wants enterprise zones in Santa Fe, I think. Santa Fe needs enterprise zones like I need a second head. Oink, oink. More pigs at the trough. Gotta go."

Vallardo smiled. Stan was a good friend. He would throw his

lot in with Vallardo, he knew. After all, the two men were cut from the same mold. Stan too was tired of grunt work, of being a mere Congressional staffer at the beck and call of the great and near great.

And suddenly, that sabbatical sounded pretty important to Vallardo too.

Chapter 16
Reviewing the Information

While his boss was scheduled to hobnob with the elite in the worlds of banking and finance at the mortgage industry meeting, Peller was digging in to meet the task at hand. His fingers tapped out yet another eleven-digit code in New York, this time Paul Chase.

"I'll bet he was even behind the scenes during Iran-Contra at some point … Friend of the Ayatollah … cagey … Looks like he's working himself into the power structure of New York, too." Steve's words, spoken half in jest last summer before Peller was even involved with this shyster Assad, came back to him haltingly. Paul would know whether Assad had been involved in any shady dealings under CIA investigation back then. He tapped the desk impatiently, waiting for Paul to answer.

"I'm sorry, I'm not in my office now. I'm searching for premium office space at the best rates in New York to meet your needs. Your call is important to me, so please leave a message. Have a good day."

Voice mail. Peller hated it. Whatever happened to human beings answering phones? And that communiqué; Paul was so button-down. On his own voice mail message, Peller usually recorded some pearl of wisdom for the week, like "Peller's Law: Opportunities multiply as they are seized, die when neglected. Let me know you called and I'll seize every opportunity to call you back." Such levity annoyed Vallardo and Derek, especially since voice mail messages at Amie Mae were regularly checked by a phone monitor. But Peller didn't give a damn, and his borrowers generally got a good chuckle out of Peller's "wisdom."

Peller decided Paul ought to lighten up. In a raspy voice, he put on his best gangster imitation. "I'm looking for some space on Second Avenue to set up a little restaurant, see? With a little bar, see? Plenty of storage room too, see? To entertain my friends late at night, see? And if you don't pull through, my friends'll break both your legs, see?" He cackled menacingly into the phone and hung up. Then he dialed the number again and left his own name and number for Paul to call him. Peller would have fun giving Paul hell about his buddy's rumored "*mafioso*" clients.

He had barely hung up the phone when it rang again, once. An inside call. "Peller here," he said.

"Louis, you won't believe it. I've searched three databases looking for Assad's assets and came up with three properties listed with his name. M.E. Limited Partnership One, M.E. Limited Partnership Two, and M.E. Limited Partnership Three. All three are in the Bronx." Steve recited the street names while Peller traced them on a huge New York City street map he had tacked up on one wall of his cubicle: "Elder Avenue, Boynton Avenue, and Watson Avenue." Peller was clicking his teeth unconsciously as he tracked them. Three apartment buildings in a once-distinguished, now-blighted portion of the South Bronx. The police had virtually given up on these streets as unpatrollable, he'd heard, given over entirely to the drug trade.

"Of course, I found out about these pretty easily by starting with the partnership name for 488 West 158th and going over the city's tax assessment database. It's altogether possible that he's got other buildings under some entirely different names. We lucked out, Louis," Steve said.

Peller was now jotting down the information. He knew it. Assad probably owned lots of properties. The guy was definitely hiding something big. "Anything's possible. Especially with this guy, Steve. Keep checking."

"I'll see what else I can find out, Lou. You know, I think we might be able to unravel this mystery man." Steve sounded keyed up too.

"Great. This is a big help, Steve. These places are in blighted neighborhoods just like West 158th. We need to know whether Assad is delinquent in his payments with other lenders. Listen, I want to go up to the city next week to meet with Leslie Russell anyway. Before I meet with her, why don't I just take myself on a little tour of the South Bronx? The condition of the buildings might confirm my suspicion that Assad's milking his properties, letting them get run down, and abandoning payment, just like the building on West 158th." Peller was talking more to himself than to Steve. "I wanna see what Assad might have up his sleeve before I talk with his beautiful advocate."

"Louis, I don't know what's more dangerous: you touring the South Bronx or meeting alone with Leslie Russell. Either way, I know I don't want to be there. But you better make sure Tommy Romano is around to escort you. You're gonna need all the protection you can get," Steve warned.

"Louis Peller takes all necessary precautions," Peller pronounced omnipotently from on high. "Don't worry about me, Steve. I'll be all right. Keep on checking, though. See if you can't track down any more of Assad's investments," he repeated before he hung up.

Good man, Steve. A born sleuth, thought Peller. Now Peller had better call Tommy back to get him to tail Assad. If Assad was visiting 488 West 158th, Tommy might be able to trail him on a circuit of his buildings, including the South Bronx apartments. No telling what else Tommy might uncover.

He dialed Tommy. Another answering machine. Peller was becoming increasingly weary of playing telephone tag. "Tommy, while you're out chasing pigeons, add one other bird to your flock: Omar Assad. If you spy him leaving 488 West 158th, follow him. Steve found out he owns some places in the Bronx. I need to know if there are any other addresses we *don't* know about. See what else he's up to. Call" *beep* "me." The machine cut off the call.

Feeling anxious, Peller walked over to the coffee machine, half hoping someone would divert him from his madness. He decided on hot chocolate and picked up a packet of the powder from a basket next to the coffee maker to pour into his mug. (It was the mug that said, "Caution: Turning 40 May Be Hazardous to Your Health," a birthday gift from Ellie.) As he filled the mug with hot water, Ellie stepped up to the copy machine.

"What's with you, Louis?" she asked. "Haven't seen you all day."

"Hi, El," he said. "I've been incredibly busy. Whoever said Mondays were supposed to be slow and easy did not work at Amie Mae."

"I've never heard anyone say that Mondays should be any different than any other day of the week. Besides, being busy has never kept you from stopping by to chat."

"I've got so much to do, Ellie. I guess I'm just feeling under the gun. Besides, I want to get things under control while Vallardo's off at his meeting. You know that when he gets back there'll be twelve new loans waiting in the in-box, and one hundred new management techniques from the banker's meeting to implement." Peller groaned in mock horror.

Ellie laughed. "Yep, it does seem like those guys get some pretty nutty ideas about running the office more efficiently every time they go off to one of those industry conferences. They ought to just stick around and work hard like the rest of us. That would do wonders for efficiency, not to mention morale."

She picked up her copies. "Say, Louis, wanna see some new pictures of the baby?" Peller could not say no to that one. He was the one who was always showing off pictures of his kids: taking their first steps, swimming, standing on their heads.

"Oh well, five minutes," he agreed. It would be a good mental health break.

****

The Bronx Zoo seemed the perfect location for Paul and Chris to work off an overstuffed lunch at Dominick's on Arthur Avenue, a borough landmark for its family-size portions, red-checkered tables, and no-menu policy. They were smack-dab in Peller's territory, and naturally, Peller had come up in their conversation. Though the zoo bordered dangerously on a white's no-man zone, the park was considered reasonably safe in broad daylight, more frequented by students from nearby Fordham University than dope dealers. The clouds were flying across the face of the sun, giving the fleeting impression of warmth, while the few remaining leaves braced vainly against the wind. The two friends were both wrapped in their trench coats against the chill.

"Your friend Louis never lets up, Paul. You know, now he's got me involved in this Sanchez woman's life. It's not enough that I got her off the hook," Chris observed, walking comfortably in stride with her old friend.

"Seems to me, Chris, that you've taken on Angel Sanchez as your personal mission, if I do read the signs correctly," Paul said smilingly.

Chris's silence was affirmation of Paul's hypothesis. She pulled her collar up against the sharp breeze.

He wrapped his arm around her shoulders for warmth. "So, what's next for thine Angel, Chris?"

"I've offered to help set her up in business, Paul. Something legit. She suggested ladies' lingerie, but I'm holding out for something a little less … suggestive."

"You may be holding out for awhile, considering the source," Paul noted.

Chris sighed and squeezed Paul's arm. The dappled sunlight danced across her face, so he couldn't quite read her mood.

"I just don't know about Angel, Paul. I think she's sincere about wanting to escape her personal hell, but how can I be sure?" Since their date, Paul and Chris had become a regular pair, although the relationship was still largely platonic. Still, his companionship meant a little more warmth in her life, a little more spring to her step. She was content to take things slow.

"You won't know until you try, Chris," Paul philosophized. "But I don't think Angel's a lost cause, and I'm proud of you for offering to help," he added. Paul too was feeling tentative about an amorous relationship. Things were so good between the two friends, he was wary of that first kiss; afraid that, in attempting to rekindle the flame, he would snuff out the friendship. But here, today, with Chris, he felt alive again. Lord only knew, romancing all the Jerri's of this city had been a deadening experience. Maybe timing was everything after all.

"You know, on that general subject, Louis seems to have calmed down considerably," observed Paul. "He left me a really funny message this morning: he's mafia, and he wants this bar, see. For his friends, see. Who'll do me in, see, if I don't give them the right price, see," Paul mimicked. "I don't think he's as obsessed with his job these days."

"Hadn't noticed," murmured Chris distractedly, kicking an empty soda can toward a nearby wastebasket. The path was strewn with litter.

"I know you're not a real fan of his, Chris, but you've got to understand, Louis is a part of my life to stay. I can't really explain the relationship, except to say there's a certain simpatico feeling."

"Skip it, Paul. I'll tolerate Peller, but don't ask me to die for him," Chris said, scooping up the can. "He's your friend." She tossed it at the basket, missing her mark by a wide margin. It landed in the soft, grassy area under a park bench. Paul snickered.

"Patrick Ewing, you're not," he called, jogging to retrieve the can and shoot it for himself.

"Aww, give me another chance," Chris started running, gaining on Paul. They both dove simultaneously and tumbled to the ground, laughing. Paul rolled on top of Chris to pin her and, looking down at her smile, spontaneously planted a soft kiss on her mouth while reaching for the can. She shrieked, toppled him, and grabbed it from his hand, shouting "gotcha," then stooped to greet his warm lips again. They were playing now, testing intimacy, testing dominance. Paul pulled Chris up to her feet and stole the can back, prying her fingers from the metal and kissing them, one by one, gingerly at first, then with increasing urgency. They embraced again, their lips tasting the fresh fruits of romance as Paul shot the can backward over his head into the trash can.

"Three points," he whispered softly, slipping his hand under her heavy coat as he pulled her toward him, seeking her body's feminine softness underneath the confines of her proper, lawyerly dress.

"I want you." The words escaped unwittingly from her thoughts.

"Me too," he whispered joyously. "Chris, let's fly away from Pellerland." He pulled her by the hand, running toward the zoo gate. "We'll leave the slums to Louis. Let's find our own paradise."

Chris, momentarily distracted by the unwarranted intrusion of Louis Peller into this moment of magic, gripped Paul's hand determinedly as they ran. "Fine with me, Mr. Chase. We'll steal away."

****

Peller returned to his desk in a considerably lightened mood. Ellie's little boy was cute, and some of the pictures were really funny: a bath where the bubbles threatened to overtake the baby and a run around his room wearing his dad's sneakers, Ellie chasing after him. The kid was wearing a huge grin. That's what life was all about, he reminded himself.

There were three messages waiting. Lana, Lana, and Paul Chase. He dialed Paul back immediately. Paul had just walked in after a reluctant parting from Chris: she to a case and he to a client. Paul still felt the cocoon of romance protecting him.

"Paul, when you were in the CIA, did you or anyone you know ever hear of this guy—Omar Assad? Could have been tied to Iran-Contra too. He's Iranian, a Muslim, and probably wired to power and money here and there."

"Louis, what a coincidence. Chris and I were just saying how much you seemed to have relaxed recently. So, how's it going?"

"It's worse than I thought, Paul. I need to know everything I can about Omar Assad."

Paul sighed. *Here we go again*, thought the much-imposed-upon friend of Louis Peller. Peller was asking him for the impossible. "Louis, you know I can't divulge anything, and besides, I got out of the Agency right around that time. I tried real hard not to know anything that was going on."

"Okay, Paul," Peller backpedalled. "I know the official line and could care less about whether we traded arms for hostages. I'm not a reporter, remember? I just need to know whether this guy has another agenda besides paying off the mortgage on a clunker of an apartment building in Washington Heights at four times its appraised value."

Paul refused to get sucked in. "Gee, Lou, if the guy's that eager to acquire overpriced properties, do I have a deal for him. Prime shopping and office space in midtown for only forty dollars a square foot. A bargain. Give him my number, pal."

"C'mon, Paul, this is serious stuff. Assad has a building that's not just part of a drug-infested neighborhood; it may be a major source of drug traffic. We suspect the super's selling crack to the tenants from his own apartment. Now I learn Assad's also got some buildings in the South Bronx, the world's worst neighborhood for drugs, robbery, and homicide. Could it be he's got a financial stake in some 'business enterprise' going on in some of them too?"

"Louis, I think you've gone off the deep end with this cockamamie theory of yours. You're totally paranoid, you know that? I mean, you have no evidence that Assad is involved in actual drug trade in Washington Heights or anywhere else," Paul pointed out reasonably.

"Maybe I am going out on a limb here, Paul, but there's more," Peller added, conspiratorially. "Assad came to the U.S. about the time as Iran-Contra and bought this building for cash, then he refinanced with Amie Mae. He happened to refinance during the peak of the buying boom, when the value of the building had gone sky high. Amie Mae lent him three times the original price of the property. He paid us on time at first. Now, as you know, the market's plummeted. He got hit bad, he says. Rental rates declined, and unemployment in those neighborhoods went up, so rent collections dropped off precipitously. He hasn't been able to make a single loan payment in two years, and he claims it's actually costing him money."

"Now, we know for a fact the building needs major repairs to the foundation, the roof, the plumbing, that he hasn't done diddly in maintenance in all this time. But suddenly, he's dying to buy this building outright for more than it's worth. For cash. Why such an Allah-forsaken place? Because, he says, it was his first investment in America, and it's got 'sentimental value' to him. To me, these excuses don't add up. So I conclude, he is either stupid or crazy or there's more to this impassioned desire to remain a slumlord in a building that's draining him of his cash reserves than we know. Assad is not stupid. And he doesn't sound crazy. Maybe he has another reason to hold this property. Could it have something to do with his business interests back home? After all, he did just return from Teheran with some new tricks up his caftan. So I repeat: does the CIA or the FBI have any information on this guy that could help explain what's going on here? I know, Paul, this is quite a leap, but—buddy, trust me here—I have the strangest feeling about this one."

Paul marveled at his friend's vivid imagination. "Listen, Sherlock Holmes, call me tomorrow when you're not having delusions. Meanwhile, I'll see if there's anything I can find out. Why I do these things for you is beyond me."

"Paul, hold on." Peller pushed another button to take an incoming call.

"Louis," boomed Joe Vallardo's voice over the line. "I have a break in my meetings, and I wanted to check in. How did the Assad meeting go last week?"

Peller put Vallardo on hold for a minute. "Thanks, Paul. You're a true friend. I'll check in with you tomorrow afternoon. Bye."

Peller punched the flashing red light.

"Well, do we have a deal?" His boss was hyped; he sounded as if he had just completed a ninety-nine-yard drive in the big game and was about to score on the opposing team. But maybe that was just Peller's interpretation of the situation. Vallardo didn't know yet that the opposing team had just tackled Peller.

Peller wanted to stall. He had been hoping to delay his official report to Vallardo until the middle of the week when he would have a better handle on Assad's other assets. He also needed to broach the subject of paying Tommy Romano bonus bucks to scope out the Washington Heights building. And Peller desperately wanted to reassure Marguerita that Amie Mae was taking appropriate steps to ensure the tenants' safety and investigating Carlos de Leon's activities a little more closely—that was where Tommy fit into the picture. But Peller wasn't yet ready to get into it with Vallardo, and certainly not over the phone.

"Well, we were sacked," Peller let slip.

"Whaddaya mean, sacked?" Vallardo sounded slightly rattled. "You were supposed to kick that ball right through the goalposts. Didn't you make a deal with Assad? Or was he just faking us out again?"

"Well, I'm afraid the answer is C, neither of the above, Vallardo. He switched game plans on us." Peller communicated in Vallardo's language. "He brought along his attorney, Leslie Russell."

"Never heard of her."

"You will," Peller informed him ominously. "She's one of the best trial attorneys on Manhattan Island. And I hear tell she's a relentless negotiator."

A trial attorney? What the hell was going on there, anyway? "Shit, Louis, why can't we just cut a deal with Assad and get this over with already?"

Peller wanted to fake Vallardo out. He needed more time before he told his boss everything. "Joe, there's a lot more to this deal than meets the eye. But I can't really explain it to you over the phone. You and I are scheduled to meet Wednesday afternoon, so I can brief you then. I'm working on some other deals now," he lied, "since I don't want to go anywhere with this one until you hear the whole story. Not to worry, Joe. We'll keep things under control. Amie Mae will still have the deal of the decade with Assad," Peller tried to sound confident, although he was far from sure of success.

There was a momentary lull on the line, then a sigh of resignation from Vallardo. "Louis, I thought I mentioned to you we're coming into some unpredictable times in this company, and there may be heads rolling. Now I swear mine will not be one of them. And you better worry about yours, too, cowboy."

Shit, thought Peller. Here came the storm.

"Something tells me I'd better skip out on these meetings tomorrow so we can talk right away, Louis. Tell Mildred I'm coming in first thing so she can work over my calendar. Meet me at eight in my office. Do you understand, Peller?" Vallardo sounded really annoyed now

"Sure, Joe. I'll be there," Peller assured him. "Enjoy the rest of your seminar," he added to the dial tone as Vallardo hung up abruptly.

Peller had to come up with a compelling story to sell Vallardo by tomorrow morning. Maybe he could test one out on Lana. Peller would call her and warn her he'd be working late tonight.

"Hi, honey," Peller began solicitously. "How's your day?"

"Ed Fishoff resigned from the editor's desk today. He's going off to start a little weekly paper in New Hampshire before the Granite State gets its next wave of presidential wannabes. You know what that means: the assistant news editor's job is up for grabs, and I'm first in line," she announced breathlessly. She hadn't really wanted to break the news to Peller this way.

Great, he thought. That's just what he needed: Lana getting a promotion. This news required a long discussion between them to hash out the "issues" and make sure Lana understood that any increase in her responsibilities and hours would mean serious deprivation to their children. Lana, he knew, would never see that on her own. But he didn't have the strength to engage in serious hand-to-hand combat just now. He decided to change the subject immediately.

"Listen, Lana," he said, injecting just the right note of weary overwork in his voice. "I know I told you I'd be staying home for a while, but it looks like I'm going to be called up to New York unexpectedly in a few days. Trip may be overnight … maybe two nights. This Assad deal is really heating up." He had informed her about Carlos de Leon and the cocaine.

She was momentarily distracted. "What now, Louis? It's 'an ill wind that bloweth no man to good,' as the Good Book says. Today's news headline?" she queried.

"Well, it seems Assad owns or has an interest in three other properties in the Bronx. I have a hunch about this guy falling into a pattern." That bit of speculation presented as fact would give Peller some leverage with his much-benighted spouse. "I've got Tommy involved now. He's watching Assad's Washington Heights property to see if he can track any links."

"Louis, you are not a PI, so don't go sniffing out clues. If Assad is perpetrating some illegal act, don't you think this investigation belongs in the hands of the New York Police Department, not the mortgage banking company you work for?"

Fair question. "Of course, Lana. But you know, I now suspect that Assad and Bud Epstein are in cahoots. I told you that Angel Sanchez mentioned some kind of relationship between those guys to Chris Boyer. Even if it isn't true, Assad is playing games with us. And Joe and Derek positively want me to pursue him." A skeptical silence fogged the air.

"Listen, Lana. I didn't want to have to worry you about this, but Joe's been talking layoffs, and I just can't afford to say no. Obviously, Amie Mae needs to find out if there are any other properties he's pulling these high jinks on."

Layoffs. That was news. "What kind of layoffs? Obviously we can't afford for you to be laid off. But what would Assad's other properties, ones Amie doesn't hold the note on, have to do with your negotiations?"

"Everything, Lana. You see, I think I can force Assad's hand a little. If I can just ascertain why Assad is so bent on keeping his property as to pay us four times its worth, I'll have lots of leverage over him. Why, for example, would he bring in his hotshot trial lawyer at this point? Assad has always done his own deals. It just doesn't add up."

She thought for a minute. Peller losing his job worried her. "Why can't you just take Assad at his word and close the deal?" She sighed, knowing that Peller would never give up his hunch. "If you are so hell-bent on pursuing this … look, Louis, you and I both know the course you're following could be a dangerous one. I beg you, ask for special security. Please."

"I'm meeting with Joe first thing in the morning. I'll make it a condition. Okay?" He suddenly felt lachrymose. "Do you love me, Lana?"

"Just make sure the life insurance policy is paid up," she responded tartly.

Peller laughed nervously. "Thanks for the moral support, dear. By the way, I'll be home late, so don't hold dinner. Oh, and I want to hear all about this unbelievable promotion they're planning for you," he threw in to appease her. He really wanted to forget she'd even mentioned it.

"I'll tell you all about it after I've started the job, Louis," she announced. "I can't wait around for you to have time to talk me out of it." Lana hung up.

More problems, he thought. Lana.

Peller stretched, but the ache in his neck and legs persisted. It was already four fifteen. Steve would be leaving soon to make the six o'clock shuttle. Maybe Peller should go have a final word with him.

He ambled down the hall, trying to contain his restlessness, anxious about the furies he might be unleashing. "What business is this of mine after all?" he reasoned, Lana's warnings ringing in his head. He reached the elevators and stabbed the up button repeatedly.

"I mean, what possible difference could any of this make in the scheme of life? Who cares whether Carlos de Leon is dealing cocaine from his apartment? Why should I get involved in Marguerita Fernandez's problems with her landlord? And what the hell am I doing putting Tommy Romano's life at risk to watch a slimy Iranian run his business?"

In his mind's eye flashed Epstein's building afire. The deplorable conditions of that building, and of Assad's, while people like Marguerita Fernandez tried to make a decent life for their families. The image of ever-solicitous Angel Sanchez. Those were the reasons that mattered. He conjured exotic visions of Angel and Epstein. Epstein and Assad, together, trying to screw Angel. Epstein and Assad, together, trying to screw Amie Mae. Epstein and Assad, together, trying to screw Louis Peller. The contortions made him ill.

Like a Poirot mystery, every suspect was vying to implicate the others. He could unravel this enigma and give Marguerita and Johnson a crack at a better existence. The intrigue was spice to Peller, though his increasing involvement inadvertently complicated everyone else's lives too. Louis Peller thrived on it.

Chapter 17
The Bronx: a Grand Tour

On Wednesday, he flew back to New York City. Throughout the entire shuttle flight, Peller was preoccupied, mentally reconstructing his meeting with Vallardo. He had recounted the facts. Assad had brought in Russell. That meant trouble for negotiations, since Russell would play hardball. It was time for Plan B, the last fallback position for the company. Peller would meet with Russell. He would settle for a half million in cash now and allow Assad to pay off the three hundred thousand dollar balance over three months. Fait accompli. Peller was still a hero.

He hadn't even bothered to mention to Vallardo his new suspicions about the drugs or Angel's allusion to a partnership between Assad and the ever-truant Bud Epstein. Vallardo would only get aggravated at Peller for sticking his nose in where the boss had determined it didn't belong, Peller reasoned.

In their meeting, Vallardo had seemed oddly agitated, pacing the same singular track in his nondescript, corporate-gray carpet, distracted, shouting about nothing in particular. The normally upbeat manager was complaining in football clichés. He swore up one side of Peller and down the other, then ranted and raved about "clearing this fucking play off the field" because the "clock was running down," putting another ball "in play," "guarding his ass," and putting Peller "back on the bench." Where was he coming from? Gradually, Peller had been able to make his boss see that, with a little extra time and one more trip to New York, he, Peller the master mediator, would be able to negotiate a sale that would relieve them of this whole mess and minimize their losses.

So there he was, winging his way north to meet with Leslie Russell, lawyer to New York's finest, to demand payment of eight hundred thousand dollars for the apartments at 488 West 158th Street, as originally promised. No sweat. So why was his stomach all tied up in knots?

Perhaps it was the turbulence. Peller looked out the scratched window as the plane hit another air pocket, and he felt his heart flutter. Clouds marbled the sky. Although they were not storm clouds, they had a kick. Peller had certainly been on smoother flights. He gripped the armrests and looked down at his worn, scuffed loafers, trying to steady his focus, regain his equilibrium. *Loafers*, he thought sardonically—the same shoes he used to wear to synagogue as a kid, when he'd find the shiniest penny in his piggy bank and wedge it in the slot to be "cool." He wasn't allowed to wear sneakers to Sunday school, but even then, young Peller couldn't give in completely to the rigors of formality; the penny was his form of protest. Now the same loafers were his casual shoes, made for walking the streets of New York and the halls of littered tenements. No pennies these days; hundreds of thousands and possibly millions of dollars were at stake.

Peller was in a hurry to begin his mission. He shifted his gaze impatiently to the seat back in front of him. He had already thumbed through the dog-eared magazine full of articles about dining a la mode at the French Open and ski vacations in New England. Nothing held his attention; he was much too preoccupied with matters at hand.

Peller's first order of business this trip, before meeting with Leslie Russell, was the inspection of three apartment buildings in the Bronx, Assad's other properties, with Tommy, chief sleuth and body watcher. And he wanted to drop in on Chris Boyer to hear Angel's revelations. Peller needed all the bargaining chips he could collect before he and Russell went head-to-head.

The plane was delayed, circling over the airport now, pushing back their arrival. Peller was a little annoyed. He knew he should have taken the eight o'clock shuttle or, at the latest, the nine. Instead he'd loafed around the house, hoping pointlessly for Lana's blessing, stalling, to take the ten o'clock. Here it was almost eleven fifteen. The delay would kill his schedule. He'd hoped to catch coffee with Russell this afternoon to renew negotiations early, but this procession of silver birds circling ahead of them, all awaiting landing clearance, effectively scrubbed that plan.

When their turn for landing finally cleared, the plane lurched on touchdown—an omen, reflected Peller in all seriousness. He walked unsteadily down the ramp and into the hustle and bustle of La Guardia Airport.

****

"So, Louie," ventured Tommy as the two men strolled out to the parking lot, looking for the Impala. "I been watchin' out at the apartment like you aksed me, and I seen a few strange things goin' on around theah."

"Like what?" Peller asked matter-of-factly, setting a quick pace as they threaded through the rows of cars parked outside.

"Like lots of people goin' in and out of de Leon's place. I carried my bird-watching binoculars," Tommy bragged.

It was a chilly, early November day. No more Indian summer. Peller walked briskly to stay warm, but the stiff breeze made warmth impossible.

"Hmmm." Peller was unimpressed. "What else?"

Tommy was a little miffed that his best creative work was being taken for granted. "Yestiday, I'd say it was about one in the afternoon or so, I remember because I was finishin' up my b'loney samwich—"

"Let's get to the point here, Tommy." They had reached the car. Tommy got in and stretched over to unlock the passenger-side door for his rider. Peller plopped down in the front seat, still feeling queasy.

"Yeah, well, as I say, it was around one, and these two white guys go into the supah's apawtment. Now I know these guys ain't tenants, right, and they don't live around there fa' shuwa, so I slumps down behind the wheel and watches 'em real careful."

"So?"

"So they was wearin' hats, and I couldn't get a good look at their faces, but I think one of 'em had a beard, not a long bush like those Hasidic types you deal with, but a regulah beard. I thought I noticed an earring in one ear too. The other guy had a tail, it looked kinda red to me, comin' out from undah the hat and all. And dark shades. I caught a Polaroid of 'em."

"Good move. Lemme see, Tommy." Peller was suddenly all ears. He grabbed the snapshot out of his driver's hands.

"Just wait a second, pal," Tommy pulled it back gingerly. "You gotta undastand, treasures like these come at a price."

"God damn you, Tommy Romano," cursed Peller. "You're not telling me you're gonna charge me for this picture? I'm paying you handsomely for this little gig already."

"Let's jus' say, I feel it could be worth a little somethin' extra for goin' above and beyond the call a duty heah, chief," commented Tommy, starting the car and weaving his way like a madman to the exit. "You know it's tough, what with Mama's health problems and all, and what with me not gettin' health insurance from Amie. Tell you what. I don't want you to think I'm rippin' you off, but I'll lay ya two-to-one odds you'll think these pictures is worth a little extra investment."

Peller frowned. The car was bouncing along over potholes of varying sizes. Tommy attempted to swerve around them when he could, but traffic was pretty heavy. Was Tommy going to be difficult about this assignment after all? "I thought we were compadres, Tommy Romano. Okay, you got more pictures?"

Tommy nodded, holding up five fingers.

"Fifty bucks, take it or leave it."

"Let's see, that's not even ten bucks a shot. I don't think so. Let's go double o' nothin', Lou. Look f'y'self. If you don' like 'em, you don' pay," the driver said with a grin.

"Okay, one hundred. That's my best offer," Peller prayed he'd accept the price, because this ordeal was already costing him to the tune of a couple hundred dollars a day. He had, at the last minute, decided not to impinge further on Vallardo's good graces.

"Or nothin'. Deal." Tommy handed the first picture over to Peller. "Heah's those guys comin' out with Carlos."

Peller could see their faces, though he couldn't make out any features too clearly; both men looked to be in their late thirties, and they were very well dressed. "Red Tail" was shaking hands with Carlos, handing him a patterned canvas sack with an African-looking design, like the curtains in Carlos's kitchen.

"Anyway," Tommy continued his narration, "Carlos left around three, yestiday and the day befo'e. He came back about six, both times, carrying a couple a grocery bags."

"What was in the bags?"

"Couldn't really tell too well from this angle. Just in case, I took a pitcha of that, too," he said, reaching into his jacket pocket. "It was getting a little dark already," he apologized, handing the darker photo to Peller.

"Could just be groceries," Peller observed.

"Could be, incept for this," claimed Tommy. He handed over a third picture, this taken through the kitchen window of de Leon's ground floor apartment. The shot clearly showed the clutter of Carlos's kitchen, including a steep pile of clear plastic bags filled with white powder. Carlos was setting down one more bag, a bag he was pulling out of the patterned sack.

"Bingo. Great work, Tom." Peller took a deep breath. So it

was true. The super was dealing cocaine. Peller was no expert, but it looked like there was a small fortune in coke on that table. "Anything else?" He was flipping again through the pictures.

"Yeah. I talked to Marguerita. You know, Louie, she's too nice to be livin' with that trash. Anyway, I told he' to keep an eye on Carlos, too. She said she'd call you at your hotel tomorrow morning."

Peller was staring through the window. They passed Shea Stadium, that bright blue coliseum, then the old '64 World's Fair Unisphere, still a symbol of hope, though it was surrounded by wasteland. Rolls of barbed wire topped steel fences, giving the place a spooky, deserted feeling. Peller had gone to the '64 World's Fair with his parents as a kid and retained happy memories of the excitement of Tomorrowland.

"Tomorrow—Thursday morning—remind me to hang around until after she calls. I have a feeling I'm going to be here a while, Tommy. Maybe I ought to postpone my meeting with Leslie Russell 'til then too. Is that it?"

"That's it, boss." Tommy grinned. "I kinda like the detective work, Lou. Maybe I can start me a new career that'll pay somethin' decent." He drove for awhile. "Hey, Lou? You gonna call the cops on de Leon?"

"Naw. The cops are probably in on the take. I've heard that New York City police on that beat are just as corrupt as the people they're hunting down.

Tommy nodded in agreement. They were moving slowly on the Queens Expressway now, passing a huge cemetery; row after row of white crosses lined the highway. Tommy veered out of his lane, dodging a speeding Jaguar driven by a glamorous-looking, redheaded woman petting the fluffy white dog in her lap. Tommy spied one of the powder-blue NYPD cars flashing its lights behind him, and he slowed down to the speed limit. Fortunately, the cop had his cap set for the redhead in the Jag.

They drove slowly past the Tudor-style houses that marked the very private Forest Hills enclave, an island of affluence.

Tommy was still on the lookout for speeding traps. Peller was ruminating.

"Tommy," he said. "I need to drop in on a friend of mine. A lawyer. Her office is in Lower Manhattan, on Broadway, near City Hall." He would pay his call on Chris Boyer first thing. Then, if he needed to, he could visit with Angel Sanchez herself.

"Whaddaya wanna go way downtown now for, Lou?"

"Trust me, Tommy. This is important, or I wouldn't even suggest it. Remember that Angel Sanchez who set fire to Epstein's place in Spanish Harlem?"

Tommy nodded. "A sweet little numba, if I recall," he commented appreciatively.

Peller ignored the interruption. "Well, I got her this lawyer to help her get off easy."

"Yeah? Why'd ya do that? Sweet on her, Lou?"

Again, Peller passed over Tommy's taunt. "This attorney did such a job getting her off, Angel's spilled her guts about what made her set that little blaze," ventured Peller with a speculative look. "And it's got something to do with Mr. Assad."

Tommy sucked in his breath then, whistling, let it out slow. "Whoa," he exclaimed.

"Exactly. Now we're gonna find out just what she knows."

"Hope it ain't another wild goose chase, Louis."

They were coming into heavy traffic: road construction. Peller was impatient. "Maybe you can make some kinda detour, Tommy."

"Ya want I should cut through the neighborhoods, Louie?"

"Whatever," Peller replied, drumming his fingers on the armrest.

"It's a little outta the way, but we can go into Manhattan through the Battery Tunnel if you're headed near City Hall. There's usually less traffic," observed Tommy. "I d'know why nobody takes that tunnel."

"Just do what you have to, Tommy."

"We can drive through Crown Heights that way. You can

see your people praying for your soul down there," declared the driver piously, pulling off the expressway.

"Just shut up and make tracks, Tommy."

"Shuwa thing. Hold on to your yarmulke," he joked. "We're on our way."

They came out in Bedford Stuyvesant, a poor, working-class neighborhood filled with storefront churches of every evangelical stripe. They drove past once-beautiful brownstones that were crumbling into decay: abandoned, with boarded up windows and litter filling the yards. They toured past an old apartment building laden with meticulous architectural detail, now in disrepair, surrounded by a black wrought iron gate, guarded by ferocious stone lions. Plastic Santa Claus faces grinned from the windows. A scrawny black girl, who couldn't have been more than fifteen, sat helplessly on the front sidewalk holding her crying baby, leaning back against the wrought iron spikes for support.

"My world. And welcome to it," mumbled Peller gloomily.

They drove on. Tommy pointed to several corner groceries. "See them yellow and red awnings, Lou?" Most of these little stores sported yellow and red canopies. "I wish I had a buck for every awning. Really, I'd be rich. They advertises drugs fa sale, I swear. And I don't mean your docta's prescriptions, eitha."

Peller knew Tommy exaggerated. Still, he couldn't help but wonder if there was truth to his claim. Crowds of derelicts were squeezed under those awnings, ostensibly to buy their fresh fruits and vegetables. But with their gaunt faces and fat children, they did not seem to be fruit eaters to Peller.

Within the space of a few blocks, but a world away physically and spiritually, they entered Crown Heights, where posters of Rabbi Schneerson hung in every shop window, like a shrine to Chairman Mao.

Peller was curious about the ultra-Orthodox. His cousins were among that clan, and he'd never understood their ways. Like the time when, as a young boy, his uncle and cousins had come to visit. They wouldn't eat at Sam Peller's house. Not even a hard-boiled egg. In fact, it had been a struggle to get his father's brother to even enter their house. No one ever explained it to Peller, just another of life's many mysteries. He watched as a young yeshiva boy flew down the street, holding tightly onto his school books. He looked up at Peller and smiled. Tommy caught a glimpse.

"Ya know, they don't usually smile, these kids, Lou," he remarked. "Nobody smiles."

They drove past the Seventy-First Precinct house, and Peller speculated on whether there were Jews on the force.

"I'll lay odds. They run everything in this neighborhood," commented Tommy.

Now they were coming out of the Jewish section. The Spanish–American Food Center marked a new culture, a new neighborhood. They drove by the Caribbean Dome, another food market next to a Haitian-owned store displaying religious artifacts like crosses, portraits of the saints, and little statues of Jesus, and a social service agency that had a line of people stretching around the block.

"They must be handing out cheese today," Tommy remarked snidely. "These people neva miss a free lunch."

"People who live in glass houses shouldn't throw stones," Peller laughed. "I've never known you to turn down a meal on Amie. Besides, my friend, you don't know what their lives are like here."

"It's you who don't know shit about their lives, Louie," sniffed Tommy. "Wid your easy life in the 'burbs. Ya gotta live aroun' heah to undestand."

They drove through the long, humming tunnel in silence. Peller was thinking there must be some way to educate Tommy. At the same time, Tommy was sure his boss would feel differently if he had to live in his neighborhood instead of dropping in on occasion. They emerged near City Hall, past the monolithic, but not invulnerable, World Trade Center towers.

"Getting out here, Tommy," Peller announced.

Tommy left Peller off on Broadway in front of the West Street building with its Art Deco facade and steel revolving doors.

"Here, give Steve this number," said Peller, handing him Chris's phone number, "and ask him to reschedule my meeting with Assad's attorney for tomorrow. Lunch." Peller allowed himself a grin. "Steve ought to be in a heat over that phone call for days." Tommy sped away.

In the small marble lobby, Peller was surprised to notice an old-fashioned elevator, complete with an operator. How quaint. On his first visit, he had sped up the stairs without even bothering to check out the lobby. Peller stepped inside as the uniformed man solicitously closed the gate and turned the key. The elevator screeched slowly to a halt just under the level of the floor, and the doorman nudged it gently up before he slid the noisy retracting gate open.

On Eight, Peller purposefully strode the long hallway with its chipping, black-and-white linoleum floor, hoping the advocate would have a few minutes for him.

He arrived unannounced just as Chris was returning from a court hearing. "Another spouse abuse case," she sighed. "Guy whipped a knife on my client one night about two in the morning, because she wouldn't make him dinner. He had just come in. Drunk, of course. Now the judge wants to set the trial back another three months. His lawyer got a continuance. I'm afraid she won't last that long in the women's shelter. She's afraid she'll lose her job as a bank clerk if she doesn't show up, and if she does go to work, he's threatened to kill her. And they call it the *justice* system." She shook her head sorrowfully, then suddenly realized that Peller had come to talk to her. "How can I help you, Louis?"

"Angel Sanchez. We never did get around to talking about her confession."

Chris sat down, remembering. Angel Sanchez. Now there was a woman who refused to be victimized. "Well, if I remember correctly, she came in my office saying she had something she had to get off her chest."

"What did Angel say?"

"Seems she wants to go legit, or at least legit enough to cover for her whorehouse. She says she wants to start a lingerie store, sort of a poor-woman's Victoria's Secret. Frankly, I have the feeling her taste might be more Frederick's of Hollywood. Anyway, Epstein was letting her run her bordello without interference, rent free and a small take out of three apartments, until she turned on him."

"How did she piss him off?" Peller asked, curious.

"She said that Epstein was complaining a lot about his 'business partner' during the time she was sleeping with him; they weren't getting along, he would say, and the partner was having trouble coming up with money—all kinds of difficulties. She decided that Epstein was making excuses. She evidently thought Epstein was trying to back off their deal to finance the startup of her store. So she decided she'd check out this 'partner.'" Boyer paused.

Peller looked at Chris expectantly.

She continued her recitation. "Well, it turns out that Epstein has a business relationship with this Assad. They bought a building or two together; Angel wasn't too clear on details. But mainly it was business and political advice that Epstein was dispensing. And Epstein let it slip to Angel that Assad was the real money man in the venture. I think she said it was called M.E. Limited Enterprises. The M.E. apparently stands for Middle East. Apparently, Assad raises the money in Iran. His brothers are in the oil business one way or another; one of them's back in Teheran, and one spends his time travelling between Mexico and Venezuela and Peru."

"You're kidding," exclaimed Peller, sitting down hard on the molded plastic chair. *Holy shit*, he thought, *they work together*. "Imagine those two scheming minds collaborating. Well, I'll be damned. That Angel's dropped quite a bomb." Peller bounced up again and began pacing. "But what does Assad need Epstein for?" Peller asked Chris.

"I guess he doesn't want to rely only on oil money, prefers to share the risk, so to speak. They pay all cash for their buildings, as you know, buy them up at a discounted price, then turn around and sell them at market value to their own partnership. The principals get to keep the difference between the discount and market price. Between Mexico City, New York, and Teheran, it would seem they've got partners around the world."

"I can certainly see why Epstein might need Assad. But I still don't understand why someone with access to as much wealth as Assad apparently controls would need a little guy like Bud Epstein," insisted Peller. "I mean, Middle East oil, for Christ's sake."

"I'm not certain myself, Louis, unless oil's been depressed for too long," pondered Boyer. "But if you think about it, Epstein's been in this game here forever, right?"

"None better. He knows the politics of money in New York real estate," Peller agreed. "In fact, no one knows how to get ahead better in New York than Bud Epstein. He can handle tenants, he understands the city's regulatory system, and he knows how to operate buildings."

"And those are all things that an outsider like Assad might not have a handle on, right?" Boyer was leading him like a witness on the stand.

"Sure," admitted Peller, the picture suddenly dawning on him. "So that's how Assad knows which politicians' campaigns to contribute to," he said.

Chris crossed her arms speculatively and watched Peller's face as he solved the riddle behind this unlikely marriage.

Peller let the implications of Angel's bulletin sink in. Not only was she servicing both his borrowers for money at the same time, but between Epstein and his real estate and Assad and his oil wells, it would appear she had her hands in some very deep pockets.

"Why would Angel tell you all this?"

"She trusts me. I got her off the hook. And she's fed up with this illicit gaming she's been involved in. She says she can't rely on either Epstein or Assad to help her out anymore. I told her I thought I could help her establish a legitimate business venture with clean money and help her get away from the barrio."

"Where did she go wrong, that Epstein dropped her?" Peller asked, still marveling at Angel's skillful, simultaneous handling of these two master tacticians.

"I guess what finally soured her tête-à-tête with Epstein was seeking help from Assad. Seems she thought the suave Iranian could help her capitalize her venture better than her other patron, the maudlin Jew, over the long haul. And she mentioned that Assad was a lot better in bed too."

"Hell to pay."

"Angel did pay. One day, Epstein walked into her apartment unannounced. He had the passkey after all, so he thought he'd let himself in for a quickie. Whom did he catch in bed with Angel, *in flagrante delicto*? None other than his trusted partner, Omar Assad."

What a soap opera. Peller doubted whether even the most imaginative of writers could dream up a script that read like this one. Epstein making it on a regular basis with this hot little Latino, while at home, his wife wouldn't even let him see her under the sheets. After all, in ultra-Orthodox tradition, consummation of sexual relations permitted no touch of the flesh except through a hole in the top sheets. That violation of orthodoxy was disturbing enough. The idea of such a preposterous *ménage à trois*—Epstein sharing Angel with not just anyone, but with a "dirty" Muslim—was truly stunning. These newest revelations were utterly beyond Peller's grasp.

"Trusted partner," Peller spat. "I don't know when any Jew ever trusted an Iranian, in business *or* in pleasure. They were partners for mutual gain, but here it seems the gain was no longer mutual. Why didn't Epstein get rid of Assad then and there? And their mistress too?"

"Angel wasn't too clear on that part of the story, except to mention that she had turned Epstein on to cocaine, which she was supplying to him. Maybe he didn't want to cut off his source," Chris speculated. "At any rate, this might complicate your case a little. Thought you might like to know."

"A little? You've thrown me into a goddamn whirlwind with this news." Peller's chest constricted in anxiety. He'd sure uncovered a pile of shit today. For starters, Angel was one hell of an operator, he realized, contriving the very clever and very dangerous ploy of divide and conquer with her unlikely lovers to advance her own business agenda. But what kind of woman was it whose scheming turned business partners, even an odd couple like Bud and Omar, against each other?

Quelle scandale. Peller speculated that it was quite possible that both these borrowers had been diverting the income from their buildings and subsidizing drugs and prostitution for the past two years: Amie Mae's money. Peller could see it now, headlines in the *Daily News*: "New York Drug, Prostitution Ring in City's Crumbling Low-Income Apartments Financed by Mortgage Banking Giant."

"Imagine this news dropping on a blue chip like Amie Mae."

"I'd like to be a fly on the wall in your office when you break that news. Whew," Chris whistled.

Peller frowned at her sarcasm. "Chris, just listen; it's all beginning to make sense. One of the tenants in Assad's building told me she thought she'd spotted bags of cocaine in the super's apartment." He figured he'd refrain from telling Chris that he'd been engaged in his own homegrown espionage. "And she also said there's a lot of suspicious-looking traffic going through his place. Now, if Assad and Epstein are in cahoots, maybe this is part of a pattern. Could it be there's drug distribution out of Angel's Spanish Harlem apartment building too?"

"I guess anything's possible in that world, Louis," replied the attorney noncommittally.

Peller wouldn't put it past Omar Assad to have Carlos clones in other apartment buildings, operating their own "business" ventures throughout the city. What a brilliant scam. Buy up buildings in the slums, set up a convenient drugstore in the super's office, and watch the revenues roll in. Drug trafficking here, a prostitution ring there, cash in the bank. He remembered Tommy's photos: the two men, the canvas sack—drug money. It was possible. After all, drug trafficking was practically sanctioned since the wise and fair-minded mayor of New York had directed police to ignore street traffickers and users. Assad could easily set up an operation that relied on small-time runners who had no connection and weren't aware of any larger organization. A cash cow. Then what to do with all that dirty money? Wash it clean: buy up more real estate.

And what about Angel's role in this scheme? Maybe Angel was using Peller to get both her lovers in trouble. *Has she also woven me into her sticky web?* Peller asked himself, unwittingly allowing this new shaft of doubt stab at his heart.

Chris remained silent, allowing Peller to speculate. Frankly, despite Angel's claims, she felt Peller was spinning castles out of clouds. Still, Chris refused to get involved any deeper … unless he wished to retain her legal services. Otherwise, Chris felt she'd done all she could. Angel was off the hook.

Peller too grew quiet. His mind was racing. He knew in his heart of hearts that he should walk away from this whole sordid affair right now. But he also knew he was already in it too deep to walk away.

"Well, er, uh, thanks for your help, Chris," he stammered, standing up with his hand outstretched. "Hope you'll call me if I can help you sometime."

"I've got your number, Louis," the attorney responded sarcastically. "Goodbye, Louis."

Good luck and good riddance, she added silently.

****

Outside, a cold, clammy November rain had commenced. He barely noticed. Peller's head was crammed with questions. He must speak to Angel himself to verify her allegations. And he would have to go about it circuitously, just in case Angel was trying to double-cross him … or throw him off some other scent. So how should he handle the negotiations with Russell, suspecting what he did about her client? What if there were drugs in Assad's other buildings too? Should Peller call the police, or had their silence already been bought?

Peller hoped Tommy would drive by soon, before his head exploded. He glanced at his watch for the fourth time; the numbers just wouldn't sink in. He was certain he'd asked Tommy to come back around two; it was already two fifteen. What if his driver had come and left again when it appeared Peller would be late as usual?

At long last, Peller spied the white Impala weaving through the heavy traffic. *Thank God*, he thought, breathing deeper. Peller was not prepared to brave a Manhattan cab ride, not today.

Peller climbed into the heated car gratefully as Tommy resumed his normal mad dash pace.

"Anything new?" the driver asked in jest. He figured that nothing could top his news.

Peller stared blankly. "Let's just say I don't think I can take much more excitement today."

Peller fished a paper containing the three Bronx addresses out of his sports jacket. "We're gonna look at these buildings. Nothing special. And no more surprises."

The wipers were squeaking across the windshield, a noise that gave Peller goose flesh. He pulled his jacket collar up, rubbing his hands in front of the heating vent.

"I been there. Ain't nothin' to see," commented Tommy, glancing at the numbers with a frown. "C'mon, Louie. I thought we agreed there were certain neighborhoods we would avoid this late in the afternoon."

"Can't be helped. Have to see them, Amie says. Besides, we're just gonna drive by. I'm not getting out of the car today, okay?"

Tommy huffed but said nothing. Inside he was seething. Either Peller was a complete idiot or he had a death wish. Or both. It was already too late to start heading for the South Bronx. But then, as far as Tommy was concerned, it was always too late. He stepped on the gas. He would hightail it up there and hightail it out. He cut back to FDR Drive, weaving across lanes through considerable traffic, at least giving the perception of speed.

Peller stared absently through the rain as the car shot ahead in Tommy's peculiar game of traffic pinball. He was trying to puzzle out the implications of Angel's confession. One thing was certain: Assad, Angel, and Epstein were three burning hot potatoes.

He was still missing large pieces of the puzzle, though at least he had some idea where the holes were. "Did you ask Steve to contact Leslie Russell's office?" Peller asked.

"Yeah," replied Tommy. "He cawled while I was theah. She's makin' the reservations fa lunch, tomorrow, one o'clock. The Russian Tea Room, no less," he observed unctuously.

"Shit. Hangout of the stars. No doubt I have to dress like a banker for that place, and all I brought was Docker's and this sports jacket. I hate caviar," he sighed, examining his attire under this new light. The old tweed was a little frayed around the cuffs, he had to admit. And his pants probably needed pressing. Oh well, she'd have to take him as he was or to hell with her.

"Sorry I can't feel too bad for you, boss, feasting at the trough with a beautiful dame. Don't sound too awful to me," Tommy harrumphed.

He didn't get it; Tommy didn't. To the big man, a free lunch was a free lunch, company be damned. It was useless to explain Peller's trepidations to someone like Tommy Romano. Instead, Peller looked out the window at the dreary day. It was raining again. Riding through this sepia cityscape was the last thing he ought to do. Louis Peller should be sitting quietly in his nice little cubicle in Virginia, pushing papers like a good bureaucrat. Why couldn't he have learned to punch the clock like everyone else at Amie Mae, he scolded himself. Too late now.

They crossed the MacCombs Dam Bridge by Yankee Stadium into the Bronx, zigging, then zagging over to Westchester Avenue all the way to the South Bronx. The scenery was bleak. Under normal circumstances, there would be colorful crowds to distract from this wasteland, but in this rain, the streets were deserted, an urban Siberia. Even stray dogs prowling the streets laid low, hiding in sooty courtyard corners in soggy cardboard boxes or huddled beneath apartment awnings sagging under the weight of the pounding rain.

They were nearing the first building, the one on Watson.

Surveying the scene, Peller had a flash of déjà vu. The rain, the pounding of water on pavement, eerily reminded him of other circumstances, when shards of bricks and mortar had rained over his head. This building looked suspiciously like the one in his nightmare. But then, he tried to console himself, all these tenements looked alike.

Peller shook his head involuntarily. Erase this specter. Lana was right; he was under too much stress. After this business with Assad was wrapped up tomorrow, he must take it a little easier, as everyone kept recommending. They would go away, someplace tropical. Saint Barth's sounded nice, topless beaches and sparkling white sands, a world away from this hell. For a moment, Peller allowed himself to imagine those sexy, bronzed French goddesses littering the beach. And Lana.

Peller sighed. The here and now would not dissolve; he had to face it.

The rarely silent Tommy was lost in thought. He glanced sullenly at Peller. He hated the South Bronx almost as much as he hated Washington Heights, and he hated Louis Peller for bringing them here. But Peller seemed blue. The big man tried to start some chatter to dispel the clouds.

"Louie, ya eveh been to Yankee Stadium?" asked Tommy, brightening. "Maybe sometime you and me could take in a game. Ya know, once the season stawts. Ain't nothin' in New York beats a ball game," he reminisced.

He scrutinized the standard-issue, post-World War II apartment building through his window. "Sure, Tommy," he mumbled. "Wait—drive slow here."

Tommy obliged, resuming his chatter. "I was a kid, we listened to the Yankees on radio. Those was the days. We didn't have no TV in our house then. I remembeh this one kid on the block, Danny Katz; his family had a TV. Once in a while, they'd aks a gang of us kids ovah to watch a game. That was the best. An' I kep' beggin' my pop to get tickets. I finally got to see a game; I was about twelve. We sat up in the nosebleeds, but I had my catcher's mitt ready, just in case." Tommy wore a boyish grin on his face. "They didn't hit many runs up that far." Tommy was the boy who would never grow up.

Peller, stirred from lethargy, muttered, nodding appreciatively. He was a baseball fan too. Baseball and summer. He had been lucky enough to catch a few Yankee games, Mets too. During college, Peller and Paul and their gang would drive down to the city to take in a double header and a couple beers. Paul was always psyched for a ballgame; in fact, Paul and baseball seemed to go together like ham and eggs. The bunch of them would sit soaking up rays on those sunny fall days before the reality of term papers and exams could dampen the high spirits of summer. The crack of the bat, the roar of the fans; those were great days, recalled Peller happily. They would take in a few games this spring, he pledged, he and Paul. Like old times.

A sympathetic silence warmed Peller and Tommy like summer sunshine.

"Did the Yankees win?" Peller asked, still lost in reverie.

"Naw. Great game anyway. And the franks were better than

any I evah tasted, before or since. I think I ate five that afternoon, and a couple bags a peanuts," he recalled.

Both men were suddenly aware how hungry they were. "Let's get a little nosh," Peller suggested, realizing he hadn't had lunch.

"If you think you're done sightseeing," his driver chided, "we can head out.

"Let's just drive past the addresses on Elder and Boynton, then you're on," Peller agreed. "I'm in the mood for some manicotti, and maybe a bowl of minestrone. Know a good place?"

"The best." Tommy, stomach growling in anticipation, set his cap on wrapping up this visit to hell pronto.

Peller took the Sony out of his jacket pocket, dictating his observations. Turning off of Westchester Avenue, they pulled up in front of Assad's building on Elder Avenue. It was typical of the many apartments Peller had gotten to know in New York: aging, shabby, and unkempt. But passable come inspection time.

"No obvious signs of decay. No one suspicious hanging around," he recorded. "The rain," he commented. Tommy nodded with an assessing glance out the window.

"Ground floor windows bricked in; may be a sign of drug trafficking around here, like other neighborhoods where dealers bother ground floor tenants." These drug dealers, capitalist phantoms that they were, were adept at hiding their stash, and themselves, from plain view. Peller had never actually witnessed such a transaction, but he'd heard stories from numerous people in a position to know.

"Location: nothing special. Same old shit," he finished, clicking off the recorder.

Tommy slowed down. "Wanna go back by that place again, Lou?"

"No, nothing unusual there. Let's look at the address on Boynton." Peller was disappointed that the place hadn't been crawling with drug traffic. "We might be out of luck in this downpour. Not even the rats are creeping out of their sewers today."

Peller continued to stare silently out the window without comment. What to do next, he pondered. This tour had been short on news so far. But what was he expecting, after all? Supers standing on street corners wearing sandwich boards that proclaimed, "Assad's Drug Stand," or a notification from the city that the place was being condemned for building code violations? More colorful murals, perhaps proclaiming Assad as the savior and drugs his miracle? No, this journey had hit a dead end. He sighed. Maybe he ought to get out and wander around the Boynton Avenue site just to make this visit worth his while.

Tommy looked quizzically at Peller. Peller was still staring at the brick shell outside his window. There was no one in sight on the street that dreary afternoon.

Dodging potholes and parked cars, they pulled back up in front of yet another six-story brick building on a street of the same. Peller noted a crevice running from a side window on the top floor to the roof of the building.

"External cracks—strike one," he announced aloud.

Behind a locked iron gate that enclosed an open courtyard in front of the main entrance, he could see graffiti scribbled on one wall. "Sylvio loves Maria" was decorated with a heart. A white peace sign reminiscent of sixties graffiti had been painted over a distinctly less romantic message, spray painted in red: "Prison ain't shit!"

As they stopped across the street, Peller noticed a figure hunched over, running clumsily out of the building, trench coat draped over his head. Two black galoshes were the only other discernible features. The raincoat looked too nice to belong to any of the residents of this dump.

Peller unlocked the door. "You ain't thinkin' of gettin' out here, are ya, Louie?" asked Tommy.

Peller ignored Tommy's scowling black eyebrows. "I'll just be a minute, Tommy. I want to take a quick look inside." Peller got out quickly and ran across the street to stop the lone soul in this concrete barrio who might be able to let him into this fortress today.

Tommy cursed him out loudly. Peller could be letting himself in for trouble. Again.

"Excuse me, I was wondering if you could help me?" Peller shouted, crossing the street.

The man peeked out from under his improvised poncho to see who hailed him. He tried to duck back beneath his disguise, but it was too late.

It was Epstein.

"Bud Epstein?" Peller looked closer. "What are you doing here?"

"I might ask you the same, Louis, but I'm not nearly so curious. Good to see you, friend. You see, Louis," he smiled wanly, caught, "I've taken your advice. Sensible shoes." He picked up one rubbered foot and waved it at Peller.

Peller was astonished. "I was just looking for the building of, um, another borrower. It's supposed to be on this block, and ..." He faltered.

Epstein did not seem at all himself. He looked worn and haggard. His eyes were tired—ringed, red, and puffy. He was still smiling at Peller, as if he had every reason in the world to be standing outside a building owned by Omar Assad in a downpour. He unlocked the gate deliberately.

For a moment, neither man spoke.

"You want to go in, Mr. Louis Peller?"

"Well, I ..."

"Please, come," he invited graciously, pushing the gate wide. "I can give you a tour, if you like."

Peller walked inside, wondering what Epstein might be up to. Across the street, Tommy leaned on the horn impatiently, then threw his hands up in despair, knowing he was now in for a long wait. Peller did not look back as he disappeared inside.

Now the growl in his stomach would keep getting louder and louder. Tommy popped a wad of bubble gum in his mouth and turned on the radio. He loved to listen to Calvin Cretin, "Mr. Conservative." People thought the guy was a pig, but Tommy thought that crabby Cal was right on target. He hadn't gone so far as to join one of the "Cal the Pal" fan clubs, but Tommy's father had—was a founding member with a bunch of his retired buddies, in fact. Tommy had attended a meeting once with his dad, just for the hell of it. The codgers sat in the same Brooklyn bar every Thursday afternoon, chewin' on their stogies and chewin' the fat while the bartender turned up the radio loud. Every once in a while, usually while a caller to the program was getting wound up about "Whatever Happened to the White Man in America?" or something just as inflammatory, one of the old guys would stand up and make a speech about the "fuckin' good old days." Then his buddies would yell at him to "sidown and shadup." Once in a while, one of the old farts would get worked up enough to call in. They were a real kick. Anyway, just tuning in to the fracas on Cal's call-in was enough to distract Tommy from his annoyance at Lou.

"I'll need to have a little talk with that boy later," he reflected before he tuned in on today's discussion: "How this whole women's lib thing laid the groundwork for the president's wife to call the shots in the Oval Office." An irate caller screamed, "I get so goddamned upset with these girls thinkin' they know how to run the country. I mean, who elected *her* president?"

While Tommy was stewing, Bud Epstein was showing Peller the apartment building. "You see, a guy I know owns this building. He wanted me to take a look, see if it's something I might be interested in buying. Seems he's in default on some other properties, and the mortgage company is ready to foreclose on him. Says that would put him over the edge financially. Guess he's facing Chapter 11. He just wants to get out intact and maybe stay out of bankruptcy."

Peller couldn't believe his ears. Could Epstein really not know that Amie Mae was foreclosing on one of Assad's buildings? He decided to play out the scenario with Epstein and find out what the old man had up his sleeve.

Epstein was knocking on the super's door. "I think he'll let me borrow the keys," he winked at Peller.

Peller was growing curious about this coincidental meeting. First, Epstein, of all people, shows up at the doorstep of one of Assad's buildings; now he was escorting Peller down the first-floor hallway.

"Whaddaya think?" Peller asked, noncommittally. "Of this place, I mean?"

"You're the expert, Louis," replied the older man. "How does it look to you?"

The super cracked his door open and peered out suspiciously. *"¿Que pasa?"* he whispered hoarsely to Epstein. The two men briefly exchanged information in Spanish, and the super disappeared to find his keys. Peller maneuvered to a place where he could spy into the super's apartment. He didn't detect anything out of the ordinary there.

The super returned with the keys. He rattled off something else in Spanish, which Peller didn't comprehend at all. But Peller was surprised; Epstein seemed to know this guy pretty well.

As they walked back down the hall, Peller observed, "I didn't know you were fluent in Spanish, Bud."

"I'm afraid there are many things you don't know about me, Louis," he said, smiling enigmatically, an empty look in his eyes.

Epstein opened the door to a vacant apartment with a grand sweep. The plaster was peeling off the ceiling. Someone was apparently using the place for storage. There were boxes—some open, some sealed—littering the dusty floor.

"Looks like it needs a lot of work," Peller observed, wondering what might be in the boxes. He tried to peek into a few, but whatever was inside was packaged pretty well; for shipping, he supposed, although he thought he noticed the corners of some clear plastic bags tucked around the edges. Could the bags hold drugs, he wondered.

Epstein noticed his lender trying to divine what secrets the boxes held and laughed. "You ain't seen nothin'," cracked Epstein. He closed the door and led Peller down the dark, dank hallway. In the janitor's closet, there was exposed wire, water stains that crept down one wall, and gobs more peeling plaster. The exposed water pipe was leaking.

Peller whistled. "This place is crumbling."

Epstein laughed. "*Nu*?" he asked with a shrug. "So why should this place be any different?"

"Care to check out the view from the roof?" Epstein asked. "I suggest we take the stairs," he said. "The elevator's a little erratic."

The two men walked to the stairway abreast. "Why are you here, Bud? Why are you showing me around like this?

"A strange thing, Louis. I haven't been sleeping too well lately. There's nothing like a little insomnia to give you time to think. I think about the concentration camps, about losing my parents, about how my uncle lived and died in an apartment like this, about coming to this country poor with a vow to escape poverty, about how empty my life is, even with as much as I've accumulated. And you know what? I realize now, all my money hasn't made me any more secure. You ever felt that way, Lou?" His borrower looked on Peller curiously.

"Frankly, no. I don't have enough money to feel that way. I feel empty without it."

"Well I spent so much time making money that I lost my humanity. My son didn't speak to me after I insisted he serve his country in Vietnam. He got blown away under friendly fire. I never knew the joy of grandchildren. My wife, well … let's just say she isn't exactly here to help me get through the night. I won't try to hide from you the fact that I haven't been the most faithful husband or devoted father, Louis. I'm done with the lies."

Peller wondered if Epstein's eyes were ringed from crying.

"At least I can stop blindly pursuing wealth. Louis, let me tell you, money won't keep you warm at night," Bud said, laughing softly at himself.

"So what's that got to do with your being here?"

"Well, I think it's more than just a coincidence that I should run into you here, Louis. I'd like to prove to you that I'm changing my ways."

"If you think this means Amie Mae will let you off the hook in Spanish Harlem, you can forget it, Bud."

"Louis, I'm trying to come clean, and you wave it in my face. Trust me on this. You'll see."

Peller was suspicious. Whenever he heard anyone say "trust me," it was time for questions. He stared hard at Bud. Peller would play along. "Tell me something, Bud. Ever see any drug activity going on inside places like this?" Peller asked, trying to appear nonchalant.

Bud laughed a long, spirited cackle. "Louis, Louis, Louis," he said, putting a fatherly arm around the younger man. "What they don't teach you about New York real estate in that country club of yours could fill a book," he said patronizingly. He laughed again, a pained laugh.

Peller was feeling chastised, like a little boy who had just asked a forbidden question of his parents and condescendingly been told he would understand someday.

The old man sprinted up the steps, slightly winded, Peller keeping pace. As usual, the stairwell was covered with graffiti, and empty crack vials lay on the landing. The air smelled of urine. They exited onto the roof, Epstein pulling the raincoat back over his head for protection. Peller, head exposed, no umbrella, toughed it.

Outside, the rain had abated a bit, and it was only drizzling. But the sky was clammy and heavy, like wet newspaper wrapping the canyon of six-story buildings. They walked silently across the tarpaper roof to the brick parapet. Rooftop antennas dangled precariously by a single bolt. Peller detected crumbling bricks and mortar. Littered in corners and kicked under the peeling tarpaper were dozens of used condoms and a few empty bullet shells. The brick bulkhead housing the elevator machinery had been chipped away by gunshot; hundreds of bullet holes peppered the brick.

Still, Epstein led him on. Now they stood beside the parapet, where the walls had been covered over with tar in an attempt to stop the mortar from crumbling. Tar was a quicker, less expensive solution to rebuilding the entire wall, but it wouldn't last. The tar was already peeling away and pulling the mortar out from between the bricks, quickening the deterioration of the building.

Peller clucked. "Lovely view," he observed. "What's he asking for the place?"

"We haven't reached a final price just yet," said Epstein. "He wants three hundred fifty thousand dollars for it: two and a half times the rent roll. I think maybe two hundred fifty thousand dollars would be more in line. Buildings around here are going for less than twice rent revenues. I haven't gotten the appraisal yet. What do you think, Louis?"

Peller was shaking his head, looking over the edge. He noticed again the giant crack from the top floor to the roof. "Looks like the exterior walls are buckling and need major reinforcement. This isn't just a face lift. We're talking arterial sclerosis."

The old man was watching Peller's reaction. "I think if I were in better shape financially …" he began. "No, it's too much for me to take on now."

"Frankly, Bud, I was wondering about that. You know, we haven't seen last month's payment on your place in Harlem, and under the circumstances, I don't know how—"

"Ah, Louis, Louis," sighed Epstein. "If you could only understand my situation."

"Try me, Bud." Peller leaned against the wall crossing his arms, then thought better of it and stood straight.

"Look at it this way. Let's say you've bought a new car that was a little more expensive than you could easily afford, but you were banking on a raise at work, and besides, you really wanted that car. You financed it through the manufacturer for convenience, even though his rate was a few points higher than the bank's."

"Can we go back inside, Bud?" The rain was picking up again, and Peller had no desire to catch a chill up on the roof. He walked back through the bulkhead door and into the stairwell again.

Epstein obliged, following Peller inside.

"Then let's say you didn't get that raise, or worse yet, you got laid off. Are you going to let them repossess that car, or are you going to figure out a way to keep it?" he asked.

Laid off. Peller hadn't anticipated Bud might know the skinny on Amie Mae's pending downsizing. No new cars for Peller. "It depends on how much I want the car, I guess." They were crowded uncomfortably together at the head of the steps.

"Exactly," agreed Epstein, a grin on his face now. "Well, that's how I feel about my little property in Spanish Harlem. I'm going to fight to pay off that loan one way or another." Peller shook his head like a wet dog. The already unpleasant odor of the stairway now mingled with the musty scent of wet wool. Where was this leading, Peller wondered.

"Even though I don't have the cash on hand, Louis, I believe I have something you might find just as valuable. It has to do with my friend, the one who owns this place," he concluded, still watching Peller carefully.

Peller looked Epstein in the eye. He was curious. He remained silent, waiting to see what Bud would pull out of his hat.

"You know, your friend and mine: Omar Assad." Bud pressed his lips tightly together.

"I don't know what you're talking about," Peller responded evenly. Let this guy play out his cards one by one.

"I mean, I know you're having trouble getting one of your borrowers by the name of Assad to the closing table. I know he promised you he'd pay off his loan in cold cash on a building on which you lent him an outlandish sum. And I also know he's erecting roadblocks to keep that from happening."

Peller was getting nervous now. What did Epstein know that Peller didn't? "That's privileged and confidential information, Bud. I can't confirm or deny any deal that Amie Mae is conducting with any of its borrowers. You know that."

"I also know that you, Louis Peller, would do almost anything to close that deal under the terms Assad originally offered," Epstein continued. "Isn't that true, Louis?"

Angel must be feeding him this, thought Peller. Or maybe it was a bluff. "What if it were true, Bud?" he asked coyly.

"As I said, I have information that might help you do what you're trying to do," the borrower repeated.

Peller was on his guard. He knew Bud Epstein was no saint. There had to be something else in it if he was willing to betray his ostensible partner.

"What's your price, Bud?"

"A little sweetener in our workout in Spanish Harlem, say, fifty thousand dollars off the principal and 6 percent interest?"

Oh, he was sly, marveled Peller. So this was Epstein's scheme: If Amie Mae would agree to forgive Bud Epstein fifty thousand dollars in principal and refinance his mortgage at a ridiculously reduced rate of interest, Epstein would spill his guts. That was bribery.

"C'mon, Bud. I can't do that for you. They'd have both our heads."

"Then what's it worth to you?"

"I'd have to talk to my boss and probably present any debt restructuring plan to the credit committee in a decision like that, Bud," Peller answered in exasperation. "Offhand, I'd say it's virtually impossible. In fact, I have to tell you, the pressure is building to foreclose on your place, because you've slithered out of our deals so often before." Truth was, no one had bothered him about Epstein since the Assad deal had come up.

"Okay, Louis," Epstein took a deep breath, preparing to come clean with his confession. "It's like this. My business has gone down the tubes. I've had to sell my other buildings. I'm practically out of the real estate game except for Spanish Harlem and one other place in which I have a small stake. My other partners have abandoned me in my hour of need. I'll admit, I got a little cocky when the real estate boom was in full swing—bet my shirt on the good times getting better. Instead, I'm going belly up. I lost the beach house in the Hamptons, I'm about to lose my supposedly humble and pious wife who, apparently, married me for richer, not poorer. Everything's gone. Everything but this information that could lead you down the trail to Omar Assad and eight hundred thousand dollars on a building we both know isn't worth a fraction of that anymore. That deal would make you a hero at Amie Mae. So, whaddaya say?"

"How do I know you're on the up and up, Bud?"

He sighed. "I swear to God, Louis. I know some facts about this man. Let's just say, I have a line on Assad's other business ventures."

There seemed to be more to this intelligence than Epstein was letting on.

"Tell me what you know," Peller insisted, crossing his arms in disbelief.

Epstein dropped a few crumbs about Assad's other real estate transactions, just a teaser. Three other buildings in the Atlantic Avenue neighborhood, the heartbeat of Persian culture in New York, off Seventh Avenue in Lower Manhattan.

"His mother lives in one of them, with a sister, I think. I guess they feel at home there. All the little shops, some of the owners speak Farsi. Those places don't look anything like the Washington Heights and South Bronx buildings. They're well-maintained, *clean*, if you catch my meaning." The emphasis was on the word "clean," Peller noted, casting a glance at Epstein to see if, indeed, he had caught the meaning correctly. Bud returned Peller's look, nodding.

"I happen to know he's got money here. Lots of it. You see, I am privy to his personal financial records too. Although, if you ever breathed a word of that to anyone, I'd deny it flat out," he admonished.

Peller was silent.

"I can help you," he pleaded. "But I need your promise, Louis. And we do this off-the-record—based on an anonymous tip, you might say—or not at all."

"How do you know all this?" he was dying to ask. He bit it off his tongue. If Epstein was willing to rat on his partner, even if it meant implicating himself, wasn't it worth negotiating a new deal with him?

"Let me talk to Joe and get back to you.'"

He saw Bud suddenly breathe easier. "Just keep the details of this conversation between us, Peller," he cautioned again.

They walked down the steps, Peller leading the way, until they reached the ground floor. "I need a phone," he said.

"There's one on the corner," replied Epstein. The rain had let up again. The two men walked out into the courtyard as Tommy rolled down the car window to yell across the street to Peller.

"Lou, we oughta be headin' out to your next meetin'," he shouted, pointing at his watch.

Peller put up his index finger and waved it at Tommy, then walked briskly up the short block to the pay phone. Epstein held back, standing behind the gate to Assad's apartment building.

"Be right back," Peller called out.

****

The phone rang in Vallardo's office. It was Peller in New York. "What's up, Louis? I thought you'd be on the shuttle back by now."

"Listen, Joe, something's come up here rather suddenly. I'm up here in the Bronx. I've got Epstein with me. Says he's ready to work with us on this—can you believe? Joe, you know this guy's an operator."

"So tell me something I don't know."

"What you don't know is that Epstein's suddenly a little down on his heels." Peller looked down at his own fifty-nine-dollar loafers and thought about Bud's expensive tastes, still wary of the borrower's motives. "He's anxious to get a little sweetener out of his repayment deal … you know, some extra financial incentive from Amie?" Peller was nodding vehemently in Epstein's direction.

"Louis, I told you to forget about Epstein. Steve's working that loan now, and you're off it. Besides, you know we can't make deals like that. We'd get leveled by the auditors if they believed there was any favoritism."

"But, Joe," interrupted Peller, "you know we won't see anything from him if we foreclose. I really believe he has no cash. So why not work with him?"

"Louis, you're savvy to Epstein's charades. I'm surprised you've fallen for the sob story. Milk the building, milk the lender—whatever he can get away with. If we start reducing the face amount of the loan and giving away low-interest loans, every red flag in this organization would go up. Every borrower in New York would be knocking at our door asking for the same deal. You know how word of these things gets out in that community. It'd be our necks. Forget it, Louis."

"Look, Joe, I think a little tweaking in this case might be worth it. It's a deal we can do quietly. Besides, Congress also wants to make sure we're supporting low-income housing, no? And New York City's the primary focus, no? Epstein's not paying us now, so what would it hurt to work out a longer term repayment of the loan and the arrears? It's better than foreclosure, where we'd only get fifty cents on the dollar. Something's better than nothing after all."

Peller was not going to let up, realized Joe. "Louis, I'll have to take it up with Derek. In the meantime, forget about Epstein and concentrate on—"

BOOM!

Vallardo heard a thunderous explosion at the other end of the line. "Lou? Louis? What's going on there? Lou?"

Peller jumped, then screamed, "Holy shit. I'm in a war zone. You can't believe what's just happened. I gotta go—" Peller dropped the phone; it was swinging with a creak of the chord and an occasional clap of debris.

Vallardo could hear hollering and confusion in the background, then sirens. "Louis? Are you okay? Get the hell out of there, wherever you are." But there was no response.

Vallardo hung up the phone. He wanted to do something, at least find out what had happened. What could he do from there? He would call the New York office and see if they'd heard anything about an explosion. Where had Peller said he was? The Bronx? Or was it Harlem? He'd said he was at Epstein's building. Or was he? But he was talking to Epstein. What the hell was going on up there anyway? Maybe Vallardo had better tell Derek. No, Derek was at a conference in Boston today. "Shit, Louis," he yelled loudly. "Why're you always making my life so difficult?"

****

Peller ran. He noticed Tommy duck behind the car and then crawl in. Debris was beginning to rain down over his head. Although he hadn't witnessed the explosion, Peller could see shards of brick and concrete falling out of the sky: a shower of fallout between him and Tommy. He hoped Tommy could start the ignition quickly and pull away.

Peller ran, trying to reach the car, another building, any kind of shelter. He desperately wanted to get out of the line of fallout. He froze, watching the concrete and glass rain down around him and hearing the drumming music going through his head. And the lyrics to an old song he had heard somewhere recently kept flashing through his mind: "Wild in the streets, we're running mad / We're out to save the earth / For us to give rebirth / Wild in the streets … the end draws near."

This is only supposed to happen in dreams, he thought, flashing back to his own worst nightmare.

He heard Tommy calling his name with increasing urgency. It seemed a distant sound. Peller was still frozen. It was forever before his mind could convince his body to run. He tripped halfway down the sidewalk and lay there, motionless. Something sharp hit his outstretched hand, but he couldn't turn his head to see.

"Louis, what're you doin'? Louis!" shouted Tommy from his car, a half a block away. When Peller didn't respond, Tommy gunned the car in reverse, back toward Peller, rear door wide open, jumped out and literally threw a dazed Peller into the back seat before speeding off.

Chapter 18
Marguerita and the Witch Doctor

"You okay, chief?" Tommy asked nervously, his eye on Peller through the rearview mirror. "Looks from here like you got mixed up with a prize fighter in the ring."

Peller sat up slowly, gingerly rubbing his head. He could feel a bump the size of a ping pong ball. "What happened?" Peller asked.

"Don' know fa sure," Tommy grumbled. "All I know is, I was sittin' theah, mindin' my own business and tryin' to get you the hell outta trouble when the top two floors of that building blew. You got quite a shiner there, Louie."

"Was it Assad's building?"

"Yup."

Peller felt battered and bruised. His lip was swollen. He tried to see how bad the eye looked through the rearview mirror, but he couldn't get a good look. "I feel okay," he tried, then he groaned as they bumped over a pothole the size of Rhode Island. He banged his knee into the armrest. It felt sore, probably where he hit the ground running toward the car.

"Guess I need a seat belt, huh?" he moaned in a pitiful voice. "What happened to Epstein?"

They were stopped at a traffic light. Tommy turned around and took a good gander at his passenger. "We'd betteh get you to an emergency room just in case, Lou. Looks like a pretty good bump to the head. Must have hit you hawd enough to stun you. I thought you'd nevah move," the driver said anxiously.

"Naw, I'm okay. No hospitals. Take me to my hotel. I need to lay down." Thank God this old Impala was sturdy as a tank. "Just tell me if Epstein got out of there okay."

The light changed. Tommy turned onto Westchester Avenue again, inching through the predictable afternoon snarl toward Manhattan. "Yeah, his car was pawked right in front. He dove behind it quick, as soon as the blast went off, then managed to open the passengeh's side door and slithehed in. The top of the car wasn't a pretty sight—looked like he'd been through a hailstorm before he pulled out of theah. Bet he was glad he didn't drive his new Mercedes; the one the fool old man pawked outside his building in Spanish Harlem when Angel set the fire," Tommy contended.

Peller tried to collect his thoughts. Two minutes earlier, and he and Epstein still would have been inside the building. Too close for comfort. He looked out the window as they crossed the river, the steely Harlem River. It wasn't raining anymore, but the sky was still heavy. He watched as they sped back downtown. At least now Peller had a good idea where they were.

"Oh no," Peller remembered suddenly. "I left Joe hanging on the line."

Tommy laughed.

"What's so funny?"

"Leavin' Joe hangin'," replied Tommy. "He's prob'ly in such a panic, he's caught the first plane out to find you himself by now. Poor old Joe."

"But he didn't know where I was calling from. All I said was I was with Epstein in the Bronx. Maybe we'd better call Shapiro and let him know we're all right."

"It'll have to wait 'til we get back to the hotel, Lou," Tommy observed. "We ain't stoppin' until we can get you somewheres you can stretch out with an ice pack on that big, fat head of yours." He was shaking his head derisively. "Anyway, what the hell was Epstein doing up at Assad's building?"

"It's a long story, Tommy. Suffice it to say, I think we may be on the verge of getting Assad to come crawling back on his original terms."

"Who cares? These guys is all crooks," Tommy retorted impatiently. He couldn't give a Sam Hill about Assad or his building. He thought the landlord was full of shit, like every other landlord Amie Mae dealt with. In fact, Tommy thought that this deal was full of shit. And if Peller didn't see all that, then he was full of shit too.

It was close to four thirty. The clouds had finally parted, and rays of sun were pouring through to give a glistening sheen to the streets and trees stripped clean by the autumn rain. If it weren't for the tall skyscrapers crowding the horizon, Peller imagined he would see a rainbow arcing in the distance.

The car crept maddeningly slow, reduced to a crawl by the traffic. The insistent blare of discordant horns screamed across rush hour. For once, Peller didn't mind being stuck in the slow lane. He didn't urge Tommy to outwit the surrounding cars or point fingers at other drivers hissing expletives at the traffic.

Tommy peered back at Peller again, worrying why his backseat rider was so silent. He caught Peller staring aimlessly.

"Look ovah theah, Louie," he pointed, interrupting Peller's somber mood. "That building, at 800 Fifth, is where Assad lives." He indicated one of the newer buildings facing Central Park. I followed him one day last week and used my trusty binoculars to find his digs. You can see his apawtment right up theah, on the thi'd floor," Tommy directed.

"Frankly, Tommy, I'm not in the mood just now," Peller barely glanced at the place. "I'm glad you're on this bastard's tail, though," he added as an afterthought.

Peller closed his eyes against the agony of his pounding skull.

Tommy glanced back at his suffering passenger. "I'm gonna take you to the hotel. Now I gotta go home; I promised Ma. But I don't want you goin' out nowheah's tonight, hear me? Call room service to bring you some food. Watch a movie on HBO, and call me in the morning. Rememba, Marguerita Fernandez wants to talk to you first thing. Then I'll take you over to the Russian Tea Room for your meetin' with that dragon lady."

Peller wasn't paying attention. He nodded so Tommy would leave him alone, but his mind was wandering. He had trouble seizing the thoughts swimming in his brain. Leslie Russell, tomorrow … stay sharp. Angel Sanchez two-timing his borrowers. The explosion … call Steve. Omar Assad. Carlos the drug superintendent. Words were moving too fast through his mind. He let them go.

Tommy pulled up in front of the Waldorf. The doorman opened the rear door ceremoniously to let Peller out. Before he rose, Peller put a hand on Tommy's shoulder. "Thanks for pulling me out of the rubble," said Peller gratefully. "Hope I can return the favor sometime."

"Let's just say I hope you nevah have to," harrumphed Tommy. "Worry about ya self for a change."

Peller sat still for a moment, steadying his nerves. "Tommy, what do you think about me going to see Angel Sanchez tonight, you know, just to see what she might be able to tell me?"

"I think *nothin'*! Now get outta heah before I carry you out."

Peller stood up shakily and watched the Impala speed off. Then he went inside, catching a glimpse of the bruises on his forehead and the black eye in one of the hotel's hallway mirrors. He looked like Rocky after a losing prize fight.

"Think I need an hour's shut-eye," he told himself grimly. "After I make plans to meet Angel."

****

Uptown that same Thursday afternoon, Marguerita was on her way to the neighborhood center to pick up her two older children. She scooped up the toddler lagging behind her, needing to move the day along and keep him away from the ruffians on the street. *Thank God my boys have someplace safe to go*, she reflected sadly. She passed a litter of kids picking fights and looking for trouble and regained her pace.

She left home a good half hour early to take a few extra minutes to watch her boys' activities and make sure they weren't mixing it up with the teenagers from the hood.

She noticed Carlos de Leon coming her way and squeezed her baby tighter to protect him from that slime. He seemed to be in a hurry, taking great strides in his gaucho boots and swinging a dapper black panama at his side as he walked. As soon as he spotted Marguerita, he slowed his pace.

"*Buenos días, Señora Fernandez,*" he said, flashing a gleaming, gold-toothed smile and bowing low, hat chivalrously positioned at his waist. "You'll be happy to know I've met with *Señor* Assad, and he has agreed to fix up our building. He's added one hundred thousand dollars to my maintenance budget for the year."

Marguerita did not smile. "*Gracias*, Carlos," she intoned. "I would like to see that in writing, if you don't mind. Now if you'll excuse me, I'm late."

Carlos, in no hurry now, loitered in front of her. "Not at all, Marguerita. Mr. Assad was very interested in helping … after I told him of your petition."

"Good. Leave a copy of your new budget in my mailbox. Now, someone is waiting for me."

Carlos was dancing in front of her, blocking the sidewalk. His hyperactivity made her wonder whether he wasn't speeding along on some of his own medicine. "Why don't I just bring it by your place in the morning? Your kids will be at school then, no?" he asked with a knowing wink.

"Yes, they'll be at school, and I'll be at work." She charged forward, determined to ignore Carlos's pursuit.

"How about later in the afternoon?" persisted the super.

"I have an important meeting," she announced without looking at him.

"Ahh, a lover perhaps?" he ventured.

"No, a lawyer." Marguerita immediately bit her tongue. She hadn't meant to let Carlos know.

"Lawyer, *Señora*? Why, there's no need for that now."

"No, I meant a friend. He happens to be a lawyer too, that's all." She couldn't let Carlos know she was consulting with anyone. Especially not Peller.

"Yes, a friend. I see," he said smoothly. There was a suspicious glint in his eye, but Marguerita didn't see it.

So she was still pursuing her folly, Carlos flashed angrily. Well, she'd regret it. "Maybe after your meeting, my lady?"

Seeing she wouldn't be able to escape without some kind of promise, she reluctantly acquiesced. "Okay. Tomorrow. I'll see you at four o'clock in the front hall outside your apartment. *Adiós*, Carlos."

He graciously tipped his hat again, the stupid grin still glued to his face. "*Hasta mañana, Señora*." As he walked briskly away, she heard him trilling a haunting melody.

"He should never underestimate Marguerita Fernandez," she sneared silently.

****

The neighborhood youth center was a low, rectangular building surrounded by a sea of concrete edged by a seven-foot iron fence rimmed with razor wire. It was the last piece of hardware that assuaged Marguerita's fears for her children. The two older boys came directly here every day after school for supervised play and homework. After they got through with their work, they had the chance to match brain and brawn with their counselors at chess or hoops on the playground outside.

The playground was eerily empty, and inside, shades were drawn. If she hadn't known better, she would have thought the center was closed. She walked swiftly and observed Freddy Sanchez waiting dejectedly behind the padlocked front door, nose pressed against the gated glass top of the door.

Marguerita hurried up the front steps and was buzzed into the building.

"*Mami,*" he called out in relief when he spied Marguerita. "*Mami.*"

Marguerita immediately went to greet him, concerned at his anxious cry. He was a very independent nine year old, the man in her household.

A cluster of children congregated close by. The counselor seemed to be talking quietly with them.

She caught his hand in hers. "Freddy, *¿qué pasa?* How is Emilio? He's okay?"

"Nothing is wrong with Emilio. I made sure he stayed inside. He didn't see anything. *Mami,* I am so afraid."

"See what? Afraid of what, son?"

"I saw something I should not have seen. I told *Señor* Smit. *Mami,* they are going to kill me."

Marguerita's eyes opened wide as she put a protective arm around her boy. "Who will kill you? Why?" she inquired.

"I saw one of the boys from our building, a big boy from the high school. He was here on our playground. He didn't think I saw it, but—"

"Wait, Freddy, slow down. Is he a boy I know?"

"No, *Mami.* He and his friends run far away whenever you're around. They call him Link. And he don't usually come here. But I know he saw me."

"Well, what was he doing?"

"He had a knapsack. I d'know what was in the bag, but it

must have been bad. It was green and red and orange striped." The boy was talking quickly.

"There's no law against carrying a bag, Freddy. Besides, you say you don't really know what was in it," she observed, puzzled at his narrative. This sounded like business as usual for the neighborhood.

"But I know this. He was waiting for someone. I saw a black man sneak up outside the fence. He sent another boy in to talk to Link. They were all talking loud, and the man had a big black hat on, so I couldn't see his face. But he looked familiar."

Marguerita's eyes opened in skepticism. "What were they talking to him about?"

Freddy nodded, relieved to confess this horror. "I'm not sure. They were talking, and suddenly, I heard the man yell, 'D.J., get him!' Link threw the knapsack over the fence at him and ran like lightening."

She saw her son's face tighten into a frown as he struggled for composure. She drew him close, steady. "It's okay, Freddy. You're fine. Tell me what happened next."

"D.J. ran very fast after him, calling, 'Link! Chain Link! You forget something?' Then I saw him pull out a knife from his boot." Freddy was sobbing now. "*Mami,* he was going to kill that boy."

"What about the black man?"

"He looked over at me. *Mami*, I think he saw my face. Then he walked away, very fast. With the bag, I think. Then one of the counselors on the playground saw something was wrong, and he stopped that boy. D.J. suddenly stopped chasing Link and played it real cool." Freddy was on the verge of tears.

Marguerita squeezed him tenderly. "My brave boy. *Mami*'s here, don't cry."

"My counselor called the police, and the policeman walked Link home. Then the cop came back here. He gave us a big speech about how you don't have to do drugs for drugs to kill you. *Mami*, I don' think that Link or that other boy give a God damn about dying."

Normally, Marguerita would have rebuked him for blaspheming God, but she was too preoccupied to notice. She walked over to Jesse Smit, the counselor on duty and a good friend to her boys. Jesse confirmed Freddy's report.

Marguerita felt a sinking in her stomach. Carlos de Leon had been coming from this direction. He was carrying a black hat, and until he spotted Marguerita, he looked as if he'd been in a hurry. She wished she knew for sure about the drugs. If her hunch was correct, Carlos was exploiting neighborhood boys. She must tell someone.

She hugged Freddy close, hurting his shoulders with her tight embrace as they gathered up Emilio for a fearful walk home. How could she meet with Carlos, suspecting what she did? She must move the children out of that building right away, someplace safe. But nowhere was safe.

She was glad she would be talking to Louis Peller. He had promised to help, and she would definitely need him now. Still, even thinking about meeting with Carlos made her flesh crawl. She made a mental note to call Eva Jones to accompany her to that four o'clock meeting. And maybe she could get the legal aid lawyer to come too. Let there be safety in numbers, she prayed.

****

Meanwhile, Peller had checked into his room and looked over the room service menu. Nothing even remotely interesting, he decided. An improvised ice pack, with cubes from the machine down the hall wrapped up in the shower cap left for guests in the bathroom, cradled his lumps.

The tube was switched to CNN, flashing images of war-torn refugees from somewhere. Bosnia, he assumed. But Peller couldn't grab onto the words the reporter recited. Cross-legged on the bed like a Buddha thinking grave thoughts, with his spare hand he picked up the remote control, aimlessly surfing through the channels. It was all meaningless anyway, he figured. He hunted down one of the local channels to see if there was any coverage of the Bronx explosion. The rapid-fire readers were rattling through the sports roundup, but for once, Peller didn't care about college scores.

Better contact Steve: alert the office before they heard a news flash, again. It was close to six, but his friend would probably still be working.

"Steve—Louis here."

"Louis, where the hell are you? Joe called up here and said you were with Epstein and he heard some kind of blast, but Bud doesn't answer at his office. I thought you were out inspecting Assad's Bronx palaces. And I've been trying to beep Tommy since four. So what's going on?"

"I'm at my hotel. You would not believe the day I've been through."

"Oh yeah? Try me."

"I'm up cruisin' the Bronx, looking for Assad's other apartments, right? Well, who should I run into coming out of one of them? Epstein. No joke. So we talk. He's looking a little ragged, standing in the rain, but he offers to give me a tour—of Assad's place."

"Why was Epstein at Assad's address?"

"It's a long story, Steve. Let me just say there's a certain relationship between Bud and Omar."

"Whoa. Wanna run that one by me slow?"

"It would take too long to explain. Steve, this is all confidential information, between us, you know. Epstein's looking to restructure his debt in exchange for offering some vital statistics about our other defaulting friend." Peller allowed himself a triumphant moment of silence to let this unusual concession sink in with Steve. "Interesting, isn't it?"

Steve whistled long and low. "More than interesting, I'd say."

"Well, I'm in the middle of a phone call outside on a pay phone asking Joe if we can cut a deal with this fox when, all of the sudden, *kaboom*! The damned building blows up."

"Assad's place? You're kidding."

"Believe me. I couldn't make this up. Anyway, all this shit's raining down on my head, I get knocked in the eye and dive for cover—any cover—and Tommy drives up and rescues me. That's how it all happened. You know," he joked wanly, "I don't see why they can't still make phone booths like they used to for Superman. A body needs protection," he asserted, head smarting.

"That's it? What about Epstein?

"He apparently managed to slip off before we did. I imagine he would not want to be caught at that scene." Peller tried for a cynical laugh. "Wonder if Epstein had anything to do with this explosion?"

"Or Assad, more likely. *Oy veys mir*," Steve groaned. "Vat a headache."

Assad. The thought hadn't even occurred to Peller.

"What caused the explosion? Do you have any idea?" Steve asked.

"Not a clue. Coulda been an accident. Coulda been insurance, like the fire. But I doubt it this time. Lots of fallout, I can tell you that. Anyway, should anyone talk to the police?"

"Not you, sweet cakes. And you can bet we won't. Why stick our necks out when it's not even Amie Mae's building?"

Peller took an ice cube out of the bucket and crunched on it thoughtfully. "Well, I'm watching the news, and I'll keep you posted."

"Thanks. Oh, and Louis ..."

"What?"

"Try to keep yourself out of trouble for once."

Peller laughed. "Yeah, I'm thinking of going to shul with my good friend Alvin Pollock. Say some prayers. Did I tell you? He wants to introduce me to his Guatemalan cantor who figures to buy some Amie properties out of default. Just what I need: the singing rebbe. Talk about painful business. See ya, Steve."

Peller felt a little better. The bump on his head was going

down, and his lip was only slightly swollen. Hunger was beginning to gnaw at him again. Maybe Paul would join him for a bite.

"Paul. It's Louis. I'm in town, buddy, and I was wondering if you had plans for dinner?"

"As a matter of fact, yes," Paul said. "Chris and I—"

"Chris? You two got something going between you finally?"

"Louis, I hate to jinx anything. It's just that we're both ready this time. Before we were just friends, and we needed to keep that physical distance. I mean, there was Sherry and Arthur—you remember the circumstances. But she's special, Chris is, a certain quality I can't identify that makes her so real, so compassionate. I need that. And I think she feels she needs me," Paul ran on, breathless.

"Paul," interrupted Peller, "I get the picture. I am happy for you guys."

"Really, Louis. It's what I've been missing for so long, and I didn't even realize it. Listen, maybe you'll bring Lana up for a weekend, and we could find a little country bed and breakfast and spend some time together soon."

"I'd like that," Peller admitted quietly. "You don't know how much some quiet time with my wife and my best friends would mean to me." He sighed.

Paul had to laugh; Chris—Peller's best friend? Paul couldn't divulge to Peller what Chris really thought of him. Well, perhaps once she recognized Peller's better qualities: his incisive intelligence, commitment to helping those less fortunate, devotion to family, loyal friendship. In fact, Paul realized, these were all qualities Peller and Chris shared. "Anyway, I'll have to beg out of dinner, Lou."

"Guess I can't compete. But you're missing out on a real opportunity."

"Louis, I know what kind of opportunity you bring, and it's one I can generally afford to live without. Thanks anyway."

Peller laughed. "Sorry about that, my friend. Maybe I have

had some bad karma. Say, that reminds me, did you hear anything about an explosion in the Bronx today?"

"Yeah, there was a news story. Showed pictures. After the explosion, the building was devastated by fire. They aren't sure about fatalities yet. No explanation for it either. That's not one of yours, is it?"

"Not exactly. But it happens I was there when the place blew up. I got a little bruised in the falling debris."

"Louis, are you hurt?"

"Oh, nothing serious. I've got a pretty good black eye and a couple of nicks and scrapes. It all happened rather suddenly, I guess."

"Peller, what the hell were you doing up there anyway?"

"It's a long story, Paul. But guess who I should happen to run into up there? My good friend and borrower, Bud Epstein."

"Epstein? Was it his place?"

"Not exactly. It's Assad's. It seems Epstein and Assad have a little partnership going."

"They're in cahoots? Are you sure?"

"Yeah. I told you, it's a long story." Peller was concerned that Chris might divulge Angel's details. He really didn't want Paul privy to Angel's allegations. After all, Paul was already convinced Peller was over the edge on this business, but it was too late for Peller to extricate himself.

As for Paul, he didn't want to listen to anything. "Listen, Louis, I'd love to hear all about it, but I'm late for my date." He hesitated. "By the way, I'm only going to say this once more. Lay off Assad. Believe me, there's such a thing as knowing too much. This business of espionage is dangerous; so dangerous, I had to quit, or it would have been my life."

"I understand there are risks, Paul," Peller responded seriously. "But things are really under control. This explosion thing was just a fluke. Really." He ignored Paul's implication, refused to dwell on the danger. "Hey, I'll probably be in town tomorrow night too. Up for a carefree evening with an old friend?"

"Maybe. Call me in the morning, and I'll see if I can fit you in. And remember, I don't want to be the one who has to identify you at the morgue. Get the picture?"

"Thanks. I'll keep it in mind." Peller hung up, suddenly lonely.

He was still feeling shaken. The tube flickered, though he had the sound off, to keep him from being alone. Peller carefully rifled through his trusty pad to record this long Wednesday in November before he lost the gory, illuminating, ever-fleeting details and the chance to ease his anguish.

He slid off the bed, changed into a black pullover, and slipped back into his loafers. An Orioles cap, with the team's new logo that he had thought to give Paul for the Chase collection, he pulled low over his bad eye.

Determined to get out of the confines of his room, he started toward the door, then paused. Angel Sanchez: he'd have to meet with her. He raised the phone, shivering, to make the appointment. No answer. Angel's answering machine clicked on after the fifth ring. "Leave a message if you're in the mood, and I'll do my best to tell you what you want to hear."

His voice trembled unsteadily when he told her he wanted to see her. As he walked out the door, he gave himself a pep talk. "Life's too short Peller. Let's get the mind off this bad news. Nothing to be done. Off to dinner." Assuming a false confidence, he opened the door, barely remembering the room key before wandered unsteadily out into the lamp-lit hallway.

****

A buzzing jarred him awake. Wasn't it still night? Peller opened one heavy eye when the phone rang again. The other eye was swollen shut.

"Damn. I didn't leave a wakeup call."

The phone was insistent.

"Hello," he mumbled groggily from under rumpled bedsheets.

"I woke you? I'm sorry, Luis. It is Marguerita."

Marguerita. He squinted in the sun-brightened room. The gauzy white curtain barely screened out the day and the close up of a nearby office building. His mind was clearing slowly. Tommy had mentioned that Marguerita would call him in the morning at the hotel. Was it Thursday already? He shut his eyes, then opened them again. Events were becoming clearer: the blast, Epstein reborn, an old new deal.

"It's okay, Marguerita." Peller stretched tentatively and sat up against his pillows. "I need to get up and moving. What's up?"

"Carlos is making promises now. He told me Mr. Assad was worried when he learned about the petition. I think Carlos is lying."

"Why do you think that?"

"First of all, he's trying to charm me. It doesn't make sense. Second, I kind of let it slip that I was talking to a lawyer. Do you think he suspects I know something?"

Peller hissed inadvertently. Shouldn't show your hand to the dealer. "I couldn't say. What do you know?"

There was silence at the other end of the line. "Well, nothing for sure, but—"

"Exactly. And you should keep it that way, Marguerita."

"No, listen, Luis. My son, Freddy, saw something on the playground after school: a drug transaction with kids from the building. I can't be sure, but I suspect Carlos was involved."

Peller thought back to Tommy's pictures. "Take extra precautions, Marguerita. And keep your children out of sight. Could you stay with your sister for a little while?" He had to warn her. He didn't want to imperil Marguerita further.

"I thought about that. Perhaps the kids can stay with Maria. I cannot leave. Carlos might get nervous and come after us. He would suspect something. He wants to meet me at four today. He promised he'd give me a budget from Assad that shows one hundred thousand dollars for new repairs to the building, including all the things we asked for. Carlos wanted to meet in my apartment, but I put a stop to that right away," she confided in whispers.

"One hundred thousand dollars? Where the hell's Assad getting the cash? He told me he was broke, Marguerita." Peller was indignant.

"I couldn't say. All I know is that Carlos promised to show me the new budget. I think he said he'd put the money into a repair escrow account."

"Hmm." Peller was thoughtful. One hundred thousand dollars didn't even come close to what the building needed to be put back into shape. Ten times that amount would be closer to the target. And Peller sincerely doubted that Assad had a million dollars laying around or, if he did, that he'd make it so obvious. Assad knew quite well that Peller would review his maintenance budgets. But he couldn't let Marguerita know hers was a hollow victory.

"You're right to keep him away. Listen, Marguerita. I'm supposed to meet at noon with Assad's attorney. I'll ask her if she knows anything about a new repair escrow. If not, I'll let you know. You shouldn't meet with Carlos. Not yet. Will you be at work this afternoon? Okay, I'll call you there, Marguerita."

It was time for Peller to find out what slick tricks his opponent had up his exquisitely tailored sleeves.

Chapter 19
Russell, Roses, and Foreclosures

The agenda for his second day in New York was quite full, and Peller settled right in to business. Thursday progressed chilly but bright, the sky cleansed from the previous day's downpour. Peller walked briskly over to Fifth Avenue, stopping in front of a newsstand to buy a single red rose from the gypsy-ish woman wrapped up and shivering in a bundle of colorful scarves and skirts. The better to distract Leslie Russell. He strolled briskly up Fifth Avenue, past the chic shops, towering skyscrapers, and luxury hotels. Horse hooves clopped ploddingly amid the cacophony of horns, the shrill of the coppers' whistles, and the restrained silences of jaded, stone-faced pedestrians who populated the avenue. Normally, he would have soaked in Manhattan's vibrancy; today, he was preoccupied. In its own sinister way, the noontime November chill that penetrated his wool blazer and blew into his heart felt ominous. Overhead, broken clouds whisked swiftly past the sun's impassive face, matching the partly-sunny, partly-cloudy mood shadowing his own battle-blemished face.

He cut across Central Park South for his meeting with Leslie Russell at the famous Russian Tea Room. He'd called Tommy to tell him not to come drive him such a short distance. Today he needed to feel self-propelled and in command, even though he still ached from yesterday's blows. Amazingly, he'd managed to sleep quite soundly. No dreaming about explosions when he'd endured the real McCoy, Peller supposed.

The morning had progressed industriously enough. Peller jotted notes on his yellow pad to buffer his case against Assad, bringing his reports up to date. And he added more personal impressions to this growing journal to try to lighten the emotional baggage with which the previous day's events had saddled him. Peller wanted to bolster his sagging confidence before his lunchtime rendezvous with Assad's attorney. This was no time to obsess over the tragedy that had come close to killing him. Outside the sports section of *USA Today*, he'd studiously avoided looking at the news. In the aftermath, he did not want to know what devastation had been wrought on the building in the Bronx.

Around eleven fifteen, Angel returned his call. He set up a meeting in businesslike tones, leaving no room for misinterpretation. Angel was equally businesslike.

The remainder of the morning passed in a battery of conversations with other borrowers, with colleagues, with Lana. He missed her and the kids; they eased the strain and made him feel better, he thought wistfully. Why couldn't he leave well enough alone and return right away for their crucial sustenance? He didn't need this madness. It was time to pull himself out of this heroic misadventure.

Confessing to Lana, Peller tried to be flippant about his pending negotiations with "the dragon-lady lawyer." Lana had been less than sympathetic to her husband's feelings of trepidation after hearing about the previous day's trauma. In fact, her voice was colder than Pharaoh's tomb. She didn't even bother to read him the riot act, warning only, "for the last time," that he had better stop taking so many risks and think about his family.

She always made him take the defensive, he thought, annoyed that he had to explain to Lana, of all people, what he was doing here. He argued, "It's my job. What do you want me to do? Quit?"

"Yes," she had replied, not what he wanted to hear. Too proud, he could never bear to admit to Lana that she was right. Still, he recognized she was.

Approaching the famous restaurant on West 57th, he spied Leslie Russell, Esquire, standing nonchalantly under the canopy. From a distance, he could appreciate her graceful but distinctive silhouette. Her skin was starkly white and smooth. She appeared cultivated and poised, swathed in fur. Her long, white neck stretched regally out of a sumptuous black mink collar. Russell the Swan. She was peering in the other direction, obviously expecting him to arrive in a cab or car. Close enough for eye contact now, he fingered the rose nervously.

As if feeling his impertinent stare, she turned in his direction. She gasped.

Suddenly, he realized what a fright he must look with his bumps and bruises—the alarm in her eyes said it all. He reddened, disarmed. As he approached, she recovered from her momentary lapse in diplomacy, pulling her expression into a professional poker face.

Peller recovered from his embarrassment quickly, his confidence reasserting itself. "Here," he said quickly, handing her the flower and grasping her delicate hand, deceptively strong. She looked quizzically at his banged-up face.

"I had an unfortunate encounter with an overhead compartment on the shuttle yesterday. I opened it to get my suit bag out, and lo and behold, all the contents had shifted … all over me." He smiled, attempting lightheartedness. "They do warn you about those things happening, but I didn't believe it." He'd be damned if he'd let her know he was anywhere near Assad's exploding building yesterday. "Live and learn. Anyway, I hope you'll still be seen with me," he joked with a charming smile.

She pursed her lips, trying to decide whether or not to believe him. "Luckily for me, I've reserved a private corner. We won't be seen," she replied evenly, in a low voice. Not even a crack of sympathy peeked out from behind her black eyes.

She walked inside swiftly, heading to a tucked-away table with a sudden determination not to be noticed. He ignored her abrupt manner, looking right and left at the assembled glitterati like a fan on a Hollywood celebrity tour. There was famed director and sometime accused child molester Gordy Glenn sitting amid two male flunkies, deep in conversation and spooning down vanilla ice cream and milk. *Why go to the Russian Tea Room for that,* Peller wondered. He spied animated leading lady Martina Jacobee entertaining an enraptured multimillionaire Wall Street investment banker—the kind of mogul whose picture appeared frequently in the business pages. He thought he spied Ivan Stephanov, born John Jack Schmidt, a has-been leading man, sloshing down his Smirnoffs solo at a table near the kitchen. Heads were beginning to turn in Peller's direction before he realized what a foolish figure he cut, a rube in this crowd of studied sophistication, and he hastened to catch up to the retreating back of the elegant Leslie Russell.

She stood in front of her chair, selecting the one that faced out into the restaurant, until he caught up. She threw the mink over the third chair nonchalantly. That obviously left him the chair facing her … and the wall. As he pulled out her chair, he surreptitiously took in Leslie Russell. The black, flowing dress hinted at femininity shrouded in mystery. Sitting, her long legs were draped in the white formality of the tablecloth. Despite his intense distrust and all protestations to the contrary, he did find her attractive. But he knew her magnetism was to be resisted at all costs. He sat down uncomfortably, his menu superimposed between him and conversation.

Finally, without looking at her, he apologized. "I really didn't mean to cause you embarrassment."

"It's okay, Mr. Peller," she replied in a softer tone. "You just caught me by surprise. I'm sorry about your accident, really."

He looked at her curiously.

"I just didn't want to attract the attention *du monde*, although there's no one in this place who matters," she explained. "It was habit, I guess. The big players in the financial community don't generally venture this far uptown on a workday, so I shouldn't have to worry about any ears that shouldn't be listening. That's why I didn't suggest we dine in the firm's dining room, although the food there is generally better than it is here. Besides, I don't need anyone from 'the street' listening in. You know how bad news gets around."

"But Assad isn't a player on Wall Street," Peller asserted.

"No, but many of my clients are. And I need to protect their integrity as well as Omar's," she explained, rather mystifyingly.

Peller had little experience with Wall Street and had no idea at all what she was driving at. He knew she, like all self-important lawyers, was full of bullshit. But he was determined to play along. "I'll try to be discreet, Ms. Russell," he replied with a constrained smile.

The waiter hovered nearby. "Let's order, then get right down to business, Mr. Peller," she resumed, motioning him to approach. "We'd like a little aperitif, I think," she ordered, looking over at Peller with a gaming look in her eye. "Join me in a Kir Royale, Mr. Peller?"

He had no idea what a Kir Royale might be, but he didn't ask; he could not allow himself to appear the rube. Never one to shy away from a contest of wills, Peller nodded.

"I always feel I can negotiate more freely after I've let go the tensions of the day."

"Of course," he agreed. He had to admit, he admired her head-on approach. He peered around the room at the rich decor. "You know, Ms. Russell, I'm not one for chic."

"Call me Leslie, Louis. You don't mind my calling you Louis? If we're going to be doing deals together, I think we ought to cut through all the crap. And I think, from what I've heard of your reputation at Amie Mae, we could work well together," she added with a sly smile.

Don't get sidetracked, he reminded himself. Ignoring the flattery, he made the first bid. "Well, Leslie, then let's start with the matter at hand: Omar Assad," he matched her man-to-man tone.

"I want to do just that," she agreed. "But first, I'd like to powder my nose. You'll excuse me a moment?"

Peller nodded, surprised at her sudden change in tactic. He couldn't understand her. One minute, she was all business, and the next? How else to describe her but "female."

She rose slowly, and he couldn't help but notice a certain swing to her walk. He considered himself a connoisseur of such details, even under adverse circumstances. After all, no crime in looking.

The waiter returned with their drinks. He was stirring his idly when she returned.

"You know, Louis, I think we ought to be able to do a lot of work together. Several of my clients are big in real estate, you know. And there are rumblings that the real estate development business is poised to make a big comeback, assuming this recession is on its last legs. In fact, I hope to be able to lure you to leave Amie Mae for more lucrative, and more powerful, playing fields."

Of course, she would have done some research about him. The first commandment in successful negotiations: know thine opponent. After all, hadn't he been quick to find out about her? Still, Peller felt he intuitively understood this ambitious woman; her tough, no-bullshit style was like his own, although she worked in a far more high-powered environment than he ever cared to. He wondered how she had found out about him; after all, he was a mere worker bee in a buzzing hive. No matter, he could certainly match her at this game.

"Leslie, I admire your balls," he shot back, taking them eyeball to eyeball in their dialectic. "And I'm prepared to acknowledge that you and I are well matched to negotiate. But you'll find I don't respond to flattery or agree to the price Mephistopheles exacts for soul selling."

"Fair enough, Louis. I wouldn't insult your intelligence by stooping to flattery. So let's drink a toast to a fair and successful negotiation—for your company and my client. Here's to you."

They raised a glass, then Russell signaled the waiter to take their order. The specialty of the house was beef Stroganoff, something that really didn't appeal to Peller. Red meat had been off his diet since college. And borscht—somehow the idea of cold beet soup was extremely unappetizing. He asked the waiter for a chicken salad sandwich on rye and again felt Leslie Russell's black eyes burning through him. The waiter raised an eyebrow at the obviously pagan tastes of this tourist, but diplomatically refrained from recommending this uncultured customer check out the McDonald's down the street when the clod's very chic companion raised her own eyebrow in warning.

Russell ordered the borscht and a salad.

Peller finished the Kir. He liked the light fruitiness of the drink and thought he might even order another, though it was his policy never to drink over business.

"Now I hate to divert this pleasant conversation," resumed Peller, who despised small talk. Forgetting his earlier ordeal, he was feeling on his mettle facing this very confident woman. He wanted to assert his authority from the start. "But I'm here to talk business, Leslie. I'm sure your client is not only willing but able to pay the token sum of eight hundred thousand dollars that we're asking from him to pay off the mortgage on his building. It's a fair price, a cost he apparently deems worthwhile to keep this prized building."

"Louis, we're interested in making a gentleman's agreement to divest you of a headache. Omar's a reasonable man, but he isn't made of money, no matter what you may believe. He can go no higher than four hundred fifty thousand dollars on this building.

"Four fifty?" he spat out, insulted. "Our brokers inform me

we can get eight hundred thousand dollars for this property. That was Assad's original offer and the one we agreed to. I'm not going to get stuck for less than fair market value, and if you and Omar think you can steal it away for nothing, you'd better think again."

"I'm sure you are aware that Omar will then have to invest at least one million dollars in major improvements to bring the property up to code. As you know, the roof needs replacing, the entire interior must be plastered and painted, and the foundation has shifted enough to warrant structural reinforcement. I wish my client had known about the underground stream destabilizing the foundation before he had invested so much of your money in the first place," she added.

Good. She obviously wasn't aware of the asbestos problem or the lead paint, he concluded. "The cost of the repair should not be so expensive, Leslie. I think you're exaggerating. I have forty-six other buildings in this town that are in various states of disrepair, and not one of them needs a million dollars to fix up," Peller blustered.

"There's no need for anger, Louis," she said coolly. "We're not here to duel."

Her cool demeanor irritated him even more. "If you'll come back to your original offer, I'm happy to work out the terms," he rejoined with a frown.

The waiter brought her soup. Peller ordered a second Kir, to break the tension, if only temporarily. He watched her taste the soup, resented her smug smile.

"I think eight hundred grand is much too high, Louis. And you know it is too. That building isn't worth more than three hundred. So tell me what you think is a fair price," she reopened the dialogue.

He was toying with his fork, thinking that he needed some more time to work the numbers. "Have you ever observed a beehive, Leslie?" he asked quizzically.

"I'm afraid I'm not much of a student of nature, no," she replied.

"Well, think of Omar Assad's building as the hive. He keeps it, but it's on my property. He wants to buy the land, hives and all, from me, but he doesn't care about the bees, just the honey inside, so he's kind of run it down. Now think of the tenants as bees living in the hive and working together to make it a safe, livable place. Can you follow that?" he asked, slightly condescending.

"What are you getting at, Louis?" she asked in irritation, impatient with his metaphor.

"Think of me as a beekeeper working to protect the lives of the honeybees against those people trying to put their hands in my hive."

Russell parried, "I'd be careful with that if I were you, Louis. I'm not sure even the best beekeepers can avoid being stung sometimes. Besides, Omar is not often bothered by bees. I'm here to make sure he can harvest the honey. And I myself am well protected against stings."

Peller insisted, "You know eight hundred thousand dollars was the agreed-upon price. It's only the terms of the payoff we're here to negotiate."

The waiter set another Kir in front of Peller and, next to it, an artistically garnished plate where cold sliced chicken lay on the plate next to a small heap of lettuce and heavy brown bread.

Chicken salad sandwich, accompanied by flourishes of pomp and circumstance, Peller noted unamused.

Russell nodded at the waiter, pausing until he left. She pushed her soup away. "The offering price has come down. Fortunately, he asked me to take over the negotiations, or he would have been totally ripped off. Even at this rate, you and I both know he's overpaying."

"Leslie, you know what I think," Peller remarked. "I appreciate your attempt to reduce Assad's offer. It is a bold move on your part. I like your style. But don't offend me by lowballing your bid," he retorted. He could set the tone here as well as she.

"Surely you can see that the difference between four fifty and eight hundred thousand dollars is unacceptable. Now, let's see how prepared you are to negotiate." He sat back, his saddle-brown eyes studying her unreadable expression.

"Oh, Louis," she sighed in exasperation. She blinked first. "You must come off that number if we're going to settle this today."

He kept on staring. In fact, he was quite willing to accept four hundred fifty thousand dollars for a short payoff of the mortgage. For a building with one million dollars of remaining debt that was now probably worth only a quarter million, four hundred fifty thousand dollars looked pretty good. But Peller still could not understand why a smart man like Omar Assad was willing to pay so much money for a building that was valued at half that price. And the news about the one hundred thousand dollars in escrow, money hitherto unavailable, left him a little peeved. Given his borrower's professed eagerness to buy, Peller still wanted to haggle a little. After all, Louis Peller was willing to wait for the deal of the century.

Apparently, Leslie Russell also felt she could wait. She appeared to relish their little dialectic, in fact. It soon became evident to both of them that their negotiations were at an impasse.

They stood as adversaries. As the meeting broke up, Leslie grabbed the check. After some verbal sparring, Peller reluctantly allowed her to pay. With a new gleam in hers, she met his eyes again, as if she'd enjoyed their match.

Not to be outdone by ceremony, Peller quickly grabbed the mink from the third chair and held it out for her. After a moment's resistance in which she measured his motives for this courtly gesture, Leslie the liberated slid her arms into the luxurious sleeves. Turning to touch him on the hand, she spoke, her tone suddenly spirited.

"Louis, I hope we can come to terms. If you have second thoughts while you're here, call me this evening. I work late at home. Believe me, this deal means as much to Omar as it does to you."

He too had enjoyed their verbal sparring match. Outside in the blustery air, she shook his hand lightly and burrowed into the sumptuous warmth of her fur then strode away, leaving him alone and at the mercy of the wind. Bereft of distractions, he suddenly felt autumn's icy finger scratch across his face, the bone-chilling herald of winter pressing in on him.

Chapter 20
The City Doesn't Sleep

By two thirty, when he finally emerged from under the Russian Tea Room's canopy, the sky had settled into overcast. Peller stepped onto the street, realizing he had a meeting with Angel Sanchez at three fifteen and no head to talk to her. His thoughts were flying in a million directions at once. Peller, mind churning, face burning, was restless and out of sorts. Leslie Russell had thrown him off his game plan. Ever since he'd arrived in New York this trip, he'd been rocked, jolted, and thwarted in what should have been a straightforward effort to resolve his problem, to work out a payoff on Omar Assad's defaulted loan. Why had this deal become so difficult? Explosions notwithstanding, his mind just couldn't absorb any more shock.

So why was he on his way toward Lincoln Center to meet with Angel Sanchez? In a dim state of consciousness after the explosion, he had believed she might enlighten him about the nature of the partnership between Omar Assad and Bud Epstein. He realized now that such information would be of no possible consequence in his discussions with Leslie Russell, whose aim was to wear him down.

Still, Angel had sounded so eager to help when he called.

"After all, Louis," she reminded him ceremoniously, "it is thanks to you I am not now in jail. I would like to help in any way I can." Well, maybe she knew something about Assad's other properties.

He walked into the very trendy Iridium restaurant at the Empire Hotel, a place that was suitably grand under its undulating copper awning and roof, blinking to adjust his eyes to the dim interior. He sat down at the bar, where Angel had said she'd meet him. He didn't know why Angel had picked a place like this, a restaurant where actors and musicians and other artsy types went to see and be seen around Lincoln Center. This was the kind of bar whose patrons never rose 'til after noon, and where the serious play began well after eleven, when the formal events at Lincoln Center finally let out. It was also a haunt for neighborhood bohemians in search of good company, good conversation, and good booze.

At three o'clock in the afternoon, however, there was scarcely a person in the joint. After waiting for fifteen minutes, he decided he was being stood up and rose to leave when finally Angel made her entrance, nervously tamping out her cigarette, which she waved about in a long, slim holder, to catch his attention. As she bustled toward him, she removed her long, colorfully woven wool sweater. She had dressed down for the occasion, wearing faded jeans and a white, opalescent T-shirt with gold studs beginning at the shoulder and parading in a stripe down each long sleeve. Even her face was plainer, without the false eyelashes and the lavish blush.

"*Hola*, Luis," she pronounced breathlessly in her singsong. "I am so glad to have the chance to thank you for helping me." Peller hadn't noticed before how breathless and flighty she acted. "Shall we have a little drink?" she asked sitting down. There were no other patrons at the glittering bar.

He shook his head, motioning that Angel should feel free to order. He already felt disoriented from the Kir at lunch. In fact, Peller wasn't sure what had possessed him earlier to raise a glass with, of all people, Leslie Russell. Angel asked the bartender for a rum and coke.

"What can I do for you today, Luis?" she asked eagerly, tapping her catlike, elaborately painted nails on the bar.

"I spoke to your attorney, Chris Boyer, the other day, Angel," he began.

"Ah, *si*, Ms. Boyer, what a nice lady," she resumed. "You sent me to her. How can I ever thank you, Luis?"

The bartender put Angel's cocktail down on a napkin in front of her on the bar and glanced incuriously at Peller. "Shall I start a tab for you, sir?"

Angel laughed and touched Peller's hand caressingly. He flinched, then nodded to the bartender. Peller was beginning to see it would be difficult to get down to business with Angel.

"Maybe you could just tell me more about what you mentioned to Chris about Bud Epstein and Omar Assad."

"Ahhh, of course. My landlord and his partner. Both are very good clients of mine," she confirmed. "Or were." She took a neat swig, emptying her glass, and motioned to the sleepy-eyed barkeep for another.

"That's what I don't quite understand. How are they partners?"

"Oh, of course. They both buy real estate. But that's something you know already, no?" Angel winked gaily at Peller. "I'm telling you nothing new."

"Yes, they're both my borrowers, you're right. But I had no idea they bought apartment buildings together."

"Oh, they don't buy apartments together, no." Angel took out a cigarette and fumbled in her purse for matches, looking over at Peller. He didn't pick up on her cue. The bartender detected her signal and offered her a light.

She nodded her head slowly. "Well, maybe one or two in the past, but that's over. No, they buy other things together: shipping lines, stocks, sexy clothing stores. Apartment buildings they own separately." She took a deep draught on her cigarette. "They don't want to manage properties together. Can you imagine," she asked, eyes wide, "the two of them arguing day and night over collecting rent and repairing leaky bathtubs?" She laughed, as if the very thought of such temperamentally incompatible characters from opposing cultures and disparate parts of the world actually conducting business in tandem was too hilarious to be true. "Bud and Omar?" she laughed again.

Peller could not imagine such a working relationship either, so he laughed too.

"No," Angel said emphatically. "The ventures they own together require only money. But they worry, because these apartment buildings are such a drain on their cash. Oh, how these men complain. Bad tenants and late rents and drugs, and bad neighborhoods. I ask Omar why he keeps them if they're such trouble, and he says, oh, he loves these buildings. But I see more," she confided. "I know he needs these apartments."

Peller looked at her, startled at her suddenly serious tone. "Why?"

"He needs your buildings to clean their money," she said, returning his stare curiously.

"Clean their money?" he repeated, confused.

At that moment, the bartender stopped back with a second glass for Angel. She winked at him, and he returned the wink with a smile. Clearly, they had just arranged something silently between them.

"Yes, clean," she said, miming the act of washing her hands after touching something dirty. "Clean money, dirty money, you know what I mean?"

Slowly, her meaning dawned on Peller. "You mean launder? They're laundering profits from illegal enterprises?"

She nodded, taking another draught of her cigarette.

"What are these other businesses?" Peller persisted.

"Well, *Señor* Peller, there's mine for one," she offered, surprised at his ignorance. "Surely you did not believe I was innocent of the prostitution charges?" She looked truly shocked at this notion.

Peller looked down at his hands. Of course he knew what she was; he just didn't expect her to admit it to him so freely. Face flushing, he looked back up at her. "No, I assumed—"

She interrupted him, waving her hand as if it didn't matter what he thought. "I am quite a successful businesswoman in my own right, Luis. I want you to know that. It's just that, since I've come to New York, well, I needed a little investment to get started, and both Bud and Omar were kind enough to offer."

"But they found out you were playing them both against each other, isn't that right, Angel?"

She frowned. "You heard this from Chris Boyer?"

He nodded.

"I'm not putting Bud up to nothing," she retorted angrily. "They are bad men, Luis. Very bad. Stay away from them, *mi amigo*."

Both were silent for a moment. "Do you know of any other such enterprises, Angel?"

"No," she answered definitively. A little too fast, thought Peller. She's hiding something. Angel sat glumly, brooding over tragedies about which he could only speculate. Maybe Assad and Epstein were threatening her against revealing any other secrets. He would let it go … for now.

Peller stood up to go. "Well, thanks for your help, Angel. If you find out anything else, call me, okay?" He plopped ten bills down on the table. "For your drinks," he said.

"Sure, Luis. For you, I will help. You helped me, and I don't forget friends like you." She winked and smiled, the cloud passing from her face.

"By the way, Angel. I understand you're interested in getting started in a legitimate business."

"Ah, yes. I want to sell beautiful nightgowns and sexy stockings for women like me, who take pleasure in pleasing men. A good idea, no? Omar and my Buddy both loved it. I am planning to get started on this very soon," said Angel. "As soon as I can get my other affairs in order."

"My Buddy." The very idea of Angel Sanchez and Bud Epstein screwing around still made Peller feel sick to his stomach. "I would do that if I were you, Angel. But stay away from the likes of Epstein and Assad. Let Chris Boyer help you go straight; she's a good woman."

"On this, we are agreed, Luis. I will stay away," she concurred. Then, seeing the look in Peller's eyes, she said, "Take your own good advice, *Señor*. Stay away from these men." Her tone was ominous.

With that, Peller left Angel to her smoking and sipping. As he slipped out, he noticed the lethargic bartender taking the stool he had vacated and moving it close to Angel.

"So much for Angel wrapping up her affairs," muttered Peller sardonically under his breath.

As Peller emerged, he pulled his jacket closer around him. The chill lingered in the autumn air, the sun played hide-and-seek behind the clouds. He wished he'd brought his overcoat. Lacking any further business to attend to in this part of town, he would head back to the office on Lexington Avenue. He idly considered taking the next shuttle for home and blowing off Marguerita, but he was too weary to move that quickly. He needed time to unwind. Besides, he wanted to rethink his Assad strategy. Maybe Steve could tell him what to make of all this. And he'd promised Paul dinner, his treat this time. He couldn't let his good buddy down. Peller would certainly require Paul's company this evening.

Up on the forty-eighth floor, through the glass doors, Julie stared at him in horror. "What the hell happened ta you?" asked the receptionist as he pushed through the door.

He tried to smooth his hair over his battered forehead. "Oh, a little accident—nothing serious. Looks worse than it feels," he explained.

"I'll say. If I didn't know bettah, I'd wonder whetheh Lana was beatin' up on you," exclaimed Julie. "I remembeh this one guy I went out with, a real loseh, he used to slap me wheneveh he got drunk and mad, which was a lot. Boy, it was tough gettin' rid a him."

"Jules, I'd love to hear all about it, but I've got a lot of things on my mind just now, and—"

"Yeah, sorry, Lou. Didn't mean that stuff happened to you," she apologized, seeing his embarrassment.

"Is Steve around? I really need to talk to him."

"Steve? He went out for a meetin'. Said he'd be gone an hour or so. I've got his numbah, though. You want I should call him?"

"Naw. I'll just use his office for a few minutes. If he calls in or comes back early, let me know."

Back in Steve's fishbowl, Peller shut the door. Feeling shamefully conspicuous, he wished there were blinds to hide his face from prying eyes. He swiveled Steve's chair around to face the window, hoping to render himself invisible. First, he would call Lana. He missed her. He should be home, not sleuthing in the barrio for an elusive drug trafficker.

There was no answer after the third ring, and he knew it would switch to voice mail. *Damned machines*, he cursed silently, then, "Lana, it's me, your ever-lovin' hubby. I'm in the New York office. Call me."

He stared down at the ants scurrying below. The sun peeped tentatively through the clouds now. A lethargy settled over him. He knew he should resume his research of New York property title transfers or check on some of his other borrowers. He twisted his fingers idly in the phone cord, unable to shake the weight that bore down upon him. There was no use digging up any more dirt on Assad, he thought. He was suffocating under the weight of his intelligence.

Then there was Leslie Russell. Her course was clear: create lots of waves, then navigate the turbulent currents on her own terms. For Peller, the murky waters made for a dangerous crossing. He'd have to create his own tempest, he knew, to divert her. He moaned. The whole thing required too much effort.

A little diversion would help. He swung back to the desk to call Paul Chase. "Dinner? Tonight? Just you and me? Whaddaya say, Paul?" he asked.

"Hi, Louis. Any new adventures to report today?" his friend questioned him facetiously.

"Well, funny you should ask …"

"Forget it," Paul interrupted quickly. "I don't want to know. Just to save you from yourself, my friend, I'll join you this evening. You know, Louis, you really ought to use that hard head of yours for more constructive purposes than as a battering ram. You realize, of course, spending time with you goes against my better judgment."

"Oh, lighten up, Paul. Let's have some fun. I need a break from this serious stuff." Suddenly, Peller felt better. He wouldn't have to kill the long night alone.

Paul somehow couldn't help but like the guy, despite his better judgment, and he didn't want Peller prowling the bars alone again.

"Let's meet downstairs at five thirty. I promise, this time I'll treat. I still have my wallet."

"Congratulations," deadpanned Paul. "Dinner for two, Tavern on the Green. On you." He hung up.

The phone rang immediately. "Hiya, Lou. Heard you were looking for me." It was Steve. "Julie said you really took some lumps."

"Oh, nothing serious, Steve. All in a day's work, you know."

"How're you going to explain this one to Lana?"

"She already knows. She really poured on the sympathy," he lied wistfully. "Wanted to fly right up so she could take care of me. I talked her out of it. Besides, the bumps have already gone down since yesterday. And the black eye, well, you can hardly see it." He peered back out the window. The shadows cast by the tall buildings over the wide avenue were growing as the sun sank.

"That's not what Julie reports, pal."

"Julie? What does she know? She gets hysterical about a mosquito bite. I wouldn't take her word for it."

"Okay, so? I'm dying … what happened with Russell? Did she eat you alive?"

"She's tough, that's for sure," Peller was forced to admit. "She says Assad's come down in his offer to four hundred fifty thousand dollars. I think she's really done her homework on this, maybe even gotten an appraisal. It would be hard at this point to get the price back up to eight hundred grand. But I'm convinced we can turn the deal around to our liking: cash at closing, no financing terms. I still believe the easiest and most doable deal is a clean and simple 100 percent payoff. Anyway, we need to put our heads together on how to pressure Assad to close this deal. When are you coming in?" Peller asked Steve, hoping to debate this theory.

"I'm afraid it won't be this afternoon. This meeting's dragging on. You know how these Wall Street types are. Goin', goin', gone." Steve made an exaggerated groan. "They don't stop long enough in one place to reach any conclusions. We're sitting in a boardroom talking when this woman, who's critical to the discussion, looks at her watch and says, 'I have to call Tokyo before the Nikkei opens. You go ahead without me.' So I start talking again, and ten minutes later, another broker gets up to leave, has to 'call the Coast' before noon. In the middle of it all, there's secretaries running in and out with message slips and transaction reports—chaos. Then the whole meeting begins breaking up before I know it, and the director I've been dealing with just smiles and tells me they all want to continue over dinner. I mean, it's wild."

Peller felt vague disappointment. He'd really been hoping to confer with Steve. "Well, maybe you can join me and my old college roommate Paul for a beer somewhere after dinner. I'm treating him to Tavern on the Green."

"Oh? What's the occasion?"

"Let's just say, I owe him. Anyway, we might go out drinking afterward. Care to join us? I can describe in full the beautiful Leslie Russell's strategy."

"I'd love to, really, but I'll have to see, Louis. I don't know how late this meeting might drag on, and I've got a lot of work to do in the morning." Although Leslie Russell was a subject he could really delve into, Steve knew that whenever Peller mentioned New York nightlife, he had something more titillating than beer on his mind. "Call me later, and I'll let you know. I'll have the pager."

It was now close to five. The long avenues no longer reflected the sun's dying rays. All New York was turning on its lights.

He remembered he'd promised to call Marguerita, although, in the heat of his meeting with Leslie, he'd forgotten to verify Assad's promise to repair the building on West 158th. He felt a pang of guilt. Marguerita would probably be upset. Well, he couldn't endure her disappointment right now; he'd have to touch base with her.

He stared vacantly, reliving the past twenty-four hours. His body ached. His mind was frozen. He felt betrayed. Afraid. Alone.

Angel's warnings alarmed him: "Stay away from the likes of Epstein and Assad." "They are bad men." But that was not the Epstein he had met yesterday. It occurred to him there was one person who might verify Epstein's change of heart.

"Johnson."

"Willie, Louis Peller here. Listen, I need to know. Have you noticed anything different about Epstein's behavior lately?"

"Well, he does seem to be checking in with me more often, Louis," offered the super. "And you know, come to think of it, he's been puttin' a little more money into the place, fixin' it up. More like the old landlord, the good Bud Epstein, before he got mixed up with that Angel Sanchez."

Peller could hear the black man's appreciation. "Making your job easier, huh, Willie?"

"I'd have to say yes. What do you think has made the difference?"

"I was gonna ask you the same question, Willie."

"Well, it's a mystery to me, Louis, but if you have anything to do with it, all I can say is, keep up the good work."

"Right. Well, I do what I can, Willie. I do what I can." He hung up, still mystified.

Meanwhile, he noticed that five thirty had crept up unawares. Paul would be waiting. He could reveal his imaginings to Paul, he realized with considerable relief.

****

Peller's talk was nonstop. Paul monitored the incessant verbal battery, helpless to turn off its flow or to know what to do with all this melancholy. He attempted to maintain calm, greeting a battered-looking Peller in the lobby of that urbane office tower. But there, right beside the obligatory contemporary office atrium cum cascading fountain, he listened as panicked words spilled from Peller's lips.

"So to make a long story short," Peller concluded breathlessly, "Epstein's offering to trade financial secrets on Assad (which I'm not even sure he knows, by the way) in exchange for a reduction in principal and lower interest on his loan, when *kaboom*! The place explodes practically over our heads. Talk about scary, Paul. I mean this was like being under attack. I was paralyzed at that moment. I couldn't think what to do, and my feet would not move. So …"

If the whole thing hadn't been so tragic, Peller's account of it would have been almost comical.

"Louis," Paul began. "Louis!" he interrupted loudly, as his friend persisted in narrating, analyzing, revisiting his hapless tale. They hailed a cab and proceeded uptown to Tavern on the Green. Peller's emotional recitation continued.

Paul had listened earnestly to the clues his friend had

uncovered and began to feel worried. After all, in his years with the Agency, he had heard of harmless-enough circumstances turning deadly. Well-meaning people had been assassinated with far less provocation. But *this* drama. Greedy landlords, rich manipulative bastards controlling and controlled by drugs and money, wreaking havoc on their tenants, many of whom were unsuspecting working stiffs trying to get on with life. Mix that scenario with the prevailing ethnic tensions of New York City, sex, violence, and scandal, and one contrived a volatile blend. Peller didn't know he was fighting fire, yet.

Paul warned, "Louis, don't get in any deeper. Stick to real estate. Let Assad make his short payoff, and get your nose the hell out of this situation. I'm telling you, nothing in New York is what it seems on the outside; it's much more insidious. Most of these neighborhoods have been handed over to the drug lords. They are *dangerous* people. Let me repeat that: they are *dangerous* people."

They alighted in front of the fairy-tale restaurant, magically aglitter with white Christmas tree lights in the midst of serenity, a late-autumn flowering meadow. Hard to imagine this place was a stone's throw from the noisy urban blight that the rest of New York City crankily endured.

Peller took in none of the spell. He was far too preoccupied with his fate. Again, the words seemed to pour from his lips. "Can you believe all this has happened in the past twenty-four hours? Paul?"

Paul ignored his drama, concentrating on how to pound the danger of the situation into Peller's hard head. "Come on, let's get a table," he suggested.

Finally, Peller stopped talking, looking around. Seeing heads turning in his direction, Peller realized he was once again attracting stares. He seemed to awaken, as from a trance, to the present. He followed Paul quietly as they were escorted to their table.

Paul was relieved to see his friend act a little more normal.

He didn't relish the role of shrink and had no idea how to help Peller out of this trauma. Although he himself had encountered many life-threatening situations in his career at the CIA, Paul had become hardened to danger. Maybe it was the repetition. Maybe it was survival. But he had never allowed himself to unravel as Peller was now doing.

The waiter came by to ask the men if they wanted a drink, and that triggered Peller's mind again. He remembered the Kir at lunch, and Leslie Russell. Leslie Russell held the key to Assad. He must find common ground.

They ordered. Paul tried to make small talk, to keep his friend from thinking about the subject at hand. "How're Lana and the kids?" he asked innocently.

Lana? Peller felt a pang of guilt. He had promised her he'd be in the office when she returned his call. Why hadn't he called her back before he went out? Now she might be dialing him anxiously, puzzled at why he wasn't there, worried about him. "She's pretty pissed off at me," he explained.

Peller tried to keep his emotions in check, not to burden Paul with his cumulative traumas, but he found he could not contain his anxiety. He launched into a mea culpa over his selfishness, not thinking of Lana and the kids, letting them down. It was beginning to be obvious to Paul that this would not be an ordinary conversation. But with Peller lately, it never was.

The food arrived, and Paul, for one, attacked it with relish. It was a welcome distraction. Peller, usually possessed of a healthy appetite and particularly fond of the massive square of three-cheese lasagna that now adorned his plate, picked listlessly at his meal.

For a few minutes, the two men were silent. Then Peller began to recount his lunch chat with Russell, whom Paul knew by reputation to be one tough litigator. While playing down Russell's skillful manipulation of the negotiations, he puzzled over her inconstant behavior: sweet and solicitous one moment, tough and businesslike the next. He mentioned his disappointment with Assad's lower offer.

In Paul's mind, this talk about negotiating with Leslie Russell was, at least, safer ground than talk of the Epstein explosion. As Peller poured out his heart about how unpredictable women were to deal with, Paul marveled sympathetically. He began admitting to Peller, and himself, his growing admiration for Chris. In a complex progression, these two friends had begun the work to lower the final barrier between them, burning for intimacy, but reticent about being burned. That admission got Peller onto the well-traveled subject of loves won and lost long ago and the question of true love. The two men recalled their various lovers, starting with high school sweethearts. They waxed poetic on this seemingly inexhaustible topic. The subject carried them through dinner and led, naturally, to what further diversion might absorb the long evening.

"Ready to go back to your hotel, Louis?"

The thought of returning to the lonely green room, that cookie-cutter copy of every sterile hotel room he had ever visited, weighed heavily. "Don't be a party pooper, Paul. It's only eight thirty," Peller noted, glancing at his watch. "How about a little of the night life, pal?" he asked hopefully. "There is a cabaret not far from here I'd like to check out. Interested?"

Paul sighed, reluctantly resigned to Peller's appetite for excitement. "As long as it's sober, I guess, Louis. Lead on, Macduff."

The "cabaret" turned out to be nothing less than a steamy, smoke-filled strip joint. Peller grinned lewdly at Paul. "Lighten up, Paul." He ordered them both rum and Coke. It didn't even register with Peller that this was the same poison Angel had imbibed like soda that afternoon.

For Peller, the sensual stimulation of the "*danseuse* disrobed" provided the ultimate escape. The smoky ambience enveloped him entirely, enabling him to forget, if only for the moment, his shock. It was a common enough reaction to New York. To beat the many stresses of the country's largest metropolis, people travelling in the fast lane were reconciled to living double or even triple lives. Life in the office was a race for the evanescent gold ring; life at home was polite. The high life—sex and drugs and gambling and love affairs—was a potent antidote for the souls of those whose lives were otherwise devoid of passion.

Paul, straightlaced as ever, tried to prod Peller from his trance. "Does Lana know you frequent these places?" he asked.

Peller appreciatively tucked a five spot under the G-string of a beautiful runway dancer who suggestively touched his chest and stroked his tender face sympathetically.

He sighed with pleasure and grinned. "Forget it, Paul. Let's have some fun."

Their drinks arrived, and tasting the sweet, burning liquid, Paul sighed sadly, disappointed over his failure to dissuade his comrade from pursuing his destructive course. He guiltily wondered what Chris would say when she found out where they'd been. Chris thought little enough of Peller as it was. If it weren't for Chris Boyer, Paul Chase might find himself delivered far more frequently into the hands of debauchery. Loneliness was a powerful magnet. He resolved this to be a moment better left unmentioned. Then, his drink warming the cockles of his heart and softening the edges of sin, Paul too relaxed.

By ten o'clock, Paul had to pour his friend into a cab downtown. Peller was dead drunk and, Paul determined, would be going nowhere under his own locomotion. Paul took along a couple steaming cups of coffee to help sober his friend up and to keep himself awake enough to make it to Peller's hotel. As long as he delivered his friend safely to his room, Paul could finally go home.

"Gotta help her. Ask about escrow," Peller was mumbling, naming Marguerita. This triggered a heartfelt moan. "Don't cry for me Marguerita," belted Peller in a booming voice, way off-key.

"Why I still put up with you is a mystery, Louis," Paul observed wryly. Peller, drunkenly deaf to the doubts of his most ardent defender, sang on.

Chapter 21
Midnight and the Neon Night

It was only ten fifteen when they returned to the Waldorf. The hotel was still alive with people passing through the large wood and marble lobby, carpeted in a luxurious red and green that was complimented by burgundy-hued flowers. In the center, the famous four-faced clock with the melodious chimes and homey wingback chairs for lounging. Peller was all for hanging out in the lobby, but Paul had no desire to sit in public with his friend in his present condition.

Paul propped Peller up in the elevator and escorted him through the maze of hallways to Peller's cozy little room, where, his self-nominated protector comforted himself, Peller could sleep it off privately. After listening for a moment to his friend's deep, regular breathing, Paul turned out the lights and crept quietly from Peller's room.

As he heard the door pulled shut, Peller lay wakeful on his bed, staring at the ceiling. The coffee was keeping him from sleep. His head felt surprisingly clear. *This ought to be productive time*, thought Peller, time when he could be making deals, doing good deeds. He decided to take on Ms. Leslie Russell, Esquire, once again. He felt he owed it to Marguerita, and to his family, to resolve this case immediately.

Peller fumbled in his pocket for Russell's card and squinted in the glare of the tensor light by his bed to decipher the blurry number she had scribbled. He pounded out the number, ham-handed, on the telephone and waited to hear a breathy voice answer.

"Leslie? This is—"

"Louis," came the silken response. "Sorry I'm out of breath, but I was relaxing with a workout on my Nordic Track," she apologized. Then, with a rumble in her throat, she added, "I was beginning to think you wouldn't call."

"Leslie, I—"

"Louis, don't let's negotiate on the phone. Come over here, and I'll fix you a healthy little digestif—a specialty of mine. Then we can talk." If you can't beat 'em fair and square, distract 'em—her motto.

"I don't want to come over," he said, beginning to clear the webs from his brain. Another drink was the last thing he needed. "I want—"

"I insist. I'll send a cab over right away, and I won't take no for an answer. Not tonight. I feel pressed to resolve this case quickly; I have other clients who need me."

I'll bet they need you, Peller thought darkly, hanging up the phone. *But I don't need you, not tonight.* He lay back down on the hard hotel pillow, thinking he'd made a mistake, but unable to call her back. Finally, he fell into a drunken sleep, only to be awakened by the insistent ringing of the telephone. His head began to throb.

"Taxi, Mr. Peller," intoned a pleasant voice from the hotel desk.

Oh well, he thought, running his hand through his hair, tucking in his shirt and straightening his tie. He found some extra-strength aspirin and tossed back two.

He descended unsteadily to the lobby and followed the cabby

out into New York's cacophonous neon night with alcohol-induced confidence. "What the hell. It's time to dance with the devil."

****

Leslie Russell purred happily to herself, hanging up the phone. Louis Peller would be putty in her hands. She checked her image in the mirror. Her body was sleek and limber, sheathed in a tight, peach-colored Lycra bodysuit. She coiled, ready to spring, like a tiger. Her eyes gleamed at the prospect of entanglement. Indeed, she was so confident of her powers to persuade and charm, she could already hear Assad's words of glee at their victory. And then, a celebration, just her and her Iranian sheik, and then …

"Oh, Omar," she sighed longingly. "I only wish it were you coming over now, not Peller."

She reached for the phone again, dialing hesitantly.

His machine. *Damn*, she thought. *Where could he be tonight?* "I have victory in my sights, my love," she announced to the phone. "Don't worry about this one; he's mine." She hung up suddenly disconsolate, doubt nagging her. She caressed the phone possessively, as if willing him to return her call. Haunted by silence, Leslie lifted the free weights to strengthen her resolve.

Peller, who had regained some semblance of sobriety, stepped into the imposing lobby of The Phoenix, home to the rich and famous. The lobby was worthy of a de Medici: Florentine gold and antique white, gilded mirrors adding to its regal splendor. Peller felt gallingly out of place but was determined to ignore his gut discomfort.

The doorman checked in with Russell while her miscast guest paced nervously in front of his inescapable reflection. To Peller, it seemed an eternity before the wary doorman finally rang the elevator and pushed the number thirteen. Peller was determined to keep things on an even keel with his adversary tonight, but he was aware of appearances to the contrary. He wished he'd had the wits about him to change into jeans and a polo shirt; he still sported the raveling tweed jacket he'd worn to lunch. He ran his hand through his tousled hair again. Aloud, he rehearsed his line: "Leslie, let's get down to business."

Upstairs, the elevator door opened out to a small foyer. The decor was ultra *moderne*: all chrome and glass, black bamboo hand painted on white wallpaper. A single red rose stretched its long neck gracefully from a slender black glass vase. It was his rose—she had expected him. There was no bell or knocker, and the interior door was open. Louis Peller boldly walked in unannounced.

Chapter 22
Keep Cool, Boy

She heard his confident footsteps and stopped her exercise abruptly, breathless from her workout, renewed. She glanced at the grandfather clock in her study: eleven o'clock. *Lucky I'm a night bird*, she mused. Grabbing an old towel, Leslie rubbed down her sweating neck and arms roughly as she glided to the front hall to greet Peller.

Peller was not prepared for this Leslie Russell. Her white skin glowed from the exercise. Her generous, red-lipped smile lit up those dark eyes and excited his smile in return. He marveled unintentionally at the grace of her long neck, surprised by her supple body and breathless voice.

"Come in, Louis," she uttered throatily. "I'm just finishing my workout. I try to do at least an hour every night. I figured I'd have just about enough time to finish, and well, here you are." She smiled. He did look a little better tonight, she thought, making a mental note to keep the lights turned low. She walked back toward her bedroom, weaving the unruly wisps of black hair back into her long braid.

"Come in," she repeated, turning as Peller remained rooted by the door. "I'll be just a moment."

He followed her slowly, stopping in the living room as she disappeared into the back of the grand apartment. This room contrasted sharply with the starkly modern foyer. It was old and exotic, cluttered yet studied, with the air of a Moroccan bazaar: a wild array of reds and blacks, copper and rattan. A ceiling fan turned lazily, blowing the richly colored batik and silken fabrics thrown casually over the back of a long sofa and covering the gold-tooled leather ottoman. He half expected to see a hookah and pipe standing on the hammered tin table knee-high in front of him. The room was rich, yet intimate. Covering the parquet floor was a leopard-skin throw. What a contrast to the condition of the ramshackle New York apartments he normally visited.

He hung his jacket over the newel post carved with the head of a lion and walked along nonchalantly inspecting the old and undoubtedly priceless knickknacks so artfully arranged. A small Calder mobile balanced delicately on her sideboard. He picked up a jade swan from the little tin table and admired the graceful cut and the solid heft of its cool, sculpted body.

Leslie reappeared. She had thrown a gauzy, brightly colored skirt over the scanty, skin-toned leotard. Her sensual lips were now painted bright red, and her long hair was swept back in a perfect braid. "Thirsty?" she asked. She pulled out a rosewood bar stool at her high, slate-topped counter and motioned him to sit. The bar was surrounded by antique mirrors and shining surfaces: copper, tin, and brass. Light reflected everywhere in the glistening trays and copper pots and kettles. They were so perfectly polished, Peller wondered if she'd ever used them.

"I could use a drink," Leslie said, smiling brightly. You?" Her face was a question mark. His gaze was still wandering.

A red, cinnamon-scented candle on the counter captured his attention, flickering, throwing shadow and light back and forth between shiny surfaces, haunting the white stucco walls. Mesmerizing.

Perceiving more than hearing her awaiting a response, he looked up in surprise. "Oh, no, thanks," Peller said, diverting his stare from the eerie shadow play. He didn't need any more alcohol tonight.

"Worried I'd try to poison you?" she asked playfully, pulling out her blender and a variety of ingredients, both healthy and lethal, pouring deftly, her agile fingers lacquered in red. "No, I prefer my dueling partners sharp." A smile danced mischievously on her red lips. "But frankly, you look like you could use some hair of the dog. I'll make you my specialty—a health shake," she said quickly, before he could protest further.

She blended the drink from behind the bar as he stared involuntarily at her quick hands, trying to digest his confusion. First, there was the sluggishness of his brain. He was not completely sober. Add to it visual chaos. And finally, but perhaps most importantly, the captivating Leslie Russell herself, swanlike and sensual. He couldn't trust her. Not tonight. Never. He must remember, his mind ticked on in slow motion. He shook his head to break the intoxicating spell.

Now she was tasting her creamy concoction foaming lightly in a handcrafted silver goblet, licking her red lips slowly in satisfaction. "Ummm," she murmured, handing him one with a gracious look. "*Skol.*" She took a long drink.

At her cue, Peller took a polite sip. The libation was cool; he tasted strawberry and banana, his favorite flavors. He took a longer quaff, suddenly dry at the mouth. Unexpectedly, this taste had a kick to it. He set the goblet mindfully back on the bar.

She selected a CD. New age. Water music, he called it.

"Now what's on your mind?" Leslie asked, suddenly all business. She settled herself on a circular-cushioned rattan seat and stretched out a foot to pull the ottoman over comfortably in front of her. Peller was perched rather awkwardly on the bar stool, but here he felt at a safe remove. He couldn't help but notice her long, sculpted leg was bare, the toes painted red to match lips and nails.

"Well," he began, trying to focus. "I've thought about your

offer. I'm not saying I'll take any less than eight hundred thousand dollars, but—"

"But nothing then, Louis. I told you, we've got no deal at eight hundred."

"Hear me out, Leslie," he began again. His mouth felt cotton clad. He chanced another sip to whet his whistle and tried to think what he really wanted to say. What he really wanted to say was that he knew all about Assad's other buildings, his other investments. He really wanted to see her reaction when he revealed he'd been less than one hundred yards away from the explosion of one of Assad's Bronx apartment houses and then to reveal his conspiracy theory and suggest Marguerita's fears, a bluff to get her to tell him what she really knew. She would try to wear him down, of course. But he was every bit her match, he reminded himself.

"I think we're close to a deal. I just want you to …" His resolve wavered under her gaze. Cast momentarily in doubt, he really wanted—what? he asked himself, looking unsteadily, his eye wandering from her blazing black eyes to her voluptuous body and her graceful dancer's foot.

So perfect, so beautiful.

He sat silent, dumbstruck. It was unmistakable, he conceded uncontrollably. He really wanted her to hold his aching head in those smooth, graceful hands and stroke it and kiss it and make him all better.

Shut up, Peller, he told himself. Aloud, he heard his voice saying, rather stupidly, "I want to make this work."

She noticed his preoccupation and was suddenly curious. "Louis," she said softly, "what is it? There's something you're holding out. Surely you can tell me?"

"Leslie, I … I believe … your client is …" he faltered.

She stood up from the chair and glided toward him. Lost in her aloneness, she sensed his. Her white face wore a concerned look, but as she walked, flame and shadow from the candle danced across that face, changing her expression to something else. He took it for desire. He stopped breathing for a moment, unsure of what she might do.

"This is not the Louis Peller I know," she said lightly and smiled again, reassuring him of their adversarial roles. She eased in back of him, brushing against his shoulder, and put her hands on his neck to rub the tension away. "How can we spar when this hard head of yours isn't really in the game? Relax, old boy," she said caressingly. "Here." She handed him his glass—half-empty or half-full, he couldn't say at the moment. "Drink some more of my magic potion. It will do you a world of good."

Unwilling but unable to resist, he took a long quaff, and after the cool poison slid down his throat, he felt the slow after burn. The strong, sensuous hands kneading his knotted neck acted with the drink as a balm to his frayed nerves. She was right, he needed possession of his faculties to duel. She was so right; the drink and the insistent massaging would put the fire back in his heart. He would take her on, in a minute. Momentarily, though, he gave himself over to his senses, watching his worries leak away behind his closed eyes.

As she felt his body relax, she pulled a stool up next to him and sat down face-to-face. She was close, their knees touching. A waft of roses mingled with sweat; the combination was not unpleasant. He opened his eyes again to notice her sober swan's eyes, aglow in the candlelight, fixed on his face. The tension was broken. He shook his gaze from hers and gritted his teeth.

She laughed as she saw the fight return. "That's more like it, Louis." She slid off the bar stool and went around to freshen his drink. "Want to talk now?"

"Yes," he said in as businesslike a manner as he could muster. "Leslie, are you aware that we're moving to put your client's building in receivership." *There. That ought to set a different tone,* he thought smugly.

She looked surprised, unmasked. "We're going to do the deal, Louis," she asserted, swan no more. "So don't mess around with any ridiculous procedural maneuvering. You and I both know that if Amie put a receiver in the building, you'd spend more to operate that building than it's worth, and your company would pay for it through the nose. You have a lot to lose if you put it into receivership." She paused, calculating. "It's just that we want a fair deal. Surely you, of all people, can understand that." She watched him carefully, leaning close.

"Leslie, I can deal as fairly as you," he said on the offensive. "Let's come to terms here. We do this deal my way or not at all. If your client wants to avoid foreclosure and possible bankruptcy, it's up to you."

Her eyes flashed, and she began to argue, then she managed a tight smile, holding her emotions in check. This man, Peller, was impossible. But he was good, she had to admit. So confident his resistance would persuade her in the end; but it was not anger that would win this competition. She immediately switched tactics.

"Louis, you are the master, there is no doubt. I'll accept your terms," she said contritely, although the fire was still sparking in her eyes.

He looked at her quickly, astonishment written all over his face, never expecting her to accede so quickly. "Then you agree?" he asked, watching her unreadable face carefully.

She carelessly pulled the ribbon out of her braid and began twisting it around her slender fingers. "I guess we have no choice if we want to do this deal," she replied, her voice businesslike and reserved, though some nameless light still shone from her eyes.

He sensed anger as her mind struggled with this sudden defeat. Yes, he had mastered her. He congratulated himself. In consolation, he flashed his best boyish grin and touched his glass to hers. They drank to their deal silently. In relief, he finished off his drink to toast his own success.

She smiled back, a forced response. He was insufferable, she thought, fighting the urge to tell him she had let him win. She had to keep her temper under wraps, let him have the upper hand, for now.

She blinked slowly, straining to cloak her rage. "I didn't

think there was anyone who could outwit me at this game, I must admit. After all, I've bested the best, you know." She was silent, her eyes downcast for a long moment. "But you've got me, and now …" Coyly, she entreated, "Teach me … show me the secret to your success." She glanced at him, lashes trembling around those deep black eyes. Quickly, she looked down again, feigning embarrassment, concealing sudden confusion. A feeling of loneliness blanketed her without warning.

He was taken aback by her defenselessness. He'd won, but of course, he realized suddenly, that would mean she had lost. Seeing her submit, he felt lost too. The phantom glow of the fire and the alcohol were playing tricks on his mind, making her seem so small, helpless. He touched her hand in confusion. It was cold. He picked it up without thinking and found himself raising that limp hand to his lips, hoping to breathe some warmth back into it. She was looking up at him now with an imploring glance he couldn't resist, drawing him into glistening black waters, closer and closer. Peller was suddenly caught like a fish flailing in a strong current. Her face loomed large. Her lips—those red lips—sucked him in, swallowing him suddenly in a bewildering kiss. Her ebony hair was now streaming over her shoulder, outlining her ivory face. Before he could think, he was touching it, fondling it between his fingers. Their lips melted together for an infinite moment, then cleaved apart.

Strangely, though only a moment before he had been empowered by his victory, he now felt bereft. Without his knowing it, he had become her conquest. Shivering, Peller needed those lips to sustain him. She bent close again. She was drawing him to her with those soft, red lips. No! He strained apart. Her arms drew him back, her mouth parted, and her eyes pulled him, swimming, drowning, into a whirling vortex of blackness, her will subverting his will in a passionate embrace. His resistance was gone, engulfed in her brighter flame. He could die a fulfilled man in those arms.

She pulled away. He felt the sudden loss of sustenance, like a fish tossed up on shore by a stormy wave. He opened his eyes wide, wondering where he was, who he was. She was watching intently, wearing a cryptic, measuring look. She stretched out her hand for his and pulled, leading him through her darkened bedroom, a place that, in his bewilderment, he did not see, although the smell of potpourri and candle wax marked it forever in his brain. He was enthralled.

Working her hypnotic spell, she peeled off the clinging leotard, slowly, indolently, her gaze never leaving his face. Her dark hair cascaded in waves now down her white back. Only the skirt remained, opalescent and flowing around her waist and hips and thighs. He wanted to stare at her supple, perfect body, but his eyes couldn't leave the magnetic lock of her eyes. He was melting in her insistent stare, helpless. And for once, he couldn't think what to do. His mind pulled him in one direction, his flesh in another.

Leslie saw him waver and slithered in. She picked up the hem of her colorful skirt and stretched her arms wide, the cloth cascading to form a translucent half-circle that illustrated the outlines of her bare, shapely legs and curving hips. She began to shimmy and snake, circling around him enticingly, weaving him deeper into her spell. Then she lifted his helpless hands to rub against her soft flesh, brushing her draped hips and unveiled torso close to him as she pirouetted tauntingly, her hair slapping across his neck and face. He saw her as if in a trance, let her rub his fingers over her body; he was transfixed by her sensuality. A mystical smile graced her face, as though she too were captive. She snaked around him bewitchingly, combing her slender fingers through his thick hair, stretching her willowy arms around to embrace him. He closed his eyes, visualizing her body dancing behind him. Suddenly, he felt a magical electricity oozing from her hands to his, awakening a passion he had never known. He stretched his hands around behind him and hungrily caressed the filmy cloth swinging over her smooth, taut buttocks, picking it up to cover his face and shoulders, entering the tempter's dance. She wrapped herself around him, touching and stroking, loosening his tie with one hand and pulling his shirt open with the other, popping buttons in her reckless haste.

He was on fire.

She circled him, fondling him from cheeks to chest, tender, tickling, teasing, then nuzzling, stroking, rubbing. "I want you," she said in that sexy, throaty voice and slid her hand suggestively under his belt. Flames erupted inside him.

He opened his eyes at her touch and gazed at her nubile body, curvaceous, unencumbered. A long moan escaped his throat as she rubbed her hands against him indolently. He couldn't resist; the flesh had won. Returning her touch with touch, he cupped her round, firm breasts tenderly and began circling, massaging with voracious excitement. He sought her lips again, and she sucked him in. He kissed her face, her neck, her breasts.

Dancing still, she slid her skirt lower and lower until it fell in a heap at her feet. Then she ripped open his belt, his pants dropping to his ankles. She knelt gracefully, her hot breath searing his skin, never relaxing her embrace. With one hand, she threw all the clothes in a heap near the wall. To stand once more, she moved her hands slowly up his legs, warming, sensuous, passionate.

Peller was swept away in a turbulent current of uncharted sensation. He had never been with a woman like this, whose eroticism and sexuality matched his own. He abandoned all thought and melted into her heat, submitting to her power and sexual prowess, moving his body in tune with hers, following a primal dance they both knew instinctively. She rose, swaying against his body, bewitching, teasing, tempting, accelerating the dance they had begun together as she tangoed tantalizingly, moving him like a rag doll attached with elastic bands to her feet as they sank into the huge, haunted cavern of her bathing room, whose centerpiece was a Roman tub illuminated by two fat, red, cinnamon-scented candles that seemed to cast their own ghosts upon the marble walls, and the figure of a white cherub sitting astride the gold-handled faucet laughed in Peller's face. Peller tried to rouse himself from the trance.

Seeing his eyes wander and feeling his body consciously tense, Russell cast another luring look into Peller's eyes. Now, she willed, Peller must submit completely. With watchful eyes, she touched him with urgent hands and pressed her lips against his shoulders, his chest.

Any thought of resistance burned away. He was a prisoner of her passion, acting only in response to the searing touch of her hands, the magnetic pull of her lips, the strength of her legs, the heaving of her breasts. The burning flame engulfed him.

She had won. Conquering the conqueror. The feeling of victory was the same as what she felt in the courtroom when she held the jury in thrall with her mastery of persuasion and her single-minded ability to tear down those opposing her. The thrill of victory lit her up like a shooting star glistening through the night sky.

Tonight, once again, she was victorious. Tonight, Russell reveled in this sexual prowess of hers, a prowess she used to dominate men and control them. Peller was her prisoner, and sex was her weapon to seduce him, to master him, to bend him to her will. She laughed aloud, a wicked laugh. There was nothing like winning, nothing. Mastery made her come alive as nothing else could.

Unbidden, solitude stabbed her. Conquest was bittersweet without love. Were this a true tango, she could let down her guard and simply enjoy the dance. Instead, she was trapped in a cycle of love unrequited. Where was Assad? She wanted him suddenly, with a desperation that overwhelmed her. But did he want her?

The seductress tightened her armor again. Stepping into her deep pool, she pulled Peller by the hand to join her. He sank in at her touch, and she slid her hands across his compliant body, down into her swirling pool of sunken marble. Then she eased in beside him, pausing long enough to adjust the steamy Jacuzzi and pouring scented oils into the spray. The hard coldness of the marble contrasted strongly with the hot, bubbling water. His eyes closed in bliss as she rubbed warm bath oils against his skin, around and around, slathering his chest, his arms, his legs with the silky ointment.

He thrilled to her touch and transferred an electric excitement from his body to hers, arousing in her an uncontrollable urge to be loved, even if it was only temporary. She suddenly needed his transcendent touch, for only the depths of his passion could guide her to Nirvana. She cupped his hand in hers and poured oil into it then guided his hand across her bare, glistening breasts, around and down so his hands skimmed soothingly across her body, pressing over her stomach, then her smooth, silky thighs.

An animallike sound escaped his lips. Fully aroused, he traced the smooth crease of her buttocks, touching her in those places she craved, until she too moaned in pleasure, and their bodies fused. He would submit. She commanded him completely. Russell was consumed by her dominance. It excited her to control him; her mastery weakened him. Victory drawn from the greedy grasp of the winner was the best victory of all. She hypnotized herself into transcendence, driving and controlling the rhythms of their bodies. Her long nails alternately scratched and stroked his shoulders, his arms, his neck. She rubbed her breasts rhythmically across his chest until he dove under the bubbling, eddying waters to kiss her nipples, to lick them, to bite them—listening to their heartbeats, like waves sounding symphonies. At the pinnacle of this primitive partnering, Russell and Peller, seducer and seduced, abandoned their souls to ecstasy.

III.
Harlem

What happens to a dream deferred?
  Does it dry up
  like a raisin in the sun?
  Or fester like a sore—
  And then run?
  Does it stink like rotten meat?
  Or crust and sugar over—
  like a syrupy sweet?

  Maybe it just sags
  like a heavy load.

  Or does it explode?

—Langston Hughes

Chapter 23
Morning Dawns Overcast

The fire was burning out of control, smoke engulfing him. He was twisting, turning this way and that to find an escape route through the conflagration. Groping, unable to see, he stumbled over something and fell to the ground. It was soft, warm. Where was he? Was he dreaming the old dream? He opened his eyes to see, blinking in the harsh light of day.

He sat up. He was sitting on some kind of animal-skin rug in a room flooded with daylight, although without sun. He still smelled smoke. It took him a moment to remember. Last night. Leslie Russell and a night of mad, primal passion. He was still in her apartment at The Phoenix. Alone.

He rubbed his eyes, hoping he might still be dreaming. But no, there was the Jacuzzi. A fire? Of course, the candles. That must have been the smoke he smelled, candles burning out as they extinguished themselves, melted in red pools of wax. He suddenly realized he was naked. He had rolled onto the floor from her bed. He flushed, distracted, feeling as if he were being observed, though he knew no one was watching.

Running to the corner by the spa, he gathered up his clothes hastily. They were in shambles, wrinkled, with buttons missing up and down his shirt. He hastily pulled on whatever was presentable, then noticed she'd left a man's button-down shirt on the dressing table for him. Just his size; *how convenient*, he thought. Catching a glimpse of his face in the mirror, he noticed it was still bruised and tender. As he began to button the shirt, he saw red claw marks raking his back. So he hadn't imagined it. The memory of their night of ecstasy awoke his flesh anew, the thrill and the shame.

It wasn't that he was embarrassed about what he had done. How could he feel shame about an act so glorious he still felt flutters? Betrayal against Lana? He discerned a twinge of conscience on that account, now that he thought of it. Still, there was something else about the seduction of Leslie Russell that disturbed him. What was it?

Peller dropped down, only half dressed, onto her bed, trying to forget and struggling to remember each glowing, no, each horrifying detail. It dawned on him that perhaps he was deceiving himself; it was not he who had been master of the seduction, but she. And why? What control did she wield for him to fall into her spell? He recalled her hypnotic dance and began to slip back into that sensual ecstasy. In bewilderment, he shook himself from her Satan's trap and hastened to draw himself back into his own skin.

It was already late; he'd overslept. Uneasy, he nosed around. Now he could see what this den of iniquity looked like. The sunken bed was covered with a black-and-white zebra-striped duvet. A low dresser was built into the walls around half the room, and was covered in black and white marble. The mirror that stretched around those same two walls reflected the cold, hard surface. The top of the dresser was free of photographs, and her few knickknacks included a silver hand-held mirror, brush, and comb set and a few magazines: *Forbes, Fortune*, and *Time*'s "Person of the Year" issue. Nothing particularly female or feminine.

He glanced across the room to the wall of windows that

looked out over Central Park. The view from the thirteenth floor was incredible, even this time of the year.

He walked over to stare outside. From the corner of his eye, he noticed the Lucite nightstand near the windows. On it, the red rose. His rose. Under the vase, there was a note written in thick black scrawl: *Thanks for the sweet dream. Had an early meeting with a client. Make yourself comfortable. Let's have dinner—I'll call you this afternoon. L.R.*

So. She too had felt … something. Maybe.

He wandered back to the bar and noticed a kitchen beyond it, gleaming with stainless steel and Mediterranean tiles. The wood-paneled refrigerator was well stocked, he noted, taking out a pitcher of orange juice that looked fresh squeezed. He wondered if she ever ate at home; anything besides "health" shakes, that was. Amazing that he wasn't feeling hungover today, he noted. Maybe that health shake did have curative qualities.

He saw copies of the *New York Times* stacked neatly on the counter. Today was Friday, November 11. He pulled out the previous day's edition, and there on page one, above the fold, sure enough, was a picture of the shell that had been Assad's building. The caption read, "Explosion Rocks Bronx Apartment Building: Gas Leak Ignited." He scanned the article quickly, noted the address, and went back to read every word closely. The superintendent, Miguel Hernando, had been interviewed and said he knew nothing. There were several people missing in the rubble. Peller wondered again about Bud Epstein. Had he gotten out of there in time? According to the *Times*, the top two floors were blown to dust, the rest, blackened by fire. He'd been lucky as hell to escape the inferno. According to the newspaper account, the owner, Omar Assad, was mentioned as being out of town and unavailable for comment. Maybe Peller should talk with this guy, Hernando.

Peller carefully lifted his jacket from the chair and put it on, adjusting the knot on his tie one more time. He was preparing to leave when the phone rang, and he froze. Should he answer, he wondered. What if it was Leslie checking in? He put his hand on the phone, debating whether to pick it up, when it rang over to the answering machine.

"Leslie, love," the voice caressed. It was Assad! "I must speak to you about the Bronx apartment. They're investigating the explosion. They want to question me about the condition of the building, and I want you there. Call me at my private number. Maybe we can have dinner afterward at 'our' place." Beep.

"Thought you were out of town," Peller muttered sarcastically to the unhearing receiver. "More Gordian knots to unravel," he marveled at this latest dispatch.

****

It was already eleven fifteen, Friday, and Peller had business left to attend to. Remorse was setting aside triumph during the cab ride as he thought of how he had betrayed his principles for one brief night of conquest, and humiliation. He couldn't keep from mumbling under his breath, berating himself for being seduced and manipulated by Leslie Russell.

Upstairs, on forty-eight, he was unusually sullen as he uttered a perfunctory "hello" past Julie to Steve's office.

"Where the hell were you last night?" his friend asked with a grin.

"What's that supposed to mean?" Peller asked, suspicious.

"Nothing. It's just that you said you'd call me … and I tried to call you."

"Sorry, I forgot."

"Jeez, Peller, who got you up on the wrong side of the bed this morning?"

Peller shot Steve a glance to determine whether his friend suspected something. Steve looked chagrined. "It's nothing, Steve. I stayed with Paul last night. A little hungover, I guess. That's all." Peller tried to smile, but his lips couldn't quite curl up.

"Sorry I missed it," Steve said with sarcasm. "Must have been a hell of an orgy."

Peller stared at his friend, wondering what his demeanor betrayed. Then he looked away. "Listen, I want to get back home today, and I still have a lot to do. Is there an empty office I can use around here this morning?"

Steve was about to make a wisecrack when he realized it would not be well received. He bit his tongue and lit up a cigarette instead. "Sure, use Vicki's," he said with a puzzled note. "She's taking a long weekend."

"Thanks," Peller answered, walking away from his colleague.

Julie buzzed him in Vicki's office. "Listen, Mr. Peller, high-and-mighty, I don't know what's eatin' you this mornin', but you might want to know that Epstein's called you twice already. Oh, and Lana called just before you came in and wanted to know what time you'd be home today."

"Thanks, Julie."

Peller immediately dialed home—he'd better face the music. "Lana, I'm sorry I didn't call you last night," he said immediately, seizing the offensive. "Honey, I didn't mean to worry you, but I got tied up in a meeting, and then I had dinner with Paul. We finally went to Tavern on the Green. You'd love it. I'll take you soon, I promise. Next month maybe. We can come up overnight, just the two of us and—what?"

"Louis," said Lana impatiently, trying to break into his monologue. "I'm in a meeting, can I call you back?"

"Oh, sure, honey."

"Thanks. I'll be done in about an hour. Ciao."

"Ciao," he said, almost wistfully. "Oh, and Lana?"

"What?"

"I love you." He hung up, guilt surging in and submerging every other emotion he may have felt. He folded his hands on Vicki's desk and buried his head in them, fighting sudden remorse like a schoolboy caught cheating.

The phone rang on Vicki's desk. Peller hesitated, one hand on the receiver. "Hello?"

"Luis," came the whispering voice.

He recognized Angel Sanchez. "Angel? How are you?"

"I am leaving the city today. This place is too dangerous." She was still whispering. "You should leave too. I called to say goodbye. And thanks."

"What do you mean, you're leaving, Angel? I thought you were going to stop playing games and get on with your life. I know it's not easy, Angel, but what you're doing is far too risky, and you can do better."

She didn't respond.

"Listen, kiddo, there's still time for you to have a good life here. Do yourself a favor, open up that lingerie store."

"You don't understand, Luis," she explained. "I can't talk, but I want to warn you—stay away from that woman."

"What woman, Angel?" he whispered back, not sure why he was whispering.

"You know, last night," she prompted.

Peller flushed again. How could Angel know whom he'd been with last night?

"She talks to *the lion*." She pronounced "the lion" in such a way as to clue him to a code name. Peller suspected there could be someone eavesdropping.

"Who's the lion, Angel?" he asked, hoping to break her riddle.

"There's *snow* in the lion's den," she responded, with special emphasis on the word snow.

"Snow? Lion's den?"

"You should be very careful. You are playing with fire. Just leave it alone, Luis. Don't put your hand in the lion's mouth. I hope we'll meet again someday, far from the devil and this hell." Mysteriously, she hung up.

What was that all about, he wondered. Was Angel warning

him to stay away from Leslie Russell? Had he been that indiscreet? And what was this about a lion?

"I don't have time to unravel cryptic messages. I've got to keep moving," he reminded himself quietly. He picked up the phone again.

"Ahh, Louis. I'm glad you called back." Epstein sounded cheery this morning. "I wanted to make sure you'd gotten away from there alive."

What a phony he was. Peller marveled at the duplicity of his landlord. Epstein would be glad to have Peller off his case. Still, Peller could not afford to cut off Epstein if he was going to find out what Assad was up to.

"And what happened to you? How did you get away safe, Bud?"

"I was lucky that my car was close and unlocked. I made a mad dash for it, Louis. But I lost track of you, my friend."

My friend. Peller wanted to spit the words back at him. Instead, he was the soul of courtesy. "Thanks for your concern, but I'm okay. Just a few scrapes and bruises."

"Well, Louis, you remember our conversation?" Epstein changed the subject abruptly. "There is another building I think you might be interested in taking a look at. Not far from my place in Spanish Harlem. It's also owned by our mutual friend," he said cryptically.

Of course, Epstein wouldn't mention Assad's name over the telephone. Probably thought it was bugged. And Peller couldn't even think the name today without feeling his bones ache. "Oh?" he asked with renewed interest.

"I could meet you there at five," offered the ever-accommodating Epstein.

"Well, I do want to get home."

"Louis, trust me. You must see this." Epstein's voice was hushed, urgent. "Just a few moments of your time."

Peller wavered. "If it won't take too long."

"Okay, let's say four."

"It's a date," said Peller, noting the address on his legal pad.

Peller had better call Marguerita this morning. And Tommy, perhaps. He scribbled himself a note on a fresh page, *Never dance with the devil,* as he listened to Marguerita's line ringing. He was doodling unconsciously—evil faces and witches masks—the doodles reminded him of the strange paintings and signs he had noted in Carlos's apartment. No answer. Of course, she wouldn't have an answering machine, he reminded himself after the eighth ring.

Just then, another light flashed. He picked it up.

"Louis." It was Leslie Russell. Her voice seemed softer. "I can't begin to tell you how much I enjoyed last night."

"I'll bet," he mumbled to himself. "What can I do for you Leslie?" he asked, polite, but distant.

"Louis, I thought you might feel ..." she hesitated. "I feel so ... well," her voice changed, more businesslike. "I thought we could have dinner, you know, just you and me, and then, how does a review of our work from last night sound?" She sounded exuberant.

He felt fragmented as shattered glass.

"I'm sorry, Leslie," he answered in monotone. "I have to get back to Washington tonight."

"I couldn't lure you with a little 'health' shake, my friend?"

He was less than confident. He had wanted to believe ... *forget it, Peller,* he thought. She's trying to rope you in. But a piece of him still thrilled to the memory; he couldn't completely forget. If he had been smart, he would have told her about Assad's message on her machine, that she did have dinner plans, with the maestro, for tonight. But he couldn't let her know that he knew; he must play along to get Assad in his own snare slowly, carefully, little by little.

He mustered a false excitement. "Leslie, I do have to return. But believe me, I could never forget last night. I promise, we will finish our work next time I'm in New York."

"When will that be?" asked the silken, sulky voice.

"As soon as I can arrange it, Leslie. Very soon."

"Wonderful," she replied, sounding relieved. "I can make you dinner at my place. I'm a gourmet cook."

That would explain all the pots and pans. "I look forward to sampling your goodies," he responded, hoping he sounded as enticing as she did.

"Oh, and Louis," she whispered invitingly, "thank you for the unbelievable evening. I never knew you could be so …" she laughed the throaty laugh he'd heard last night in the fog of their fantasy, "so persuasive. Persuade me again," she begged.

"Me too. Goodbye," he whispered, remembering. He hung up. Was he deluding himself? She sounded as if she wanted him too. Maybe she really felt it, that overwhelming magnetism between them. He loved her smooth sensuality. But she had another side to her too: dark, calculating, duplicitous.

And then there was Lana.

He needed a few minutes to recover from Russell's surprise call. He glanced in shock at his legal pad and realized his doodles were growing ghoulish. He had to get it all out of his system somehow, a catharsis. He began to write … and write … and write.

****

Before he knew it, it was three thirty.

If he was going to make it uptown in time to meet Epstein, he would have to leave right away. Peller decided not to bother Tommy who, he hoped, was out somewhere watching the ever-intriguing escapades of Omar Assad. Peller hopped into another cab.

He carried his yellow pad with him, reading over his confessions. The eight hand-written pages he had filled that morning were not merely a step-by-step recap of what he had learned wading through this muck, but a confession, a baring of his increasingly troubled soul. Starting with Bud Epstein and Marguerita, the narrative spiraled ever outward and seemed to reach no ending, like the creation and expansion of the universe.

And like the theoretical course of the universe, he anticipated a time when everything now unraveling would come crashing back in on itself, and him.

Before he could make any more sense of it, they had arrived in Spanish Harlem. If Peter was keeping track accurately, this was the eighth apartment building they looked at. This one was in no better condition than the others Peller had visited.

Epstein was waiting inside the doorway. He still was not looking quite himself, and Peller noticed a shiny red bump on the landlord's balding pate. The erstwhile real estate magnate still sported the foolish-looking trench coat and galoshes.

Epstein greeted him with that same cheer Peller had noted on the phone. So out of character, speculated Peller; this man normally wore a serious expression. He shook his borrower's hand and noticed his eyes looked red-rimmed and vacant. He appeared as one in a trance.

Epstein approached Peller with this cryptic tale:

"Do you know the story of the wise man and the fool? The wisest man in the village studied day and night, seeking knowledge, truth, and righteousness. The good, simple people of the village asked him every question under the sun: 'How was man created? Why are there stars in the sky? How come there are four seasons?' To which the wise man, their rebbe and teacher, after thinking deeply and scratching his chin, would reply, 'Because God, in his unsurpassed wisdom, has willed it.' And the people would always exclaim, 'Indeed, it is so,' and thank the wise man, leaving him gifts and flowers. The man was a scholar: who could refute his wisdom? As it happened, there was a child living in a nearby village, a child who did not know any father and whose young and frivolous mother had abandoned him to the care of a neighbor, an outcast woman. This young boy was not like the other children of his village, for he possessed a keen and quick mind. He too asked questions, but the questions were troubling; they raised the fine distinction between good and evil, demonstrating how fuzzy the line was and how often the people he knew crossed it. The villagers, who had long ago stopped seeing their own weaknesses and transgressions, shunned him as an instrument of demons."

"What's your point here, Bud?" Peller asked, irritated at being preached at with old Jewish folk tales.

"I think you'll find this most interesting, Louis," Epstein replied mysteriously. "This rebbe had heard of this curious boy, and he made a great to-do about how he must be possessed by evil spirits. He was at pains to stay away from the boy at all costs, and he warned the villagers to shun him. He told everyone that if the boy were to get near him, the youth would cast his evil on the village and harm the good rebbe.

"This worked for a long time. As it happened, the winter was a long, cold one, and all the cows and goats and chickens in the wise man's village died. Devastating spring rains kept the plants from growing. The people were hungry. When the villagers asked the wise man, 'Why?' he answered, 'It is that boy.' And they all nodded, terrified, and went back to their homes and locked the doors.

"Well, one day, the young boy was playing in the woods just outside his village. He wandered off and got lost, and the harder he tried to figure out where he was, the more confused he became. The day grew colder, and another heavy rain threatened. Thunder grumbled in the distance. When it was nearly dark, the child stumbled on the house of the wise man and knocked on the door. 'Can you help me? I am lost,' he cried. The wise man recognized the voice and knew it must be the evil boy and did not answer. 'Can you help me? I am lost,' the boy cried again. Again, the man ignored the child, hiding from this evil spirit. Meanwhile, the heavens opened, and a torrential rain let loose. In desperation, the boy entered the house. It appeared empty. He was cold and wet, and he found a blanket and a roaring fire to warm himself. He was hungry, so he ate the plate of food that was left on the table, food the wise man had hoarded for himself, and the child was grateful for this miracle. While he ate, the wise man was silent, huddling under his bed. After dinner, the boy felt tired. The bed looked warm and clean, so the boy laid down on it. He fell asleep. The wise man under the bed couldn't move, for the sagging mattress was resting on his back, and he feared he would wake the boy. In the morning, the boy rose early and went away, and the wise man came out, relieved this trial was at an end, and prayed to God that demons would not infect him.

"The wise man stepped cautiously outside. Miraculously, the sun was peeping out from behind its rainy curtain, and the ground was moist and fertile. A rainbow stretched across the sky, and birds sang. Where there had been nothing the day before, plants were growing in abundance. A rooster was crowing happily to a chicken from yesterday's empty coop. And the wise man realized that the boy he supposed to be evil was a messenger of the creator.

"He strode urgently across his yard, where the boy must have run, and yelled, 'My son, come back!' But he was nowhere to be found.

"He asked the townspeople if they had seen him, for this boy had performed a miracle. He wandered beyond the village to search and got lost. Desolate at what he had missed, the rebbe set out to find his son. It was forty years before the wise man found his way back to his village, without a sign of his son, the boy he had long before turned his back on. By then, he was an old, bitter man.

"The children of the villagers he had known, living now in prosperity and happiness, discovered him late one afternoon, dazed and alone. They asked him, 'Who are you?' and 'Where do you come from?' to which he replied, 'I was your rebbe, and now I am the village idiot.

"The villagers stared at the old man, incredulous. 'What has happened to you, Rebbe?' someone asked. A young man laughed cruelly, 'You are no teacher, old man. You are a fool.' Everyone laughed at the forsaken figure standing stooped and sorry in the village green, to which the old fool replied solemnly, 'It was God's will.'"

Epstein looked at Peller expectantly.

Peller missed the import of this parable. He tapped his foot impatiently, arms crossed. "Bud, I have a plane to catch this afternoon. Now, why are we here?"

Epstein was patient. "Don't you understand? The man had ignored the one thing that mattered in his life, not even recognizing his own son. By the time he realized it was not only his son he was shutting out but the Lord, it was too late."

"Too late? What's too late, Bud?"

"Acceptance. Forgiveness. Giving something back. Louis, for me, I hope it is not too late. The 'wise' man turned out to be a fool." Bud Epstein was talking to himself as much as to Peller. "I'm done being the fool, Louis." Epstein saw sadly that the story had missed its mark. "I don't want to waste what's left of my meager life searching for something that's been right in front of me the whole time."

Peller wasn't buying it. That speech sounded too pat.

Bud sighed and turned with a tired wave of his hand. "Come look. This too is one of Omar Assad's apartment houses. You will find more things here that will tell you more than you want to know. But you must swear you'll tell no one of its existence."

Peller nodded, impatient with this warning, and followed Bud into the building. There was something familiar in the old man's bearing. *Of course*, thought Peller. Bud Epstein reminded him of his father. Sam Peller and Bud Epstein were of the same generation, and both of them were lost in stories of their youth, telling and retelling worn-out parables. With Sam Peller, it had been tales of valor fighting as an American in the South Pacific during World War II. With Epstein, it would be fables from the old country. As far as Peller was concerned, these myths were all irrelevant. Bud Epstein was put on this earth to remind him of his crusty, crotchety father, a man who had never been satisfied with his son. *May he rest in peace*, Peller thought with guilt. His father never offered affection, and his kindnesses often came with strings attached. Peller had learned at an early age that nothing comes free, not even from a father, let alone a sly curmudgeon like Bud Epstein.

The first floor hallway was noisy, crawling with people of dubious moral judgment, rundown, like any other building in the neighborhood. But Peller was beyond being interested in whether the cracks in the walls were structural and whether the pipes were made of brass. Epstein took him to the stairs. "Think we'll avoid the elevator," he said. They walked down one long flight and into a half-finished basement, one that would have been used as a bomb shelter forty years earlier, had there ever been any need for one. The dusty yellow-and-black sign still hung on the wall. The noise sounded louder here. Peller could hear voices calling, singing, shouting beyond the wall in front of them.

Epstein pulled out a large key ring from his coat pocket and unlocked first the steel gate, then the heavy door that barred this part of the building from prying eyes and sticky fingers.

Inside, a small crowd: seventy-five or one hundred people, Peller judged. The cellar had a red and gray linoleum floor and gray painted walls and was set up with long card tables and chairs. Behind the tables, men stood—big, menacing men—with their shirt sleeves rolled up and their eyes in constant motion. Poker chips and dice rolled on every table as people bellied up to take their chances. Peller noticed signs on the walls for craps, blackjack, poker, roulette, and a place to bet on the horses. On a platform in the front of the room stood a drum set and a keyboard.

Nobody noticed the two visitors, so intent were the gamers at winning.

Epstein was watching Peller carefully. "Gambling?" Peller whispered.

"Tonight. Small crowd, so far. Every Friday and Saturday night," clipped Epstein with a small smile.

"Who's running it?"

"The superintendent. With the blessings of the landlord."

"You mean Assad knows about it? He knows gambling is illegal. Why's he permit it—of his super, no less?"

"Part of their bargain. Assad pays the super a pittance. Pathetic really. The guy's a street-smart entrepreneur from the Dominican Republic, right off the boat. Assad tells him he can run this underground casino, invite all his family and friends, and keep the take. Except for Omar's 50 percent … rent."

Peller laughed cynically. "Some scam."

"No kidding. I don't need to tell you that, in addition to the sodas and pretzels they serve here, the neighborhood gang brings in a little illegal refreshment to supply the crowd."

Indeed, Peller spotted evidence of some hush-hush transactions taking place as a teenage boy circulated in the crowd, money sliding through his fingers and into his baggy pants.

"They all work for Omar."

Peller was watching the teenager as he passed stealthily through the crowd. A man in his path was accusing a second man of cheating. They both appeared drunk, or stoned; Peller couldn't tell which.

"Why don't we call the police?"

"The police? They're in on the take. Or so I'm told. Things can get pretty rowdy down here."

The boy unwittingly passed close to the yelling pair, and without warning, the crowd closed in to watch the fight, pitching the waif off balance and throwing him in their midst.

The angry man pulled a knife. "No one cheats me," he called, and when the boy froze, showing wide eyes and empty hands, he thrust the point into the stomach of the boy. "Anyone else?" he challenged. The man immediately pulled out a bag of crack vials from the dead boy's pants. The noisy crowd hushed and immediately drew apart to allow the disturbed man his space as the second man tried to run for the door. Panic and chaos.

Peller started toward the fallen young man, but Bud pulled him back. "You don't want to get involved, Louis," he whispered quietly, pulling Peller quickly toward the door. "We're getting out of here."

They stumbled through the rumbling crowd, past the tables, out of the gates, and up the stairs, Epstein panting at the exertion, Peller blindly following in shock.

"Let's get out of here, Louis," Bud pushed him as they neared the borrower's car. "Slip in. We'll drive down Broadway until we're back in safer territory."

A long silence enveloped the car. Peller was shaken. It took several moments before the pounding in his heart subsided, the trembling in his knees eased. They drove down Broadway and over 106th to the relative calm of Columbus Avenue. Far from Harlem.

Finally, Peller swallowed. He felt composed enough to talk. "The drugs?" queried Peller.

"Assad," confirmed Epstein. "Coke. Crack. Smack. His supers sell it to the tenants. Omar supplies it."

There was no doubt about it. Epstein had the goods on Assad: hard evidence, not just suspicions, like Marguerita's, or circumstantial, like Tommy. Epstein could provide the linchpin that sealed Assad's fate.

But then there was Russell. What of her? Peller felt a flush rising to his face as he broached the subject. He tried to sound nonchalant. "One other thing I wanted to ask you about; do you know Assad's attorney?"

"Russell? Of course. She's in on it too. Poor girl; one of New York's best turned bad for the love of money. And a bad man."

Russell ... Assad ... Peller began to feel tension building behind his eyeballs. She was playing him. He had to act cool.

"*Leslie Russell?* In on what?"

"She's a shareholder in three or four of his properties. Apparently, Assad wanted to distance himself from direct control, so he had her set up shell corporations; she's an officer. Ditto the partnerships; her name's on as managing partner. Gave her shares. It's amazing what money can really buy."

Peller was eyeing Epstein carefully. What a scheme. Leslie Russell got a piece of the action too. And to think, he'd just slept with that cunning, game-playing, cold-hearted bitch. But she couldn't be as manipulative as all that; what they'd felt last night wasn't calculated, it was real. She'd just admitted as much. He felt his stomach churning.

"Stop here, Bud. Talk to me. I still don't understand why you're telling me about this."

Epstein pulled over to the curb near the Hayden Planetarium, leaving the car to idle. Bud put his hand on Peller's arm. "I want you to expose Assad and put him out of business. But you must protect me," he spoke confidentially.

What a sly old codger he is, thought Peller with grudging admiration. *He swore me to secrecy, then implicated himself in this impossible story, and he knows there's nothing I can do about it*, Peller thought.

"Why, Bud?"

Finally, Epstein spoke, and there was something animallike in his eyes, wild fear in his face. "Assad's got a contract out on me."

"What?"

"The Bronx explosion? He knew I was nosing around there. The fact that you were almost blown to hell with me was coincidence. But Assad is deadly, and he has me in his sights. He turned Angel on me. Just before she left town, he cut her off, had one of his goons strong-arm her. And now he's threatening to take me down. After all I've done for him," sighed Bud wistfully. "As they say, 'there's no fool like an old fool.' Louis, I don't want to be a dead fool."

"But his building—" began Peller.

"Building, schmilding. What does he care? He collects the insurance and goes on to the next scam until that gets too hot."

"So much for sentiment," Peller retorted caustically. He looked Bud levelly in the eye. What to believe. Bud Epstein was tough and couldn't be trusted. He had lived a hard life, Peller knew. But this Bud seemed different: old, frail, frightened. Peller could help him. He nodded slowly.

"Can I count on you?"

Peller nodded and squeezed Epstein's bony hand firmly.

The two men exchanged a final glance. "I'll drive you to the airport, Louis."

Looking into the face of his father, Peller replied, "No thanks. I'm taken care of. I'll just grab a cab. Goodbye. I'll let you know what happens."

The trip home, Peller was consumed with writing, to cleanse his soul of so many sins: pride, stubbornness, arrogance. The very qualities he'd hated in his dad. Sins of the fathers, sins of the sons.

Chapter 24
That Old Black Magic

On 158th Street, an age-old tribal ritual was occurring. Carlos de Leon had come to call on Marguerita Fernandez and would not be put off. The night before, Marguerita had stood him up for their meeting, and Carlos, angry, was determined to personally serve this budget with the extra one hundred grand for repairs, showing that Marguerita's demands would be met.

For her part, Marguerita was prepared to play hardball. She conjured up Carlos's hard face and felt fear and revulsion. She had been avoiding Carlos, because Peller hadn't called her back. As of this morning, Peller still hadn't phoned. But now, Carlos was knocking on her door.

Marguerita cracked the door ajar, safety chain attached. "Carlos," she said. "What do you want?"

"I wasn't sure you'd be here at this hour. I only want to show you what I promised I would, *Señora,*" he grinned. "The budget and the list of repairs, as you requested."

"Slip it to me through the door so I can read it," she said, on her guard. She had, in fact, come home to begin packing.

"I would like to come in and talk it over with you, make

sure nothing was left out, Marguerita," he explained, charmingly patient.

She opened the lock reluctantly and stepped out into the hall, closing her door behind her.

"Thank you," he said, a little disappointed that he hadn't been invited in. "Where are your children?"

"They're at my sister's house this afternoon," Marguerita answered, immediately sorry she had told him anything. "Listen, Carlos, if you think I'm going to put up with any funny business from you …" she launched into a fury.

"No, nothing of the sort. Calm down. I was just trying to be neighborly," he said.

She looked at him again and realized she was probably overreacting. After all, she had no real evidence Carlos was connected to the playground incident. "I'm sorry, Carlos."

"No problem," he said still smiling.

Marguerita returned his smile measuredly and put on her glasses to review this document drafted in tortured legalese, slowly.

"I think everything must be there," he said after a long, silent while.

"If you don't mind, Carlos, I'd like to take this to my attorney to review," Marguerita said, finally looking up.

"Sorry, my lady. I can't let you have that. It's the only copy," said the apologetic super.

She held tight to the paper, staying her ground in the hall.

"Hey, I know; come to my apartment, and I can make a copy for you," he exclaimed. "I have a fax machine that will copy this."

She looked skeptical and shook her head.

"I swear my intentions are honorable," Carlos pleaded mockingly, holding his hands turned up by way of innocence.

"Okay, Carlos," Marguerita conceded. "But no funny stuff, or I'll call the police." This might be an opportunity to catch

Carlos with more evidence showing, the evidence with which he would hang himself, she thought.

Carlos could not suppress his smile at her threat of calling a so-called officer of the law. He'd paid them all to look the other way long ago.

They walked down the dimly lighted hall, Marguerita trailing a few feet behind Carlos. He turned. "Why do you hate me so much, Marguerita?"

"I do not hate you, Carlos. I just don't trust you, that's all. I've lived here long enough to know that you don't keep promises."

He frowned and walked on.

As the pair entered Carlos apartment, it looked suspiciously free of anything shady, Marguerita noted. No drugs in sight today. And yet, there were the masks and saints and incense, thrown artlessly, as before, in dark corners.

Carlos noticed her interest. "Those are handicrafts made on my island," he noted with pride. "Although I do not practice Voodoo as a religion now, not the way my ancestors did in Haiti." He picked up a painting to show her, a colorful primitive. "Here's St. Patrick who, in *Vodun*, as we call the religion, represents the *loa*, Dambala, an intermediary to God. He is like Moses of the Jews."

Marguerita, a devout Catholic, cast a skeptical look on Carlos, then looked down again at the picture of the saint as if he'd been vilified.

Then Carlos picked up a carved wooden snake laying on the floor in a corner of the room that seemed to have been converted into a little alter, with a straw mat, woven pouches hanging on the walls, and a small table piled with bowls made of gourds, incense, beads, masks, and empty rum bottles. He waved the snake menacingly in her face. "Both Moses and Dambala carry the rod, which they use as their magic to turn into a serpent and frighten their enemies." He looked over at Marguerita who, with her impassive face, was clearly not in the mood to be entertained with tales of witchcraft.

Carlos continued. "I showed this to a Jewish man who was visiting me here, someone called Louis Peller." Carlos watched Marguerita's face carefully while he recited his tale. "He confirmed to me that Moses had such a rod and threw it in front of the Pharaoh in Egypt, turning it into a snake. But then," he smiled, "you must know that from your reading of the Old Testament."

At Louis Peller's name, Marguerita looked up suspiciously, wondering if Carlos knew anything about their acquaintance.

He grinned at her again, as if agreeing he didn't believe this folk wisdom either. He was suddenly curious; Peller could be using Marguerita to spy on him. "I think they make interesting wall hangings, although, as you can see, I don't have much hanging at the moment."

It was true, she noticed. Since her last visit, he had removed almost everything from the wall.

"Fresh paint," he explained, turning on his fax machine in another corner of the room. "I figured, if we're fixing up the place, I might as well treat myself first."

She frowned. "I hope you're true to your word, Carlos, because I've been discussing this with my lawyer, and—"

"Whoa. There's no need to bring lawyers into this. Check me out, and see if I'm not telling you the truth about this budget," he reassured her, handing her the copy. He patted her on the shoulder.

She stared him in the eye, aggravated by his impudence. "That's it. If you so much as touch me again, I'm calling the law on you, Carlos. Believe me, I'd hate to see what they might do to you," she stormed and, turning quickly on her heels, strode away, slamming the door.

He scowled at the door. Then he laughed a low, terrible laugh. Threatened, denied satisfaction in the wake of this human tornado, Carlos fumbled through some paraphernalia in the corner until he found what he was looking for and said, suddenly menacing, "We'll see who gets what's coming." He picked up the mask of the goat, drawing a long match from a box on the table and struck. "We'll see," he growled, suddenly transformed, as he passed the mask in front of his eyes. He touched the flame dangerously close to the goat's head. With the other hand, he thumped menacingly on a voodoo drum. And again, he laughed his low, sinister laugh.

****

While Peller was airborne, Paul Chase was frantically trying to track him down. Finally, he got Lana on the phone.

"Lana, hi, it's Paul. Yes, I'm fine, but I'm worried about Louis. After the explosion, he didn't look too good, and he's acting, well, crazy is the only word for it. And now, some, umm, friends have given me some rather important information that he needs to know."

"I know he's acting strange," Lana replied, distracted, worrying about her deadlines. It was three, Sabbath was approaching, and she too wanted to get home. "I tried to tell him not to get so involved, and then I begged him to come home Wednesday night, but you know how stubborn Louis can be."

"Do I ever," Paul commented and recounted their discussion at Tavern on the Green, gracefully omitting their nocturnal revelries. *Let Peller deal with that trespass*, he figured.

"What can I do, Paul?" Lana was truly puzzled. She had never had much influence with Peller once he set his mind on some goal, and although she was worried about him, she just didn't see how she could redirect his course.

"If I were you, I'd try to be home when Louis arrives. Cook him a good dinner. Wear your sexiest clothes. Do whatever you can, but keep him away from this city. Whatever has gotten into him, he seems to have some kind of obsession with his borrowers—a death wish, I'd say, judging from what he's told me of these guys."

Lana sighed. "I will try, Paul. But you know how stubborn my dear husband can be." Someone handed her a dummy of the newspaper's first edition. Frankly, the news took precedence over whatever Louis's latest escapade might be. Or so she tried to convince herself.

"Paul, I'd better go. I've got a newspaper to put to bed." She hung up and turned back to her computer, glaring at it angrily, now entirely distracted from her deadline.

****

Peller suddenly felt a stab of conscience. Lana was probably wondering where he was. But he couldn't face her, not now. He extracted a credit card from his wallet and the handset from the seat back in front of him. On impulse, he dialed Paul's number.

"Paul, listen, I have a feeling I might have dug myself in here ..."

"Louis, listen, whatever you've gotten yourself involved in, get out immediately. I contacted a couple of my sources, and they've had their eye on your guy for some time. I can't talk on the phone, but understand this: your landlord's brother is in New York from Mexico. Wants to buy some New York apartment buildings, in the slums. Does the name M.E. Limited Enterprises ring a bell?"

"Paul," Peller whispered, "I have to know. What's going on?"

"Not here. When you get in to National, I'll be in touch. Just hang loose, old buddy," urged Paul quietly.

Peller was on edge until the shuttle touched down after interminably circling National Airport in the normal Friday-afternoon backup.

Peller carried his overnight bag and briefcase off the plane and wondered where to go. He realized there was a bank of telephones in the main part of the terminal, but he didn't want to stand in full view of everyone charging through the airport. Instead, he looped back behind the men's room and waited expectantly at the phone there. He dialed Paul back.

"What's the story, Paul?"

"Louis, I can't tell you everything, because it's classified. But what I can say is that the Agency is running an operation out of Mexico City, investigating an international drug smuggling ring. The drugs are going from Colombia to Mexico City and somehow jumping the border and getting into New York, Washington, L.A., Chicago—the usual destinations. What's different about this operation is that it seems to have a financing source in the Middle East. The money is going through a bank in Teheran. But here's what sent buzzers off in my brain. When I checked with my buddies, they confirmed that three of the suspected ringleaders have the same last name: Assad."

Peller was tense. "Bud said he was supplying drugs. I wasn't sure if I should believe him."

"Sounds like your friend has his hands on a limitless quantity of primo cocaine, Louis. And he's getting it from a close relative."

Peller was thinking. "I suspected Omar might know about Carlos dealing from his apartment, but I never really thought Assad was the supplier," he mumbled, almost to himself. "That explains the heavy drug activity in Assad's building in Washington Heights."

"I'm afraid it's much bigger than one building, or even all of Washington Heights, Louis. Remember the building that exploded?"

"Remember?" Peller exclaimed, rubbing his forehead tenderly, thinking of Assad going after Epstein, his "partner."

"That place followed the same pattern: drug infested, suspicious activity. The super was dealing from the building."

"Damn. I'll bet Assad's got all of his supers pulling in a fortune from this drug operation."

"There's an understatement, Louis. To top it all off, we suspect he bought all these other apartments for cash, with the drug money."

Laundered drug money? Angel had warned him. That would fit, Peller realized. "Do me a favor, Paul. I was visiting a building in Spanish Harlem this afternoon. It's his too."

"I can guarantee it: same pattern. The FBI has been following him around town for months. They're just waiting for the right moment to bust him."

The CIA knew all about it. The FBI was waiting to sting. The enormity of this news was mind boggling. One thing was clear, Assad was not hurting for cash. Not that it mattered now, not after what Peller had just learned.

"Louis? You still there?" Paul sounded concerned.

He whispered. "What should I do, Paul?"

"Get out. The Feds know how to handle crooks like the Assad brothers. And you're messing up their operations. Stay away."

Peller felt stung. "Right. Stay away, Louis. Okay, Paul. I'm convinced."

Chase was suspicious at his friend's sudden turn of mind. "Louis? You're going to drop it, this digging into Omar Assad's problems, right?"

"Right. Just as soon as I get my eight hundred grand from Assad. Paul, you've got to tell your pals: Assad's after Epstein. He'll need their protection. I gave him my word." Peller hung up the phone.

At the other end of the line, Paul heard the dial tone and nodded his head in despair. "God damn it. Won't he ever learn? Louis, Louis, Louis."

****

Peller decided he had to get back to New York as soon as he could to close this messy deal. There was little time. From the sound of Paul's voice, the authorities were close to shutting down Assad's operations. If the Feds got to him before Peller could close the deal, Amie would not get one penny out of Assad or the property. It would be a total loss. He dialed Leslie Russell.

"Leslie, it's Louis here."

"Louis," came back that honeyed voice. "I knew you wouldn't stay away."

"As a matter of fact, I'm planning to come back up first thing Monday, and I need to see you right away."

"I'm all yours, you sly boy, you. Would you like to come to my place again, or shall we try something a little more exotic? I have a friend who—"

"Leslie, this is business. Listen, there's something I didn't tell you. Those bumps and bruises on my face?"

"Yes?" she asked, immediately on her guard.

"I was in the Bronx Wednesday, an apartment building on Boynton Avenue blew up, literally in my face."

"You were in that terrible explosion? Why?"

"Don't act innocent, Leslie. I know it's Assad's, and I've learned a few other interesting facts about your client since I visited that place."

"What are you talking about, Louis?"

"Don't play dumb with me, Leslie. Just make sure you and your client are at Amie Mae at nine thirty sharp Monday morning."

"Louis, please believe me. I knew nothing about any of this. I didn't want to face it. I realized, after I, after we were together … I thought I loved him. I've been all wrong. I've got to cut myself off from him. But, Louis, I don't know how. I'm afraid …"

Her plaints sounded hauntingly familiar. Threats. First Bud, then Leslie.

"I will try to protect you, Leslie," he said mechanically, bereft of emotion in the face of the twin confessions he had heard today. "But you must not show him what you're thinking. Bring Omar in Monday. Keep up appearances until I figure things out."

Who could be trusted, wondered Peller as he hung up the phone.

Peller wound his way home the long way that evening, feeling he'd aged twenty years over the past three days. He blocked the mounting melodrama and his impossible promises from his mind. First things would have to come first.

He was in no hurry to walk through that fabled door to

domestic tranquility with the weight of his deception about him. He had a lot of explaining to do, and he didn't have a clue about how to begin. He knew Lana would immediately suspect he'd been up to something. He was a terrible liar, and Lana could always see through his lies. No, he would have to think of some way to hold her off tonight; he didn't have the strength for the pitched battle a true confession would undoubtedly trigger. Peller had to admit, though, Lana would have good reason to leave him after this transgression. Peller knew he himself would explode with rage and pack his bags immediately were she ever to be unfaithful to him.

But he knew, deep down in his heart, Lana would never betray him. And that made him ashamed.

****

Omar Assad was a *very* busy man. So when his secretary tracked him down at a Wall Street brokerage house with his brother, he was quietly annoyed.

"I'm sorry to interrupt you, Mr. Assad. I know you said no calls this afternoon, but it's one of your superintendents. Building emergency, he says."

"Couldn't it wait, Miss Rasheed?"

"He says no, or believe me, I would not have interrupted you."

"Fine. Put him through. No—wait a moment."

To his brother and their broker, Assad nodded his excuses. To be interrupted like this, in the middle of a critical business transaction—couldn't be helped.

"Omar, I'm sorry," Carlos intoned. "It's just that your friend from Amie Mae is becoming more than a nuisance. He knows … something. I have it from a reliable source; he's been nosing around. He saw the operations in the basement of our Spanish Harlem building."

"How could he find out about that property? I own it free

and clear, no mortgage. It's registered under the partnership name. Who's ratting on me?" he asked immediately, black clouds gathering across his brow.

"I wouldn't necessarily jump to any conclusions about informants, Omar," Carlos said, trying to calm him. "I just think we underestimated Peller. He's damn good."

"Well, I can't afford to have someone who's 'damn good' breathing down my neck. Do what you must to throw him off the scent," he instructed his foremost henchman. "Where's Russell?" Incompetent bitch. Why wasn't she doing her job? Though Leslie Russell was a tough attorney, Assad had noticed that she was sometimes a bit too easily led. Certainly, in their own tumultuous and tempestuous relations, she had shown herself vulnerable to the attentions of a charming and sophisticated admirer. After all, he thought contemptuously, she was a mere woman.

"Boss, I thought she was meeting with you this afternoon."

"In just a little while," he admitted. "Good." With a conscious effort, Assad forced himself to deliberate. They'd have to shut down all their operations for a few days to make sure that Peller didn't stumble on anything incriminating. The guy smelled blood, Assad reflected, and he wouldn't let up easily. *Well, let him sniff.*

"Carlos, get word out on the street. No more selling, no more gambling, no more trafficking until I give the signal."

"Sure. I understand. And, boss?"

"What is it?"

"Want me to stop Peller too?"

"Do that, Carlos."

Assad hung up the phone feeling slightly relieved. Good man, Carlos. Reliable in a pinch. He strode back into the conference room, where his brother and their bond trader were talking.

"Yoseef? Come with me. George," he said, offering his hand to the broker. "Emergency's come up, and we've got to go. We'll have to come back sometime next week."

"But Omar, we were discussing some bonds that have just hit the street," complained his brother.

"Sorry, but there will be others." He smiled forcefully, and grasping his younger brother's arm with firm control, Assad steered him through the door and down the long hallway to the elevators. "I'll call you, George."

They were on the elevator. "What's your hurry, Omar?" asked Yoseef, angry that he'd been cut off in front of their broker.

"Can't tell you here. Can you call Mexico City right now and tell them to halt everything? It's only four there, so your people will still be working. I'll explain later."

"What in the world? Omar, have you lost your mind?" They hurried out onto the street. Omar flashed a convincing frown, pinching his brother's arm.

"Yes, Omar," whined his brother. "You've made your point."

****

Carlos was busy arranging his amulets and potions. The shades were pulled down, and his apartment was black, incense smoking in every corner. He had magic to do, a *mystere*, a spirit to summon. He stood before the altar in his apartment, now draped with cloth. He donned a red robe, marked the altar with ashes and gunpowder, and invoked the name of Baron Samedi, spirit of the dead, as he lit several candles over the altar to that *mystere*. The overwhelming scent of perfumes filled the air in the small apartment. There was a bowl next to him on the floor filled with wine mixed with blood.

The ritual was critical. First, a drink of the blood. Then he donned the goat-head mask and began swaying, moaning, pounding on the drums. The spirit entered Carlos. He began to dance and chant in unrecognizable words, both Creole and African, invoking the *zombi*—the soul-less one—offering to serve. He pricked his own finger sharply; the blood flowed out onto a paper. *Carlos the Lion*, he wrote in his own blood, then he put the paper in a jar along with some rum. "*Mange moun*, Louis Peller," he cried. Carlos resumed his singing and swaying as he signed his bargain with the devil. Finally, he tore off the mask and stopped his haunting moan.

Carlos picked up the phone. He dialed the phone number for Amie Mae's New York office. Everyone had gone for the day, as was the custom in New York prior to the Jewish Sabbath, except Steve who grabbed the phone just as he was walking out the door.

"Louis Peller?" asked the accented voice.

"He's not here," Steve replied. "Can I take a message?"

"Yes. Tell him this: One of his children will disappear if he doesn't walk away from temptation."

"Temptation? What are you talking about?" Steve said, thinking this might be a prank. "Who is this?"

"Just tell Louis Peller not to stick his head in the lion's mouth. He will understand."

Steve heard the phone click at the other end before he could respond. The lion? Who? Temptation? What the hell was going on here? What kind of trouble had Peller gotten himself into this time? Steve was panicking. One of his kids, disappear?

Chapter 25
Evil Enterprise Unlimited

Lana left work early. She finished what she could, which wasn't much under the circumstances, and then walked out of the newsroom without a word to her boss or anyone. Brooding about Peller, she wondered what might compel him to continue his crazy inquiry into this one truant landlord among the millions in New York City. At this point, it seemed this foray into the psyche of his borrower was no harmless study in psychology. Peller had been seduced by danger and the scent of success, deduced Lana. The only other possible motive for his obsession with Assad could be that he was trying to prove something. Prove to his long-dead father that Louis Peller really was capable of contributing something to the betterment of the world; put that ghost to rest at last. Whatever his motive, it had gone well beyond reason. "Damn you, Louis," she cried.

She walked in the door, and Sofia was talking on the phone, motioning Lana over. Sofia looked worried.

"Hello?"

"Lana—Steve. I'm looking for Louis. Is he home yet?" His voice sounded strained.

"Not yet, but I think he should be back any minute. Paul

Chase was looking for him a little while ago too; I think he paged him. Anything wrong?"

Steve wondered what Paul had wanted. "Lana, I think you ought to take the kids and get out of there as fast as you can."

"The kids? What are you talking about, Steve?"

"I mean some crazy guy with a heavy foreign accent called just a few minutes ago threatening your children."

"My children? Why?" Lana repeated automatically, uncomprehending.

"Louis has gotten himself in too deep this time, Lana. Whomever he's been tracking and whatever he's learned, they're crazy. I don't know who it is or why, but knowing your husband, I think we ought to take this threat seriously."

"But Steve …" Her heart was racing.

"Do you have somewhere to go?

"Well, I guess we can go—"

"No, Lana, don't tell me. The phone might be bugged."

"Steve, you're scaring me." Lana felt her stomach tighten, panic overwhelming her.

"Just get out of there, quickly. You can let me know where later."

Lana hung up, trembling. She couldn't collect her thoughts. Leave—where? Danger, go!

Her brain wouldn't work. Her hands were clammy. Unconsciously, Lana began to pace. She went to Sofia. "Sofia, listen carefully. I'm taking the children to my mother's in Cleveland," she whispered. "Get their things ready, and I'll load the car. We must do this quickly."

Sofia's eyes grew wide. "What is wrong?"

"We can't stay here, or we may be in serious danger. I don't know anything more than that. I know I've got to get the kids out of here right away, that's all. Leave right after we do. Make it seem like nothing's out of the ordinary. Later this evening, I want you to call Louis here and let him know we're safe. Then call this number," she said hastily, jotting down Steve's home phone number. "It's a friend, Steve. You can tell him where we are. Please, hurry."

****

Steve was feeling rattled after talking to Lana. He kept trying to page Peller, but there was no response. What if something terrible had happened to him? And after all the stress and strain of this most recent trip to New York, how would Peller react to the news of a threat against his own children? With the rancid muck he'd been raking up, and everything that had befallen him, there was no predicting Peller's state of mind.

Steve decided on the spur of the moment to track down Peller. He needed to contact Paul Chase. Hadn't Lana just mentioned that Paul too was trying to get ahold of him? Maybe if they shared what they knew, they could unravel this latest mystery. He thumbed through the phone book, determined to find Paul. The guy brokered commercial real estate; he had to be listed.

No Paul Chase's in the book. He'd have to work his way through the long listing under P. Chase. The fourteenth call to a P. Chase, this one on East Sixty-Ninth, proved to be the ticket. "Paul Chase? Is this the Paul Chase who went to Syracuse and lived with that nutso screwball Louis Peller who's now gotten himself into a hell of a jam? This is Steve Shapiro; remember me? I work with Louis Peller in the New York office."

"Of course, Steve. How are you?"

"Tell you the truth, Paul, I've been better. I just took a call here that was directed at Louis. Anonymous. Someone threatening to take one of Louis's kids if he didn't stop what he was doing."

"Does Louis know? I mean, have you called him?" Chris, wearing trekking shorts and a "Save the Whales" T-shirt, was standing over an open weekender on Paul's bed, helping him pull together a few necessities for their long-awaited escape to the country. She looked inquiringly at Paul who was startled by the news. "I just talked to him about an hour ago at National Airport."

"I've been trying to page him, and he isn't answering. I called his house, and Lana answered. I told her to pack up the kids and go."

"Lana? Oh my God. She must be scared out of her mind. I'm afraid I already had her worried to death, because I spoke to her earlier, trying to reach Louis myself. Is she okay?"

Paul nodded at Chris in disbelief. Chris walked over and put an arm around Paul's shoulder. He lifted the receiver so she could listen in with him.

"No, she's very upset. I mean, how would you feel if someone said they were going to get one of your children? Listen, Paul, what's going on here?"

Chris gasped.

Briefly, Paul recounted what information he knew—at least the stuff that wasn't classified. Steve listened, anxiety growing.

"Paul, I'm going to Maryland to meet Louis. I can't imagine what might happen if we just broke this news to him over the phone. He's already stretched to the breaking point."

Paul thought for a moment. "There are a lot of things you don't know about this case. I can tell you this, Steve: it's gone way beyond Louis Peller and Amie Mae. You say that Lana's going to contact you to let you know where she's going? Good. Stay where you are. I'll go track Louis down."

Steve was relieved. Other than watching his friend fall to pieces when he told him about the threat against his family, Steve had no idea how to help Peller. A dyed-in-the-wool city boy whose world did not extend much beyond the famous map on the old *New Yorker* cover, he knew he would probably get lost trying to track down Peller's house in the wilderness of Washington's suburbs. Might as well be Oklahoma, for all Steve knew.

"Good. Thanks, Paul. You've known him a long time. I'm sure you can help. Keep me informed, and let me know if there's anything I can do."

"Give me your home number," said Paul. "I'll be in touch."

Paul hung up the phone, exchanging quizzical glances with Chris.

"Damn it all."

Refraining from an "I told you so," Chris confidently took charge. "You're going to have to track him down again, you know."

"But, Chris, how many times do I have to bail this guy out? What about our weekend?" he asked rhetorically, holding her hand tightly. Once again, Peller had destroyed Paul's plans through his idiocy.

"I've warned you Louis is trouble, but he's still the best friend you've ever had. You can't leave him to hang in the wind. Go." She pushed him toward duty.

He turned and pulled her toward him, overwhelmed by love. "My good conscience." He kissed her tenderly. "How could I have been so blind all these years?"

Chris laughed lightly, a wry laugh. "Seems you have a blind spot in each eye, my love. Help Peller." She kissed him yearningly, repeatedly on the lips. "We'll have another chance, Paul. I promise. But Louis may have only this one chance."

"Louissss," Paul rallied, a battle cry as he pried himself reluctantly from their embrace. He picked up his overnight bag to set out for Silver Spring, Maryland.

****

Postponing the inevitable confrontation with Lana, Peller dillydallied the whole way home. Driving through DC, which he rarely ever did, he decided to stop and pick up a bite for dinner at Popeye's Fried Chicken. It was great stuff for clogging the arteries, he knew, but what the hell. If he was already flirting with danger, what difference could the clogging of his arteries make? Driving home up Sixteenth Street to Colesville Road, he decided on impulse to check out a movie at the big multiplex at City Place, in the heart of the "revived" Silver Spring.

Place was deserted. Peller slunk to his seat, hoping to be amused. *Dancing with the Devil* had an all-star cast. It was supposed to be a comedy about an unhappy suburban yuppie couple trying to revive their marriage on a dream vacation in some remote banana republic with untamed flora and fauna, when they unsuspectingly discover a colony of the twentieth century's most notable dead and deposed despots, from Trotsky to Papa Doc Duvalier, alive and evil, living in exile and plotting to do each other in—part of their unlikely quests to conquer the world. Our heroes get caught in madcap adventure and are arrested for alleged spying, set to boil in the cauldron by the tyrants, who then can't agree on who has the most right to stew the captives. The premise sounded corny enough, and he was dying for a laugh.

Unfortunately, the film turned out to be a dud, but at least it bought Peller time. Maybe by the time he got home, Lana and the kids would already be asleep. Or else Lana would be too angry at his being late to talk to him anyway. Either way, he wouldn't have to confront her tonight.

By the time Peller pulled into the driveway, it was close to ten thirty Friday night. He was a little surprised not to hear Manny-dog yipping noisily, but supposed that he too had turned in for the night. The front porch light was on.

He opened the door quietly and tiptoed in. He noticed the kitchen was dark, but he detected a glow from somewhere in the back of the house. A cold dread pulled at his heart. What if Lana was waiting up for him in the den? He had to have some explanation ready.

Footsteps in the hall: not Lana's. Sounded like a man. What if Lana … but no, she wouldn't do anything. Besides, she knew he was coming home tonight.

"Louis?" said a familiar voice in a stage whisper. At the sound, Manny woke and made a mad run in Peller's direction.

"Paul?" Peller was squinting at the silhouette framed in light. "What the hell are you doing here? Where's Lana?" he asked loudly in surprise. Peller squatted down to pet his furry friend between the ears.

"Louis, I don't want you to panic. Lana's not here. She and the kids … went away."

"She left me?" Peller's voice rose as the possibility struck him. How could she know? A wave of guilt engulfed him. "How could she just leave?"

Paul was standing in front of Peller by now. His friend still looked battered and bruised, and his face was frozen, a sheet of white. "I think you'd better sit down. I need to explain."

"Explain what? Stop the guessing game, Paul, and tell me what the hell's going on."

"After I spoke to you this afternoon, Steve intercepted an ominous call that was meant for you. Someone, some foreign man, called and threatened to harm your kids. The message they left you was, 'Stay away from temptation.' He said, 'Don't stick your head in the lion's mouth.' What's that all mean, Louis?"

The lion? Where had he heard that before? Peller's already pale face went even whiter. "I don't know any 'lion,'" he replied, something familiar nagging at him. "Where are my babies? Is everyone all right? Does Lana know about this?"

"Luckily, Steve called here to warn Lana."

"Where are they?" queried Peller in alarm.

"Your babysitter called here a few minutes ago. She wouldn't tell me anything. I think you should call her immediately."

Peller dialed the number Lana had posted on the refrigerator. He had never before called Sofia at her home; babysitters were Lana's job. Dread filled his face, and his fingers were trembling. He paced the floor.

"Sofia. This is Louis here. Tell me, where's Lana? Where are the kids?"

He shook his head, stopping his pacing momentarily to concentrate. "Um hmm," he replied. "What time did they leave? I knew I should have come right home," he reproached himself.

He began writing while he listened. "Okay, Sofia. Thanks. Listen, stick by the phone, and I'll call you to check in. Bye."

Chase looked at his friend expectantly as Peller replaced the receiver.

"Lana went to her mom's in Cleveland. I've got to call her. I'm going there too."

"Whoa, pardner. First of all, I don't think you ought to call her there from this house. Too risky; they could trace her whereabouts. And before you jump back in the saddle, there are a few things you need to think about. First off, you look like hell. I recommend you stay here tonight, rest up and shower and leave in the morning. You'll never be able to drive through tonight under these circumstances."

"What about the threats? Has anybody notified the police?"

Paul shook his head. "No need. Not yet, anyway. First of all, I suspect it's an amateur, someone trying to scare you, but who has no intention of following through, although you can never be sure about threats like these. I've already checked the house for listening devices. There are none. I'm concerned about your safety anyway; whoever is behind this sounds unpredictable. At any rate, I'll stay here with you tonight. If anything happens, we'll notify the police right away. Second, I don't think you should drive your own car anywhere. I've got a rental here. I parked it on another street so no one would see it standing in your driveway and pick up the connection. Drive that one so no one will follow you or miss seeing your car here. Now, think—who's the lion?"

Peller shook his head in frustration. "Someone warned me about the lion before," he recalled slowly. "Not long ago. Someone warned me not to put my 'head in the lion's mouth.'"

"Who?" Paul asked insistently.

He could hear the voice, whispering in his ear … of course. Those were Angel's words to him, just before she left.

"It was Angel, Angel Sanchez. Remember the woman who set fire to Epstein's building? The one Chris got off the hook?" Peller looked nervously over at Paul who was obviously trying to puzzle out the pieces to this mystery. "This is really dangerous, isn't it, Paul?"

"Welcome back to Earth, Mr. Peller," said his friend sarcastically. "I've been trying to tell you that for months, and I understand I'm not the only one. If you'll recall, Angel Sanchez is the reason you got yourself into this disaster to begin with. Now she has something to do with the threats on your family—or at least she knows who does. She warned you, too. You're an idiot, you know that Louis? A fool to put your family in such jeopardy, not to mention yourself."

The village idiot. The very thing Epstein had warned him against in his cautionary tale. Peller buried his head in his hands, trying not to let go in front of his friend. He was really frightened now. And ashamed. He'd opened Pandora's box, and all the serpents were crawling out right in front of his face. 'The lion's mouth' … what could it mean? "What should I do now, Paul?"

"I would pray for a guardian angel if I were you." Paul looked at his friend with compassion and pity. Peller didn't need any scolding from him; he was already suffering from his own self-inflicted torment.

Paul put a firm hand on Peller's shoulder. "Listen, pal, I'll worry about things from here. You just get yourself to Cleveland tomorrow. I have some friends in the private security business—they used to be in the Agency too—and I'm going to make sure they're watching you and your family, twenty-four-hours a day, for now. Meanwhile, I want you to call your boss in the morning and tell him you're going to take a little sabbatical … just until the heat dies down. You can check in periodically, but I wouldn't leave any numbers where you can be reached. Understand?"

Peller nodded without looking up.

"Any other idea who could be behind this?" Paul asked.

Peller shook his head. "Only other crook I've got on the line now is Assad, but there's no reason for him to think—" he began, then stopped and looked Paul in the face.

"I did talk to someone else by phone while I was at the

airport, someone who knows Assad, but I know she wouldn't say anything."

"Who is it?"

"Leslie Russell."

"Leslie Russell? The shark? Assad's attorney? What did you tell her?"

"Well," Peller hesitated, not wanting to tell his friend about being seduced by legal counsel for the opposing side.

"It's important, Louis. You've got to tell me," Paul urged.

"Well, we had a little meeting the other night, after you brought me back to the hotel from dinner."

"Holy shit, Louis. I put you on the bed dead drunk. How could you?"

"I guess I was sober enough to dial the phone but too drunk to know I was too sloshed to handle myself," Peller explained, embarrassed.

Paul just stared, stunned.

"Anyway, I went over to her place thinking I might put a close to our negotiations and ..."

"And?" Paul demanded impatiently.

"And I guess we both kind of let ourselves get carried away," he admitted, his face red with shame.

Paul guessed that this little indiscretion had not stopped with an argument over interest payments. "Louis, you don't know who you're dealing with. Leslie Russell is a whore, and I don't just mean the legal kind. Her reputation for winning in New York stretches up and down Manhattan Island. And it's a well-known fact that if Leslie Russell can't beat you at the bargaining table, she can sure as hell beat you in the bedroom."

"You don't understand, Paul. Russell and I reached an agreement. She will cooperate." Even as he said this, doubt shrouded his thinking.

"What did you say to Russell?" Paul pressed him, ignoring Peller's chagrin.

Peller was fidgeting with his keys. "I told her I wanted to

meet with her and her client Monday morning," he answered, noncommittally, his eyes down.

Paul was watching Peller with hawk's eyes.

"And I told her I'd been in the explosion in the Bronx. That I knew the building was Assad's. And hers."

Paul stared at him in disbelief.

Peller nodded his head, his face red with shame. "I found out she's a partner in every one of his properties. Epstein—you remember I ran into him in the South Bronx? He confided in me. Apparently, Assad wanted to distance himself from direct control of the buildings, so he had her set up the shell corporations. She's an officer. Ditto the partnerships."

"Louis, when are you going to stop throwing lighted matches into oil wells?" exploded his friend the ex-spy. "You're provoking dangerous professionals. Leslie Russell's suspect because of her limitless ambition and her willingness to do anything to further her client's—and her own—interests. On top of that, Assad is a major player in an international drug cartel, wanted by the U.S. government and several others. You don't even know what the CIA has on this guy. I dug up some old intelligence from the Iran-Contra debacle. Even back then, we suspected there were some drugs-for-arms swaps going on. I think Omar and his brothers played a significant role." Paul looked at Peller in complete exasperation. "Do me a big favor, Peller—get the hell out of town first thing in the morning and stay out until I figure out how to extricate everyone from this disaster."

Paul's tirade was met by Peller in utter defeat. "Leave me alone, Paul," muttered Peller. He turned, head down, and walked up the stairs without a word.

****

There was a light glowing at the end of the darkness. From the all-enveloping blackness of the hallway, Peller wasn't sure where the light was coming from, but he knew he had to find out. He walked slowly, thinking the source of light would be just around the corner, but there was no corner where he assumed it to be. There were cracks in the floor, and Peller strained his eyes hard to avoid them. He walked quicker. The floor was slippery beneath his hard soles, then, as he continued to walk, it became pitted with potholes he could not see, swathed, as he was, in a black darker than night. It was difficult to proceed. He should have worn sneakers, he realized suddenly; how could he wear hard-soled shoes to inspect this terrible building?

Unexpectedly, he heard someone approaching behind him. No one was supposed to be in there, he thought. This building was condemned. He could feel long, phantom's fingers reaching from behind to tap him on the shoulder.

From the darkness, a woman's voice whispered softly, so softly he couldn't hear any words, just an indistinct hum.

"Who are you? Why are you here?" he asked, approaching again slowly, peering through the dark, trying to see something, anything. A shadowy shape, feminine in form, reappeared. Something about it was familiar.

"The light," he thought he heard her say. The voice reminded him of someone. Frightened, he turned, looking for light.

Instead, there lay a snake.

Suddenly, he felt a cold wind whistling around him, through him. He began to shiver. The hissing wouldn't stop.

"Louis? Louis, wake up."

He opened his eyes. A bright yellow light shining in his face made him squint. Paul.

Paul turned off the flashlight. "Louis, you were sweating and moaning in your sleep. I thought you might be having a seizure of some sort. You must have been dreaming."

Peller sat up slowly and rubbed his eyes. "It was bizarre, Paul. I've been having a lot of nightmares lately. I was running from something dark and scary."

"It's the anxiety. The message from 'the lion' and all. I think once you get out of here, you'll feel better. Now, you'd better go back to sleep."

"Sure, Paul. Thanks. What time is it?"

"It's two fifteen. Get some rest."

"Yeah. Goodnight."

Paul shut the door, and Peller shut his eyes, trying to go back to sleep. But he kept remembering his dream.

Must be the stress, as Paul said. How could he rest easy when his family was in such serious danger? Could he wait until morning to make sure they were safe? No, he had to go right away, to keep danger from tapping anyone else on the shoulder.

Peller quietly dumped out his overnight bag and picked out a couple of clean shirts and some underwear, throwing it back into the bag. He pulled on his sneakers, jeans, and a sweater and padded down the steps.

Peller looked around cautiously. Paul had fallen asleep on the sofa with a newspaper over his chest and a light on. For once, Manny didn't wake up to greet his master, content just to have a warm body to sleep against. Peller watched him slumber, so peaceful, cuddled tight next to Paul, his head resting on Paul's chest, a beam of moonlight shining on his silver coat.

"You've got a good friend there, Manny," whispered Peller as he picked up his keys. Manny opened his eyes and lifted one ear in acknowledgment as his master slipped silently out the door.

Chapter 26
Facing Lana

When he was safely on the highway, Peller breathed a sigh of relief. He checked the radar detector to make sure it was working. He'd be at his in-laws' by eight. At least then he could make sure everything was okay. At any rate, it was better than tossing and turning in bed all night.

He left the car in neutral to slide down the driveway so as not to disturb Paul. He kept checking the rearview mirror to see if he was being followed. He didn't see any cars at all until he turned onto the Beltway, then he headed out I-270 for Interstate 70 west. Cars were stretched out evenly on the highway; even at that hour, there was a long necklace of taillights threading its way west, he marveled. He relaxed his mirror vigil, satisfied that no one was following him. Not that he'd ever been tracked before, but the coast seemed pretty clear.

He pushed the car to seventy-five miles per hour. The major advantage of nighttime travel, he decided, was speed and discretion. He needed to make good time. Watching the speedometer climb, he noticed he was low on gas. Better hit a rest stop before he got too far from civilization, he thought. Besides, a cup of coffee might do him some good.

He pulled off the road near Gaithersburg, Maryland, and found an all-night gas station with a convenience store. After pumping gas, he stocked up on a few provisions; a giant-size mug of coffee, some pretzels, two candy bars, and a bag of trail mix ought to get him to Cleveland.

****

It was already four thirty in the morning when Paul woke up on Peller's couch. He was awakened by the dog nuzzling his hand and licking him insistently. It took Paul a minute to remember why he was here. He stretched and yawned, petting the dog absently on the head. At least Louis hadn't had any more bad dreams, he thought.

He shouldn't have slept, Paul knew, but he couldn't help it. He was exhausted. Besides, he was no longer a young man. Those all-nighters he used to pull in college and night watches for the Agency had been performed by a lean, tough, young recruit who thrived on excitement and a Spartan existence. Since then, he'd grown old and soft. He needed coffee.

Finding his glasses on the coffee table, Paul stood up. He let the dog out in the fenced-in yard and found a coffee maker in the kitchen. He opened the refrigerator to look for coffee. Good, they had caffeinated coffee, thought Paul, measuring out four scoops. Better make a cup or two for Peller too. He'd looked exhausted last night and had a long drive in front of him.

The dog was scratching to be let in. Paul slid open the door and, looking in the driveway, noticed that Peller's car was missing. "That asshole," he cursed under his breath and ran up the stairs, hoping against hope that Peller was still there. He cracked open the bedroom door and, seeing no one, walked in. Paul was furious. He saw Peller's dirty clothes dumped in a heap by the bed. There was his briefcase. No suitcase; Peller must have packed it. A planned escape, and he'd been sleeping, Paul thought, knowing it was his own damned fault. He could kick himself—what if the perpetrators had come after Peller? Some guard he was.

Now that the breakout was concluded, there was nothing Paul could do about it. It was too early to call Lana, and he didn't want to worry her any further. Besides, at the earliest, Peller wouldn't get to Cleveland for another few hours.

Paul was still unclear about how this thing had come to such a pass. Maybe there were some clues to help him understand the kind of danger Peller was in. Papers and a travel kit were filed in the briefcase, but the papers were drafts of workout agreements. Except for toothpaste and shaving cream, there was nothing inside the small zippered case. He walked carefully around the dirty clothes to the other side of the bed. There, Paul noticed a yellow legal pad with Peller's handwriting, and a small tape recorder lay on top of it.

Forgetting all about his coffee and his fatigue, Paul picked up the papers. Several pages were flipped back, and the one showing began as follows:

> I might have underestimated L.R. Went there last night to conclude deal. She was working out when I arrived and had barely anything on. What a body! What a Jacuzzi! A night of rapture.

He was embarrassed. This was Peller's diary. Paul couldn't read this personal stuff. But what should he do? If he was going to help Peller, well, he'd better sit down.

****

By the time Paul finished reading through the scrawled journal about seven thirty, he had a headache of monumental proportions. The sun was creeping close to the horizon. Paul pulled off his glasses and chewed on the stem. What to do?

The document he had just read was very revealing. He'd tried to concentrate on the professional notations referring to M.E. Limited Partnership and Epstein and Assad. There was quite a bit of evidence against them, mostly circumstantial, he realized. Still, that was a good place to start, and the information was certainly consistent with what the Agency had compiled on Assad. But the personal stuff—Russell's seduction of Peller and Peller's records of his wild wanderings through New York—pretty damning. Paul sighed. Poor Lana.

Lana. He'd better warn her about Peller. He couldn't call from here though, just in case the Pellers had eavesdroppers. In less than a minute, he dropped the papers, ran downstairs and out the door.

****

"Lana, it's Paul."

"Paul? Where are you?"

"I'm at a McDonald's not far from your house."

"My house? What are you doing there?"

"Trying to save your compulsive husband from himself."

"Is Louis okay? Is he at home? Is the house okay?"

"The house is fine. Yes, I saw Louis, and he's quite shaken up, as you might imagine. In fact, that's why I called … he's on his way to you now, and you need to know he's not in the most stable state of mind. I'm not sure what time he left; I must've dozed off. Anyway, be careful. He drove his own car, which I asked him not to do. He may have been followed. There's just no way to know."

Lana babbled angrily into the phone. "Paul, what has Louis gotten involved in? How could he do this to the children? Who in the hell does he think he is anyway, scaring the daylights out of everyone?" She too was on edge, and understandably so. He sympathized but wasn't really listening. Paul was preoccupied with his own moral dilemma: should he tell Lana about the journal?

Aside from the allusion to Peller's tryst with "L.R.," there were notes on that pad that could incriminate Peller's borrowers.

"I hate Louis for doing this to me," he heard her say in angry sobs.

He broke into her impassioned monologue. "Listen, Lana. I want to send something to you—to Louis actually. It may be important evidence if anyone should be asking questions. These people may be trying to blackmail Louis into not divulging anything he suspects about them. Based on these notes, and from what I've learned, it would seem Louis knows a great deal. At any rate, the papers—Louis's notes and things—shouldn't stay here."

She sniffed, trying to stop crying. "I hope Louis is done asking questions, Paul. That's what put us into this predicament in the first place," Lana sniffed cynically.

"Lana, I won't kid you. This guy's not gonna put up with Louis's meddling politely. Protect yourself and the kids, Lana," Paul warned. Then he paused, trying to decide what else to say.

"And, Lana, keep an eye on Louis. I'm worried about him. This time he really needs you to stand by him. To show him you love him."

Something in Paul's voice triggered Lana's suspicion. "What do you mean, Paul, he needs me? Of course I love him. As crazy as he is, he's just trying to do the right thing for those suffering people living in despondency. I hate this situation, but why wouldn't I stand by him 'this time'?"

"No reason. No reason I can think of. Really, believe me. Just watch him." Paul's voice sounded guilty. "Listen, I gotta go now. I'm at a pay phone, people waiting, understand? G'bye. I'll overnight that package to you—to Louis—there." Ethical problem neatly trumped: leave it to Peller to explain his own infidelities to his wife.

He hung up, torn. He wanted to help his friend, protect him, but he had to send those notes. Feeling guilty, he ripped out the offending pages about Leslie Russell just to be safe.

Lana hung on the line for a long moment, the dial tone

buzzing in her ear, wondering ... worrying about this news. Peller was coming, and he needed her. Why wouldn't she support her man? And as for love, she had decidedly mixed emotions right now. Well, whatever conflicting evidence there might be, it was almost certainly contained in the package Paul was sending. Lana had a feeling she'd better look out for it herself.

****

Peller was in Wheeling now, about to cross over the Ohio River. Day had broken without his even realizing it. Normally, he would have enjoyed this clear, starlit drive through the Appalachian foothills; today, however, he hardly noticed, though the skies were bright. He'd been preoccupied, brooding over his seduction by Russell, over stumbling on Assad's dangerous tracks, over what to say to Lana. Such a tempest. And to think, all his problems had started simply because he'd been determined to unravel the mystery of why Omar Assad was willing to pay a fortune to hold onto his decayed, junky, hellhole of an apartment building. But then he'd gotten greedy, trying so hard to hold Assad to that ridiculously inflated price. Peller cursed his own gluttony.

He turned north on Interstate 77 and slowed his speed. It was daylight now, sunny and clean, the kind of cloudless day when cops would lay speed traps. Peller wouldn't give them the benefit. Besides, he was in less of a hurry now that his conscience was knocking. He began a dialogue with himself, debating back and forth.

Peller: I can't tell Lana about Leslie Russell. I'll just tell her I've learned that Assad is using the apartment buildings as a front for his drugs and gambling, that I've learned his brothers are supplying the stuff, his supers are distributing it, and he's afraid I'll blow the whistle, so he's threatening me so I'll shut up. That's the truth.

Conscience: She's gonna ask you if Assad's attorney knows about his illegal activities.

Peller: I don't know, and I don't care is the answer.

Conscience: Peller, you know you're a terrible liar, and Lana knows when you're lying.

Peller: What should I do?

Conscience: Come clean. Tell her the truth.

Peller: What truth? That a beautiful, sexy but demonic lawyer seduced me to blow me off the scent? And that I fell for the trap? She'd leave me quicker than you could say—

Conscience: Abracadabra. But there's no wand that will make Assad's black magic disappear. Peller, don't lie. Your lies will just come back to haunt you.

That was the crux of the matter. Up until now, his lies had been small lies—innocent, face-saving lies. Even so, those small lies had spun more lies, and more, until they'd grown and grown, leaving him twisting and spinning in a giant cyclone of deceit.

It might cost him his marriage, but he'd tell the truth, Peller decided, gritting his teeth.

He drove the next fifty miles without his conscience bothering him. When he left the highway, nearing the comfortable old neighborhood where Lana's parents lived, he patted himself on the back for bravery; he'd tell her everything. He turned onto the street and saw Lana, looking disheveled and preoccupied, picking up the newspaper from her parents neatly manicured front lawn. All confidence vanished. He smiled sheepishly.

"Later," he commanded his ringing conscience.

****

In New York City, day was not yet breaking. Morning would dawn without warning—somber, overcast, and threatening. Tommy gulped down his third cup of coffee, parked outside Assad's Fifth Avenue condo, watching and waiting for any evidence that might incriminate the bastard. Steve had called him last night and told him about the threat against Peller's kids. "The lion" was roaring, whatever that meant. No matter. No one pulled that kind of bullshit against any of Tommy Romano's friends, that was for sure. So he was waiting out the night to do a little window shopping, see what kind of shit Assad had started.

Tommy slung his pigeon-watching binoculars around his neck and moved his car around a couple of times so the police wouldn't think anything fishy was going on. So far, he'd seen nothing.

He peeked at his rearview mirror again, searching for cops or suspicious characters for the umpteenth time. He noticed a man walking his dog across to Central Park. One of those sissy little yappy dogs Tommy despised. The doorman was out looking around now too, so Tommy would probably have to move again.

Then he saw her, wrapped in a voluminous black cape. That bitch of a lawyer, Russell; he identified her immediately by those incomparable gams. What was she doing here this time of day? He watched as she strolled casually up to the building, greeting the doorman. So the doorman knew her; maybe she'd done business at Assad's apartment before, thought Tommy suspiciously. He decided to disappear around the block and drive down the side of Fifth closest to the park. From there, he could peek into Assad's apartment. Why such a fat cat would take an apartment on a low floor was beyond Tommy who knew that the toniest people lived in penthouses; most rich folks wanted to be as far away from street noise as possible. Ha! Tommy laughed. The very idea of staying away from the street in New York was laughable. Fa'gedaboutit. This was no country retreat.

At any rate, Assad's choice of the third floor was a lucky break for Tommy. He had already checked it out on several occasions, even spying on Assad during a romantic interlude with some high-priced-looking dame who wore only diamonds to bed. Lots of diamonds.

He found a spot and cleaned off the spyglass, then realized he'd better get this for the record. He loaded film into the brand new thirty-five millimeter telephoto camera with all the bells and whistles that Peller had bought at Forty-Seventh Street Photo; Louie wasn't satisfied with the little Polaroid, didn't work too good in low-light situations like this one. This baby would sure come in handy now, Tommy admitted.

He got out of the car. The view from the street was clear. He peered through the viewfinder. Shit. The windows were shuttered today, and lights were on in the living room and Assad's bedroom. There was no detectable activity at the moment.

Tommy looked back down the street, prepared to start shooting pictures of pigeons if anyone asked any questions. After all, pigeons, to Tommy's mind, were much more trustworthy than people. People always screwed things up, while pigeons you could count on. There went the man with the yappy dog, back into the building. Tommy saw another man getting out from a cab. He nodded at someone or something, apparently inside the building, then started talking to the doorman. He couldn't see the man's face from here. He put the camera back up to his eye to get a better look. It was Assad.

Immediately, Tommy pointed the camera back up at Assad's windows. He saw Leslie Russell looking out the window now. She must have her own key: a rendezvous. Tommy started snapping away—first Assad, then Russell. He turned as if to focus on something in the park and walked a few slow paces to detract from any attention on the street. He could wait.

When he turned back, Assad too was in the apartment. Like Russell, he was staring out the window. Perhaps they were expecting someone else. They seemed to be in heated discussion; Tommy wished he could hear what they were saying. Snap went the shutter. Omar Assad walked away from the window.

The attorney had her back to the street now. She was gesturing angrily. Omar was walking back toward Russell. He slapped her. Then, in one swift motion, he grabbed her and pulled her roughly into a forcible embrace. After a long moment, the kiss ended, and then, reaching for her hand, he pulled her away from the window. They weren't arguing anymore.

Snap, snap, snap.

Tommy looked around one last time to make sure no one was watching. Just as he was about to get into his car, he noticed one more familiar figure hastening down the street: Carlos de Leon.

Carlos spelled trouble. If Carlos noticed Tommy taking pictures, he would immediately suspect something and report it to Assad. Tommy didn't want to stumble in his own trap. He plopped into his car in a hurry, hiding his face behind his straw cap, and melded in with the rush hour traffic. But not before he stole one final shot.

Chapter 27
Let the Home Office Fix It

Lana was staring at Peller, even as he studiously avoided her eyes. The two of them were poised at opposite ends of her mother's overstuffed sofa, arms crossed tightly. Lana wore her robe tight around her body; a frown creased her face. Peller had bags under his eyes and a heavy stubble on his chin. That, plus his rumpled clothes, gave him the air of a street person.

All was not sweetness and light in this room. When Lana saw Peller approaching, she'd seemed frightened and worried. He had tried to hug and comfort her, even hoped she would comfort him. Instead, she threw up her hands as if to ward him away. Sensing the tension, their children cleared away, instead pestering Grandpa to make them waffles. They didn't want any part of a "discussion" between Mommy and Daddy.

Now Peller was mired in explaining the unexplainable.

"Louis, try clearing this up for me: why didn't you warn us there was serious danger?"

"Lana, I swear I didn't know anything about it until I got home and saw Paul sitting in our family room waiting for me."

"That's another thing. How the hell did Paul get in there?"

"I don't know, to tell you the truth. I didn't even think to ask him, I was so surprised. I suppose Shapiro must have called him after the threat came in and—but that's all besides the point."

"And the point is … exactly?"

What was his point, Peller wondered. "I want … I mean, I hope you will stay here for a while, until things cool off at home. You and the kids will be safe. You can probably even work from here, with fax machines and phones. I'll even explain it to your boss, if you'd like."

"Louis, you can't even explain it to me."

"Look, Paul has already arranged to provide security for us … all of us. Meanwhile, I've got to figure out how I'm going to resolve this situation."

"Good thought, Louis," she said in quiet sarcasm, face set, placing her hands on her hips and locking him away from her. "But that thought should have occurred to you six months ago, before you put your children's lives in jeopardy."

He grimaced. This line of attack hurt, for she had honed right in on the crux of the issue in her quiet, accusatory way. She had every right to scream, strike, and condemn. Instead, she chose the quiet voice and the cold heart. This stoic assault was more destructive than any verbal or physical violence could ever be.

She turned away, remembering Paul's words: "He really needs you now." She saw her husband's turmoil, and yet, she couldn't console him. He had inflicted this pain on his own family blindly, carelessly; she could not forgive him for that. She had every right to be angry.

Sullenly, he said, "Then there's nothing I can say or do that will make you understand?"

"Right. Don't talk to me. Just make sure nothing happens to those kids. You'd better go talk to them now, because they're pretty confused, being whisked off in the middle of the night without their daddy. They *need* you, Louis."

At least someone did, he thought gratefully, retreating from Lana's icy presence.

****

He lay down for a rest in Lana's childhood bedroom after offering the kids hugs and kisses, reassurances for his concerned father-in-law, and a promise to go grocery shopping for his mother-in-law. There was no question that Lana and the kids would be better off here, around attentive people who could look after them.

But Peller couldn't figure out what to do next. Should he turn Assad in? Or leave it to the CIA? Should he press his advantage and collect for Amie Mae before the Feds moved in? Or ask to be taken off the case? He wasn't a cop, he reminded himself, just a businessman trying to save his company some money. And help some desperate people, he reminded himself: Marguerita, Bud, and Angel. But at what cost to himself and his family?

He closed his eyes and fell into an uneasy sleep. He was in a hallway again. He recognized it: his grandmother's building in the Bronx. The place looked like any of a hundred of his buildings: rundown, dank, and depressing. He smelled gas. Something shook the building: an explosion.

He ran into his grandmother's apartment, but he couldn't find her. The building was rocking. He had to get her out. "Nana," he called.

"Let her go," boomed his father's voice. "Let us go."

Then he saw a light flooding out from her bedroom door. The white light was blinding in its celestial splendor. Her comforting voice called him from his pain: "Louis." Her voice was soothing, familiar.

"Louis." The voice sounded urgent.

He opened his eyes. It was Lana, standing between him and the window, surrounded by a halo of light. He couldn't see her face in the glare.

"Sorry, I must have dozed off." He rubbed his eyes like a kid trying to open them from a particularly deep sleep.

"I'll say. You were twitching and talking as if you were possessed."

He wanted to touch Lana and beg her to hold him safe, but she still looked unapproachable. "What time is it?" he asked instead, hugging his chest with his arms.

"Close to two. Don't you think you ought to call your boss and warn him about this trauma? Maybe you can get Amie Mae to do something."

"Vallardo? On a Saturday? What would he do?"

"I don't know, Louis, but he deserves an explanation," she said in annoyance. "We all do," she grumbled under her breath.

Peller sighed. "I tried to explain, Lana."

"Well, I just don't understand. But maybe Joe will. You'll have to tell him sometime. Go ahead, Louis, get it all off your chest."

She sounded angry.

He picked up the phone to dial, looking sideways at her implacable face, begging forgiveness but finding none.

He got Vallardo on the phone. Lana made herself comfortable on the chaise across from the bed. It was apparent that she was planning to listen to the whole conversation, thought Peller with a sinking feeling. He'd better measure his words.

"Joe, sorry to bother you on a Saturday. I got back late from New York, and I thought there were a few things emerging after my, um, meeting with Leslie Russell that you ought to know."

"Louis? I've been expecting to hear from you. I mean, I had to hear about your stalemate with Russell through Steve for God's sake. And now this threat against your family? What is it with you, Peller, that you can't pick up the phone and keep me informed?"

"Joe, Joe … just listen a minute. I'm sorry. I took some time to go with my friend Paul Thursday night to relax after that huge explosion and everything, so I didn't get a chance to call … anyone," he ventured, glancing at Lana's stony face. "I mean, after all, it was a hell of a two days, between the explosion and Russell. "

"So what's the deal with Russell?" interrupted Joe, impatient to learn details.

"Well, we had a second, uh, discussion," Peller kept his eyes away from Lana's, "about selling the building. She brought Assad's bid down to four hundred fifty grand in their offer over lunch, as I guess Steve mentioned, and then relented and said Assad would meet his original price."

"That's great, Lou," shouted Coach Vallardo. "Way to play the game. I knew you could run with this ball. Helluva play."

His boisterous response was greeted with silence.

"Right, Louis?" ventured his boss.

"Well, not exactly. See, it turns out that my hunch was correct about Assad. Listen, Joe," he interrupted himself in sudden panic, "you gotta swear you won't tell anyone about this, not until I figure it all out. They're threatening my family—my *family*, damn it."

"Okay, okay, Lou. I swear. But maybe we can do something to help. What did you discover?"

"I found out that Assad uses his apartment buildings as a front for a drug ring he runs with his brothers. One brother operates in Mexico City and another brother in Teheran."

"He what?"

"That's it; it's a drug ring. Drug money and gambling apparently finance his real estate investments all over town. Epstein showed me this gambling operation he uses to subsidize another building in Spanish Harlem. Operations were in full swing, and we just about made it out of there—"

"Wait a minute. You're going way too fast for me here, Lou. They're buying real estate with drug money?"

"That's the long and the short of it, I'm afraid." Peller felt a little better having revealed the facts to his boss. It was a company problem, this conspiracy. After all, Amie Mae couldn't let disaster befall one of its trusted employees on the job.

There was a long silence at the other end.

Assuming Vallardo was confused, Peller launched into further explanation, ever mindful of Lana's intense interest. "He gets a great price on these places—a cash discount, right? Then he turns around and sells partnership shares at inflated rates. What's more, he enlists a few of his trusted supers to sell drugs to his tenants and the neighborhood. Guys like Carlos de Leon. He pays them with proceeds from the gambling and the drugs. It's gotta be a fucking mint."

Vallardo was frozen, but not from confusion. What he was really ruminating over was the possibility that he might somehow have gotten himself caught in Peller's little trap. Assad bought New York apartment buildings. If he bought them at a discount, he could turn around and sell them to his partners for a higher price and make a significant profit. The quick-profit scam rang a bell in Vallardo's head. His investments in distressed New York real estate, the quick profits, same damn pattern, he realized, kicking himself. He had bought himself a piece of Omar Assad's drug ring with his investments. Then there was the recent expansion of the partnership's investments into oil drilling and the purchase of a South African shipping company. Teheran. It struck him. The report sent to the partners was signed by one Ibrahim Assad. Just another Arabian prince. The name "Assad" had not registered … until now. Vallardo's heart was pounding. This was no coincidence, this investment opportunity he had been tipped off to by a borrower. They were probably all in cahoots: Epstein, Assad, Cinoletti, and now Joe Vallardo. Business made strange bedfellows indeed. Vallardo's fantastically profitable investment was a money-laundering front for Assad's drug ring.

Meanwhile, Peller was droning on with details, details now undeniably linked to Joe Vallardo's suddenly collapsing future. *Take a deep breath. Calm yourself, Joe. Maybe you're wrong, and the partnership has no connection with Louis's borrower*. After all, everyone in the Middle East was named Assad.

But he was forced to admit, with a sinking feeling, that he'd allowed himself to get sucked in.

Peller stopped talking. Vallardo still couldn't respond. Peller pressed him. "Joe, you see, I've got to make sure my family is safe until we figure out what to do. Joe, what do you think the solution might be?" Peller questioned him.

"Sure, Lou, whatever," he replied in a complete non sequitur. "I've gotta go, Louis."

"Go? But, Joe, you have to help me," Peller insisted.

"I gotta go … little Joey's crying," Joe lied. Dumbfounded, he realized he'd tied up his whole life's savings in this very illegal deal, deceived his wife in the process, and gotten deeply involved in something that presented a clear conflict of interest to his one true success, the job at Amie Mae. What if Stan Sponzelli's reform-minded congressmen got wind of this endgame after Vallardo had tipped off Stan to his windfall investment? Shit. He was out of the game. Out for life.

"Wait, Joe, you gotta tell me what to do," Peller persisted, confused, wanting direction from his boss.

"Never get involved with the devil, Lou," came Vallardo's reply in a surprising echo of Peller's own conscience. There was confusion in Vallardo's voice. "S' long, Louie." Vallardo hung up.

Peller looked over at Lana with a shrug, mystified.

Hearing Peller recite his story again, Lana still wasn't satisfied. There was something about Peller's behavior that wasn't adding up. And it wasn't just stress or fatigue, she decided. He wouldn't look her in the eye.

"Louis, tell me what else is on your mind."

He opened his mouth to confess, then closed it again. He knew Lana wouldn't understand his vulnerability or how he had deceived himself over what Leslie Russell was offering him that night. He couldn't tell Lana the truth and lose her, lose everything.

He said nothing.

"You know, Louis, I've always been honest with you. And despite everything, I believe you've always been honest with me. Or I did anyway. If there's something you're keeping from me, you know I'll research the facts thoroughly to find out. So you'd better tell me yourself."

"Really, Lana, you heard the whole story. Like I said to Joe—"

"Fine, Louis. If whatever you won't tell me is worse than our kids being kidnapped or killed and worse than being caught in an explosion that rained bricks on your head, I'll have to insist that you leave this house."

"Lana. You can't be serious," he pleaded. "Where do you expect me to go?"

"Go home if you want and get your friend, Paul, to babysit you against the threats of your hit men. Or if you don't want to stay at home, find someplace else. A place of your own. I don't want any part of it. I can't help you."

His own place? Was she serious? He finally looked into her eyes. They were blazing. He would have to go. Unless he told her.

"Okay," he sighed, looking down again. "I'll call you from … somewhere. Lana?"

She said nothing, face turned to stone.

"I'm sorry."

Peller walked down the stairs, ashamed, bag in hand. He tried to joke with the kids as he explained he had to leave again. Lana remained ensconced in the bedroom she had grown up in, her only remaining bulwark against whatever terror Peller had wrought.

Three children grabbed their father's arms and tugged on his legs to keep him from leaving again. "Why do you have to go home, Daddy? Stay here with us … Why can't we come with you, Dad? … Want Da Da," begged their puzzled little voices.

Waving, attempting a smile, Peller pulled out of the driveway slowly, soaking in the memory of three tearful, pleading faces, hoping they would all come back home to him soon.

His heart was heavy. Retracing his drive through the suburbs and back to the highway, Peller tried to sort through a plan of action. Where could he go? What could he do? If he went home, who knew what hazards might await him? They'd already threatened his family. If Peller so much as opened his mouth to the authorities, if he drew attention to what he knew, he was afraid those innocent little faces would be wiped out in a flash. And it would be his fault. But they couldn't all live in perpetual terror either. He had to do something. What?

****

Steve Shapiro had Tommy Romano in his office. He'd jogged into work on a Saturday to meet up with the driver after Tommy's panicky phone call early that morning. The two men, Peller's friends, had called a tacit truce to their ongoing feud under these circumstances. They were huddled over Steve's desk, studying photographs.

"See, that's Assad. He was coming into the building around six thirty this morning. And look, theah's that Russell woman," Tommy said, pointing at a face peering through a window.

That was Leslie Russell all right, sporting a body-hugging, rose-colored minidress. Steve whistled.

"You say she was already in Assad's apartment before he got back?"

Tommy nodded. "I saw her tawking with the doorman. Maybe she and Assad have some kind of arrangement, if you know what I mean."

Steve Shapiro thought Omar Assad was one hell of a lucky guy. "So what's this got to do with Louis, Tommy?"

Tommy flipped through the photos. Assad and Russell in a tight clench. Russell arguing with Assad. So what if the lawyer and her client were having a fling? That wasn't any of Steve's affair … damn it anyway.

Tommy got to the final picture. Carlos de Leon, dreadlocks and all, passing in front of Assad's Fifth Avenue digs. "Here, Steve, this is the shot. Look at the one I took this morning next to these others." Tommy set that morning's photograph next to the earlier snapshots of Carlos and his two friends exchanging sacks, then Carlos's kitchen and the cocaine. He was carrying the same bag.

"That's Omar's super, isn't it? From the building on West 158th?"

"Yep. Carlos. Carlos de Leon … the lion."

"'Don't put your head in the lion's mouth,'" repeated Steve aloud. "That's it—it's Carlos de Leon!"

"I thought you might be interested," Tommy said grimly.

"I'll call Louis and describe the photographs. But I think we've got to get these pictures to him right away, Tommy, so he can identify them himself. Can we fax them immediately?" Steve was pacing the floor, worrying, fingering an unlit cigarette.

"I can fax them to the home office, chief."

"Good. I'll call Louis and warn him to go directly to Amie Mae to watch out for them right away."

****

When the phone rang at Peller's house, Paul was half dozing in front of the television, curled up in his annual winter hibernation. Peller had called him from the road to alert him that he was on his way home, that things were okay in Cleveland, but Peller needed to figure out how to fix the situation. He'd spoken cryptically. Paul had tried to talk him out of it, but there was no changing Peller's mind once it was set on something. S-T-U-B-B-O-R-N.

The phone kept jangling, finally lodging Paul from his slumber. Paul picked up the receiver suspiciously. "Hello?"

"Is Louis there?" came the man's voice.

"Who's calling?" Paul asked.

"It's Steve."

Paul sighed with relief. "Thank God it's just you. This is Paul, Steve. Louis isn't here just now."

"Paul, where is he? Is he okay? I've got to get some important information to him right away. Is he at the office by any chance?"

"Nowhere near. Can't say where he is just now, but I think I'll see him soon." They were to meet at a diner outside town. Paul warned Peller against coming directly home. He was still on the lookout for strange faces.

"Can you get to his office? I'm faxing some materials he might need to review. Fast."

"Is there security on the weekends?"

"There's a passkey in his briefcase. That's the only security."

"I'll check it out."

"Go there right away. His cube is 2-C-8 on the second floor. The fax sits in a room behind his cubicle. I'll have Tommy wait a half hour before he sends the stuff. Will you be okay, Paul?"

"I can handle this stuff, understand, Shapiro?"

"Right," Steve said, sounding worried himself. "Get word to me about Louis, okay?"

"Okay."

Paul went to search Peller's briefcase for the passkey. He was a little concerned about the possibility of someone sneaking into the house to plant listening devices while he was gone, but the risk would just have to be taken. Besides, thought Paul with a sudden grin, there was killer beast Manny dog to protect the place. That schnauzer yapped like a maniac whenever strangers approached. Scared Paul every time.

Out the door Paul dashed.

****

The greasy-spoon diner Paul had picked to meet him was just that: greasy. Truckers and good ol' boys from Berkeley Springs, West Virginia, and surrounding towns on both sides of the Mason-Dixon Line stopped off here to shoot the breeze and trade news. Just a couple hours west of Washington DC were communities where, except for the advent of satellite dishes and VCRs, time virtually stood still, where it could still be 1953. Berkeley Springs was pretty far off Peller's beaten path, but then, he didn't have any particular destination in mind at the moment. At any rate, Peller, weary and preoccupied, was relieved that Paul would be meeting him there.

Peller sipped on a cup of stale coffee and managed to find a two-day-old Washington newspaper to read. Paul was supposed to meet him by eight that evening, and it was already eight fifteen. Peller was nervously studying the sports pages, for the third time.

Finally, Paul strolled in. He had Peller's briefcase under his arm and was wearing a blue felt cap, flannel shirt, and jeans. He fit right in with the locals, the picture of calm and control.

Peller felt his spirits rise immediately. Of course, Paul would assume the perfect disguise; "blend in with the locals" was his modus operandi.

"Goin' huntin' tonight, friend?" Peller asked, trying out a bad joke.

"How ya doin', buddy?" Paul returned jovially, punching Peller on the arm.

Paul sat down across from Peller and motioned to the waitress, a sour-faced woman staring from behind the counter, to bring him a cup of coffee.

"Louie, I'm glad to see you're still alive," he exclaimed, mindful of ears listening in, suspicious of any outsiders passing through. "How's the family?"

The waitress brought over the coffee. "Care for any pie, fellas?"

Paul grinned. "My pal here will have two pieces of your apple pie. Really, you've gotta eat, Louie. Ya look a little peaked," he told his friend sympathetically.

When the waitress was out of earshot, he changed his tone. "Louis, you look like hell. Why didn't you stay with Lana and leave me to get you out of this mess?"

"Couldn't, Paul," he said. They were both quiet as the waitress brought over the pie.

"Made it fresh this mornin', boys," she announced mischievously, waiting for Peller to dig in. "Hope ya like it." The enormous slice of pie she set down in front of Peller looked, in fact, like petrified wood. He managed to swallow a stiff bite and smile. Satisfied, she ambled back to her counter.

"Ya know, Paul," Peller rambled, catching on to Paul's local-yokel act. "There's some nice parcels of land not too far from here. Beautiful country, isn't it? Far from the Beltway and close enough you can still buy the *Washington Post* for a quarter. High investment return. What say we mosey on out of here and take a look at those properties down the road apiece? Maybe a place to retire someday?" Despite the cardboard-like quality of the pie, Peller shoveled it into his mouth. He was famished. He washed down the pie with thick, brown coffee.

"Love to, Lou. Name a time, and I'm there. We can set up shop together, I promise. Even Chris says it might be nice to escape the city, be a country lawyer. But you've gotta promise me you'll stay out of everyone else's business and concentrate on your own."

"Naw, I'm done worrying about someone else's housing disasters. I just want a nice, quiet life down a long country lane and my wife and kids safe at home." Peller choked on his words.

Paul placed a reassuring hand on Peller's shoulder. Quietly, he asked, "What happened, Louis? How are Lana and the kids making out?"

Peller set his jaw. "Lana kicked me out. Said I wasn't being completely honest with her and she couldn't help me." He recited this fact as if he were reciting from someone else's script.

Paul's face turned serious.

"Let me confess something right off, friend. I saw your journal. I know the truth about your meeting with 'L.R.'"

Peller almost spit out his pie. He looked into Paul's face

pleadingly, guilt written all over his. "Why'd you read my personal stuff, Paul?"

"I had to. I thought it might contain a key to getting you out of this tight corner you've painted yourself into."

Peller looked stricken. "Don't tell Lana," he whispered.

"Well, it's funny you should mention that, Lou."

"What kind of funny, Paul?"

"I sent the journal to your in-laws' for safekeeping."

Peller's face turned red. He was furious. "You what?" he wheezed, in anguish over the news that not only did his good and trusted friend know about his grand deceit, but now Lana would know too, after he'd lied and told her there was nothing else to confess.

"How was I to know you would leave before the package arrived?"

"Great. I'm dead."

Paul relented. "But I removed this," he announced, holding up several wrinkled yellow pages.

Peller scanned the scrawls quickly. "Thank God. Don't scare me like that anymore, Paul. I've seen enough spooks already this week."

"There's one other thing," his friend said. "These just came in over the transom."

Peller took the fax printout of the pictures from Paul's hand. He studied the first one: Leslie Russell in front of some apartment building. He groaned. It resembled Assad's place. Then Leslie inside an apartment that Peller knew wasn't hers. The third shot, Omar Assad. Either Leslie had tricked Peller again, or she was doing an exceptional job of keeping up appearances.

Peller turned up the next picture, of Assad and Russell kissing. His face burned. He slumped back in his chair, the wind knocked completely out of him. Leslie. Omar. He'd been seduced by the maestro's mistress. Peller began to laugh a long, cynical laugh that startled Paul.

"Louis, are you okay?" He hadn't thought the pictures would

have such an impact. Maybe he'd underestimated Peller's mental state.

Then Peller put his head down on his hands, exhausted, ashamed, afraid. Paul put an arm around his friend's shoulders.

"How could I be so conceited?" Peller mumbled. "I thought … I really thought I conquered her. But I was bargaining with the devil." He lifted his head, still red faced, and looked at Paul. "I forgot who she was, Paul." His lip trembled as he struggled for control.

"And I destroyed everything," Peller moaned. "Lana despises me for what I've put the family through. She thinks I'm a selfish, self-centered bastard for bringing on this trouble. And she doesn't even know I cheated on her yet. And you know what?" he asked rhetorically. "She's right. I'm nothing but a no-good, two-timing, overzealous idiot." Another sob escaped his throat.

Paul looked around the room, embarrassed. "Louis, try to pull yourself together," he whispered. "You can't make a scene here."

Peller made another effort to stop, wiping his eyes with the back of his hands. He tried to smile, to show those staring strangers tuned in around them that he was okay. He sullenly attacked the pie again.

"Stop beating up on yourself, Louis," Paul coaxed quietly. "You know what you've done wrong. Now you have to do something to make it right. Look here. There's one more picture you've got to see, Louis."

"What? Seeing Russell in the clench with Assad is not shame enough?"

"Stop wallowing in it, Louis," Paul ordered and handed him the final shot.

"Carlos de Leon," Peller said softly, rubbing the paper between his fingers. He looked up at Paul again. "Carlos … the lion?"

Paul nodded. "I think we know who's behind the threat against your family, Louis."

Chapter 28
The Plan

Early Sunday morning, Louis Peller came home. His fearless dog leaped joyfully onto his master's chest as soon as Peller stepped inside the front door.

Paul walked in behind Peller, completely wrung out. After four hours spent trying to convince Peller that he was putting himself in greater danger by going home, Paul gave up in utter defeat. At least Paul had managed to follow Peller back home, despite his friend's kamikaze course. Finally, Peller was determined to face down the maestro.

Paul resolved to shadow Peller as closely as possible, not leaving him alone for more than a few minutes at a time, swearing he would stay at Peller's house that night and every successive night until the danger subsided, though Peller tried to convince his friend he was fine alone. Paul thought not. He would a damned sight rather endure the night red-eyed and wakeful, chugging coffee, with Peller safely tucked in his own bed. Louis Peller would not sneak out tonight.

Peller slept amazingly well that night, not waking until nine thirty Sunday morning. He hadn't slept that late since he was a teenager. Peller guessed it was fatigue that finally overcame his anxiety that night. When he finally opened his eyes in his own bed, it was on the heels of yet another dream—roars and cries rose eerily from Carlos's apartment, and they were ritual sounds of drums, chants, and moaning. Screaming. An open door poured light: escape. When he arrived at the doorway, beckoning white sands sparkled in tropical splendor. And Lana. He awoke with a smile, feeling rested.

The sun was also bright outside his window, and it gave him hope. Hope that all was not lost. Hope that he was, in fact, doing something right. With a last foray into the jungles of New York Monday morning, he could put to rest the nightmares of the adventurer and find contentment, the peace and happiness with his wife and family that he now realized were balm to his soul. He stroked his dog's furry coat in contemplation of better times to come. Home. Normalcy. The love of his wife, the warmth of this house, the innocent and honest affection of his children, and friends, these were what made life worth living.

That day, Peller would start a fresh chapter in his life. Maybe he couldn't repair all the damage, but the mending process must begin.

Paul was brewing his second pot of coffee. "Feeling better, champ?" he asked Peller, feeling rather gritty himself.

"Never better." Peller smiled his first sincere smile in days. The bags and bruises in his face were fading, and the old sparkle was back in his eyes.

Paul was astonished. Just last night, he had been talking to a defeated man. "Coffee?" he asked hoarsely.

"No thanks, Paul. I think I'm going to give the stuff up. Nightmares."

Paul sat down. "Glad you're doing so well this morning, Louis. What's your plan for the day?"

"That's just it. We've got to plan. I want to take Assad down screaming. Sink his whole fucking ship. And you've got to help me do it."

"I don't think I'm going to like this, Louis."

"Paul, I promise. I've got to finish what I've started. Help me this one last time, and I'll treat you to season's tickets to the Mets. Shea Stadium. Box seats."

Paul lifted his eyebrow suspiciously. "Louis? You can't afford box seats."

"Then I'll give you Omar's." He winked. "After all, he won't be able to use them in jail. C'mon, Paul, we've got work to do. I want to fly up to New York tonight to be there in plenty of time for my meeting with Omar Assad and Leslie Russell."

"I'll scheme with you if you'll just let me catch forty winks, and promise me you won't steal away anywhere," warned Paul.

"Deal," announced Peller triumphantly. "It will give me time to read today's newspaper for a change."

****

In Cleveland, Lana was still fuming. Peller had some nerve, coming here and telling her he was sorry. As if he expected her to forgive him, just like that, for putting the family in jeopardy. And the way he acted, so contrite. Well, he'd just have to get them all out of danger and stop getting involved in mischief and mayhem for the sake of that ever-lovin' job of his, she thought in disgust. When the going got tough, Joe Vallardo abandoned him. So much for company loyalty and corporate responsibility.

The doorbell chimed and jarred her from her brooding. Her parents had taken the kids to the park for a picnic, thinking, correctly, that she needed time to herself. She opened the door, and there was Federal Express. Of course, the notes Paul had sent.

"Luis Peller?" asked the delivery woman with a hint of a Spanish accent, a curvaceous, alluring redhead with pouty lips—a standout, even in her standard-issue uniform.

"Sorry, he's out at the moment," muttered Lana. "But I can sign for it. I'm his wife." Lana noted that the woman seemed to be looking past her. For Peller? But he wasn't there.

"I have instructions to give this directly to Mr. Peller," the woman noted with a frown.

"And I said Mr. Peller's not here," Lana said testily. "I know what this is. His associate, Paul Chase, alerted me the package was coming."

The driver looked at the name on the package. Paul Chase—it matched. "Well," she began to relent. "I do have specific instructions ..."

"Look," said Lana cooperatively. "Here's my driver's license. See? I'm Lana Peller. Oh, and here, here's my husband's American Express card, see, Louis Peller." She held up the IDs, smiling. Lucky she'd forgotten to give Peller back this credit card. It was the only card he'd left home in Silver Spring the night he'd been pickpocketed in New York.

"Well, okay." Sizing up the attractive wife, the delivery woman handed over the package. "I hope I don't get fired for this," she said.

"On the contrary, I will write a letter commending your caution and thoroughness," Lana responded graciously. She really intended to help this woman. "What's your name?"

"Angela Sanchez ... um, Angela Sanchez-Smith," she corrected herself, showing Lana her own identification. She pronounced Smith with a long "e" and ending with a "t"—Smeet. She lingered a moment, still peering into the house as if she were waiting for a ghost to appear.

"Mr. Peller, he's coming back?"

"I will give this to him right away, Ms. Smith."

"I hope he's okay," murmured the driver incomprehensibly. Then she added, "Thanks, Mrs. Peller. Have a nice day." And she hopped into the truck and drove away.

"Have a nice day," Lana mimicked. *You too, Mr. Peller*, she thought tartly, wondering what Peller would say if he knew what she was about to do. And she hurried inside to delve into whatever dark and dangerous secrets this package might contain.

****

Hours later, she lifted her eyes from the long-lined sheets to note that lengthening shadows were stealing ominously across the room. It was well after two, and Lana was more terrified than ever. It was obvious to her now why their family was in danger. Peller had been dealing with seasoned criminals. How could Peller be so smug—or so naive—as to think he could toy with these people? Peller was a fool.

But she was puzzled. There was nothing personally incriminating in this record. Just Peller gallivanting around town in those strip joints and sleazy night clubs. But he'd told her about that stuff. Seemed juvenile to her, hardly the kind of thing to make Paul, of all people, concerned.

Then she noticed that several consecutive pages had been ripped out. Must have been done in a hurry, for she could detect fragments of sentences on the edges, where the pages hadn't come out at the perforation. *Wore a swinging black dress*, said one. Probably more of that Times Square sludge, she thought. *She stripped in front of red candles that*, began another. That confirmed it: a strip joint. She'd really have to confront Peller with that unnerving habit of prowling through the night; it wasn't right. Then she unfolded the phrase, *L.R.'s passion* and *ravished me*. She thought back to Paul's baffling warning: "This time he really needs you to stand by him. To show him you love him." And then Peller on the phone with Vallardo, hesitantly alluding to a "second meeting" with Leslie Russell. "L.R."

Damn him. Her kids lives were being threatened, and he was out screwing some bitch legal counsel to the opposition. "Smart, Louis, real smart." But sarcasm wasn't the point here. He'd cheated on her. She *hated* him. He had fucked Leslie Russell. Finally, the depth of his deception hitting her, she screamed in despair, "Why'd you do it, Louis, you two-timing bastard? Why'd you do this to *me*?"

At that instant, she heard brakes in the driveway. The kids

and her parents clamored out. She tried to collect herself and ran into the study with the legal pad. She couldn't let anyone else witness this.

"Hi everyone," she announced, all smiles. Lies. "How was the park?"

"Great," her father smiled, relieved to see Lana less morose.

"We loved it, Mommy," Alexander said.

"But we missed you," joined Alison.

"Da Da," cried out Ashley.

"I'm glad you had fun," their mother said. "Now Mama needs some time to write, so you go out and play."

Her father looked at her quizzically.

"Oh, just a deadline I have to meet for a story that's got to run Tuesday, Daddy," she explained. "I thought I mentioned it. I can fax it from up the street at the copy shop to the newsroom."

"I don't recall—"

"No big deal, really," she interrupted. "Shouldn't take me more than a couple hours to type out. Still have the old Underwood?"

"Come on, little fishies," Lana's mother called out. "Who's going to help me bake chocolate chip cookies?"

Lana ran up and gave her mom a kiss. She turned to her father. "Thanks, Dad," she smiled warmly. His eyes were worried. "Nothing to be concerned about. Life must go on."

She disappeared into the study and quietly locked the door.

****

"Paul, I have to go back up there and meet with them. Don't you see? If I don't conclude what I started, my family will remain in danger."

Paul tore at his hair. "Louis, I'm telling you, it's suicide." Paul began pacing, exasperated at his friend's insistence on such folly.

"It's the only way things will work, Paul. The *only* way. Humor me on this one."

"I'd advise you this time to turn things over to the authorities."

"And if I do that, my family will still be in danger, Paul, because they'll go for Assad, not his henchmen. It would be impossible to trace all the members of Omar's drug organization. If Assad's other men are anything like Carlos, they're fiercely loyal to him, and they'll carry out his business for him, even if he's behind bars. No, I could never rest easy. No thanks. I want my family to get out of this alive, not afraid to walk or play or go to work every day."

Paul raised one eyebrow and said nothing.

"Can we point the finger at Carlos, Paul?"

"Yeah, with the pictures, I think there might be something we can do."

"I mean put him away for good, Paul, not just a few years on Rikers for drug trafficking."

"We'd have to have more direct evidence of Carlos's threat on your children to really nail him, I think. Short of that kind of proof, we're looking at killing Carlos."

Peller looked at Paul with a malevolent grin.

"Forget it, Louis. We are not going to carry out a murder plot here," Paul contested angrily. "Don't even consider it a possibility. Are you entirely off your rocker?"

"It was just a thought, Paul," responded Peller registering chagrin. "A fantasy, should we say?"

"A nightmare is what I'd call it," mumbled Paul cursing Peller out until he realized his friend was merely engaging in wishful thinking that he could climb out of this hole so easily.

Back and forth, Peller and Paul worked through the day on a plan to entrap Assad that would effectively implicate the lion.

"I go up there tomorrow, carry out my meeting with Russell and Assad, and at the end of the meeting, we send in the police with a warrant for Assad's arrest. Epstein could provide reams of evidence," Peller theorized.

"We need them to find the drugs. Would Epstein know when Carlos is scheduled to receive a shipment?"

Peller nodded eagerly. "Paul—it's worth a shot. We've gotta

try." He picked up the phone to dial Epstein's pager. "Can we nail Assad too?

Paul considered. "If the case goes to trial, we'll have to figure out how to protect Epstein from reprisals. If I were him, I'd want some guarantees."

"And just before they throw Assad in jail, I'll make sure he comes up with enough money to pay back every penny he owes Amie Mae, with interest. Otherwise, my problem will be collecting from the United States government after they confiscate Omar's 'sentimental attachment.'"

Epstein rang back immediately. Peller spoke cryptically. "They're expecting a shipment of contraband within the next forty-eight hours? Are you willing to tie the shipment to our friend's operations? If you testify, we'll go for full immunity." He hesitated.

"I'll be in touch." Peller nodded at Paul as he hung up the phone. "We've got our plan, Paul. I'll play the innocent with Assad; he knows I suspect something, of course, but I'll assure him I'm only interested in doing our deal and nothing more. Which is true, by the way. Epstein says there are deliveries in Washington Heights every four days or so. I call the police and tip them off and *voilà*, the lion is caught in his lair."

"That's a nice, clean illusion, Louis, but a million things could go wrong with the scenario," Paul warned.

"Of course, we need protection for Epstein; maybe Chris can help us there. Epstein fingers Assad as we conclude our morning meeting," sketched Peller, ignoring Paul's objections.

"Assad could get to the lion, Carlos or whoever he is, before we do and order him to follow through on his threats—or worse, Louis. It's a very risky strategy." Paul sounded ominous.

"I'll make sure Tommy's constantly scoping out Carlos's apartment. It's the best I can do. Look, Paul, I'm aware of the risks. But what else can I do? I'm in this so deep now, I have to try something drastic."

They concluded their business around dinnertime. Paul had

a long, private conversation with Chris, avoiding Peller's ears. Reluctantly, she promised to work on the details of Epstein's immunity. The trap was set.

"Let's blow this joint and grab a bite, Louis. I need to relax," Paul suggested wearily.

But Peller was all fired up. "Sorry, Paul, but I want to go up to New York tonight, to mentally prepare for this showdown."

"Louis, Louis, Louis. I won't let you go up there alone, unprotected, to stay at some hotel where that Carlos de Leon could arrange to greet you with the snub nose of a pistol. Fly up first thing in the morning. Or else, I'm coming with you."

"Can't let you do that, Paul. I need your help on this end, to keep an eye on the house and to be my eyes and ears in case Lana tries to reach me. I can't tell her that I'm going back up there, not now. Besides, I'm going to stay with Steve. He has security in his building," Peller lied coolly. "I'll be okay. Just make sure the house and dog are safe."

"Let me just go on record as protesting yet another foolish Peller move, Louis." Paul was furious. "I won't cover your ass this time, you jerk."

"Fine. Let the record show," mimicked Peller solemnly, "that Paul Chase is against this stupid Peller idea. And he's probably right."

"As usual."

"As usual."

"Louis, you scare me. You really do," Paul replied soberly, cautioning. "I hope, after all is said and done, you'll take a very long sabbatical. You and Lana."

"If she'll have me back," he answered gloomily. Then Peller brightened, landing a friendly punch on Paul's shoulder. "Thank you, my friend. I know I couldn't do this without you. I owe you."

Paul mustered a skeptical smile. "Shalom, Louis. May God be with you."

****

After Peller drove off in Paul's rented car, Paul grabbed a beer out of his friend's refrigerator, called up Domino's for a pizza with the works, and turned on *60 Minutes*. He generally liked Andy Rooney's cranky commentaries. As chance would have it, the show's lead story tonight was about the Dominican drug ring in Washington Heights. Paul watched it intently, hanging nervously on every word about the terror, crime, and violence inflicted by the community's uncrowned Hispanic Mafioso, and shuddered at the unnerving coincidence.

Life was too real for Paul tonight. He turned off the television. The house was eerily silent. He peered out a front window through the split in the curtains for the Domino's delivery. There was Peller's car in the driveway. The neighbors had their lights on. The street seemed calm. Paul called the dog in from the yard to keep him company, grateful that this crazy, loyal mutt was around to warn him of anyone who might approach.

Still, Paul was suffering a bad case of nerves. This, he recalled, was one reason he'd finally left the Agency; constant stealth and dread were too hard on the nervous system. He decided he must escape this anxious state of mind; a video might do the trick. Peller had an extensive collection: musicals, cartoons, animated classics, the entire Hitchcock collection, and a few other oldies. Something light was in order tonight. Unlike most men, Paul rather enjoyed the old romance films: *Casablanca, Breakfast at Tiffany's*, movies that depicted a nostalgic, innocent era in America. On occasion, he dipped into a few cult classics like *The Rocky Horror Picture Show* and *Blue Velvet*. Tonight, he chose *Breakfast at Tiffany's* to enjoy the revelry of the impish Holly Golightly in a far less brutish depiction of New York.

The VCR was set up in Peller and Lana's bedroom. Paul, exhausted from the previous two days of trying, unsuccessfully, to protect his best friend from his own bull-headed destructiveness, could finally stretch out on a real bed to relax. Lights off, TV on, he laid his aching head against a billowy buffer of pillows, comfortingly stroking the affection-crazed dog snuggling up against him. In the dark, the flicker of the television screen and another beer combined to create a hypnotic effect. Paul, gazing hypnotically at the TV set, was soon pleasantly immersed in the flighty fantasy, Peller, peril, and pizza forgotten.

So he didn't hear the newly greased glass door in the back of the house slide open. He wasn't aware of the stealthy footsteps climbing the stair. Manny, petted into submission, was so content to be the center of affection that, for once, he didn't sense anything out of the ordinary.

When the light from the hallway was suddenly blotted out by a dark figure with a wild mane of tangled hair materializing in the bedroom door, Paul sat up instantaneously. Too late. A clean, silent shot through the chest knocked his body back into the nest of pillows and stilled Paul the protector, forever. With the sudden convulsion of the master holding him, the high-strung dog leapt ferociously at the intruder, whelping and barking. In midair, his head was pierced, penetrated by a second silenced bullet.

The irrepressible Holly Golightly flickered on, unnoticing.

Fleet of foot, the lion fled.

Chapter 29
Assad's Final Offer

Sunday evening in Steve's living room, Peller laid out his plan in all its beautiful simplicity for his colleague. It was important to perfectly orchestrate the play whose finale would see Omar Assad arrested and convicted. Whatever Peller knew about Assad, he would promise not to divulge; he was only interested in getting the best possible payoff on the property and washing his hands of the whole affair once and for all.

Bright and early Monday morning, the two men walked briskly to their office. Feigning calm on this extraordinary day, they waited for Assad and Russell to arrive. And waited.

By ten thirty, when there was no sign of the duo, Peller decided to call them. Peller dialed Assad's apartment and his office. No answer. He checked with the receptionist at Russell's law firm. She was there, with a client. This forced a change of setting; Peller would taxi to Leslie Russell's office.

He arrived without announcement and informed the protesting receptionist that Ms. Russell was expecting him.

Peller banged open her closed office door unceremoniously. As luck would have it, Assad was there. Russell was annoyed at any interruption, ready to read the riot act to unwelcome intruders.

Peller marched in. Russell and Assad froze, stunned. A look of terror settled over Russell's stony eyes. Assad had just spoken to Carlos, who had informed his boss proudly that he had "fixed" their problem with Amie Mae. Peller was supposed to be dead.

"Seems you must have misunderstood our date, Leslie," Peller announced with a patronizing smile. "I told you we would meet this morning at Amie Mae."

Russell stuttered incomprehensibly. Her heart was barely beating. Peller was alive.

"But that's okay," continued Peller, smiling. "I brought the papers here with me, so we can complete the payoff right away. Are we agreed on eight hundred thousand dollars?"

As he stared at Russell, she turned away, unable to meet the challenge fixed in his eyes.

"Here are the terms we're prepared to accept," began Peller, launching into the script. Without allowing so much as an objection, he came to the bottom line. "In exchange for meeting your original price and completing this transaction today, I'll agree to leave you alone," he concluded, winking conspiratorially at Russell.

Taken completely by ambush, the attorney and her client had no counteroffer.

"Well," suggested Peller, taking their silence for assent, "I took the liberty over the weekend of having everything drawn up for our meeting. Why don't we just get the paperwork signed?" He pulled a stack of documents out of his briefcase. "Then we'll be finished. Omar, the building will be all yours, free and clear, to do with as you will." Peller smiled graciously. "Now, if you'll excuse me, I need to call my office to attend to another matter."

Assad angrily attempted to protest Peller's cavalier treatment. Peller smiled enigmatically and ignored his borrower's complaint as he left the room.

As soon as he left, Russell's phone rang, leaving the attorney and her client no time to reconnoiter. She had been unable to convince Assad to attend the meeting at Amie Mae. Instead, he had insisted on meeting her here. When he revealed the hit on Peller, Russell had been genuinely frightened. If Assad would murder his adversary in cold blood for mere suspicion of his possessing information, what would he do if he found out about her complicity with Peller? And then for Peller to appear like this, risen from the dead? She tried to control her shaking hands. Assad couldn't suspect …

She cradled the phone between her shoulder and her ear so he wouldn't detect her fear. "Russell here."

It was the receptionist. "There are two detectives here looking for Mr. Assad," she announced shakily. "What should I do?"

Leslie's black eyes were wide, her pale skin even whiter than normal. "Show them in."

Louis Peller made his reentry flanked by the officers. "Here's the agreement, as promised," he announced cheerfully, handing it to Assad.

The officers politely demurred to this transaction. "Mr. Omar Assad? We have a warrant for your arrest. You are charged with drug trafficking, operating a gambling establishment, money laundering, and mail fraud."

A rattle deep down in Assad's throat signaled the snake's recoiling.

****

There it was Tuesday, front page of the *New York Times*, above the fold: "Iranian Real Estate Magnate Arrested in Drug Sting: Feds Suspect Drug Money Used to Acquire Properties," by Debora Starr.

Steve had left for his predawn run, sneaking out while Peller slept peacefully. Peller, waking at first light, had dashed out to grab the first edition.

Ace reporter Deb Starr was an old friend of Lana's who had been a cub reporter at the *Times* when Lana was in J-school at Columbia. Debora had given her friend research jobs, then used her as a stringer on a few assignments, launching Lana on her reporting career. Although Peller had met Debora a couple of years ago at a family gathering, he'd always found it best to stick his nose out of Lana's professional life and made it a habit not to consort with her newspaper friends. Except now, when he needed one of them. And Debora, sensing a hot scoop, had been more than happy to oblige. Peller scanned the article and noted that the writer had made good use of the facts Peller had sent her, adding a few astonishing revelations of her own, like the fact that Assad owned at least thirty-five buildings throughout the city, most of which were centered in the South Bronx and Washington Heights. How had she uncovered that astonishing count, he wondered. She verified FBI interest in the Assad brothers and inserted a particularly incriminating anonymous quote, one that must have come from Epstein:

> Omar Assad pieced together an organization of such sinuous complexity that not even he could completely trace its path. Superintendents in three of his buildings in Washington Heights and the Bronx hired tenants and neighborhood teenagers to sell cocaine and heroin on the street. The supers' apartments serve as drug distribution outlets, and their workers line up outside the apartments, awaiting their assignments and remuneration. Noted a former Assad business investor, who declined to be identified, "He is shrewd, I tell you, with a diabolical mind for detail, a master strategist. In his head, he has masterminded a labyrinthine international organization for his clandestine operations." Mr. Assad allegedly distanced himself from the drug business by using intermediaries. Devising an entirely legal ruse to avoid any personal connection with his operations, Mr. Assad set up shell corporations in which his attorney is chief officer. Noted the former business partner, "I invested in two of Assad's buildings before I learned what was really going on with

this real estate. But you can bet, as soon as I saw the nature of these investments, I sold my shares."

Although it is not uncommon to find drugs being sold in some neighborhoods of Washington Heights, the size and scope of this drug ring is unprecedented in New York. New York Police Chief Albert C. Jerome cites this as "the bust up of a major operation that has been a scourge to this city since as early as 1988. NYPD has been working with the Federal Bureau of Investigation to gather sufficient evidence to close down Omar Assad's shop for some time. We are convinced that this bust will contribute significantly to the department's efforts to clean up the drug problems in Washington Heights, Spanish Harlem, and the South Bronx. This operation has grown in scope enormously over the past few years."

Federal authorities, including the Drug Enforcement Administration and the FBI, have been investigating a drug cartel in Washington Heights for the past eighteen months. Law enforcement officials were tipped off to an unusual volume of drug activity in an apartment building at 488 West 158th Street. The trail led to owner Omar Assad, whose other apartment investments were found to mirror similar drug activity as that uncovered in the Washington Heights property. Assad's former associate commented, "I learned of some of the problems visiting the buildings myself. As a major investor in a deal, I reserve the right to inspect the properties. What I saw would appall you: kids of all ages using the stairwells to urinate, because the toilets in their apartments did not work; old people walking down four crumbling flights of stairs, because the elevators haven't been in operation for months; rat infestation. And the super is sitting like a king in his apartment, dealing dope to the riffraff, dope delivered in Omar Assad's private jet from sources he and his brothers control in Colombia and Mexico. The money

> just rolls in. Meanwhile, a super from one building would not even know his counterpart in another building. He isolates each building into its own cell, reporting to a separate chain of command."
>
> Authorities have uncovered evidence that the couriers, the suppliers, and the growers, many of whom are members of the immigrant superintendents' families who remained in Santa Domingo or Caracas, each perform specialized tasks in an underground network of drug transactions and money laundering.

"Bravo, Deb," Peller commended aloud to the empty apartment. He was sitting cross-legged on Steve's couch. Good old Deb Starr; she sure lived up to her name. One of these days, Peller would have to take Deb and Lana out to celebrate, just the three of them.

Peller flipped over the *Times* to read any related news; Deb had hinted at another bombshell that might drop on this case. And there, sure enough, was a picture of Russell and Assad, apparently talking inside Assad's apartment (with a photo credit for Tommy Romano). The picture was captioned: "New York socialite and prominent attorney Leslie Russell (left) has been implicated with Middle East real estate investor Omar Assad (right) in an illegal drug trafficking, gambling ring." As requested, Amie Mae's name and Peller's involvement in the affair went unmentioned.

Boy, thought Peller, Starr had really nailed Russell. Even the caption had been written to point the finger at Assad's attorney. Peller had mixed feelings about the accrued legal evidence implicating Leslie Russell. Though she had, for all intents and purposes, double-, no, triple-crossed him, even as she avowed her sincerity. The despair and betrayal he read in her eyes as they placed the cuffs on Assad's wrists to lead him away bespoke feelings of tenderness, of loss, and, Peller believed, of remorse.

The second story inside the *Times* focused attention on the soaring career of a stellar New York attorney who, through greed and manipulation, had set herself up for a fall. "Russell's Next Defense to Be Her Own—Special to the *New York Times,*" announced the headline. There was no byline. As Peller read the story incriminating Russell for her complicity in Assad's business—for setting up partnerships and corporations designed to conceal Assad's majority shareholder status by naming herself managing partner and concealing his illegal drug dealings—he was shamed anew by his tryst with the attorney who, it now came to light, had been in bed with Assad in more ways than one. The details struck home. How could he have been drawn in by this seductress while she was sharing her sheets and her considerable legal prowess with Omar Assad? Peller could hardly admit he'd been lured by a calamitous attraction to her flawless white skin, mysterious black eyes, and tempting red lips. All the sordid details recounted in the story, including the information Peller had gotten from Bud Epstein, pointed to the fact that Leslie Russell was a knowing partner of Assad. Peller had prided himself in knowing that he had conquered her, and yet, he had lost. No firebird would rise triumphant from the ashes of the swan.

Still, there was some satisfaction to be gained from Omar's arrest. Carlos's apartment had been searched in the wee hours Monday after investigators, tipped off by Tommy Romano's stealthy vigil, witnessed the routine delivery of a large shipment of cocaine and caught several of Carlos's accomplices in the act. But Carlos was nowhere to be found. Still, Tommy was busting with pride about his role in fingering the notorious lion of West 158th.

Assad and his brothers soon would be swept tidily off the streets of Washington Heights, Harlem, Brooklyn, and the Bronx. Peller had done what he could. A wiser man today, Peller was no longer naive enough to believe that other profiteers in the same mold wouldn't spring up in their wake. He rubbed his hands over his face to wash it clean of fear and shame.

Was it worth it? He got his payoff: eight hundred thousand dollars. At last, Louis Peller's work was complete. But his life was a shambles. How to approach Lana was the remaining question. Utterly anguished and humiliated, Peller now had the monumental task of repairing his broken marriage and renewing faith with a few hurt and confused children.

Steve's phone rang. Peller ignored it, not wanting to answer for Steve. It flipped over to the answering machine, and suddenly, he heard Lana's voice on the recorder: "Louis, I hope you're there. Pick up, someone. It's urgent."

He jumped for the receiver. "Lana," he answered nervously. "I was just thinking about you. Honey, I … I mean, please—"

She interrupted, her voice coming out in gulps. "Louis, we have to work it out later. Something awful's happened. I just found out. Paul—"

"I know. I asked him to stay overnight at the house last night. I promised I'd call him later to let him know how the thing played out—"

"Louis. Listen. Paul's … dead."

Dead. It didn't sink in. Dead? No, not Paul. It wasn't possible, Peller decided. What could she mean? He opened his mouth but couldn't speak. Sobs wracked him. Paul, his friend. His partner. His protector. He felt again the bricks stinging him on the head. He felt the wind knocked out of him. He felt he would die.

Filling the excruciating silence, Lana blurted out, "I didn't know where to find you, Louis. Or what to say. I found out a few hours ago." Checking in with her former mentor Deb Starr at the *Times* to see if Lana's anonymous story devastating Leslie Russell had run in the first edition, the reporter informed Lana that the wires were carrying the story of a murder in suburban Maryland, motives and suspect unknown. The street address was theirs. Apparently Sofia had gone in the house to check on the dog and discovered the bodies.

Softer, Lana recounted, "Sofia found him lying in our bed … shot through the chest."

Who? What? When? How? Paul was shot in bed. Not his bed. Paul Chase had been sleeping where Peller should have slept. A million doubts coursed through his brain, but he was too stunned to utter them aloud. His best friend was dead, shot with a bullet that had been reserved for another target: Louis Peller. Paul was dead.

"Louis?" Lana cried. "Say something. Are you still there?"

"It's my fault," he managed to choke out in a gasp.

"I'm so sorry, Louis."

He buried his head against the back of the couch in shame and fear, holding back sobs. Finally it dawned on him; that's why Russell and Assad had been so astonished when Peller marched into her office: Louis Peller was supposed to be dead. Carlos, or whoever, was their hit man, had reported success. Of course, Carlos couldn't have been in his Washington Heights apartment at the same time he was in Maryland murdering Louis Peller. And Russell had known all about this? Suddenly he was not the least bit sorry Russell was under suspicion. Jail would be too good for her.

Out of fear and long-suppressed anxiety, Peller began to shriek. "Lana. Lana. They got Paul. Don't you see? I'm so sorry. They got Paul, Lana, but they meant to get me."

She heard him and sat down, too shocked to answer. The thought had never occurred to her. Of course. A killer had entered *their* bedroom. He hadn't been aiming for Paul Chase. Paul was the unwitting stand-in for the real target—Louis Peller—who knew too much.

"Louis," she yelled. "Louis." She had to break through his hysteria. "Louis, get somewhere to safety. We have protection here, don't worry. This, this killer …"

Dimly, her insistent plea rang through his frenzied brain, self-reproach mixing with fear. Peller had to hide. Carlos was still at large. Carlos would know Peller had fingered him. Peller was a marked man. But who could he turn to for protection? Paul had always been his guardian. Now a guardian angel. A shiver wracked his body.

Lana grieved for Peller—so devastated already by the chaos

he had set in motion, this news about his sole confidant was shattering. She too was despondent over the cold-blooded murder of their good friend. Still, she could not help ease Peller's grief. In her outrage, she held him largely responsible.

But hearing his sobs over the phone, she relented—a little. His anguish was so deep. She hadn't the heart to mention that police had also found the body of Peller's other best friend lying in a wasted heap on the floor next to the bed. Pitying, even through her anger, she gathered her wits about her, took a deep breath, and recited quietly, unemotionally, "It's all so horrible. What has happened, Louis? Did you *gain* anything by this act? You've lost your closest friend." After a moment, she added, "We've all lost." And unable to offer anything more, she hung up.

Peller's brain didn't register the dial tone on the other end. When he finally dropped the receiver, the buzzing phone line muffled against the couch, he was unaware of it. He sat staring blankly, nothing registering on his consciousness except the fact that his buddy was gone because of him. Brutally murdered. Dead. Mistaken for Louis Peller. Peller couldn't get beyond that fact.

Steve came back from his run, newspaper tucked under one arm, and quietly unlocked the door, thinking Peller might still be sleeping. He tiptoed into the room, only to find Peller on his couch, newspaper unfolded at his feet, shivering uncontrollably.

"Louis? Louis," he called. Peller began to moan. "What's wrong?" Steve touched Peller on the shoulder. His colleague hid his head in his knees and doubled over. Steve sat down gently beside him, patting him helplessly, trying to still his shaking.

"Louis? Please tell me what's happened. Snap out of it," he called to no avail. Peller seemed to be in shock. His eyes were dazed. Why? Steve was clueless. Then he noticed the phone receiver buried behind a cushion. He picked it up to listen; the phone was dead.

Whatever news Peller had received must have been devastating, thought Steve, wondering what new horror he could have learned. He had to get Peller to talk. He hung up the phone and paced the floor, watching his friend to detect any sign of recognition. Nothing. He poured a glass of cold water from the fridge and pressed it against Peller's lips, hoping he might drink. His friend was shaking so uncontrollably, some of the water splashed over his face and ran down his cheeks, a rain of tears.

Finally, the shivering subsided. Peller's body relaxed. He looked up at Steve, his eyes still glazed, and whispered something incoherent. Steve had to bend his ear close to Peller's lips to hear him.

"Paul was shot."

This revelation knocked the wind out of Steve. He sat down hard, silent. Of all the people involved, Paul Chase was the last one who should have been hurt. He was just trying to protect his friend, Louis the stubborn, Louis the compulsive, Louis the obsessed. Steve stared long and hard at Peller's tensed face: anxious, angry, outraged. Finally, he mastered his feelings to ask the ultimate question, the one at whose answer he had already guessed: "Who did it?"

Steve could detect Peller's visible struggle to shoulder his pain. He heard him take a deep breath. "Carlos," Peller blurted out finally. "He meant to get me." And the mask Peller had tried so valiantly to fasten over his face cracked with pain. He wept.

Chapter 30
Made for Television

She watched in trepidation as Omar Assad was arrested in her office. Dutifully, she accompanied him to the precinct house, where her client was to endure a humiliating and very public detainment. Mechanically, she denied all accusations, advising her client to maintain his silence. Finally, Leslie Russell went home exhausted, determined to flee before she too was fingered.

She passed a tense hour in her apartment, pacing. She had shed her clothes nervously while she packed, clad only in a bathrobe. She had nowhere to go. Three suitcases lay strewn with clothes in her bedroom until she decided to take only a small overnight bag for maneuverability. Each time she picked it up to make her escape, some noise in the hall spooked her. Assad would send one of his killers after her. After all, she knew everything about his operations. He was a vicious, vengeful man. She had no one to turn to.

With a hand on the phone to reserve a spot on the next plane bound for Costa Rica, she hesitated. What if her phone was wired? The look on Peller's face, his victory in entrapping Assad, it was the same euphoria she had experienced in vanquishing him in the bedroom. Peller would stop at nothing now to see her defeated. Loneliness and fear wrapped her in their smothering embrace.

Three dull thuds of her door knocker, a coiled brass snake. Panicking, she felt that snake coiling tightly around her throat. A woman called out, "Police."

They were there already. What did they want? What should she do? Was her least objectionable course the NYPD, or Assad? The press would be lined up for the kill in a high-profile case like this.

"Get a hold of yourself, Leslie," she muttered under her breath. "You're the master of the courtroom. You can talk yourself out of anything. You've always been able to talk." She began hesitantly toward the door, then reconsidered. *If they find how deeply I'm involved in Omar's businesses, I'll be ruined. My reputation will be in tatters*, she thought. *If I'm disbarred and, worse yet, imprisoned … what life will I have left?*

She glimpsed a white, frightened face in the mirror and covered her eyes with her hands, sliding those slender digits over her face and neck as if to erase herself magically from the scene. No. She wouldn't let them see her weak. She pulled her features into a cold, glittering smile and outlined her lips in her blood-red lipstick. *I won't let them break me. I'll mount my own offense against that devil, Omar Assad. And the assault starts here and now.*

She called out, "Just a moment. I'll be right with you." Jumping into her red Lycra dress, she slipped on pale, opalescent stockings and stepped into the black pumps with spiked heels lined up carefully at the foot of her bed. "Come fuck me" shoes, they were called. Defiantly, she laughed. Quickly, she passed a brush through her thick, black hair, arranging it to flow seductively over her shoulders. She hoped all the TV photographers were men. They wouldn't catch her with her guard down.

She talked to herself as she applied her makeup ever so skillfully. "You can beat this, Leslie. Give nothing away, nothing. They have no evidence you've knowingly done anything wrong. Only Louis Peller's damn theories."

Carefully, she set her face again in that proud, imperious smile. "Leslie Russell never loses," she told herself assuredly. She could not afford to lose everything she'd worked so hard to build. No matter the cost. She was resolved to clear her own name of a man she had once loved criminally, desperately.

The glitter of suppressed tears still hung on her black lashes, and the tight smile clung to red lips as she opened the door. At once, a chorus of voices sang out the accusations, asking her to reveal the details of Omar Assad's conspiracy. Captivating and beguiling, she met the battery of cameras, spotlights, and microphones thrust in her face with ready words to unmask Omar Assad's treachery, denying any knowledge of his schemes.

As she opened her mouth to respond, two police officers in blue stepped forward and grabbed her wrists roughly. "Leslie Russell? You're under arrest." Before Leslie could speak, the female officer recited the accusation: "You are an accessory by concealment to setting up illegal corporations for the purposes of money laundering," pronounced the Amazonian black woman on Russell's left, showing her a warrant. She then read Leslie Russell her Miranda rights. The second officer, an older, bald-headed man with a paunch, obviously a longtime veteran of the force, adeptly slapped handcuffs on the proud Leslie Russell and began to march her unceremoniously down the hall. Reporters fell in behind, barking out their own interrogation. Jaw set determinedly as she walked, struggling to maintain her composure during this mortifying processional, a haughty Leslie Russell was guided silently under the brilliant illumination of television lights, their spots burning shame into the back of her head and shining her way, casting her larger-than-life shadow down the hall.

Epilogue
Peller's Penitence

Steve sat on the edge of the couch, patiently determined. Peller held the phone receiver in one hand, a glass of water in the other. He was paralyzed.

"You'll have to tell her sometime," Steve reminded him gently.

"I can't do it, Steve. Me, of all people. She hated me before …"

"You were Paul's best friend."

Peller looked stricken. Paul took the receiver out of his hand in frustration. "I'll get her on the phone."

He dimly heard his friend apologizing for disturbing Chris Boyer in respectfully hushed tones.

"Louis, I want you to pull yourself together," Steve announced, hanging up the phone. "Chris is coming over here so you can tell her."

"My God, how can I look in her eyes, Steve?"

"Find a way, Peller. Steel yourself."

Chris buzzed up fifteen minutes later. Steve disappeared into his bedroom.

"I wanted to hear the details first hand. Did your plot work out as planned, Louis?" Chris asked anxiously, searching Peller's ashen face for details.

"Chris," he whispered, trying to control himself. "We got Assad. But Carlos de Leon wasn't there. He was …" choked Peller.

"Get a grip, Peller," Chris urged. "We'll find Carlos. I know you're worried. He'll be brought to justice. I'm working on Epstein's testimony. Looks like the DA's office will give Bud partial immunity for 'fessing up. Really, Louis, it's all good news."

"Not all," gulped Peller, unable to confront her. "Chris … they hit him."

"Louis, Louis …you told me that already. I know," she said, mystified, looking from Peller to Steve and back again.

"No!" he shouted. "You don't know. Paul—Carlos got Paul."

A stunned silence.

Bracing her with his arms, Peller somehow found the strength to tell her. About how he'd left Paul home, for security. About the case of mistaken identities. About Peller's absolute ignorance. As he felt her weight collapse against him, he sat her on Steve's couch. "Chris, believe me, I blame myself entirely. You have every right to hate me."

He watched her anxiously, as if her condemnation would absolve him of guilt. Her face was wiped clean of emotion, as if nothing he had said registered.

Peller picked up her hand to comfort her, comfort himself. Suddenly, she struck at him, swinging blindly. As if a wall had collapsed between them, tears began streaming down her face. "It's my fault. I made him go to you. He didn't want to go. I even told Paul that I would tolerate you, Louis, tolerate your insane drive, but he couldn't expect me to die for you. And now, he's … Where is Paul? I have to see him. I love him," she cried.

Silent, Peller felt doubly stung, realizing he was not only the cause of Paul's death, but he'd abused the privilege of Paul's friendship. He felt his eyes well up again at the knowledge. He finally whispered, "Me too, Chris. He was my best friend. I loved him too."

"How can you say that, Louis? How dare you. You drew him in, deeper and deeper, as you've tried to involve me. And your family. How can you talk about love?" Chris's fury rained down on Peller like hail.

He felt his throat constrict as he hesitantly confessed, "I have been blind, Chris. Blind to the bounds of common sense, the binds of family and friends. Blinded by my own nightmare of ambition and stubbornness and pride. I have no excuses."

Chris stared at Peller, grief over Peller's catastrophic folly mingling with pity for a man without a friend. "I hope you've finally exorcised your demons, Peller," she whispered.

Peller was suddenly determined to retrieve some remnant from the ashes. "Chris, we must bring Paul's death to justice. Help me fix the system so he won't have died in vain."

She could not return his fervor, his compulsion to make things right. She sensed that Peller was trying to make sense of his trauma, to bring something positive to this disaster. But so devastated was she over the loss of her lover, she could not even sort through her own confusion, much less guide Peller.

"Chris, Paul would have wanted us to fight on for those in need. Look at what you've promised to do for Angel Sanchez. What you and I might be able to do for Marguerita and Willie Johnson."

She considered wanly through her tears. *Press on, Louis,* she urged telepathically. *Press on toward redemption. But don't ask me to get involved.*

There was a long, black silence between them in which they both grieved independently, thinking of Paul and his strength. Chris moaned, a deep mournful sigh. And before she even realized the words had escaped her lips, she heard herself promising, "Perhaps. For Paul."

There was a glint of hope in the depths of his sorrow. "For us all."

****

Spring was sweeping Washington in bounteous Technicolor, crocuses and daffodils dotting the hillsides. Tommy had never been this far from Brooklyn before. He stood in Peller's office in McLean, the office that had once been Joe Vallardo's. Poor Vallardo. When he'd offered his resignation under a cloud, no one had defended him but Louis Peller. Vallardo had resigned just before his involvement in the Assad partnership came to light. Thanks to Peller, the company would probably not pursue the matter, but Vallardo was clearly ruined, both professionally and personally. Nobody, including Vallardo's wife, Andrea, knew exactly where he was hiding out.

"Hey, nice cap, Pelleh." Tommy stuck out his hand and gave Peller's a vigorous shake. He carried a bag of bialys. "Theah fresh the way you like 'em, Louie. Listen, pal, now that I'm not workin' for the company, I want to thank you personally. You been like a brother to me, man. I woulda never thought ta go into the private eye business if it hadn'ta been fa you."

Peller, sporting Paul's Yankees cap turned backward, took the bag smiling. "Tommy, that's the nicest thing anybody's told me in a long time."

"I says to myself, Tommy, you can't just let a friendship like this disappeah."

"Tommy, I owe you my life," Peller reminded him quietly. "My kids' lives too. Without you on the case—"

"Fa'gedaboutit. I did what any friend would do. Say, I'm sorry to hear about Paul. He was a good man."

Peller absently touched the brim of the baseball cap. "I miss him, Tommy. I think about him every day. You know, he and I were going to be partners, invest in a little property and do what my good borrowers are doing, only not in the city and, of course, not at the expense of the tenants." Lost in the reminiscence, he looked downcast.

"You mean what you did for Marguerita and Willie Johnson?

Setting them up to run their own buildings and all? That was good, Lou. Steve told me all about it. Says it's workin' real good. That Marguerita. If she can clear the gangs out of West 158th, she's one tough lady."

"Yeah," reflected Peller. "Like that, Tommy. I think Paul's friend Chris might help me carry on the dream. I'm hoping."

"Well, good luck with it. Say, whaddaya think of your buddy Shapiro?"

"Steve? You mean this matchmaker thing?"

"Yeah. Imagine him going to some old yenta to find a nice Jewish girl. What an old-fashioned thing to do."

"Stranger things have worked out, Tom," replied Peller with a wink.

"Don' I know it? Well, I'm off. Gotta pair a tickets to Laurel racetrack. Never been there befoeh."

"Still bettin' on the ponies, eh, Tommy? Thought you were off the gambling."

"Can't change all my bad habits, Louie," winked his buddy. "Anyway, I'm takin' my new flame. Say, that's right, you know her. Julie—Julie Hudson."

"Whoa, Tommy. Way to go."

"Listen, Lou, you keep in touch, okay? Come up to Brooklyn, and I'll introduce you to Mama Romano. The best Italian cookin'."

"It's a date, Tommy. And I wanna see those pigeons race, okay, pal?"

Tommy gave Peller a friendly punch. "S'long, my friend. Give that go'geous wife a yours a big kiss for me, will ya?"

Peller smiled emptily and watched Tommy leave, loneliness tugging at his heart. "Yeah, Tommy," he mumbled. "A big kiss."

****

Lana came home, finally, at the end of March. Five long months had passed while Lana and the kids attempted some sort of normalcy in exile. At last, the exile was at an end. At her request, Peller had moved into a little efficiency nearby. Lana had not seen Peller since Paul's funeral, which she had attended by his side, ever the dutiful wife. Still, she had not forgiven him.

The children were running around the yard, crowing like banshees on the bright spring day, happy to be home at last. They knew very little, except that their unexpected vacation was at an end and their daddy was going to be living somewhere else for a while, somewhere close by, but not in their house. It was too confusing to analyze the distance between their mom and dad right now. They were just thrilled to be home.

Lana too was relieved to be back, ready to resume her life after five long months in self-imposed exile, caught and caged in her childhood home. She hadn't dared bring the children back until the media stopped snooping around the house, until police were through deposing Peller and investigating the evidence of Paul's murder. Until the ghosts disappeared. At last, she felt ready to take up the mighty pen once again, if only to edit someone else's copy. Ironically, she mused, her shining moment as a journalist—the article incriminating Leslie Russell for her involvement in Omar Assad's affairs—had been anonymous, a revelation Lana had surfaced at the expense of her own marriage, and her integrity.

The house was oddly still without Manny's joyous greeting. Lana was feeling wary. She strolled through the kitchen and the family room and stopped cold, peering through the sliding glass door. With a shudder, she conjured the image of voodoo-man Carlos de Leon sneaking catlike through the family room, tiptoeing up her stairs, carefully cocking the gun. She could not go up those stairs just yet. She was too spooked to enter their bedroom, to touch the place on their bed where Paul … no. The image was too horrifying. She opened the front door, breathing deeply, hoping the chatter and banter of the children would drown out the gruesome sound of gunshots that echoed in her imagination.

They were safe now, she repeated, trying to convince herself. Omar Assad was on his way to serving time in a federal penitentiary. Leslie Russell had made sure of that. In mounting her own defense, she had incriminated Assad, spelling out in glorious detail every strategy he had devised to amass a legal foothold in the slums and turn it into an opportunity to organize one of the largest drug networks the city had ever seen. In the process, she managed to create a carbon for every petty drug dealer scheming to get rich quick. As usual, the authorities held their news conferences, promising to take extra measures to clamp down on suppliers. As usual, the politicians were divided over remedies, erecting a wall over which they could hurdle new accusations about the futility of the solutions created by the other side.

Amid all the hue and cry over remedies and prevention, Leslie Russell got off lightly, seven to ten years, suspended sentence, five hundred hours community service. Some deal she struck with her old friends in the DA's office: "She had no idea her client had purchased the properties with laundered drug money and used the shell corps and her to distance himself from the business, Your Honor." Although, Lana noted with some satisfaction, she was barred permanently from practicing law, no small defeat to the queen of the advocates. It was sickening how this bitch who called herself an attorney would betray her client to try to save her own soul. Of course, Russell's client was the devil incarnate, and Leslie Russell had sold her soul to him long ago. She was not human, Lana reminded herself angrily. Meanwhile, Lana derived considerable gratification from the fact that her article in the *Times* had played no small part in Russell's arrest and disbarment.

Carlos de Leon was holed up in a New York jail, where he would stand trial for drug possession and distribution. Whether he could practice voodoo under such circumstances remained to be seen. Carlos was also wanted in Maryland for murder in the first degree. Her friend, Debora, had written the story in the *Times*: "Assad's Super Arrested for Drug Dealing; Mastermind of New York Drug Ring Is Murder Suspect in Maryland Case."

Police, in investigating Paul Chase's shooting, had found a clean set of fingerprints on these very sliding glass doors. The lion had been careless. Lana was glad Carlos would be standing trial for Paul's murder in Maryland. She wondered whether Maryland had the death penalty. Death was the only sentence fitting this heinous crime, she thought bleakly with helpless vengeance.

Now it was time to confront Peller. She was still furious. He had phoned daily while she was at her mother's, begging forgiveness. She kept refusing to speak to him. Now, pacing the floor of their house with tears streaming down her face, it was obvious the very foundation of their marriage was splintered. Peller must see that.

She rehearsed her speech aloud: "This is no small screwup, Louis, that I can easily forgive. You can't keep flying on your kamikaze course and expect me to accept, 'I'm sorry, Lana.'" She gritted her teeth against his anticipated verbal assault, his defensiveness. "You've changed? Prove it."

"It's not easy for me to prove I've really changed," a voice interrupted softly, startling her. Peller. He was standing fifteen feet away in the doorway, looking pale and tired. How long had he been there? He'd changed? How? He was unshaven, crumpled. He must have seen her arguing with an invisible husband, she realized, suddenly embarrassed.

"Louis. I didn't hear you come in."

He stood by the door, vulnerable, carrying a single yellow rose. "I walked in through the back door. I didn't want the kids to see me yet. Not 'til we had a chance to talk." He held out the rose: a peace offering.

He wanted to touch her, run his hands through the light, silken veil of hair to kiss the smooth cheeks streaked with tears. He felt a sob rise in his throat at her obvious suffering, all because of him. Lana, lovely Lana. He wanted her to take his face in her tender hands and forgive him with her soft, warm lips.

She stared at him. Peller looked so small, defeated. She was susceptible to his guilelessness. A ruse, she reminded herself. He was no naïf, especially not after what he'd seen in the depths of this hideous escapade. She could not let him charm her. "Damn you, Louis. You're not supposed to be here. I don't want to see you right now." She steeled herself to resist his entreaties to let him come home.

Disappointed, he remained rooted near the door, still clutching the posy. Peller tried to catch her eye, hoping to inspire a smile on that lovely, guarded face, but to no avail. His own smile faded, and left despair. He sighed, sorry for her pain, unable to sustain her reproach. Once again, she was right, right to hate him.

"I have some good news, Lana," he said to lighten the heavy veil separating them. "Remember Marguerita? She immediately took over the property management in Washington Heights. The building went to foreclosure, but Marguerita organized a group of tenants to buy the building outright. Amie Mae is allowing her to assume the mortgage. I put her together with Willie Johnson, over in Bud Epstein's old building, and the two of them are going like gangbusters, cleaning out the skeletons and the rathskellers. Isn't it great? Her dream was to make her home safe to raise her kids. You should see the way they've rooted out the drug element, what with Carlos under wraps now. It's a wonder what a little determination will do, isn't it?"

"I'm really happy that's worked out for her, Louis," Lana replied courteously. She couldn't share Peller's zeal, though she appreciated what a difficult road Marguerita had in front of her. "Whatever happened to Epstein?" she asked, a little curious about this man whose life-changing transformation had almost robbed her of her children and her husband.

"Bud's lying low. He worked a deal with the DA to provide immunity for spilling the goods against Assad. Sold off all his apartments and bought a little place in the Catskills, where he's set up the Steven Epstein Foundation, in memory of his son. Gives away money to folks in need. In fact, it's partly his money that put Marguerita and Willie in business. Could you ever have imagined?"

"Humph," murmured Lana; the irony wasn't lost on her.

"Oh yeah, after a trial separation, his wife took him back. She saw how much he'd changed ..." Peller's voice trailed off. He hoped Lana would see the parallel as clearly as he intended it.

"Louis, let's not talk about this now. Not today. I need some time," she recited, looking down, refusing to meet his puppy-dog eyes.

It wasn't working, Peller confessed, this begging to come home.

"Lana, I've been thinking. Maybe we weren't meant to be," he offered instead, unexpectedly. "I know I'm a difficult person to live with. I took too many risks with too many lives, including yours and the children's. You deserve someone more reliable, even-keeled, someone who will take care of you."

She studied his face to see if he was baiting her. But no. Surprisingly, he looked sincere. Still, she felt duped. How dare he? How could he just charge right in and give up without an argument? Did she want him to leave? She didn't know what to say.

"You don't have to decide right away. I'd stay close by, to be near the kids, of course. That is, if you don't mind."

This kind of solicitous accord was completely uncharacteristic of Peller. He must have something up his sleeve. She decided to play along, see where it went. "Okay, Louis," she responded.

As soon as she spoke them, she regretted her quick words. Maybe she didn't want someone reliable. She wanted him.

Peller looked crestfallen, like a little boy whose favorite old teddy bear had been given away. He had hoped she would see how much he'd changed. He thought she might want a reconciliation as much as he did.

"Lana, I'm sorry," he blurted out. He had to tell her. She had to understand.

In confusion, she crossed her arms and set her face against him. She couldn't let him see how his words touched her, Lana the strong told herself. Wavering, she brooded over her course. Why not, asked Lana the forgiving.

Resolute, she turned her back to him. "It doesn't matter anymore," she replied in a small voice.

Peller, for his part, felt desperate. "But it does matter. Oh, Lana, you don't know how much." He wanted to plead with her to take him back, to start over. He would promise to make it all up to her. He craved her forgiveness.

"Lana, let's start over. We'll focus on us for a change, I promise," he faltered as he realized how hollow his promises must sound to her.

He heaved a sigh and turned sadly to go, his goal still elusive. Everything was detached from reality, as if he were living a dream. But this scene was real, and he was about to lose the only things that mattered: Lana and the children, a last chance at happiness.

"I love you," he said simply, sewing his heart on his sleeve.

She turned back to face him finally, her eyes still shining with tears. "I know, Louis," she whispered softly.

"I'll prove to you I've changed if you'll let me," he offered eagerly. "I can give you my love, unconditionally. And time. Take them. Take all you need, Lana. But don't leave me. I need you so."

He looked at her again, framed in light. The light from the window created a halo around her. He caught her hand; it was small and warm between his icy palms. He felt a slight pressure as she squeezed, then pulled away slowly. Not angrily. But like a promise. Oh, how he hoped the promise was real.

The children had just realized their father was home. "Daddy!… Hugs and kisses, Dad!… Where you been, Da Da?" Their spontaneous outpouring of love warmed him like no other force on Earth.

He glanced at the door, then back at Lana, wanting her consent. She nodded, waving him outside, toward their clamoring tribe. Feeling more at peace, Louis Peller opened the door, blinking out the blinding glare of the day as Lana receded into the shadows of the dark hallway. Feeling suddenly lighter than air, he walked out into the warmth of love, into a dazzling profusion of light. Everything felt so familiar, so right.

"Louis," her voice called after him.

The dream. Again.

Printed in the United States
215466BV00001B/2/P

9 781440 124433